PRAISE FOR LA[UREN]
STAY T[UNED]

"Riveting and much..."
MIDWEST BOOK REVIEW

"If you're a fan of Sophie Kinsella and Emily Giffin, then I think you will truly enjoy this novel."
MANDY REUPSCH, *THE ROMANCE BOOKIE*

"A great read!"
REBECCA BERTO, *NOVEL GIRL*

"Kudos to Ms. Clark on a wonderful debut...I look forward to reading more of her books."
KATHLEEN HIGGINS-ANDERSON, *JERSEY GIRL BOOK REVIEWS*

"Realistic and refreshing!"
MICHELLE ADAMS, *BOOK BRIEFS*

"Clark's first attempt at story-telling - fiction story-telling - is a prize for any reader to have on his or her shelf."
BECKY HOLLAND, *MACON EXAMINER*

"As fast-paced as a real-life newsroom."
DEVON WALSH, WKRG-TV ANCHOR

"A great read! Lauren Clark writes so well you can feel what the characters feel."
LAUREN DAVIS, WVLT-TV ANCHOR

"Stay Tuned is fast-paced, fun, and a downright treat."
KIRA MCFADDEN, AUTHOR, *THE INRUGIAN CHRONICLES*

"The characters in Stay Tuned grab hold and demand you live the story right along side them."
EMLYN CHAND, AUTHOR, *FARSIGHTED AND OPEN HEART*

"Loved it and you will too. The book will draw you in and leave you wanting more."
ANNE RICHTER, WWNY-TV ANCHOR

Dancing Naked in Dixie

ALSO BY LAUREN CLARK

STAY TUNED

Dancing Naked in Dixie

LAUREN CLARK

MONTEREY
PRESS

Copyright 2012 by Lauren Clark

Library of Congress Control No: 2012937009

ISBN 978-0-9847250-4-5

For information contact:

MONTEREY
PRESS

Monterey Press LLC
57 North Monterey Street
Mobile, AL 36604

FOR MARK

Chapter One

"THE NEW EDITOR NEEDS YOU, JULIA." A stern summons from Dolores Stanley leaps over the cubicles and follows me like a panther stalking its prey.

"Just give me a minute," I beg with a wide smile as I sail by the front office and a row of hunch-shouldered executive assistants. Steaming Starbucks in hand, my new powder-white jacket stuffed in the crook of my arm, I give a quick wave over my shoulder.

I am, after all, late, a bit jet-lagged, and on deadline. A very tight deadline.

A glance at my watch confirms two hours and counting to finish the article. I walk faster. My heart twists a teensy bit.

I don't mean to get behind. Really, it just sort of happens.

However, that's all going to change, starting today. I'm going to organize my life, work, home, all of it. I'll be able to check email on the road, never miss an appointment, and keep up with all of my deadlines.

Just as soon as I can find the instruction manual to my new iPhone. And my earpiece.

Anyway, it's going to be great!

So great, that I'm not the least bit panicked when I round the corner and see my desk; which, by the way, is wallpapered in post-it notes, flanked by teetering stacks of mail, and littered with random packages. Even my voicemail light is flashing furiously.

Before I can take another step, the phone starts ringing.

In my rush to pick it up, I trip and nearly fall over a pile of books and magazines someone carelessly left behind. A thick travel guide lands on my foot and excruciating pain shoots through my toes. My coffee flies out of my hand and splats on the carpeting. I watch in horror as my latte seeps into the rug fibers.

"Darn it all!" I exclaim, snatching up the leaking cup and setting it on my desk. Other choice expressions shuttle through my brain as I catch the edge of the chair with one hand to steady myself. I frown at the offending mess on the floor. *Who in the world?*

Until it dawns on me. Oh, right. I left it all there in my hurry to make my flight to Rome. My fault. I close my eyes, sigh deeply, and the strap of my bag tumbles off my shoulder. Everything—keys, mascara, lip gloss, spare change—falls onto the desk with a huge clatter. Letters and paper flutter to the floor like confetti in the Macy's Day Parade. Just as Dolores sounds off again, her voice raspy and caffeine-deprived.

"*Now*, Julia."

My spine stiffens.

"Be right there," I call out in my most dutiful employee voice. Right after I find my notes and calm down.

As I start to search through my briefcase, a head full of thick silver curls appears over the nubby blue paneling.

"Hey, before you rush off," Marietta whispers, "how was Italy? Was it gorgeous, wonderful?"

"Marvelous," I smile broadly at my closest friend and conjure up a picture postcard of Rome, Florence, and sun-drenched Tuscany. Five cities, seven days. The pure bliss of nothing but forward motion. "From the sound of it, I should have stayed another day."

Marietta studies my face.

It's the understatement of the year. I hate to admit it, but the prospect of inhabiting an office cubicle for a week intimidates me more than missing the last connection from Gatwick and sleeping on the airport floor. Claustrophobia takes over. I actually get hives from sitting still too long. Most days, I live out of suitcases. And couldn't be happier!

I'm a travel writer at *Getaways* magazine. Paid for the glorious task of gathering fascinating snippets of culture and piecing them into quirky little stories. Jet-setting to the Riviera, exploring the Great Barrier Reef, basking on Bermuda beaches. It's as glamorous and exhilarating as I imagined.

Okay, it is a tad lonely, from time to time, and quite exhausting.

Which is precisely why I have to get organized. Today.

I sink into my chair and try to concentrate. What to tackle first? Think, think.

"*Julia Sullivan!*"

Third reminder from Dolores. Uh-oh.

Marietta rolls her eyes. "Guess you better walk the plank," she teases. "New guy's waiting. Haven't met him yet, but I've heard he's the 'take no prisoners' sort. Hope you come back alive."

All of a sudden, my head feels light and hollow.

I've been dying to find out about the magazine's new editor.

Every last gory detail.

Until now.

"I'm still in another time zone," I offer up to Marietta with a weak smile. My insides churn as I ease out of my chair.

Marietta tosses me a wry look. "Nice try. Get going already, sport."

I tilt my head toward the hallway and pretend to pout.

When I glance back, Marietta's already disappeared. Smart girl.

"Fine, fine." I tug a piece of rebellious auburn hair into place, smooth my suit, and begin to march. My neck prickles.

I'm not going to worry. Not much anyway.

My pulse thuds.

Not going to worry about change. Or a re-organization. Or pink slips.

Focus, Julia.

The last three editors adored me.

At least half of the North American Travel Journalist Association awards hanging in the lobby are mine.

The best projects land in my lap. Almost always.

Well, there was the one time I was passed over for St. Barts, but I'm sure what's-her-name just had PMS that day. And I did get Morocco in February.

This last trip to Italy? Hands-down, one of the choice assignments.

I round the corner and come within an inch of Dolores Stanley's bulbous nose. As I step back, her thin red lips fold into a minus sign. Chanel No. 5 wraps around me like a toxic veil.

Dolores is the magazine's oldest and crankiest employee. Everyone's afraid of her. To be perfectly honest, Dolores doesn't like *anyone*, except Marietta—and the guy in accounting who signs her paycheck. And that's only twice a month.

Most of the office avoids her as if she's been quarantined with a deadly virus. "Good morning, Dolores," I say with forced cheer.

As expected, she ignores me completely. Instead, Dolores heaves her purple polyester-clad bottom up off the chair, and lumbers toward the editor's office. Breathing hard, she pushes open the huge mahogany door, frowns, and tosses in my name like a careless football punt.

I follow the momentum, shoulders back, hoping Dolores

doesn't notice my shaking hands.

Stop it, Julia. No worries, right?

Dolores pauses and murmurs something that sounds like 'good luck.' *Wait. Dolores wished me luck?* That freaks me out completely. I want to run. Or fall to the floor, hand pressed to my forehead, prompting someone to call the paramedics.

Too late. The door clicks shut behind me. The office already smells different. Masculine, earthy, like leather and sand. I crane my neck to see the new person's face, but the high-back chair blocks my view; an occasional tap-tap on a keyboard the only sound in the room.

I fill my lungs, exhale, and wait.

Light streams onto the desk, now piled high with newspapers, memos, and several back issues of *Getaways*. A navy Brooks Brothers jacket hangs in the corner.

I gaze out the window at the majestic skyscrapers lining Broadway, a blur of activity hidden behind a silver skin of glass and metal. A taxi ride away, three international airports bustle with life. Jets ready to whisk me away at a moment's notice. My pulse starts to race just thinking about it.

"Not in a big hurry to meet the boss?"

The gruff voice startles me. My knees lock up.

"Sir?" I play innocent and hope he'll blame Dolores.

The chair spins around. Two large feet plop on the desk and cross at the ankles. My eyes travel up well-dressed legs, a starched shirt, and a red silk tie. They settle on a pair of dark eyes that almost match mine.

For a moment, nothing works. My brain, my mouth, I can't breathe. It absolutely, positively may be the worst shock-of-my-life come true.

"David?" I stutter like a fool and gather my composure from where it has fallen around my feet.

The broad, easy grin is the same. But the hair is now a little more salt than pepper. The face, more weather-beaten than I remember.

"I told them you'd be surprised." David's face flashes from smug to slightly apologetic.

I say nothing.

"They talked me out of retirement," David folds his arms across his chest and leans back. "Said they *had* to have me."

"I'll bet," I offer with a cool nod.

His face reveals nothing. "Not going to be a problem, is it?"

Of course, it is! I dig my fingernails into my palm, shake my head, and manage to force up the corners of my mouth.

"Good." David slides his feet off the desk and thumbs through a pile of magazines.

I stand motionless, watching his hands work. The familiar flash of gold is gone. I glower at his bare finger, incensed to the point of nearly missing all that he is saying. I watch David's mouth move; he's gesturing.

"...and so, we're going to be going in a new direction." He narrows his gaze. "Julia?"

I wrench my eyes up. "A new direction," I repeat in a stupid, sing-song voice.

David frowns. With a smooth flick of his wrist, he tosses a copy of *Getaways* across the desk. He motions for me to take it.

"The latest issue," he says.

Gingerly, I reach for it. And choke. *That's funny.* I purse my lips. *Funny strange.* The cover story was supposed to be mine. My feet start to tingle. I want to run.

Instead, I force myself to begin paging through for the article and stunning photos I'd submitted—shots of the sapphire-blue water, honey-gold beaches, and the lush green landscape.

With forced nonchalance, I search through the pages. *Flip. Flip. Flip.* In a minute, I'm halfway through the magazine. No article. No Belize. No nothing. My fingers don't want to work anymore. I feel sick.

"Julia, what is it? You seem a little pale," David prods. He leans back in his chair and stares at me with an unreadable expression.

I continue looking. *Where* is my article? Buried in the middle? Hidden in the back? More pages. I peek up at David, who meets my dismay with a steady gaze.

What kind of game is he playing?

I yank my chin up. "No, nothing's wrong," I say lightly, "not a thing."

Inside, I'm screaming like a lunatic. *There must be a mistake.* My bottom lip trembles the slightest bit. I blink. Surely, I'm not going to…lose my…

"It was junk. Pure and simple," David interrupts, the furrows on his forehead now more pronounced. He jumps up and folds his arms across his chest. "Bland, vanilla. The article screamed boring. It was crap."

Crap? Don't mince any words, David. He might as well toss a bucket of ice water on my head. I shiver, watching him.

"Let me ask you this." David stops walking back and forth and puts his fists on the desk. "How much time did you actually spend writing and researching the article? Just give me a rough estimate. In hours or days?" David's finished making his point. He sits down and begins glancing through a red folder.

My mind races. Last month? Right. Trip to Belize.

Focus. Try to focus.

I fidget and tap out an uneven rhythm with my shoe. Excuses jumble in my head, swirling like my brain is on spin cycle.

David clears his throat. He opens a manila envelope, thumbs through the contents, then gazes at me with the force of a steam-driven locomotive. "Are you taking care of yourself? Taking your … prescriptions?"

The words cut like a winter wind off the Baltic Sea.

I grope for words. My thoughts fall through my fingers.

My attention deficit isn't exactly a secret. Most everyone

knows it's been a problem in the past. But, things are under control … it's all been fine.

Until now.

I start to seethe. David continues to gaze intently and wait for my reply.

What are you, a psychiatrist? I want to spout. *Not to mention all of the HR rules you're breaking by asking me that.*

"I'm off the medication. Doctor's orders. Have been for several years," I answer, managing to give him a haughty *the-rest-is-none-of-your-business* stare.

David backs off with a swivel of his chair. "Sorry. Just concerned," he says, holding one cuff-linked hand in the air. "So, *exactly* how much *time* did you *spend* on the *article*?" David enunciates each word, stabbing them through my skin like daggers.

"Five hours," I blurt out, immediately wishing I could swallow the words and say twelve. "Maybe seven."

David makes a noise. Then, I realize he's laughing. At me. At my enormous fib.

My face is scarlet, glowing hot.

Head bent, David flips through a set of papers. He pauses at a small stack. I recognize the coffee stain on one edge and the crinkled corner. My article.

"Let me quote verbatim to you, Ms. Sullivan," he says, his tone mocking. "Belize offers the best of both worlds, lovely beaches and a bustling city full of good restaurants. Visitors can find fascinating artwork and treasure hunt for souvenirs downtown."

He stops.

Surely, my article was better. He must have the draft. Oh, there wasn't a draft. Oops. Because I hadn't allowed myself much time. Come to think of it, I banged most of it out on the taxi ride from the airport. I accidentally threw away most of my notes in a shopping bag, which wasn't really my fault. I was late for my plane. And then…

"So, I killed it." David ceremoniously holds the papers over the trash can and lets go.

I watch the white papers float, then settle to their final resting place. Maybe I should jump in after them? My legs start to ache. Why did I wear these stupid Prada boots that pinch my left heel?

"But, all is not lost," David says dramatically. "I'll give you a chance to redeem yourself." He drums his fingers on the desk. "If you can up the caliber of your writing. Spend some time. Put your heart into it."

I don't say a word. Or make a sound. Because if I do, I'm sure to sputter out something I'll regret. Or, God forbid, cry. *Redeem myself? Put my heart into it?*

Deep breath. Okay, I can afford to work a teensy bit harder. Give a tad more effort here and there. But, the criticism. Ouch! And coming from David, it's one hundred times worse. The award-winning super-journalist who circled the globe, blah, blah, blah.

David cracks his knuckles. "Look, I know it's been tough since your mother's illness and all." His tone softens slightly. "Her passing away has been difficult for everyone."

I manage not to leap over the desk and shake him by the shoulders. *Difficult? How would he know?* My blood pressure doubles. *Stay calm. Just a few more minutes.* Doesn't he have some other important meeting? An executive lunch?

David drones on like he's giving a sermon. I try to tune him out, but can't help hearing the next part.

"Julia, it's affected your writing. Immensely. And look at you. You've lost weight. You're exhausted. I want you to know I understand your pain—"

"You *don't* understand," I cut in before I can stop myself. My mother died two years ago. She was sick before that. I still miss her every day. *Damn him. Get out of my personal life. And stay out.*

We stare each other down, stubborn, gritty gunfighters

in the Wild West.

"Fine," David says evenly and breaks my gaze. "So, as you've heard, the magazine is going in a new direction. The focus group research says ..." He glances down at some scribbled notes. "It says our American readers want to see more 'out of the way' places to visit. Road trips. A Route 66 feel, if you will."

Focus groups. I forgot all about that obsession.

David pauses to make sure I'm listening. For once, he has my undivided attention.

"According to the numbers, they're saturated with Paris, London, the Swiss Alps. They want off the beaten path. Local flavor. So, we're going to give it a shot. We'll call it something like 'Back Roads to Big Dreams.'"

What a horrible idea. I swallow hard. Our readers don't want that! Who did he interview in these focus groups? The Beverly Hillbillies?

David continues, immensely pleased with the concept. "The emphasis is going to be on places that offer something special—perhaps historically or culturally. But the town or city must also be looking toward the future. Planning how to thrive, socially and economically. It's going to be part of a new series, if it turns out well." David puts emphasis on 'if' and shoots me a look. "What do you think?"

Is he joking? He doesn't want my opinion. Does he honestly think I like the idea?

David pauses. Apparently, he expects a response. An intelligent, supportive one.

"Sounds ... interesting," I manage to squeak out and shift uncomfortably. I predict that I'll be spending a full day spinning half-truths. I'll likely be offered a lifetime membership in Deceivers Anonymous if I don't die first.

David snatches up his glasses. *Glasses?* When did he start wearing glasses?

"I know you're our token globe-trotter, but I'd hoped

you'd be more enthusiastic." He taps his Mont Blanc on his desk calendar and then points to the enormous wall atlas. "I'm thinking Alabama."

Something massive and thick catches in my throat. My head swivels to the lower portion of the map. I begin to cough uncontrollably.

Ever so calmly, David waits for me to quit.

When I catch my breath, my mind races with excuses. The words stumble out of my mouth, tripping over themselves. "But, I have plans. Tickets to the Met, a fundraiser, a gallery opening, and book club on Monday." I don't mention the Filene's trip I'd planned. Or the romantic date I've been promising Andrew, my neglected boyfriend.

David waves a hand to dismiss it all. "Marietta can handle the magazine-related responsibilities."

From the top drawer of his desk, he produces an airline ticket and a folder with my name on it. He sets them on the edge of his desk. Something I can't decipher plays on his lips.

I keep my voice even. "What about Bali?" I had planned to leave for the South Pacific a week from Friday. "It's on my calendar. It's been on there…"

David shakes his head. "Not anymore."

The words wound me like a thousand bee stings.

"Alabama," David repeats.

I swallow, indignant. He's plucked me off a plum assignment without a thought to my schedule. My new boss is sending me to who-knows-where, and he looks perfectly content. I narrow my eyes and fold my arms.

"Seriously David, you're sending me on an assignment to…Alabama? *Alabama*?" I sputter, searching my brain for an appropriate retort. "I'd rather—I don't know—*dance naked* for my next assignment than go to Alabama!"

The announcement comes out much louder than I intend and reverberates through the room. Dolores probably has her ear pressed to the door, but the phrase bounces off my boss like a cotton ball.

David smothers a chuckle. "Suit yourself."

"It's a done deal, isn't it?" I finally manage, my voice low and uneven. The answer is obvious. The airline ticket and folder are within my grasp. I don't move a centimeter toward them. For all I know, the inside of one of them is coated with Anthrax. For a brief moment, I picture myself, drawing one last ragged breath, on the floor of David's brand-spanking-new office carpeting.

"It's your choice." David swipes at his glasses and settles them on his nose. "Deadline's a week from today. That's next Wednesday. Five o'clock. Take it or leave it."

I stifle an outward cringe at his tone, and the way he's spelling it out for me. Syllable by syllable, like I'm a toddler caught with my hand in the cookie jar.

Take it or leave it.

Not the assignment. My job.

It's your choice.

David's fingers hit the keyboard. Click-clack. "Oh, and leave your notes on Italy with Dolores. I'll write the article myself."

That's it. The meeting's over. I'm fuming. Furious. I want to rip up the papers an inch from his face and let a hailstorm of white scraps fall to the carpet.

Take it or leave it.

I start to turn on my heel and walk out like we'd never had the conversation. David will come around, won't he?

Then, I stop. It's a joke. An awful, terrible joke. Do I have other job prospects? Do I want to change careers? What about my apartment? What about the bills?

Fine. Okay. Have it your way, David.

I catch myself before I stick my tongue out. He probably has surveillance cameras set up on a 24-hour loop.

David knows I'm beaten.

So, I bend, ever so slightly. In one quick motion, I reach

out to tuck the folder and ticket under my arm. In slow motion, the papers slip through my fingers like water between rocks in a stream.

Damn! The clatter of David's awkward typing stops.

So much for a smooth exit.

On the ground lies a square white envelope and matching note card. I swoop down to gather my mess.

Though I'm trying not to notice, I can't help but stare at the delicate pen and ink lines on the front of the card. There's no lettering, just thin strokes of black that form the outline of a majestic mansion and its towering columns. Before I can stop myself, I flip open the note card, expecting a flowery verse or invitation. Some event I'll be expected to attend for the magazine? A party?

There are only a few sentences inside, barely legible, scrawled in loopy, old-fashioned writing. *David, Please help*, I can make out. Underneath, a scribbled signature. An *M*, maybe?

Hmph. There's no end to what people will do to get a story. Gifts, money, flowers, I've seen it all. Traded for a snippet of publicity.

I refold the note and hand it across the desk. It must not be particularly important, because David takes the card and sets it aside without glancing at it.

Necessary papers tucked securely in the crook of my arm, I straighten up, flick an imaginary piece of lint off my skirt with my free hand, and begin to walk out. My feet brush the carpet in small, level steps.

I reach for the doorknob, inches from the hallway.

"Have fun! Don't forget to check in," David calls after me. "Oh, and send a postcard."

I scowl. His voice is ringing in my ears.

That's low. Lower than low. He knows I collect postcards. Make that *used to*. In my past life. I want to stomp out—have a proper four-year-old temper tantrum. Be in control, I tell myself. Keep your chin up. Walk.

David can go to Hell!

I make the most horrible, gruesome face I can think of.
Surveillance cameras be damned.

Chapter Two

MY DAY IS ABOUT TO GET WORSE.

I'm in trouble. Big trouble. The sort of trouble that ends careers. And every single person in the office knows. Eyes track me like bloodhounds. My ribcage contracts like I've been caught in a lasso. When did my cubicle get so far away?

What, did David send out a memo announcing my punishment? I can picture the subject line now. Something catchy and stolen from a trashy tabloid magazine. *Julia Sullivan Strikes Out Again. It's Alabama or Bust!*

Now, to my immense irritation, some idiot is whistling. What's that tune? Then I know. John Denver. *Country Roads.*

Coincidence. Pure coincidence. I shake it off.

"Yee haw!"

My head jerks up.

A fluke. It must be.

Still, it rattles me. I remind myself that a shift in management brings out the worst in people. Employees expect a shake up, some casualties, and a few empty desks. Every man and woman defends his or her own worth. I've been lucky. I'm usually off on assignment halfway around the globe.

Until now.

I see the straw cowboy hat. It's perched jauntily on the entrance to my cubicle.

This is personal.

My eyelids flutter, while my steps slow to the pace of a slug in dry heat. And I realize everyone within a hundred-mile radius is watching to see what I'll do.

The first thought that pops into my mind, quite sincerely, is to snatch up the hat, throw it on the ground, and trample it with the wildest abandon of a Nairobi warrior.

I swallow.

And walk past Marietta's empty cubicle to my desk.

I gather my purse and down jacket, then shut down my laptop, which gets jammed into my leather bag with the folder and airline ticket. From the corner of the room, there's a sneeze. Or a snicker. When I twirl around to leave, at least a dozen faces peer up at me.

Hell's bells! I have an audience. Think Julia. Don't lose your cool. Think.

Ever so casually, I force an easy smile, stroll to the hat, and settle it on my head. I twirl a piece of hair and assume my best Daisy Duke pose. I grasp the edge of the cowboy hat and tip it ever so slightly. And wink.

"Bye, y'all!" I swing my hips toward the elevator.

No one makes a sound.

Mercifully, the elevator is empty and waiting. The doors shut behind me. I collapse against the wall, toss the hat to the floor, and press my cheek against the cool metal.

Question: How much does it suck when your new boss is the one person in the world you can't trust?

Answer: A lot. Especially when it's your own father.

I start to bawl like a baby.

The elevator offers a ten-floor reprieve from any human interaction. I cling to the metal handrails, praying the doors don't open before we reach the first floor. The light moves, ticking down from nine, then eight, and seven. At the third floor, I sniff back my tears, wipe at my face with both hands, and pick up the hat. I cram the straw appendage under my arm, holding back a desire to crush it under both feet. With my luck, if I do it, someone will cite me for littering in my own workplace and fine me two hundred dollars.

A ding signals we've hit ground level. *Rock bottom, I think. How appropriate.*

The wind's picked up since this morning, gusting in bursts that seem to push me down the sidewalk. Sleet pelts my hair. Balancing my bag and the stupid hat, I shrug on my white jacket, zip up, and re-position my scarf. Barrier up, I almost sigh in relief. *There. Better.*

Teetering on the heels of my boots, I hold my breath and squeeze into an opening in the crowd, just as an elbow catches me in the ribcage. *Sheesh.* I wince in pain and bump against a man's shoulder. He glares at me from under his faux fur-lined hood.

"Sorry," I squeak and resume jostling for position. A flash of bright yellow speeds by, sending a spray of wet, gray slush. There's a yelp of outrage, some fist-shaking, and a few choice cuss words lobbed after the taxi. I glance around the angry mob. *Why is everyone in Manhattan looking for a cab?*

The answer comes a moment later, when I overhear two women exchanging shrill weather reports. They're both clutching iPhones, tapping and sliding manicured fingertips over the glossy screens.

"We're going to get buried," one hisses. She tucks her black cashmere wrap over her pearl choker and adjusts her Louis Vuitton clutch.

"Six to ten inches of snow before midnight," the other confirms. Her red Chanel lips are pursed. "The whole city may shut down."

A tap of panic hits me between the shoulder blades. *If the airports close, how will I get to Atlanta? I have to get home. I have to pack. I need a taxi now.*

With a surge of energy, I push through the group, balance on the curb, and wave my arms at the oncoming traffic. "Taxi! Taxi!"

In one miraculous instant, three yellow cabs pull up. With a rush of activity, people swarm the vehicles. I manage to latch onto a back door handle and yank it open. The weather-report ladies are on the other side of my taxi, deflecting dagger-looks from a pair of men who arrived a few steps too late.

The driver is honking his horn, waving us inside. "Come on, ladies," he urges with a nasal shrill. "Meter's running."

"We were here first," Chanel Lipstick calls over the roof of the cab at me. I watch as her mouth curves into a satisfied smile. Obviously, the woman always gets what she wants and is quite comfortable taking it away from someone else. This makes me angry and slightly hysterical. I say the first thing that pops into my mind.

"I-I'm sick," I declare, making my best wide-eyed and pitiful expression. "I can't last out here much longer."

This announcement makes both women stop. Cashmere Wrap throws me a dubious glance. I wrack my brain for an illness. Something awful that will make them regret trying to steal my taxi. The Flu? Salmonella? Mad Cow disease?

"Athazagoritis," I announce, shocking even myself when the words spurt out of my mouth. This gets the desired reaction. The women offer simultaneous pitying looks, almost as if they've been practicing.

Chanel Lipstick waves a gloved hand, acquiescing. "Get in, dear, we can ride together."

The trip to my apartment is an exhausting exercise in humiliation. Every mile, I curse my impulsive nature, swearing on my mother's grave that I will never lie again—even to strangers who are mean to me—blizzard conditions or not.

The two women rapid-fire questions at me like I'm the subject of an FBI investigation. *How did I learn that I had this illness? When? How many treatments do I have to have? Does it make me very sick? For how many days? Who is helping me at home?*

I stutter through answers, wanting to smack my own forehead for ever saying it. Of course, Athazagoritis isn't real. The word popped into my head because Marietta's forever teasing me about being so scattered and missing appointments. She says Athazagoraphobia—fear of forgetting—might actually be a good thing for me.

Cashmere Wrap presses gloved fingertips to her rouged cheek. "Is it terrible?"

I think fast. "It's somewhat rare," I say, darting my eyes toward the snow-covered sidewalks, wishing I could jump out. "I'm able to work, but I get really tired."

"Oh, you poor dear," Chanel Lipstick says. "A career girl. What is it that you do?"

"I'm a writer for *Getaways*," I admit, relieved that I don't have to fib about that part.

"The travel magazine? How glamorous," Cashmere Wrap purrs. "I hope you get your strength back. You're so young. I would never have guessed you were ill."

"Thank you," I whisper and sink lower in the seat.

Then, the taxi stops and the driver announces my address and the fare. *Thank goodness. I've managed to answer everything, every single question. Now I can get out of here.* I reach for the door handle, lift, and swing one foot out onto the street.

Chanel Lipstick presses a hand on my arm. She's holding on, and I'm not sure she'll let go. "Oh, my dear," Chanel Lipstick whispers. "I have to know. Is there any cure?"

"Yes, um. Sure."

Finally, she releases her death grip on my arm.

Outside the cab, I hear my name. Someone is yelling "Julia!"

Relieved at the thought of escaping the taxi, I spring onto the sidewalk, then catch myself. It's Andrew, my boyfriend, striding down the sidewalk in a long wool coat. His hair, despite the storm, is combed in place. He looks a bit worried, with his shoulders hunched, both hands shoved deep into his pockets.

Actually, when I come to think about it, there aren't many

moments when Andrew *isn't* concerned about something. He worries about numbers because he's a CPA. He's employed by a large firm, a very prestigious company, where everyone scurries around doing very important accountant things, especially during tax season. His job, I've learned, is about managing forms. There's the long form and short form, and forms with different titles: W-2, W-4, 1099, 8863, 941. I can't keep them all straight.

Being good-natured, Andrew always laughs at my confusion. He says he can't identify all of the stamps on my passports—with emphasis on the plural—and that makes us even. I'm not about to argue.

"Andrew, w-what are you doing here?" I sputter as he kisses my cheek. I fumble inside my bag for cash to pay the cab driver. Of course, I'm short a dollar or two. My boyfriend, prepared as usual, chips in the remaining bills.

My new-found friends are fascinated by his sudden appearance. Four gloved hands cling to the open window. Both women, in turn, edge the other one out for space.

"Take care of her now, she's not feeling so well," Chanel Lipstick calls out first.

Andrew throws an arm around my shoulders and gazes down at me, concerned. "What's wrong, Julia? Rough flight, sweetheart? Bad day?"

"You're right about that," Cashmere Wrap accuses him, almost hanging out of the cab to berate my innocent boyfriend. "Her Athaza—"

Andrew blinks at the women as the cab driver guns the engine and drives off, vehicle fishtailing back and forth in the slush.

"What did she say?" My boyfriend's brow is crunched into a deep line.

I scramble to cover the gaffe. "I think she was trying to tell you—" I glance at the collar of his pressed shirt, then down to the red swatch of his tie. "Ah, that's a sweet boyfriend."

Andrew grins and buys the cover-up.

I pat his shoulder and paste on a wide smile. "Let's grab dinner." With a firm hand, I steer him away from my apartment and up the street toward our favorite pizza joint.

It's crowded and loud, brimming with music and noise. My ears usually ring for hours afterward, but the food is worth it. They have brick-oven pizzas, all kinds, with toppings like Porcini mushroom and Gorgonzola cheese. The restaurant also offers fifty-two exotic beers on tap, a concept Andrew claims to adore. Of course, tonight, like every other evening, he places the same request.

"Red Stripe, please," he says to the server, who nods and doesn't move to jot it down on her notepad.

"Merlot?" she asks me, pencil poised. I'm a little less cautious than Andrew, choosing a Shiraz or Cabernet on special occasions. She appears almost crestfallen when I nod, but perks up when Andrew orders Napoli pizza.

"Adventurous," I comment.

"You're just back from Italy," he grins and winks, as if needing to remind me.

I don't dampen his enthusiasm by reminding him that Rome and Naples are a few hours apart. The cities are nothing alike. The food is half a country apart. The people, ditto. I don't bother because Andrew doesn't like to travel outside the United States. He's phobic about public transportation, airlines, trains, and cruise ships, which rather limits our romantic vacation possibilities.

Our relationship works—and has for years—likely because I'm so exhausted from logging frequent-flier miles that I don't want to leave the City once I'm here. Andrew loves that I never beg him to take me to the Hamptons, the Adirondacks, or Vermont.

Nope, I'm content in my pajamas and socks, snuggled up with my fleece blanket next to Andrew, watching movies all weekend. Of course, I'm usually asleep halfway through the first film. Jet lag always gets me.

Andrew says he doesn't mind—likely because I have no earthly idea what we're watching; probably back-to-back reruns of *The Apprentice* while I doze off. Andrew has a real thing for Donald Trump. I told him, if he ever gets a wild idea about adopting a comb-over, he can forget it.

"Tired from the trip?" Andrew asks as the server plops down our drinks. "You seem distracted."

"A little," I agree and take a long sip of wine, trying not to gulp. "Sorry."

"Well, we need to plan our anniversary dinner," Andrew reminds me, offering a shy smile.

An immediate pang of anxiety hits me when I hear the word 'anniversary.'

Andrew reaches a hand to rub my back. He looks so hopeful, so sweet. "So, are you here for longer than a day? Aren't you staying for a week this time?"

"Afraid not. New boss. Big change in plans," I shake my head.

"Oh," he replies. Andrew is used to me cancelling plans.

I avoid his gaze, not wanting to hurt him, but unable to be completely honest. I'm not happy about the trip, but I'm almost relieved to avoid the momentous anniversary celebration.

Andrew knows I'm not a romantic. Hallmark cards and flowers give me hives. And I haven't really shared this with him: The idea of *forever* really freaks me out.

I twirl my wine glass by its stem and change the subject. "I'm off to Alabama."

There's a rush of noise and a gust of chilled air blows through the restaurant. A crowd of people breeze inside, stomping snow off boots, calling out to friends. Much to my dismay, they settle at the empty table right next to us, the loudest drunk to my immediate right.

Andrew sets down his Red Stripe and stares at me. "What

did you say? Atlanta?"

"Al-a-ba-ma," I sound out the word, enunciating each syllable so that he can hear me over the shouting.

"Alabama?" Andrew is baffled and rightly so. He expects me to announce a place like Amsterdam, Alaska, or Albania. An exotic, exquisite, or unusual locale. Not small-town U.S.A. "Is he crazy?"

"Yeah. Screw him!" I say. All around me, heads turn.

The drunk behind us perks up. "Yeah, that's right. Go for it! But, um, get a room," the guy warbles, his words slurred. Swaying a bit, he turns his chair to leer at me.

I flush a deep shade of fuchsia-pink. Andrew shoots the guy a withering look. The man grins and winks. Then, like a good drunk, he goes right back to his friends.

"Thanks. It's a long story," I murmur. Suddenly, I am exhausted. I don't want to talk about work, my new boss, or my assignment. I don't want to talk about my possible unemployment. Most of all, I don't want to talk about the future. Our future. My future. Or anyone else's future.

I would like—very much—to go home.

Ever the gentleman, Andrew complies, hailing me a cab, prepaying the driver, and rattling off my street address. The snow's tapered off now, the night sky is clear, and stars wink at me overhead. I smile, thinking about Chanel Lipstick and Cashmere Wrap's predictions. Not even close to the dire storm the ladies expected.

That's weather in New York. Unpredictable, at best. As is my life.

Andrew presses a kiss on my forehead. "Get some rest, Julia. Call me," he says. After I scoot inside the cab, he closes the door behind me, and waves as the taxi pulls away from the curb.

I watch him from the rear window. His hair is still perfect. He's so kind and thoughtful. He's a saint. And there's no way I can marry him.

The deep pit of guilt is still there when I climb the steps to my apartment building, unlock my door, and close it behind me. I peel off my coat, then the first layer of clothing, kick off my boots, and strip off my stockings.

With a sigh, I collapse on my small sofa and curl up with a fleece blanket. And I think about my mother. I miss her so much. She'd know what to do. My mother was the logical one in the family. The planner. The cautious, measured, safety-first parent, even at the very end, right before she died. My mother—stuck full of needles and tubes, injected with medicine—was calm, rational, and uncomplaining.

I'm nothing like her. Polar opposite. The negative to her positive.

My fingers trace the edge of the soft fabric. This was her blanket. One of a few keepsakes I managed to collect before my father had her apartment cleaned out. It had been all of twenty-four hours after the funeral and I unlocked her apartment door to find each room empty. There was a uniformed mover inside—someone David hired—packing the remaining items into a solitary box.

"What are you doing?" I demanded. "Where are my mother's things? Who are you?"

The poor guy explained that he was asked to remove everything from the apartment and dispose of it.

"Dispose of it," I remember shrieking, "like trash?"

The man backed away, holding up both palms as if we were launching into a Jackie Chan martial arts battle. Without another word, I heaved the box onto my hip and left the building. After a stop at my apartment to drop off my mother's belongings and pick up one very important item, I went straight to my father's office at *Forbes*.

I stormed inside the building, ignoring the receptionist, and leapt around scuttling secretaries. My father was at his desk. He looked up, brow furrowed, when I entered the room.

"Julia," he said, getting out of his chair.

"How could you?" I asked, keeping my tone low and soft. I was not going to lose control. I would act like an adult.

"What are you talking about?" my father asked, sitting back in his chair with a frown. But he knew. I could see it in his eyes. He knew.

"You're throwing out everything. You hired someone to *dispose* of my mother's things. You didn't tell me. You didn't ask me. How dare you try to erase her memory?" The steadiness in my voice wavered. I waited for an answer. A flicker of emotion. Anything.

My father shifted in his seat. He leaned forward and clasped his hands. His cufflinks caught the light. The flash of silver irritated me. Then, I realized why. He was wearing a gift from my mother; cufflinks for his fiftieth birthday.

"Give those to me," I said and held out one hand.

"Pardon me?" my father appeared taken aback.

"The cufflinks. My mother gave them to you." I began to tremble. My palm felt damp. I made myself stand straight. Unwavering.

My father stared back at me. He didn't move. He didn't remove the cufflinks.

I expected as much.

With a swift movement, I yanked the book from under my arm and slammed it down on his desk. The pages flew open. For a moment, I caught myself. *Was I really doing this?* The album was a collection of postcards—places we'd visited during my childhood, my teenage years, and in college. It was my mother's idea. She loved postcards—wacky ones, beautiful ones, every sort of postcard she could find. It was a way to remember all of my travels. That's what she told me when she bought me the first one. My mother sent them when she was on trips. When I was older, I mailed them to her. It was a way we had connected.

My heart thumped as I peeled back the first page. I

glimpsed my mother's writing on the back. After a moment's hesitation, clutching the thick rectangle between my fingers, I tossed it at my father's head.

The first one was the most difficult. After that, it became easier. I launched another, and another. Pictures of Myrtle Beach, The Poconos, and Napa Valley flew past David's head. I followed up with New Mexico, Dallas, and the Florida Keys. The floor around my father became a sea of color. The air filled with picturesque scenes—beaches, mountains, lakes.

The Grand Canyon bounced off his nose. Las Vegas landed on his shoulder. The Seattle Space Needle slid past his elbow. In a final rush, I sent postcards of St. Simon's Island, Cancun, and Knoxville, Tennessee into my father's lap.

For my grand finale, I held up the remaining pages and dumped them into the trashcan. David didn't even blink.

"Good-bye." I let the door to his office slam behind me.

He never answered.

I CLOSE MY EYES AGAINST THE MEMORY, tucking my body into a smaller ball on the sofa. As my knees press against my chest, I sigh. I wrap both arms around my legs, hugging them closer.

For the thousandth time since my mother's death, I wish I'd kept the album. I wish I'd kept even a few of the postcards. A tear escapes from the corner of my eye. It runs down my cheek and splashes onto my arm.

Most of all, more than anything, I wish I had my mother back.

Chapter Three

THE BEST BUTTS IN ALABAMA, the huge billboard above my head brags. A robust pink pig, dressed in blue overalls and a cowboy hat, winks down at me. Next to the hog's turned-up nose, royal blue letters read 'Phil's Bar-B-Q.'

Phil certainly knows how to make a first impression. As does Mother Nature.

The sunshine beats down on my shoulder through the window. *Is it always this muggy in December?* I swipe at my forehead with the back of my hand and do quick surveillance.

Where is the historic, elegant city I was promised in the letter? There *is* a normal-looking church across the street, a run-of-the-mill real estate business to my right, and a tiny hole-in-the-wall place called The Donut King, which seems to be doing ten times more business than the Winn-Dixie grocery store I just passed.

So far, all I see of Eufaula, Alabama is more in-your-face commercial than traveler chic. Of course, I'm not in the best frame of mind to become one with my surroundings.

After a lousy Thursday morning of sulking and a rushed packing job, I sent an RSVP with regrets for the fundraiser, gave away my tickets to the Met, left a voice mail for Andrew, and changed my ticket to an earlier departure.

Hours later, after fighting through JFK security and surviving the cramped flight to Atlanta, I spent the night in Buckhead, Georgia. This morning I picked up my enormous rented SUV—it was either that or a red minivan—and began driving the three-and-a-half hours to reach my pinhole-on-a-map destination.

All to save my job.

Along the way, Marietta and I burn up cell phone minutes playing our version of Trivial Pursuit: "Famous Stuff about Alabama." The short edition.

Celebrities? Lionel Richie and Condoleezza Rice. Songs? "Oh, Suzanna!" and Lynyrd Skynyrd's "Sweet Home Alabama." Books? *To Kill a Mockingbird* and *Crazy in Alabama*, which Marietta insists is about a woman who carries around her husband's head in a hatbox. I definitely have to put that on my to-read list.

Famous movies? *Close Encounters of the Third Kind,* and my personal favorite, *Sweet Home Alabama* with Reese Witherspoon. Remember the opening scene with the gorgeous white mansion? It was—drum roll, please—filmed in Eufaula, Alabama. Marietta checks Google to confirm it.

Food? Never mind. Phil the pig has that covered.

Marietta's saying something about SEC football and a cult-like following of college teams when I turn into the paved parking lot of a Citgo gas station.

"You mean like the KKK?" I park and glance behind the SUV for any white-hooded marauders. "Or a David Koresh kind of spooky, everyone-kills-themselves-cult?" I pause and cut the engine. "Wait a minute, the Branch Davidians were in Waco, Texas."

My best friend chortles. "Yes, Jules. I don't mean an actual 'cult.' I mean everyone loves it—like when the Yankees are on a serious winning streak. It's what everyone talks about, just warning you. The state of Alabama doesn't have any pro teams, so the college teams kind of make up for it."

"Ah, thanks for the heads up." My best friend is my unofficial source for all things Southern. Before settling in at *Getaways*, my good friend spent the better part of two years in Jackson, Mississippi after her husband's job transfer. According to Marietta, who grew up in Jersey, she loved the area, but when a position opened up in Manhattan, they moved back.

We say good-bye, I park and step out of the car, stretching my legs. As I slide my card into the gas pump reader, the rev of a tractor-trailer engine makes me jump.

The Expedition drinks up the fuel like a camel left in the desert for a year with no water.

Finally, *clunk*. The gas pump clicks off. The monitor displays seventy-one dollars and ninety cents. I stare at the numbers in shock, double-checking the gallon total. No wonder I drive a Prius.

I fight with the nozzle to get it back in place and accidentally give the handle another quick squeeze.

Splash!

Ugh. Double ugh. Gas on me, the ground, the Expedition. The slight breeze and sun dry my arm in seconds. I now reek of rotten eggs, and I'm hoping the Citgo has a semi-clean restroom. Bells jingle above my head as I push open the glass door. A blast of air conditioning hits me full-force.

"Hey! How are ya, sugar?" A gum-snapping woman of about fifty waves at me wildly from behind the counter. "Hot one already. WTVY says it's gonna be dang-near 80 today. Can you believe that? Sakes alive, it's December."

I stop in my tracks. There are only three of us in the convenience store, and she certainly isn't talking to the half-asleep, scruffy, red-haired, hasn't-bathed-in-two-weeks looking man in the corner. The clerk follows my eyes.

"Don't pay Stump no mind. He's harmless. Just drunk." Her hot pink fingertips waggle in the air. She tilts her head to the side and looks me up and down. "You ain't from around here, are you sugar? Bless your heart. Passin' through?" She waits expectantly for an answer.

"Visiting for a few days," I swallow and remember to be polite, "for the Christmas Tour." Does everyone here talk non-stop? Where is the restroom?

The woman snaps her gum and clasps her chubby fingers under her double chin. "You'll love it. You have to see Fendall Hall and Shorter Mansion, of course. Where are you staying? Are you by yourself? Where did you say you're from?"

This seems eerily similar to a police interrogation. Even Stump is taking an interest now. So much for flying under the radar.

"Um, New York. I'm supposed to find… a Mr. … Jordan." I strain to remember the name on the business card.

"Oh. *New York*," she drags out the words, impressed, "and you must mean *Shug*…and his last name is pronounced Jerr-dan."

"Jerr-dan," I repeat, red-faced. *Nice faux pas, Julia.* What in the heck kind of name is *Shug*? I thought it was a misspelling. His name had to be Stephen. Or Shawn.

I don't have to wait long for an answer. "His mama and daddy are big Auburn fans. War Eagle!" The woman shakes her fist in the air and whoops. At the slightly surprised look on my face, she lowers her voice an octave. "You know, Auburn University? *Coach* Shug Jordan?" She says the name as if he is the Pope or British royalty. "Even named that sister of his after Coach Pat Dye. Bless her heart." The clerk flutters her glued-on eyelashes to the ceiling.

Auburn University. Coach Dye. Marietta wasn't kidding about football being a religious experience in the South. "I'm sure I'll hear all about it." I smile widely, and that seems to satisfy the clerk. "If you'll excuse me, where can I find the ladies' room?"

"Straight back, sugar. Watch your step."

I step into a broom-closet sized bathroom, close the door

behind me, and lock it. Who knows who might follow me in here? I heave a sigh and turn on the water to soap up my arm where the gas permeated my skin. I scrub until my arm turns red, then splash my face. Much better.

"Sugar?"

I'm barely out of the restroom. I pick my way around some cardboard boxes stacked in the aisle, grab a Diet Dr. Pepper, and make my way to the counter.

"You don't want that," she says flatly. Her lip curls up.

"Um, pardon me?" I actually do want it. Very much.

"The Diet Dr. Pepper," she replies and moves the bottle toward the register. "Here! This is what you need. On the house." She reaches under the counter, plops a bright blue can down and slides it toward me, along with two small, wrapped cakes. Apparently, I'm taking them whether I want to or not.

The packages crinkle when I pick them up. I'm guessing fifty grams of Trans fat. Each.

"Moon Pie," I read aloud. "The only one on the planet. And RC Cola." I drag the ice-cold can toward me. "Thank you. I do need the Diet Dr. Pepper, too, though."

The clerk nods, slightly offended, as if I'm asking to buy beer on Sunday morning. "You'll have to pay for that." Her fingers fly across the register. "One-oh-nine, sugar."

I fish a dollar and nine cents out of my purse. Fine by me. "Thank you," I repeat.

She bags up the drinks and Moon Pies. "Anytime. Come back and see us." The woman snaps her gum one more time and smiles at me.

Stump waves.

Both of them watch me closely as I slide back inside the Expedition and crank the engine. I fight a sudden urge to punch the accelerator, do a screaming u-turn on two wheels in the middle of the highway, and head straight back to Atlanta.

But, of course, then I wouldn't have the story. Or a job.

And I can't bear the humiliation.

I don't crack open the Diet Dr. Pepper until I'm well out of sight.

Chapter Four

I DO SOME QUICK CALCULATIONS IN MY HEAD. If I'm able to finish the first interview this afternoon, get a quick tour of the town, and then take some photos, I can wrap up another interview or two in the morning. On that schedule, I can easily make my 6:01 departure out of Atlanta tomorrow night.

That means I can stop by book club Monday, make an appearance at the fundraiser, and enjoy the gallery opening. Reschedule my date with Andrew. Go to Filene's and hope they have something left. Best of all, I'll have plenty of time to write the article before David's deadline.

My father will get the surprise of his entire rotten existence when I turn it in early. Perfect.

The tiniest nudge of hope edges its way inside of me. I can do this. My job will be intact. I can go back to living life as usual, and David might just give up on this crazy 'Back Roads' idea. Or, he could get abducted by Martians. Whichever comes first is fine with me.

The thought makes me grin as I bump over railroad tracks, pass a stately Presbyterian church, chug up a small hill, and ease into downtown. No aliens in sight.

At the stoplight, I glance at the return address of the letter perched on my dashboard. 201 North Eufaula Street. Straight ahead.

Yes. Now this is more like it. Bluff City Inn to my left, bustling coffee shop to my right. Stately brick buildings, wide sidewalks, graceful trees. Everything's decorated in red and green for the holidays. Even the air smells sweet as I roll down the window.

I inhale deeply, slow the Expedition to a crawl, and search for building numbers. Whew! Finally, there it is. The Historic Chattahoochee Commission. The loose stone driveway crunches under the massive wheels as I pull into a makeshift space and park. The Expedition groans a sigh of relief when I shut down the engine.

Purse and notebook in hand, I check my face in the mirror, do a quick finger-comb of my hair. My red-gold highlights catch and hold the sunshine. I smile back at my reflection.

Ready or not.

I ease open the door and jump down what seems like five feet to the ground.

Slam-crack!

On instinct, I duck behind the door. What the—! Was that the windshield? I inch up to get a better look.

Slam-crunch!

A chunk of gravel hits the side window. Another rock zings by my head. Sheesh! So much for Southern hospitality. If this is how the locals roll out the red carpet, I'll find somewhere else—

Slam-crack!

The glass now bears a spidery star-design. The rental people will be thrilled. *Did I remember to get the extra insurance?*

I brace for another onslaught.

Nothing.

Nothing.

Then, I hear a high-pitched squeal.

"Noooo," a child's voice wails. "I don't want to go into the house! I want to stay here! You can't make me!"

Ever so slowly, I creep out from behind the door and inch my way to the back bumper of the Expedition.

A wisp of a girl, feet flying, is wrestling valiantly with a dark-haired man three times her size. After a few seconds, the man squats down with the girl, gently holds her wrists and forces one hand open, then the other. Defeated, the girl lets the stones fall like hail in a thunderstorm.

I step from behind the vehicle. A much too-thin, agitated woman rushes out the back door. It bangs hard behind her.

"Ella Rae Sweet, you come here this instant." Her face a mix of frustration and frown lines, the woman storms for the steps leading down to the parking lot.

For a moment, the woman becomes my mother, and me, the child. The lines soften into a round blonde woman in an apron and skirt. I'm six years old again, my usual headstrong-self running away from trouble. I've likely broken a vase or knocked over a table.

The wood on the stairs creaks, an eerie loud crunch. We all look up in time to see the second rung crumble into several pieces beneath the woman. As she falls forward, her mouth opens in a silent shriek of dismay, too late to make a sound.

Like a tight end in a pro-football game, the dark-haired man springs into action. In one fluid motion, he shoots to the bottom of the steps, crouches down, and catches the woman in both arms. Touchdown!

Wow. I blink at the impressive display of athleticism.

"Nice Superman catch," I call out and wave at a safe distance as the bodies untangle.

Three pairs of eyes flicker my way. Confused? Curious?

Okay, maybe the superhero comment was a little over the top. Maybe superheroes are frowned on in the Deep South. Maybe I'm just paranoid.

I force a smile and start to ask if I'm at the right place. "I'm looking for …" My mind goes blank. Great. What's his name again?

The man stands, brushes off his pants, and walks toward me. He pushes back a shock of black hair with his fingertips. The corners of his eyes crinkle as he sticks out a hand for me to shake. "Shug Jordan," he says simply, with a hint of a southern drawl. "So glad you made it."

"Oh, it's you," I exclaim, then wish I could swallow the words. My hand flutters as it reaches for his. "Julia Sullivan," I say hurriedly, give a firm handshake, and collect my professional persona. "*Getaways* magazine. It's a pleasure to be here."

Shug turns to survey the Expedition. "Sorry about the windshield. We'll take care of it. This is my niece," he pulls on the sleeve of the rock-throwing sprite, and then grins, "and, Julia Sullivan, meet Patricia Dye, better known around these parts as PD. She's Ella Rae's mother."

Before I can open my mouth, PD interrupts. "Ella Rae, apologize for the window, young lady." She flashes her daughter a stern look.

"Sorry, ma'am," Ella Rae faces me and replies dutifully. Her eyes, a startling cornflower blue, peek out at me under a veil of blonde curls. She scuffs the gravel with her toe. An impish smile plays on her lips, hidden from her mother.

"Don't worry about the truck. It's a rental. I have insurance." I try to lighten the mood and smile at PD. "I was just thinking how much I was like your daughter when I was young. My mother always said I was full of energy and into everything—"

"You must have been a load of trouble, then," PD says, hardly moving her tight lips. Her eyes shift from me to her daughter.

I swallow at the barb and maintain a pleasant air. "Yes, I—"

"Trouble, trouble, trouble," Ella Rae parrots, much to the dismay of her mother, who now radiates even more annoyance. I think PD may reach nuclear reactor status.

"Oh, I *rarely* get in trouble these days," I joke, to lighten the conversation, and wink. It's a little white lie, but Shug appears pleasantly amused by the whole situation.

My comment makes Ella Rae giggle.

At that, PD turns, chin held high, and stalks off. Her heels sink into the bumpy driveway, making her gait awkward and uneven. Obviously, no points scored there.

Shug hides a chuckle. I bite the inside of my cheek to keep from laughing.

"Ella Rae Sweet?" PD calls, pausing at the stairs.

"Ma'am?"

"Come get your things. It's time to leave." PD's slender hand grips the railing. "And, by the way, Shug," she pauses for emphasis, maybe for my benefit, "I'd appreciate it if you'd try and set a good example for your niece."

Ella Rae scampers after PD like a naughty puppy to her master. The door bangs shut behind her so hard that the windows rattle.

I blink after mother and daughter, not entirely sure what just happened.

"That's my sister for you. I'm thirty-five years old, and everything I do still aggravates her." We exchange a smile.

"Um, I'm not related, and I feel like I'm annoying her," I reply, keeping my voice hushed.

Shug grins. "PD has her hands full, trying to start her own business. It's extra tough, because PD's a single mother." Shug continues apologetically. "Ella Rae's a wonderful girl, bright, loving…but she can be a challenge, especially since her daddy took off."

The mere thought stabs me in the chest. The way it did when my own father left.

"I'm an only child," I offer up, and then stop myself. Opening up about family leads to questions about my mother, my father, then my general lack of a life—no husband, no baby, not even a dog. I just can't go there.

"Lucky you," Shug answers with an easy grin and steps toward the Expedition to get a better look at the damage.

I start after him and admire the easy way he carries

himself. Unruffled by his niece's misbehavior, relaxed about his neurotic sister's comments, not bothered in the least that a complete stranger will be following him around for the next few days.

My mind flashes to Michael J. Fox in *Doc Hollywood*. The character ends up trapped in South Carolina for weeks because a couple of backwoods mechanics can't get his Porsche fixed—or won't.

Gosh darn, now who's being neurotic? I tell myself to say something funny and lighten the mood.

Shug turns away from the windshield and runs a hand through his dark hair. "We'll get this fixed up in no time," he snaps his fingers. "Promise. Just like magic."

I'm immediately relieved. Okay, no superstition here. And, unlike his sister, he has a sense of humor.

"Just like magic," I repeat, teasing him. "Any other superhero powers I need to know about?" I strike a mock pose. "Able to fix flat tires? Leap tall buildings in a single bound?"

Shug stops and eyeballs me. "Nope. I wish." His face breaks into a smile. "How about you? Any tricks up your sleeve?"

"Oh, some mind-reading," I deadpan. "Sometimes, I'm psychic."

"That sure would come in handy," Shug says. "I thought..."

A long, loud horn and the screech of tires cut off his train of thought. Shug peers at someone behind me and makes a comment, momentarily distracted. The thunder of a truck engine drowns out his words.

The noise covers the obnoxious rumble of my belly. I ignore it and press a hand to my stomach as some teenagers pass by, hanging out the window of a souped-up Yukon, followed by more girls in an SUV with 'Panama City Beach or Bust' painted on the window.

"College kids. They'll freeze at the beach," Shug says

dismissively. He ignores their waving and smiles down at me. "Hungry?"

Darn it all. He did hear.

"How'd you know?" I ask, feigning shock as we begin to walk.

Shug flashes a mischievous look. "Read your mind."

Chapter Five

"ARE YOU ALWAYS IN SUCH A HURRY?" Shug asks, his voice slow and steady compared to my frantic pace. My usual velocity is hyper-drive. Get there as fast as I can, I don't care if I break my neck, or the speed limit.

"Oh, sorry," I slow my brisk stride into a leisurely walk, "hazard of living in the City. Everyone's in a rush, twenty-four seven. Always someplace to go, somewhere to be. When I was younger, I used to wish I didn't have to go to sleep—you know, so I didn't miss anything."

Shug gives me a strange, amused look. If he thinks I'm crazy, at least he is polite enough not to say so.

"Where are we going anyway?" A towering statue of a Civil War soldier stares off into the distance as we cross the intersection.

"Honeysuckle Diner," Shug answers, "just down the street a piece."

A piece. How cute.

Shug describes the thick French toast and warm, buttery cane syrup. Fluffy eggs. Sausage and grits. Suddenly, I'm famished. Seconds later, we arrive at the door.

"Yoo-hoo," a simpering voice calls out from across the street. A car door slams.

No. We can't stop. The smell of fresh-baked biscuits makes me weak. I try to tell Shug telepathically that I'll die if we don't go inside now. I look longingly at the Honeysuckle Diner. Shug is completely distracted.

And then I see why.

Thigh-high boots on a pair of long legs, a short red skirt over tights, and a sequin-trimmed sweater. Topped off by a thick, shiny mane of white-blonde hair and a mega-watt smile.

The girl blows a kiss and waves, as if we might somehow miss her or the white Mercedes convertible she just poured herself out of. Gosh, people are friendly down here. And gorgeous.

I glance down at my standard New York garb—black head to toe. What else did I pack? Oh, right. Almost everything I own, down to my panties, is black.

So what? I argue with myself. Why compare myself to a random girl on the street? Someone I'll *never* see again.

"Um, that's my girlfriend," Shug leans closer to explain. "Mary Katherine." He gestures for her to come across the street.

Of course. So, she's not a random girl. *Lovely.* I'll bet we'll be seeing her every day.

But Mary Katherine shakes her head coyly, points a finger to her cell phone, and steps onto the opposite sidewalk. By the time I decide to wave back, she disappears around the corner.

Shug doesn't seem bothered in the least. He holds open the door to the diner.

Sweet salvation.

My knees weaken at the sight of steaming breakfast plates on every table. Raucous laughter, animated conversation, and the clang of pots and pans from the kitchen make it almost impossible to hear. Shug motions for me to follow him, but stops every few feet. He shakes hands, exchanges back slaps, and chuckles as we move through the crowd.

Curious stares follow us. Polite, inquisitive looks. A wrinkled forehead, pursed lips, a raised eyebrow. If I make eye contact, which I'm trying not to do, the person smiles brightly and chirps a greeting.

Great. I can imagine what they are dreaming up. Star magazine-type rumors, followed by a heinous paparazzi photo. I see it all too clearly. The headline will read: *Who's that girl? Is Shug Jordan cheating on Mary-what's her name?*

Oh well. There's always food. At least I'll die embarrassed and happy.

I center my attention on the tiny empty table in the back corner. Mentally, I push Shug toward it. When I start walking, I almost kick him in the ankle. Closer, closer, there you go. A few more feet.

Without warning, another roadblock appears: A short, round, heavily made-up woman stops Shug to hug him and kiss the air next to his cheek. And then someone, who must be her daughter, goes and does the same thing. No one's in a hurry. Except me.

Five long minutes and three stops later, we make it to the table and sit down. I pick up the narrow menu, hold it in front of my face, and scan the list. Grits, biscuits, red-eye gravy—

"It must be overwhelming," I hear Shug say.

I edge the menu to one side and peek out. He gives me one of those open and honest looks, with piercing eyes. Like an actor on daytime television about to reveal who killed so-and-so's sister's cousin's mother.

"What must be?" I tilt my head in his direction, thinking Shug must mean the menu. It certainly wasn't what I'd call gourmet, but even ostrich eggs and endive smeared with peanut butter would do at the moment. Can't he tell I'm about to gnaw apart the table?

"All of this." Shug makes a sweeping gesture at the rest of the room. "I'm used to it. I was just thinking, to an outsider, well ..." Shug seems to lose his train of thought. He glances down at his own menu, suddenly self-conscious.

Very observant. Pasting on a big smile, I grasp for a witty and off-hand remark, which comes out a jumbled mes... no, not at all. It's different from New York, but I'm not u... fortable. Quite the contrary. I feel right at home."

Shug gives me a thoughtful nod and picks up his m...

It's not the truth. Me being right at home in small-t... Alabama is the equivalent of Kim Kardashian never shop... again.

In New York, it's all about anonymity. No one cares ... you are, unless your last name is Trump. No one says hello... waves, unless it's to grab a taxi.

A waitress hovers nearby. I hurry to take a look at th... menu, and then realize she's not just wiping down the tabl... next to us. She's staring. Shug hasn't even noticed.

Another server appears, and two hands plop down... glasses of light brown liquid. "Good morning, y'all! Cute hair, sweetie," the girl, who appears to be all of nineteen, is calling me sweetie. She inspects my roots and chews on the eraser of her pencil. "Did I hear you say New York?" Her voice raises several octaves. "I've always wanted to visit New York. Rockerfeller Center at Christmas time. The big tree. All of the lights."

I try not to visibly wince at the mispronunciation, but keep my lips buttoned. The minute I correct someone, I'm certain to butcher some Southern phrase in front of a dozen people.

Shug speaks up. "Julia's here to do a preview on the Pilgrimage for *Getaways* Magazine."

The girl's eyes widen like I'm a movie star. Her voice rises a few octaves. "A real magazine reporter?" Several heads swivel near our table. "Can you interview me? Can I be in the article?"

I attempt a serious look at Shug, who stifles a laugh, entertained by the entire situation.

"Um, I'll do my best to include everyone."

That seems to placate her. The waitress prattles on, wav... ing her notepad. "If you feature the Honeysuckle Diner wi...

. "Oh,   ler lip, "Brad Pitt could see it and come
com-   n London, and Europe. Zillionaires." She
                p and down.

enu.   n in my seat and reach for the closest glass.
own   d, I take an enormous swallow.
ing   s so syrupy-sweet I gag. My eyes water. The
                ound in my mouth and I long to spit it on the
ho   t think about it, I instruct myself. Just do it. I
or   down my throat in one big gulp.

                tart to choke. Then cough. I can't stop.
e   s your heart!" The girl drops her notepad and starts
e   my back so hard I'm certain my ribs will crack any
                'She's choking. Oh, my Lord! Someone help her!"

Chapter Six

ALL AROUND US, people stand up and gawk. Shug jumps to his feet. He pushes the waitress away, wraps his arms around my waist, and shoves his fists into my diaphragm. Over and over. In fact, I almost can't breathe.

Doesn't anyone realize I haven't eaten a morsel? *It's the awful tea*, I want to scream, but I'm being squeezed too tightly; the helpless prey of an anaconda.

Somehow, between compressions, I manage to gasp, "I'm fine."

Mercifully, Shug lets go. I want to fall to the floor and roll around in pure joy. But I can't move. "Are you sure you're all right?" he whispers, inches away from my ear. His hand still rests on my waist, which after all the drama, feels rather cozy. I lean against his arm and close my eyes briefly. And inhale.

Oxygen. Blessed oxygen.

My eyes blink open. How embarrassing. But, thankfully, because I haven't spat a chunk of food across the room or gone into convulsions, the diner patrons have already lost interest and are back to gossiping about someone else.

"Julia," Shug says urgently when I don't answer. "Are you okay?" He circles back around the table and sits down across from me. As he does, his hand slides from my waist to my fingers, which he squeezes tightly. "Do you need a drink? More tea?"

With his free hand, Shug holds up the offending liquid.

Between my elbow pressed into the table and Shug's grip

on my hand, I shudder but keep my balance. I realize if I don't answer, Shug's likely to leap back into rescue mode. Or make me drink the tea, which will cause me to vomit.

"I'm okay. Absolutely," I say, attempting to appear perfectly normal and refreshed, like I haven't just made a spectacle of myself in front of thirty strangers eating breakfast.

I actually somewhat lost my appetite. Especially when I see Mary what's-her-name heading straight for the table.

Mary Kate?

Mary Anne?

Mary Katherine. That's it.

"Yoo-hoo," she chirps at us, making her way toward the back of the room, all white and sparkly. Like a hummingbird, Mary Katherine flits from one group to another, pausing momentarily to preen in the large mirror hanging on the far wall.

Except I realize she's not looking at her reflection; she's scrutinizing me. The girl who happens to still be holding her boyfriend's hand.

At that moment, I jump back and grab my fingers like I've been scalded, but it's too late. Her eyes probe my face as she moves toward us. I take it all back, what I said earlier. She's not a hummingbird at all. She's a lioness stalking a defenseless—

"Well, hey, y'all!" says Mary Katherine sweetly. "What do we have here?" The words slide off her lips like beads of honey.

No. No. Don't sit down, I beg silently.

I need to start my interview. I'm already behind.

Of course, she's sitting down.

On cue, Shug bolts up from the table and offers his seat to Mary Katherine, who slides into the modest wooden chair like it's her royal throne. He clears his throat. "Mary Katherine, this is Julia Sullivan. The writer from the magazine I've been telling you about? In New York." His tone is important, solid, all business.

Mary Katherine's mouth forms a slight 'o', but if she's impressed in the least, I can't tell. She gives me a thorough once over, pausing at my black jacket, black pants, and then my black shoes. At any moment, I expect that cute couple from "What Not to Wear" will jump out from behind the partition that hides the kitchen.

I start swinging my foot, a bad habit, but it tends to soothe my nerves.

The waitress is back. "Try again?" she asks innocently. "You feelin' better darlin'?"

Mary Katherine swivels to look at Shug. "Oh dear, did I miss something exciting?"

The waitress is staring at me. I motion for her to stay quiet, widening my eyes in alarm.

Evidently, she thinks it means recap the entire choking event in vivid detail. Then embellish on the facts. I flush cherry-red up to my hairline and do my best to examine my fingernails and cuticles.

Holding the entire restaurant spellbound, the woman launches into her story. Five excruciating minutes later, she wraps up with flourish, probably because the manager is glaring in our direction.

"... and he practically saved her life," she says, finishing with a little bow at the end.

Mary Katherine's eyes narrow. Shug is flustered.

I have to say something. I have to fix it. "It really wasn't like that at all," I interject.

"Aw, sweetie, go on. It's all right." The server winks at me. "We needed some excitement around here." She taps her pen on her notepad. "So, can I take your order?"

Fabulous.

"May I please have some water?" I ask in a meek voice. "And some ..." I scan the menu. "Grits. No cheese. And bacon please."

The waitress scribbles on her pad and turns to Mary Katherine, who's scowling. This isn't going at all like I planned.

I steal glance down at my watch. "Look at the time," I exclaim. "We have to get busy."

Shug looks confused—something that translates into 'you said you needed to eat, now we need to leave?'

"Oh, after breakfast, I mean. We have a lot of ground to cover. A schedule to keep, right?" I chirp and wave a hand as if he shouldn't worry, then pretend to check my iPhone.

What am I talking about? *Schedule* is not even in my vocabulary, unless I have a plane to catch. Schedules mean confinement, like the four walls of an office. I don't schedule. I rely on my local contacts for who to see, what to do, and where to go.

It's worked so far.

Well, maybe not every single time.

There was that luggage mix-up in Greece when I ended up with someone else's suitcase. Little did I know it was full of nothing but cigars, condoms, and a pair of men's red silk pajamas. *Gag.* Five seconds later, I was back in a taxi on the way to the airport to find my real baggage.

And I did get lost in Madrid, but only for a few hours. This I-thought-they-were-nice couple took pity on me, offered me a ride, and then wanted to stop off for a glass of wine. I was all for it until the husband propositioned me. He thought a threesome with his wife would be delightful. I begged off, citing a recent Hepatitis flare-up, fingers crossed behind my back the whole time. The man deflated like a stuck balloon faster than I could say 'adios.'

Then, there was a hotel snafu in Cozumel, when I ended up sleeping in a youth hostel. After my roommate left her taco half-eaten on her backpack, we had a midnight bug infiltration. Big. Huge. Bugs. Thank goodness I was on the top bunk.

Anyway, it all worked out, in the end.

And here, in Eufaula, Alabama, Shug seems every bit the

reasonable, responsible host. I can rely on him to point me in the right direction. "So, what's on the agenda?"

"I do have some things in mind," Shug wrinkles his brow. He's probably trying to remember if I asked for a schedule. I'm not about to correct him. He takes a long drink of the dreaded sweet tea. Ugh! How can he stand it? My teeth are rotting in my head just thinking about the cavities. Dentists must make a fortune around this place.

"Great! I can't wait to get started!" I exclaim.

Mary Katherine giggles like we've just shared the funniest joke ever. The sound crawls right up my back. "Shug has been beside himself—we're thrilled that you've decided to come to Eufaula and do the article!"

I smile at the 'we' comment. And have a sneaking suspicion they've known about this little project a lot longer than I have.

With a nudge at Shug, Mary Katherine throws me a hopeful look. "If I'm *lucky* enough to be in the article, I'll need to buy at least thirty copies and send them to everyone. All of my friends in Birmingham and Mobile," Mary Katherine ticks off names on her fingers. "There's Stacey, Melissa, Candy, Alicia…"

Shug clears his throat.

Mary Katherine pauses, "You do know I'm on the Pilgrimage committee, don't you Julia?"

I don't know this, but nod anyway.

"Breakfast," Shug announces, no doubt as glad as I am for the interruption.

One by one, the plates are set in front of us. On Mary Katherine's is one slice of toast, no butter, and a plain bowl of sliced melon. Shug has what looks like several biscuits topped with gravy and something else I can't identify.

My grits and a side of bacon arrive seconds later. "May I have some brown sugar, please?" I ask the server. She gives me a strange look, then disappears.

Mary Katherine lowers her eyes and takes a tiny nibble of her toast. At this rate, we'll be here a million years.

I dip my spoon carefully into the creamy-white grains, as if I'm testing the water of a swimming pool the first day of summer break. A bit of it sticks to the end of my spoon. Looks harmless enough. I close my eyes and put the spoon to my lips. Hmm. Bumpy and kind of bland. A little salty.

When I open my eyes, Shug is staring at me with an amused look on his face. "You really should try it with cheese," he recommends.

"Oh, no," I say, horrified. The brown sugar arrives and I am totally distracted. I dump half the bowl into the grits and begin to stir. The sugar melts into a lovely taupe swirl. Without hesitating, I spoon some into my mouth. Mmm. Pure heaven.

"So, tell us about how you became a writer," Shug asks.

I smile, grateful he's changed the subject. "I grew up around it, so it seemed like a natural career fit for me, too. My father's been a journalist all of his life. He started out as a newspaper reporter in the South, worked his way up the East Coast, then went to New York and got into the magazine industry."

Even Mary Katherine looks impressed. "Shug's in the family business," I hear her say.

"Really? The travel and tourism business?"

"No," Shug tries not to laugh. "She means that I'm part owner of Jordan Construction and so is my sister. My father runs the business. The Historic Chattahoochee Commission is my full-time job."

"For now it is," Mary Katherine adds tersely. "It's a great service to the community. But it's so demanding and keeps Shug here all of the time."

Somehow, I don't think I'm getting the full story. I focus on my grits and brown sugar.

"Traveling is so glamorous." Mary Katherine sounds wistful, almost human. "I'll bet you've been to all of the most wonderful places. Paris, London, Rome."

"I'm just back from Italy. Belize before that," I say, nodding.

"Do you love it?" she asks, hopeful, leaning closer.

"I do. I see so many different places and different people. I don't have any commitments. I'm not stuck anywhere."

Then, I see Shug staring off into space. *Have I upset him?*

Staying here is probably what's expected of him. Like the mafia, but not as clandestine and illegal. He does it for family. A sacrifice.

"But there's nothing wrong with living in a lovely place like Eufaula." I look at Mary Katherine with an apologetic grin. "Besides, travel isn't all that glamorous. You lose your luggage, miss flights, the weather can be awful, and hotels can lose electricity. I never get my mail."

Mary Katherine looks unconvinced and takes another bite of dry toast. Doesn't she have somewhere to go? Something to do? Exercise? Haircut? A job?

Which reminds me about my own career.

I put down my spoon, dab at my lips with a napkin, and prepare myself to listen, forcing my body to be still.

"So," I say, "Tell me all about Eufaula."

Chapter Seven

MARY KATHERINE LOOKS IMMEDIATELY PAINED and purses her lips, as if someone poured a pound of salt in her sweet tea.

"Oh, my. Gotta run, y'all," she twitters and pushes back her chair. Ever the gentleman, Shug jumps to his feet again.

She pecks Shug on the cheek and turns to me with an apologetic look. "Have to get to Dothan. I'm squeezing in a mani-pedi before my meeting at the bank. Can't be late."

The thing is, as I gaze in her direction, Mary Katherine's fingernails and toes look immaculate, like tiny shells painted a pale coral color. Not one chip.

She gathers her purse, then takes time to fuss with Shug's collar. I'm certain the gesture is a sign, a symbol, perhaps a warning to me. Mary Katherine is marking her territory, making sure that I know what's what. She might as well hammer a sign above Shug's head, "Private Property. No Trespassing."

Don't worry sweetheart, I want to say. It's all business. I play with the straw in my water glass to illustrate just how detached I am from the whole scene. I wonder why someone as beautiful as she is has to put so much effort into demonstrating ownership.

Andrew wouldn't know what to make of it if I acted swoony. I'm the first to vouch that my boyfriend deserves more attention. He always teases that he's going to file a missing person report when I'm off on assignment for more than a week.

With men, staking a claim doesn't do any good anyway. If they want to leave, they just do. Take my father, for example.

"Julia," Mary Katherine is trying to get my attention. She waves a finger in front of my face. "Thought we'd lost you for a minute there."

"Oh no," I recover, "just running through some ideas." I certainly can't tell her the truth. That she's a possessive girlfriend with security issues.

Mary Katherine wrinkles her brow.

"For the article," I explain.

"Oh, sugar," she claps her hands. "I meant to ask you, Julia … and I'm sure you won't mind, Shug."

Uh-oh, I'm already thinking. Shug looks a tad uncomfortable.

"Please join us for dinner tonight at the Jordan's. It'll be great. You can ask all kinds of questions about Eufaula. And meet the rest of the family. They have all sorts of photos and books from the old days. Don't they, honey?"

"Sure. Good idea," Shug chimes in, relieved.

What? He was supposed to disagree. I'm already shaking my head no. I need a bubble bath and a glass of wine. Then, sleep. Dinner can be Diet Dr. Pepper and a Hershey Bar.

They both look at me expectantly.

"I think I need to rest, with the long trip and all…" I start to explain.

Mary Katherine immediately pouts. Shug looks taken aback. Great, I've just broken some long-standing rule of Southern hospitality. Never say no to an invitation. "You need to meet MeeMaw. And Aubie and TJ."

Who is she talking about? Does everyone have crazy nicknames?

My resolve crumbles. "Well, I suppose I can if it's no trouble."

"Good. Then it's all settled. Say, about six-fifteen? See you then!" Mary Katherine reaches over and squeezes my hand like we've been best friends for years. "Can't wait to see you tonight."

Then she's gone.

"Whew!" I don't mean to say it out loud, but somehow it escapes from my brain and travels out my mouth before I can catch it.

Shug starts to chuckle. He throws a twenty and a ten on the table. "She's something, isn't she?"

"Um." I'm not sure how to answer.

"Don't worry about it. Mary Katherine operates at 150 percent all of the time. She tries to make a good impression. She wants everyone to like her. I'm sure she just wants to make sure you feel welcome."

"Oh," I say and feel slightly guilty. Maybe I judged her too quickly.

"You ready to go?"

"Absolutely."

"We'll grab your bags and drop them off so you can get settled. Probably best if you leave the SUV at my office. No need to drive around with a shattered windshield."

Balmy air hits me as Shug holds open the door. We step outside, and I am blinded, the way immediate bright light shuts down your senses. When I regain my focus, I get the strangest feeling. Then, I realize that the sidewalks are almost empty. One person wanders up ahead, window-shopping.

It's so peaceful. So quiet. So not New York. In the City, there's the rushed crackle of electricity on the streets. Everyone in his or her own little world. People too busy to strike up a conversation, every head on the subway buried in the *Wall Street Journal*. Hot dog vendors on every corner. Street salesmen hocking knock-off designer purses and jewelry.

There's none of that here.

"It's funny to think that folks managed without air conditioning for eons," Shug is saying as we start to walk. "Of course, if you've lived here all your life, it's not that bad."

"I wouldn't have made it," I say, half-joking. "I'm not that tough. What does the temperature get to in the summer? Ninety-nine in the shade?"

Shug laughs and nods.

"If I had to stay outside in July, I'd probably melt." I shade my eyes at the glare as we round the corner, and I try not to run toward the trees lining the street and sidewalks up ahead.

"Oh, I think you're wrong," Shug says with a sidelong glance at me. "We all underestimate our own strength and determination." He pauses, thoughtful.

And I realize he's not talking about the heat at all.

"Almost three hundred years ago," Shug says with a sweeping motion toward the expanse of antebellum houses and trees in front of us, "none of this existed. Only Creek Indian tribes and wildlife lived here. Then, two hundred years ago, the first white settlement was established. The people built a steamboat wharf, which boosted trade between Alabama and Georgia."

I nod, taking it in.

"None of it would have happened unless someone first believed it could be done, put the plans in place, and led the charge."

He's animated now, talking about the history of the region. I imagine he sees women with parasols and hoop skirts, the men in hats and long coats, horse-drawn carriages with the clip-clop sound of progress.

"My office is the Hart House," he explains as we pause in front of the building. "It's Greek Revival; constructed in the mid-1800s. One of Eufaula's original settlers, John Hart, built the home. We've been able to keep the integrity of the original structure virtually unchanged."

Shug's eyes caress the small cottage, its hipped roof, and the six white columns that shelter the front porch. "It's home right now, which horrifies my parents, especially my mother, who'd love me to buy the Pitts-Gilbert House or the Russell-Jarrett—"

The confusion on my face makes him stop.

"I'm sorry," he apologizes. "Many homes in the area are named after the families who lived there. Those names are often combined with the families who live there or own them now. For example, my parents' house is Jordan Manor, down the street is the Couric-Smith Home— it was featured several years back on the *Today* show. Katie Couric traced her own family history."

I raise my eyebrow, impressed, and bite my lip. Perhaps if I would have taken the time to do some research, I'd have realized that. I find my keys in my purse, pop the trunk on the Expedition, and take out my lone piece of luggage.

"You travel light," Shug comments and takes the handle of my suitcase. "Mary Katherine needs a trailer or two."

"Years of practice," I grin and hit the button to lock the SUV.

"Am I giving you information-overload about Eufaula?" Shug takes a step back to scrutinize my reaction. "Mary Katherine says I tend to do that. She teases that I know the ghosts from the past better than I do the people living around me." He shrugs his shoulders. "Maybe it's true."

He's joking, but I sense a hard edge to his confession.

"Not at all," I reply. "I'm fascinated."

"Okay, good." Shug smiles and waves for me to follow him.

"So," I ask, "with all the generations of families, and with naming these mansions, it seems like every house would have its own story."

Shug smiles. "Exactly. And every good story starts with asking the right questions." He flushes. "I'm not trying to tell you how to do your job. It's just my opinion. I've always wanted to write a book, maybe about Eufaula. I just haven't found the time."

As I half-listen to his explanation, I wonder if David warned him.

The right questions.

I brush off the hint of doubt creeping up my spine with the shake of my head.

Surely, David didn't say anything.

I know how to do my job. I know how to get a story together. I know how to delve in, ask questions, and find the heart of the issue.

I'm a seasoned journalist, after all. I've won awards. I'm a professional who works for a national magazine.

But, the nagging uncertainty won't disappear. It lingers with the persistence of a gnat buzzing in my ear.

Go away, David, I want to shout. *Leave me alone. I know what I'm doing.*

It's the heat, I finally decide. The humidity is seeping into my brain.

We arrive at the bed and breakfast. It's lovely, with huge, beveled glass doors and a sprawling porch. "Let's get you inside. You might melt, remember?"

We both laugh, causing a passerby to stare.

"Meet you back here in an hour?" Shug grins again, his entire face lighting up. He's really handsome, thoughtful, and smart. The total package. No wonder Mary Katherine is so protective.

"Okay," I nod and smile as a shock of hair falls over his forehead. Adorable.

Down the street, a car honks, yanking me back to reality. *Stop it Julia. You're in Eufaula on business, not to gawk at the South's not-so-eligible bachelors.*

As I watch Shug disappear around the corner of the building, David's words float into my mind—rising and popping like air bubbles reaching the surface of a lake.

I'll give you a chance to redeem yourself. Put your heart into it.

No sugar-coating there.

No hand-holding.

No promises or guarantees.

I straighten my shoulders and take a deep breath. I can do this. Piece of cake, right?

My personal pep talk doesn't do much good. One thought—one niggling, twisting thought—shakes me to the core.

What if my best isn't good enough?

Chapter Eight

I DESPERATELY WANT TO:

- Put my feet up
- Be alone for five minutes
- Unpack my wrinkled clothes
- Put on some lip gloss
- Wash my face

Not too much to ask, right? But, when I see what—or should I say who—is waiting for me inside the B & B, I know I can forget all of it.

The owner—it has to be—is dressed like someone off the cover of last month's GQ. His dark hair is close-cropped; his high cheekbones are set off by immaculate sideburns. Starched pale pink shirt, tiny wire-rimmed glasses, trim suit, and flowered tie.

In contrast to the massive walnut dining room table in the center of the room, he's thin and wiry, with delicate hands. His body is bent slightly over a vase of flowers, like he's telling a secret to the huge arrangement of lilies—all listening intently with upturned faces.

He swivels around and straightens at the sound of my footsteps on the hardwood floor. The door had been propped open as if he knew I was about to arrive.

"Darling Miss Julia!" he exclaims in a heavy British accent. His arms fling open, and he rushes over to greet me. "I'm Roger."

Before I can speak, Roger hugs me to his chest, kisses

the air on both sides of my cheeks, and then holds me out at arms' length. "Gorgeous, simply gorgeous. You're lovelier than anyone said. Naughty them." He wags a finger, then asks, admiring my outfit, "Donna Karan, darling?"

I nod and my head swirls. *Naughty them?* Who is he talking about?

Roger takes in my blank expression with arms folded elegantly across the breast of his suit. "The girls at Honeysuckle Diner, of course. And Elma from the Citgo. They all called my cell the second your big, bad Excursion pulled into town."

"Oh," I manage, a little in awe and somewhat bewildered that my arrival had been announced in a phone chain from the local gas station.

My host lets his gaze linger over me, appraising everything from my upturned nose to my bare left ring finger. Roger draws a breath. "We can't wait to read your article. I mean, it's not everyday someone from New York is here. Of course, you'll be previewing the Pilgrimage. The Christmas tour will give you a little taste." He looks dreamily at the wall. "Historic Eufaula by candlelight is unparalleled."

I suddenly feel a little ill. How many people are banking on my very presence in this sleepy town producing the article of the century? I hadn't even written the first word.

Perhaps I look blue—in an oxygen-deprived sort of way—causing Roger to snap his fingers in front of my face. "I know just the thing to help!" he says, carrying away my bags before I can stop him. "If you need background information," he lowers his voice, "I know a little about *everybody*. I can be your 'source,'" Roger adds with a sly wink. "Don't worry. By the end of this week, you'll feel right at home."

I'm not celebrity gossip columnist Liz Smith. I'm only staying one night if I can manage it—two at the very most.

Roger's already disappeared around the corner. "Follow me, sweetheart," he calls out.

I step cautiously onto the plush Turkish rug. The parlor to

my left is filled with antiques, gun cabinets, and writing desks. A poker table sits in the middle of the room. To my right, the ladies' parlor is draped in expensive burgundy fabrics, a piano in one corner. Portraits and gilded mirrors grace the walls.

From down the hall, I hear Roger whistling. My Lord, he's probably unpacking everything in my bag as I'm dawdling in the foyer. I follow the sound to the second bedroom on the left. Roger's already placed my suitcase near the closet door. He's lit an enormous white candle and is blowing out a match as I enter the large room. The scent of gardenia drifts from the flame.

"And so?" Roger says, not pausing to gauge my response. He's flitting around, plumping pillows, rearranging towels in the adjoining bathroom.

"It's lovely, thank you," I say and look longingly at the antique four-poster bed. I'd love a nap. I would give my favorite Prada boots to a stranger for eight hours of sleep. Instead, when it's obvious Roger's not in a hurry to leave, I perch on the edge of the bed.

"New York," Roger looks past me at the wall, this time sounding not at all like he's from the UK. "I'm so jealous. It's a huge dream of mine. Go to the city. Get my big acting break." His eyes brighten as he speaks.

"Have you ever been to New York?" I say, curious. "I thought at first you were—"

Roger claps his hands. "A world traveler? From London? Magnificent. You've made my night."

That wasn't exactly what I was thinking, but …

Roger's still talking at warp speed. "Darling, I wish. I grew up in tiny Newville, Alabama, on a farm. Henry County, just down the road." His nose wrinkles as if he's smelled manure. "I didn't fit in at all," he laughs, sounding a little forced. "Still don't."

This answers quite a few questions. "So, why don't you go? To the City?" I ask.

Roger's brow puckers up, like I've just asked him to explain the theory of relativity.

"To follow your dream?" I clarify, reaching over to stroke one of the pillows. It's soft as silk, with elegant tassels and trim.

Rogers bends near the bookcase to brush off an imaginary piece of dust. "Oh, you know," he says casually. "I'm so busy here. I'm involved in theatre productions in Dothan. The Understudy, SEACT. I've done *The Music Man*, *Grits on the Side*, you name it. And I do have my small social circle ... supper club, book club. And up until this very minute, I didn't know anyone in New York." He looks at me, lashes fluttering, his words pointed and meaningful.

I giggle at his dramatics. "Well, now you do." The words slip out before I can think. What am I doing? I never offer anyone a place to stay—especially to men—although Roger is far from intimidating. I swallow. "I'll be sure and give you my number, so you can look me up."

Roger's face is a mix of sheer terror and delight. "Bless your heart! That's so kind. So wonderful. I just don't know what to say. I just didn't think ..." He rubs his hands together and wiggles around so much I think he's going to start dancing. "I actually know someone in New York," he says to himself in a whisper. "You probably have all kinds of connections; being a magazine writer and all..."

"Magazine writer," I repeat and slap myself on the head. Oh no! In all of the fussing and chatting, I'd almost forgotten about dinner. I jump off the bed, grab for my suitcase, and fumble with the handle. "What time is it? Oh, no. I'm going to be late."

"Late?" Roger echoes. "Is there a big soirée I've not been invited to?" He pouts a little.

Gosh, I hope not. Ignoring the comment, I unzip the silver track on my suitcase. Frantic, I dig through my clothes to find my makeup, jewelry, and a decent dress.

Roger hasn't moved. He's still waiting for my reply.

"Um, I don't think so. Dinner at the Jordan's tonight." I find the makeup case and hold it up triumphantly. My watch face glints in the candlelight. It reads five-forty-five. Phew. Still some time.

Roger is tapping his fingers along one dresser. "At the Jordan's? Meaning his parents' place ... with everyone?" He peers at me intently. "Not the little shack of an office Shug calls home for right now, I hope. I do have to get him going on my decorating plans. I'm thinking *Southern Living* meets *Metropolitan Home—*"

I shake my head vigorously. "No, I think it's a casual family get-together. His mother, his sister. His dad, maybe? I'm really not sure."

A sudden thought hits me. I imagine a throng of people, elbow to elbow, and I won't be able to see or hear because of the crowd.

"Well, well." Roger adjusts his tie and takes a few steps toward the hallway. He pauses in the doorway, then half-turns to look back at me. "That should be interesting." A strange expression crosses his face—halfway between amusement and fascination.

It's obvious there's something I don't know. It's also clear he has no intention of telling me. I know I should let it go, allow him to leave, and find out for myself. Three seconds later, I can't stand it any longer. My insides are twitching every which way, but I keep my tone even and calm. "What do you mean?"

"You'll see," Roger says. "We'll chat tomorrow, darling. Catch up."

With that, he struts out the door. It shuts behind him with a gentle click.

I shake my head. Catch up? What's with these people? I think for a moment. Well, I guess that's what normal people do when they sit still long enough.

Come to think of it, when I'm home, I can't be bothered with office gossip. It seems I'm always a dozen episodes behind on who's dating who, who's getting a divorce, or who's having a baby.

All this worrying isn't good for me. My breathing is shallow and fast. My throat is scratchy and dry. I glance around the room, slightly panicked. No mini-bar, no bottled water. No Diet Dr. Pepper because I drank it already.

Do I dare get that RC? And the Moon Pies?

Desperation knows no bounds when I have to quench my thirst. I start to fish around in the pockets of my tote bag. Ah ha! Gotcha, I think triumphantly. Except for the Moon Pies are hot and half-melted. The RC is a bit warm too.

Ice. Surely they have ice here. I take a step toward the door. No, I can't bother Roger. If I do, I'll never get to the Jordan's.

Bathroom sink. They have to have one of these. Behind the door, a lovely white pedestal sink sits in the center of the far wall, a huge claw-foot tub to the right.

I take a peek in the mirror; run a hand through my hair. The handles of the faucet creak when I turn them. For a moment, nothing happens. Then, blessed water! I let it run, then tuck my hair behind both ears and stick my mouth underneath. Water is dripping across my cheek and up to my ear. Even so, it's delicious, wet, and cold. Refreshed, I throw myself into getting ready.

Black skirt, matching jacket, a pair of deep red, open-toed heels, dash of lip gloss. There.

It's six o'clock on the dot. Certainly, I don't want to be early. Or late. I glance at the directions. Shug has written down an address on North Eufaula Avenue. It's not far.

I walk over to the window and hoist the wooden frame up a few inches so that a slight breeze can come through the screen. The room is taking on a golden glow from the setting sun. A sudden gust blows past my arm. Several papers, which were neatly stacked on the writing desk in the corner, flutter to the floor. Stationary, envelopes, and a few brochures about the Pilgrimage, thanks to Roger. There's a postcard, too. I pick that up last.

It's a lovely one, actually. The towering white structure cuts an impressive figure against a turquoise blue sky. Bright pink azaleas hug the columns and steps leading up to the veranda.

I flip it over and read the back.

Shorter Mansion. 340 North Eufaula Avenue. Built in 1884 by Eli and Wylena Shorter, the home took on its present Neoclassical Revival appearance after its 1906 renovations. Headquarters for the Eufaula Heritage Association. Open Year-Round.

Out of habit, I reach for a pen, uncap it, and hold it above the white rectangle.

Wait. Who am I going to send it to? Emptiness fills my chest.

Andrew would like it—he'd probably die of shock, actually. The man's not used to impromptu displays of affection. Better not start now. I'll be expected to keep it up, then disappoint him when I don't.

Marietta would appreciate it, but it wouldn't be quite as special as sharing it with family.

And David? I begin to laugh out loud, then cover my mouth. I'll send him a postcard the moment I start craving red eye gravy and biscuits. Or say y'all.

As I think, I run a finger along the edge of the postcard, rub the glossy coating with my thumb. There's only one person I want to send it to, and she can't get mail.

Mom, I really miss you.

Chapter Nine

OUTSIDE ROGER'S BED AND BREAKFAST, I feel a little bit like Alice in Wonderland. I keep waiting to hear the angry honk of taxis and the squeal of tires. I expect to smell motor oil and see clouds of smog dotting the tops of silver skyscrapers.

Like many city dwellers, I find comfort in the anonymity of New York's sidewalks. You can vanish into a sea of bobbing heads, ponytails, and baseball caps. The constant noise, jostled elbows, and the steady crinkle of shopping bags provide a buffer from anything remotely personal. Sunglasses shield every eye, even when it's cloudy. On any given day, the line in front of the hot dog stand stretches a mile, where people stand closer than husbands and wives, yet are strangers. Amidst it all, brakes squeal, horns honk, and cell phone conversations buzz from all sides.

Here, it's quiet. Really serene. The azaleas and gardenias, full to bursting with pink and white blooms, have obviously been tricked into thinking it's spring because of the warm weather.

By accident, a person might fall in love with a place like this. It's the silliest thing in the world for me to think. I'm not one of those sentimental types. I prefer the hustle, bustle, the noise, and the action. I'd be bored and restless in a place like this. At least, that's what I've told my friends. And myself.

I actually can't remember a time in the last decade that I've spent more than five minutes in a small town. Okay. There was the time I was handed a whopping speeding ticket in La

Jolla on my way to San Diego, but that really doesn't count. A three hundred dollar fine does tend to dampen the moment.

Here, though, at this very moment, the sky turning a deep shade of violet, but it's clear enough to see a sprinkle of stars overhead. Under the streetlights, crickets begin chirping, and the air is so sweet and heavy with moisture a person could almost drink it in. My breathing is slower, my heart doesn't feel quite so heavy, and I'm letting myself stroll along, absorbing the details of everything around me.

I pass Shug's office. One light burns in each window opposite the center door; the building is still and quiet. Next to his office is the Eufaula Library, a two-story red-brick building with light yellow trim. The large hanging eaves under the hipped roof give it a stately feel; long, narrow balconies face north and west.

Up ahead and across the road, a dark, gothic-looking church strikes an imposing figure as I come nearer. The bricks are pale, set off by dark, tall, stained-glass windows. Beneath a small white cross, the centerpiece of the church is a rose window set between the two main towers. To the left, a fountain sits in the center of a stone-paved garden.

I cross the street to get a better look at Shorter Mansion, which stands out in bright white with its Corinthian columns. A balcony sets off the double wooden doors and leaded-glass windows beneath. Dentils and a balustrade run along the top of the structure above a frieze of leaves and scrolls. It is certainly worthy of its stature as one of Alabama's most magnificent historical sites.

The home next to it is a dark, sprawling estate with an expansive porch and a tower that must reach three stories high.

Up ahead, both Highland and Cotton Avenues branch off of the main street—North Eufaula Avenue. I watch for house numbers, and then I see it. An amazing creamy-tan stucco home comes into view. It must be the Jordan's. I gaze up at it, impressed. Its enormous rotunda entrance with six columns shelters a wide balcony.

When I step from the sidewalk to get a better look by a young magnolia tree, the lawn feels like a cushion under my shoes.

The terrace seems empty, so I close my eyes a moment to think about tonight's gathering. It's a chance to get great background information for my story. I'll have to remember to ask about the—

"Ow! Ouch!" I almost leap out of my skin as something sharp bites at my ankle, then my toes. My skin is burning, like someone lit a match under the arch of my foot. I jump around, brushing at my legs and peer down at the mound of dirt and grass.

In the streetlight, I see that it is swarming with minuscule red ants. An army of them. There must be five hundred, all on a mission from the devil himself to suck the blood out of my body.

I step onto the sidewalk and almost lose my balance trying to get my shoes off. The ants are clinging to my wrist and finger, munching on whatever they can find. I slap at my hand and manage not to fall, somehow kicking off one my shoes across the lawn.

All at once, someone grabs my waist to steady me. It's Shug, who calmly bends down, smacks at my ankles with a plush, white hand towel, and wipes away the bugs. I am too busy knocking the critters off my knuckles to care about the burn of his hand on my skin.

With a splash, he pours a cool liquid on my ankles. The intense smell makes me want to pinch my nose, but I'm so relieved that the pain is gone that I don't even care about being drenched in stinky, chilled vinegar with a hint of apple cider.

When the jug is empty and I'm satisfied Shug's taken out the last ant, I look down at my legs and feel a little nauseous. This man kneeling in front of me is inspecting my toes. On top, between, and below each one of them. Thank goodness my feet are clean and my pedicure is relatively intact. The shiny red of my toenail polish glints back up at me.

I steady myself with one hand on Shug's shoulder. If I let go, I think I might fall over.

"Okay, you're safe. They're all gone." Shug flashes a concerned smile in my direction.

"W-what are those evil, blood-sucking monsters?" I spit out. My ankles are puffy and red in spots. I'm trying to ignore it and maintain my dignity.

Shug starts to laugh. "They don't suck your blood. They're fire ants. They bite." He nods down at my feet. "And inject a kind of poison."

I bite my lip. Poison.

My rescuer takes in the sick look on my face. "Some people are allergic," Shug says quickly, "but you'll probably be okay."

I nod and try to put on a brave face, but can't help that I shudder. It still feels like ants are crawling up my skin with tiny legs.

Shug tilts his head to get a better look at the small welts knotting up on my toes and the tops of my feet. "You'll get little blisters. They'll go away in a few days."

I try to ignore the ugly welts. It's impossible.

"C'mon," he says, "let's get you to a safer place."

I hobble along behind him, humiliated. Despite the slight breeze, I'm covered with a slight sheen of sweat. Thank goodness, the rest of his family wasn't here to witness—

"Ah-hah," I hear from behind one of the porch columns. It's PD, eased back in a rocking chair, the motion of it almost too slight to notice. "Shug to the rescue again."

I'm on guard, but since this afternoon, the sharp edge to her voice has softened.

"Hello," I call up to her.

She looks at me, smiling. "We'll have to start calling my brother the caped crusader."

"And this could be Wayne ..." I wink at her, "I mean, Jordan Mansion."

Ella Rae appears from nowhere, clambering down the steps. "Who's Wayne?" she asks, throwing herself around Shug's leg.

"Bruce Wayne," I start to tell her, trying not to reach down and scratch at my blistering skin. Ella Rae looks up at me blankly.

"The guy who plays Batman," Shug adds, swinging his niece up into his arms and hugging her tightly. "Just like Superman is Clark Kent."

"Oh," Ella Rae shrugs. Before anyone can finish explaining, she's off again like a shot, at the other end of the veranda, amusing herself by weaving in and out of the columns like they're a personal obstacle course.

PD leans forward, unruffled, extends her hand, squeezes mine lightly then releases. Her skin is cool and smooth, the sensation of laying a hot cheek against a marble slab.

"So we didn't scare you off with the broken windshield?" PD asks, a slight smile playing on her lips as if she's keeping a secret. "I'll warn you. The entire Jordan family at once can be quite overwhelming."

So I've heard. I can't decide whether she's trying to test me, so I'll just be truthful.

"Can't be any worse than the chaos of our office in New York," I joke. "At the magazine, it's always a dozen phones ringing, fax machines spitting out paper, and people yelling about the printers running out of ink."

The creak of the door interrupts. Shug and PD, who are facing me, turn their heads at the sound. I smooth my shirt.

"Shug honey, be a dear, and come hold this door," a musical voice comes from inside the house.

Before I can blink, Shug's already there, and a curvaceous woman with flushed cheeks and flame-orange hair bursts through the door holding a tray of ice-filled glasses. They clink with every step, and all are filled with sweet tea. I'm certain of it.

My parched throat starts to close up at the sight. For a moment, I indulge the idea of "accidentally" spilling the sugary sweet tea all over my ankles so they'll stop making me fidget. After another second, I realize than every mosquito and fly in a five-mile radius would then dive-bomb my legs.

After a slight bobble, Shug's mother balances the drink tray on the small table between the rocking chairs. She then whirls around like an aged ballerina.

"This is my mother, Aubie Jordan," PD leans forward in her chair, frowning.

"And you must be Julia," Aubie sweeps over to hug me. As she exhales my name, I am enveloped in a cloud of Estee Lauder *Pleasures* and Jack Daniels.

I hold my breath and try not to cough as the air is squeezed out of my lungs. Over her shoulder, I see Shug exchange a glace with PD.

His mother releases me to reach down for a glass of sweet tea. Her hand shakes slightly as she offers it to me. "Here you go, honey. The best in Alabama."

"Thank you," I grit my teeth into a pleasant expression. She's looking at me expectantly, so I pretend to take a sip. A piece of sugared ice slips into my mouth. I run it over my tongue, and the sensation chills my taste buds.

Satisfied, Aubie takes a shaky step and slides into the seat next to Ella Rae, scolding her for not helping out in the kitchen. She looks young, but Aubie must be in her mid-fifties. Dressed in a trim cream pantsuit and heels, her unlined face bears only a hint of make-up. Like PD, there's a dab of gloss on her lips and sweep of light shadow on her eyelids. Her charcoal dark eyes match Shug's in color with a layer of mascara to open them up wide.

As I'm analyzing the familial similarities, I realize she's still talking to me.

"I'm sorry," I say at the awkward lull in the conversation. "What would you like to know?"

Aubie smiles widely, revealing two gleaming-white rows of perfect teeth. "Now, where do you go to church, up in New York? You must have a church family?" Her eyes are wide and soft, like a puppy's. She looks almost hopeful, like I'm a lost soul to rescue.

I blink, hold my breath, and digest the question. Before I answer, I scan my memories like I'm thumbing through a cabinet of file folders. I stop when I see the portrait of my mother in the vestibule of First Presbyterian and hear the tinkle of wind chimes in the distance.

The question has caught me off guard, and I'm angry with myself for letting it. I remind myself I'm in the Bible belt, not New York. Marietta warned me that church, family, and football supersede global warming in the Deep South. No doubt, she would be rolling on the floor at this little situation.

"Mother, please," Shug is saying. Clearly embarrassed, he tries to read my reaction.

Undeterred, Aubie takes a delicate swallow of sweet tea, which now I'm suspicious is spiked with something 80 proof. And waits.

I make my face a blank canvas. Nevertheless, I am trapped. I have to respond, sooner or later. And, as a travel writer, sometimes even the most overt, awkward question about religion or politics has to be overlooked in the interest of getting an article done—this particular story being the most important since it's now directly connected to the rest of my journalism career.

I turn my head, cough lightly, and hold a hand over my mouth. "I'm Presbyterian," I manage to get out, hoping she doesn't ask for evidence of the last time I sat in a wooden pew and listened to a sermon. Or whether I've been saved.

Saved from what? I'd probably ask after a few drinks.

My mother was convinced of her faith—even after Amyotrophic Lateral Sclerosis sapped all of the strength from her body. As I watched her waste away from ALS—Lou Gehrig's disease—the beliefs I'd been taught to hold onto so tightly began to chip away, pebbles loosened from cement after sun, wind, and rain take their toll.

Why would a benevolent God take away the most valuable things in life when you need them the most? And how do you fill the void that's left behind? My questions are hollow and deep, like the indentations a metal scoop leaves behind in a container of ice cream. Before my insides melt, it's back to the freezer with the memories of my mother, lid on tight— where the air's too cold to think.

I consider telling Aubie I have no "church family" or any other "family" for that matter, but that's not entirely true. There's David, my once-estranged father and new boss.

However, before I can form a response to her question, she's already moved on to sensitive topic number two. She's staring at my fingers. The left ring finger, to be specific. I watch Aubie drain her sweet tea and mystery mixture. She dabs at her lips thoughtfully.

"And how about a boyfriend, dear? A fiancé?"

I knew it was coming, yet a blush of red creeps up the back of my neck and spreads into my hairline. PD is openly ignoring the conversation, staring at the roof of the home across the street. Shug shakes his head and walks toward Ella Rae, who, thank goodness, is oblivious.

I keep hoping a butler or a maid will ring a chime and announce dinner. Or a convoy of fire trucks could race through town, whistles blaring, lights flashing. Instead, the street is quiet, and a mockingbird calls in the distance.

I wrinkle my nose. "Um, Andrew and I have been dating for a while, but I'm in no hurry to get married," I admit. I'm about to give the rest of my standard answer, which I've rehearsed a thousand times. My career comes first. I'm not ready to give that up, and it wouldn't be fair to a husband or child to split my attention. And besides, if forty's the new thirty, what's the rush?

But Aubie tilts the empty glass to her lips and a stricken look crosses her face. "Excuse me, y'all," she whispers. "I have to check on supper." And with three unsteady steps to the door, Aubie disappears.

PD sighs, jumps up, and follows her mother at a hurried pace. The door slams behind her. I allow my shoulders to relax, but I avoid Shug's gaze. I don't say a word about Aubie. I'm sure it pains him to watch her.

Shug breaks the silence between us. "My mother's an alcoholic. Has been ever since I can remember. I thought, since this was so important—having you here, representing the magazine—that she could take a break for a few hours." He shakes his head.

I crease my forehead and put a finger to my lips. "You don't owe me any excuses. It's none of my business, Shug. Really, I'm fine."

"Maybe I should have given you a disclosure list." Shug allows a small chuckle.

"Your sister mentioned that it might be a little overwhelming," I reply.

Shug hesitates, frowning, then takes a deep breath. "Julia—"

I clear my throat and look him directly in the eye. "Please give me a little credit. I'm here to learn about the Pilgrimage and Eufaula, not flush out Jordan family secrets. I work for a wholesome, family-friendly travel magazine, not *US Weekly or Star*."

Visibly relieved, he reaches out to squeeze my hand. "Thank you for understanding."

I squeeze back, then pull away, lowering my eyes. There's a good chance my cheeks are Hello Kitty-pink, so I turn my head so that Shug can't see. His touch still tingles all the way up my arm to the back of my neck.

We take a few steps toward the house. Inside is filled with candlelight, and the sound of silverware and serving spoons clinking. Whatever's cooking smells heavenly—distinctly rich with butter and cream.

Shug's not talking. He's staring out—at nothing—lost in thought.

How did the mood get so serious? I have to say something to lighten it up.

"Now, listen," I give him a quick elbow in the ribs. "If *People* magazine calls and offers me a million dollars for an exclusive, I might have to think about it." I pause and wink. "So be on your best behavior, sir."

Shug grins—ready to tease me back—but freezes in place as he glances over my shoulder. His face turns ashen. "Stop!"

Chapter Ten

"LOOK AT ME," says a childlike voice behind me. I spin around.

Ella Rae is up on the railing at the far end of the porch. She's balancing in the air, her arms outstretched like a tightrope walker. One step, swing of the leg, next step. Oblivious to the sharp edges of the boxwood branches below that may cushion her fall or snap her neck.

A sudden urge overwhelms me. I want to run, scream, catch her before she falls. Under his skin, I believe Shug's muscles are aching to sprint across the smooth pavement, yet neither of us makes a move. It's like we've both unconsciously agreed sudden movement will scare her and she'll fall for sure.

Shug moves his foot a few inches, then another. He's barely picking up the soles of his shoes from the concrete. Only his hands give him away. They're open wide, ready for his body to lunge forward.

I hold my breath as Ella Rae performs a slow pirouette on the banister, then extends one leg behind her. Her hands flutter, grasping at the air for balance, then she steadies herself.

Shug is closer.

Ella Rae has noticed. One eye on her uncle, she moves her leg perpendicular to the ground and dismounts with the grace of an Olympic athlete. In one smooth motion, Shug grabs Ella Rae underneath her arms and swings her up onto his shoulders. Ella Rae squeals with delight and claps, as Shug makes her bounce like a rider teaching her horse to canter.

"I'm thirsty, Uncle Shug," Ella Rae announces with a sweep of her hand. As Shug sets her on the ground, Ella Rae breaks into a run. I realize she's heading in my direction—for the pitcher of sweet tea, and six glasses beaded with condensation.

I concentrate on willing Ella Rae to stop before she plows into the end table next to my elbow. Just in case, I hold out my arms to brace the impact. I mean, really? How much damage can a 40-pound six-year-old do?

"Julia!" I hear Shug say with a hint of urgency. "You might want to—"

It's already too late.

Ella Rae hits the table like a bowling ball; the glasses wobble like pins. One falls, then another. In slow motion, the rest knock against each other, crack apart, and tumble to the ground in pieces.

It's a bit like a car crash, when you know you've made a mistake. You're already in the middle of the intersection and the other vehicle is about to rearrange your fender. Everything's in slow motion, and there's not a thing you can do about it. You just sit and wait for the situation to play out.

"Yikes!" I can't help but say when the tea and ice cubes hit my legs. It's freezing cold and I'm now drenched with the syrupy brown liquid. Drops of it cling to my hair and cheek. I move my head to shake them loose.

I expect to see blood. But, on the ground to my right, Ella Rae's managed to roll away unscathed. From a half-circle of broken glass, Shug deftly plucks his niece from the mess and sets her next to the front door.

Out of nowhere, laughter bubbles up in my chest. I try to cover my face with my hands in mock despair, but can't because they're bathed in a sticky film. Ella Rae, now pasted flat to the stucco wall, manages a smile.

"Are you okay?" Shug gives me a strange look of bewilderment.

I gasp for breath, but can't stop giggling. How much worse can this get? In the span of several hours, I've had my rental SUV attacked, been accosted by fire ants, my religious life questioned, my Diet Dr. Pepper almost refused. Now, I've been bathed in a drink so sweet I'll probably stick to the dining room chairs.

I inhale through my nose and try to swallow. Okay, there, you can do it. Focus.

"It's just … it's just," I glance at Shug's incredulous face and start to giggle again. I bend over and hug my knees, then pinch myself to get a grip. I try again.

Looking amused, he whispers to Ella Rae. She slips inside the house without a sound.

"It's just that I am supposed to be in Manhattan. And I'd probably be out at a very nice restaurant where nothing ever gets spilled, and people are very, very serious about their meal, and equally serious about their hundred-year old scotch."

Shug picks up a piece of glass. It glints in his hand, winking at me.

"I'm supposed to be *there*," I say. "But I'm *here*." Which is thousands of miles away from home, twenty degrees too warm, a trip that is—so far—just short of a complete nightmare.

Things aren't turning out anything remotely like I planned. I haven't done the first interview. And I'm starving. I tap my semi-soaked shoe, trying to gather my thoughts. With every movement, my heels squish. But I'm not unhappy. Not in the least.

"And so?" he echoes, not taking his eyes off me.

I glance down at my outfit, which I have to admit, isn't completely ruined. It will dry.

"Not what you expected?" he prompts, his face is awash with worry.

"Something like that," I laugh and dab at my face with the

edge of my sleeve.

"Well," Shug hesitates. "It would mean a lot if you'd stay."

I'm about to unleash a silly comment when I see his face. And melt.

"What I meant to say is that I'm fine. I'm not leaving," I muster a determined look and crouch down. "I'll help clean this up." My fingertips find the rough concrete as I steady myself and search for shards of glass.

"I have an idea. How about this?" Shug says.

I think he's found something unusual, so I look up, and we nearly bump heads. Shug sits back on his heels and pushes his palms against his khakis. "We'll start over," he explains. "From scratch." His hand stretches out to me again. "Shug Jordan. Nice to meet you."

He has my attention now. Anyone who passes by this porch will think we're insane. On hands and knees, I lift one arm and slide my hand into his waiting palm anyway.

The door swings open as Shug touches my hand. And doesn't let go.

"Shug? Julia?" I hear a female voice call.

When I glance up, I wrench my arm back and my fingers wiggle free as PD takes in the shattered mess and spilled tea. Traces of liquid are left, but most has soaked into the crevices and cracks.

I paste on my brightest smile and direct it at Shug's sister. "Care to join in? We've been doing gymnastics. Ella Rae was first on the balance beam."

Beside me, Shug lets out a snicker.

PD just stares as if I've sprouted another head.

"Shug was trying for a handstand, but he's not very good," I said breezily.

"I think I'll pass," PD shoots a strange look at both of us. "Anyway, dinner's ready. You'll probably want to get cleaned up."

The screen door creaks and closes.

"Julia," Shug begins, "why—"

"It's fine," I cut in, straightening up and brushing off both hands.

"You didn't have to take the blame." Shug's eyes search mine, curious. "Why did you?"

I don't know quite how to answer. There are a million tiny reasons, all equally valid.

Just pick one, I tell myself—I was the same way, a little out of control, on the edge of everyone's nerves?

Or, I could tell Shug that Ella Rae might have ADHD. Or something like it. And remind him that she's already been in trouble once today.

Finally, there's this answer: Given a little time—say, the next ten years—maybe Ella Rae will outgrow it. Or learn to manage it better. And she'll be okay.

I don't explain.

Instead, I sum it up this way.

"She reminds me ... of me."

Chapter Eleven

UNLIKE THE STREETS OF MANHATTAN, the twenty square feet of the Jordan dining room leaves little space to disappear. I press myself against the wooden edge of a side-table, out of the way.

When Mary Katherine and Shug's father arrive at precisely the same time, the family sweeps them up into a hugging frenzy.

Shug's father turns to greet me. From his profile, I've already noted the same dark hair, the identical angled jaw line. There's an air of nonchalance in the way he carries himself, a hint of mischievous little boy.

"Julia Sullivan," I say and extend my arm to shake his hand.

"Toomer Jordan, but you can call me TJ." With the force of a steamroller, I find myself being crushed, arms flailing, against the barrel-chested man whom I just laid eyes on a moment ago. My feet lift off the floor, and I struggle for air.

Aubie saves me. I hear the kitchen door swing behind her. "Thomas Jefferson Jordan, put her down." The words, slightly slurred, are rigid, nonetheless.

Immediately, I'm back to Earth, and the soles of my shoes slam against the carpeting.

"Thank you," I gasp. *Do that to a stranger in New York and you'd likely be slapped with an order of protection or get sued.* Clearly, behind the Mason-Dixon Line, life is much cozier.

"Aw, Aubie, I didn't mean nothing," TJ's voice lies. He

winks in my direction and moves over to bear hug Ella Rae. TJ growls like an animal, and his granddaughter screams with delight as he throws her in the air, millimeters away from the fifteen-tier crystal chandelier. PD watches, tight-lipped.

"May I help with anything?' I offer, as Aubie makes her way toward the kitchen.

She shoos me away with a firm push of her hands.

"Enjoy yourself, dear," she urges.

I watch in awe as Aubie transports plates heaping with food to the dining room. She disappears, and I count five seconds, then she's back with another dish, this time fried chicken, glistening gold. She sets down the plate, puffs of steam rise. Then, she's gone again.

When I think no one's looking in my direction, I snatch a moment to check the puffy, red skin on my ankle. As I twist my leg in the light, trying to see, Mary Katherine breaks her conversation with Shug to rush over and inspect my leg.

"Lord have mercy, bless your heart!" In four-inch heels, she tiptoes over and examines the raised, angry spots. "Did Aubie get you with the vinegar?" Mary Katherine asks, covering a smirk with wide-eyed innocence.

Before I can take a breath, Ella Rae pipes up, "Shug dumped it on her. A whole jug of it." She sniffs the air, "Can't you smell it?"

"Young lady," PD cautions, giving her daughter a pointed look and shaking her head.

Mary Katherine, ignoring the insult, lays a cool hand on my shoulder. "You just be careful, honey. Things aren't the same here as in New York."

So I've noticed.

"I'm going to get MeeMaw," PD calls out.

"Everyone find a seat," Aubie says over a pot of beans she sets in the middle of the table. She takes a wobbly step back to survey the scene.

Mary Katherine does her best not to scowl across the

table as Shug sidles into the chair next to me. Before I can offer to swap seats, TJ lumbers by.

"You gonna watch Duke this weekend?" He yanks back the chair at the head of the table and nods at Shug. The chair groans as he plops down, leans back, and props one elbow lazily over the armrest.

"If I get time," Shug answers. "And I think Carolina looks good."

"Eddie Jackson's got a pool goin'. Big money. *Big.* You want in?" With a muscled hand, TJ yanks at the napkin from beside his plate and flicks it open with the snap of his wrist. The fabric flutters in front of his ample stomach and disappears under the tablecloth.

I blink and take in the exchange, watching Shug react to his father.

"No thanks," he says, offering an easy smile. "I like my money right where it is."

TJ shakes his head and rolls his eyes, like Shug has just told him the world is flat, not round. "Son, we're talking easy cash."

"There's no such thing," PD snaps from the doorway. She is guiding a tiny woman in a wheelchair into the only open spot at the table. As they walk closer, PD pauses next to me. I turn to stand up and greet her.

"MeeMaw, this is Miss Julia Sullivan," Shug's sister yells, close to the woman's ear. "From New York City."

"Nice to meet you," I say and take her tiny hand in mine. The woman looks as frail as balsa wood. Her skin is the color of parchment paper. MeeMaw's white hair is swept away from her face into a simple chignon.

I expect to see the cloudiness of cataracts, the result of age and wear, but her eyes are a sharp, deep, black-brown mahogany. A small notepad and pencil are cradled in the folds of her long, blue cotton skirt.

MeeMaw nods hello, and PD nudges the chair further

down the table, fussing over her with tenderness.

Shug bends his head close to mine. "Daddy's mama. She had a stroke and can't talk."

The notebook and pencil make sense now. I can't imagine losing the ability to speak. Everything would bottle up inside me, fill to the top, and burst.

Aubie downs another swallow of spiked tea. "Say the blessing, TJ," she commands as she sets her glass on the table.

TJ clears his throat and lifts his arms like the conductor of an orchestra. Everyone, except for me, joins hands with the person next to them. I slide my palm to the table and let it rest there. Shug finds my fingers. Ella Rae's tiny palm slips into my other hand.

Heads bow around the table.

"Heavenly Father," TJ begins, "We thank you for this day and all the blessings you have bestowed upon this family. We are humbled in your very presence, Oh Lord, and feel you working in our daily lives. I pray that we may be forgiven for our sins, and remember that you sent your only Son to die on the cross so that we may have eternal life in your magnificent kingdom of heaven." Shug's father continues in this fashion for at least another five minutes, adding in blessings for the community, the governor of Alabama, and members of the Auburn University football team.

I try not to wiggle. My right leg is asleep, and my neck is starting to spasm. My eye opens a sliver, just enough to see Ella Rae glance at me from under the fringe of her hair. TJ keeps talking and we sit, smiling at each other.

"And thank you, dear Lord, for sending us Jessica from New York City ..."

"Julia," Ella Rae interrupts and I try not to laugh.

TJ clears his throat. "Thank you dear Lord, for sending *Julia* from New York City. Watch over her and keep her safe as *Julia* visits our fine city." He takes a breath. "Finally, Heavenly Father, bless this food to our bodies and us to your service. In

Jesus' name, Amen."

Shug squeezes my hand and lets go. With a clatter, forks and knives are picked up and the conversation begins again in earnest. As I pass the platters, taking a sample of each, I notice that Mary Katherine chooses the tiniest drumstick and scoops only five beans onto her plate. She eyeballs my portion with a touch of satisfaction and sweeps her napkin onto her lap.

No wonder she's so thin. Oh well.

"Okra." Shug's voice pulls me away from worrying about Mary Katherine. He hands me a steaming bowl with pellet-sized pieces of vegetable, each green piece coated with a golden breading. A tangy but sweet smell tickles my nose. I hesitate, then scoop a small helping onto my plate. At least three pieces bounce off onto the table and leave grease marks behind.

I hurry to pass the dish and hear Mary Katherine start to titter. That is, until Shug snaps up the okra pieces from around my plate and pops them into his mouth like candy.

PD, who's been feeding MeeMaw with microscopic spoonfuls, stops and makes a face at her brother. Mary Katherine glares in Shug's direction, like he's just licked the floor clean. Ella Rae giggles and mimics her uncle, but a few of her okra pieces hit the floor.

"Shug," PD whispers. "Manners."

Shug winks at his sister and digs into his mashed potatoes with vigor.

Aubie, who's missed the whole performance, is wobbling to stay upright. "Julia dear," she slurs, "we are so excited you're here to preview the Pilgrimage."

Before I can answer, TJ cuts in. "Now Aubie, I know that's your pet project." He turns to me. "There are big plans for ramping up tourism in the area, and not just in the historic district."

I see Shug frown into his dinner plate.

"Just remember, there's a lot more to Eufaula than just the Pilgrimage," TJ lifts his fork at me to emphasize his point.

Aubie ignores her husband's comment. "When I was just seventeen, in 1965, the city held the first-ever Pilgrimage." She sighs and clutches her napkin, dabs it to her lips. "There was this reporter."

PD clamps her mouth tight and closes her eyes.

"It was the event of the century, with lovely parties and so much celebration." Aubie pauses, her eyes resting on a photograph to her right. I follow her gaze, taking in the young girl in a billowing skirt. A young man is by her side, unsmiling.

"He took that photograph," Aubie says dreamily. "That reporter. I can't remember…" Aubie rubs her forehead with his fingertips.

"I get to wear a dress like that to the Pilgrimage. It has a pink bow!" Ella Rae pipes up.

"Shhh!" PD scolds Ella Rae, then directs her attention to Aubie. "Mother, I'm sure Julia would love to hear about the actual Pilgrimage, not—"

"He was so handsome," Aubie persists, swaying with the memory like she's dancing. "A real gentleman. And I wore that dress. I still have it, you know, in the closet." She tries to take another sip of sweet tea, and then scowls into her now-empty glass.

At this point, everyone's stopped eating. TJ is red-faced, rebuffed. Ella Rae plays with the vegetables on her plate, lining up the okra and creamed corn into a smiley face.

Shug shifts in his seat, watching his mother. I forget about my tingling leg.

Aubie leans her chin toward her open palm. When she does, her jaw misses her hand and lands on the table. The impact makes the silverware bounce and the water in my glass slosh dangerously close to the edge.

"Mama!" PD's words come out a gasp, but it is Shug who pushes back his seat and springs up. Mary Katherine, annoyed, tries to grab his wrist. Shug shakes off her touch and bends over his mother, whispering in her ear.

I'm holding my breath. Aubie doesn't respond. Her cheek is pressed against the tablecloth.

"That's enough," TJ slams a heavy hand on the table. Ella Rae jumps and begins to sob silent tears. Her small shoulders quiver. TJ doesn't notice. He glares at Aubie.

"Bless her heart," Mary Katherine murmurs to herself, her fork poised in the air. She's not looking at Aubie, though no one else notices. Her gaze is focused on TJ, like he's the only person in the room.

Shug heaves his mother to her feet. As they step out of the dining room, Aubie clings to her son, head lolling back like a rag doll. Their awkward footsteps sound down the hallway. *Clump-slide, clump-slide.*

Ella Rae finds her feet and rushes off. I don't stop her. Neither does anyone else.

A door closes on the other end of the house, and in moments, Shug is back at the table. He grips the napkin he threw down on his plate.

"Ella Rae's in her room," he says to PD. He makes no mention of his mother.

I swallow and wonder how many times a month this happens. And whether anyone reacts any differently.

"So, Julia," Mary Katherine dabs at her lips with her napkin, the smile of a Cheshire cat behind it. "Tell us all about New York City."

So, this is how it is, I think. Hit rewind, and it's like Aubie was never here. I glance at Mary Katherine's plate, still arranged with her pitiful chicken leg and five lonely beans.

My appetite has disappeared. "What would you like to know?" I answer, keeping my voice even.

Mary Katherine peppers me with questions about shopping and shows, celebrities and clubs. I describe restaurants, exotic dishes, and talk about museums and new projects.

"There you go," TJ booms. "New buildings, renovation, growth. So much opportunity. Just what Eufaula needs."

"I don't know about that …" I struggle to answer. "Speaking of construction, why don't you tell me about what's happening in Eufaula. Give me some background for my article."

TJ looks pleased at my suggestion and Shug's eyes light up.

"That's why we're so excited that you're here," Shug begins. "We have some significant renovation projects we're trying to get off the ground. The Bluff City Inn, next to the Honeysuckle Diner, was built in 1885 by Dr. Reeves as a one-hundred room, three-story hotel."

TJ clears his throat, looking bored.

"There's also the Lakeside Hotel and Restaurant. It's on the shores of Lake Eufaula. Another eight miles up the road is the area's state park," Shug adds. "It's in sore need of modernizing, but we're trying to tackle the project with some funding from the government."

TJ now drums his fingers on the table. "Are you done?" he asks, when Shug takes a breath. "Mr. Encyclopedia of Historical Knowledge over there." TJ jabs a thumb across the table. "Aubie's brainwashed him into thinking we need to save every shack in Barbour County."

"It's my job," says Shug, his jaw set.

"Well, if you got your candy-ass over to the construction company full-time maybe we could go ahead with some of those building projects I want to tackle." TJ's voice is fiery hot. "Some of them houses—"

"I figure you've got it covered, Daddy," Shug says calmly.

"What I think is that you need to get yourself a decent house instead of that office you're living in. It's a disgrace," TJ fumes. "A *Jordan* living like he don't have a dime to his name."

Mary Katherine forces a giggle. "You boys are always fighting. Y'all don't want to leave Miss Julia with a poor impression of our sweet town with your arguing, now do you?" She dabs at her lips daintily, but her eyes shoot fireworks at both men.

TJ throws his napkin on his plate but doesn't answer. Shug flushes red.

"I'm looking forward to seeing all of it," I interject into the silence. "The new work and any plans for the future. That can be part of the article—just as much as the history."

Mary Katherine claps her hands. "Yay! You'll be so impressed with all of the work Jordan construction is doing. Why, *we're* one of the oldest family-based companies in Eufaula. MeeMaw's father started it, back in the day." She pauses to give Shug a loving look.

The *we're* strikes me as oddly territorial, yet no one has corrected her. I can't resist asking, "What about you, Mary Katherine, how are you involved in Jordan Construction?"

Her eyes fly open wide, then flicker in embarrassment. "Well, no. Actually I'm not. I'm in commercial banking. In my spare time, I do some modeling, some pageant coaching—"

TJ coughs and pushes back from the table. "C'mon Shug, let's see who's playing."

I immediately stand and start stacking dishes as Shug and his father exit the room. As I grab for the empty platters, PD touches my arm. "You don't have to help clean up."

"I insist." The dishes clank together noisily as I balance a few glasses on a plate.

The kitchen door swings shut after PD. MeeMaw appears to be dozing. As I bend to collect her plate, the glint from her ring blinds me. I have to blink and turn my head.

"It's lovely, isn't it?" Mary Katherine muses, almost talking to herself as she gazes at the huge diamond. "I'll have this one or one like it soon."

The dishes almost slip from my hands. I glance around, wishing Shug or anyone else in the family would come around the corner and hear what she's saying. MeeMaw's eyelashes flutter the slightest bit as I pick up another plate, concentrating on not breaking dishes.

Mary Katherine gives me a coy smile. "They love me.

And I adore them of course." I watch as she gazes around the room like she owns it. "Isn't it a great house for entertaining?"

She doesn't wait for my response.

"PD's the celebrity chef in the family. You'll have to try some of her desserts," she confides. "Silly old Shug won't let me near the kitchen. He doesn't trust me. Last summer, I turned on the gas stove and forgot all about it."

I swallow hard as Mary Katherine titters and continues her story.

"He came in, sniffed the air, switched off the gas, and yanked me outside. You should have seen him." She spreads her arms wide, "Five seconds longer, and Whoosh! The whole place could have blown up!"

"Wow," I cringe, imagining the house exploding into smithereens.

"Close call, right?" she bites her lip and shrugs. "I'm so much more careful now. I have to be." Mary Katherine lowers her voice to a hush. "This is all going to be mine soon." Her words are concrete, like the mold's already been cast, the tiny pieces left over smoothed and sanded away. Her blue eyes are granite, determined. "Mine and Shug's. Someday. Very soon."

Chapter Twelve

THE NEXT MORNING, Marietta calls before I'm out of bed. I rub my eyes with both fists, trying to wake up.

"So, spill it. What's it like?" she asks. I can see her twirling a piece of hair, feet propped up, laptop open. "Do you love it? Is it like *Sweet Home Alabama*—or more *Deliverance*?"

She is joking, of course. "The city's lovely, there are some gorgeous homes," I confide. "Now, I have met a few characters," I describe Elma and Stump at the Citgo station and can't help but giggle out loud.

The sound rings across the room and I cover my mouth. Other people could be trying to sleep. Or enjoy the quiet. For that matter, I don't know if Roger is in the next room. And he doesn't need more to gossip about.

In the background, someone yells for Marietta and she muffles the phone. "That's David, for the second time," she finally whispers. "You didn't tell me he's such a slave driver."

I wince and want to shrink into my skin. *Workaholics are like that.* "Sorry, I should have mentioned it. I guess they misplaced the perfectionism gene when they got around to me. I was handed the can't-pay-attention unless the room is on fire DNA."

"Well, you rival each other in the patience department," she whispers. "I've got another fifteen seconds before he blows a gasket. Just have to finish typing this memo."

"Good luck," I say.

"Okay. Hurry back." I can hear Marietta clicking on her

keyboard as we talk. Another phone rings in the background. "Bye."

"Bye," I say to the dial tone and roll out of bed.

With a stretch, I begin my morning routine. After a quick shower, I get dressed, and fix my hair. With a glance at the clock, I realize that somehow, I'm ahead of schedule. *That never happens.* I don't meet Shug for another twenty minutes.

With a cursory glance around the room, I confirm there's nothing else to do. I packed last night, and Roger promised a late checkout, so I leave my bags lined up by the wall.

I ease over to the door, unlock it, then turn the handle as gently as possible. Mercifully, it doesn't squeak. The wooden slab protecting me from the rest of the world swings open, welcoming in the perfume of freshly-baked biscuits and bacon.

The sound of whistling lifts through the air, followed by the bangs of pots and pans, the rush of water in a sink. An off-key voice sings the lyrics. Roger. *Camptown Races here we come, doo-dah, doo-dah. Camptown Races …*

Gingerly, I take a step onto the hallway onto an oriental rug so thick my heel seems to sink several inches. I pull the bedroom door shut behind me and it clicks into place. *Doo-dah, doo-dah …*

There's a small piece of guilt clinging to me. *Roger took the time to make a nice breakfast.* His singing trails off into a soft hum. I continue to tiptoe, arguing with myself the whole way to the foyer. *If I stop, I'll never leave the house, I'll be late for my appointment, and I'll never get back to New York and the rest of my life.* A little drastic, yes, but enough to convince me to keep moving. I ease toward the front of the house. Just three more steps.

"Julia?" Out of nowhere, Roger appears.

I scream in fright.

Roger squeals and leaps out of the way, clutching a large wooden spoon and his striped apron in panic. "What is it?

What did you see?" His eyes dart back and forth, searching every nook and corner. He's up on tiptoes, prancing like embers are smoldering under his feet.

"I'm not sure," I gasp.

A few startled guests peek around the corner. Roger spots them and immediately assumes his cool persona, letting his apron drop. "Nothing to be worried about, y'all," he coos. "Julia almost tripped. Frightened her to death, bless her heart."

Reassured, one by one, the faces disappear. "Be right there with the biscuits," Roger trills after them.

I inch toward the door.

Roger puts a finger to his lips then creeps toward me. "Was it Mr. Wiggles?"

"Who?" I mouth.

My host holds up his palm, turns it up to the ceiling, and makes his other fingers crawl across the flat of his hand. "Mr. Wiggles," he breathes.

It dawns on me. He's talking about a mouse. "I-I don't know," I say, making my voice tremulous.

Roger looks sick. His face is purple. "I thought those people took care of him," he sighs, wipes his brow with an embroidered handkerchief, and shakes his head. "They were supposed to catch him and set him free," he confides in a hushed tone.

"Oh," I say and press my lips together. I should tell Roger the truth, but he's already rushing me out the door.

"Run along, dear," he tells me, steering my arm with a firm grip. "Roger will take care of everything. Including Mr. Wiggles." His voice is ominous. "Don't breathe a word, sweetheart. Bad for business."

"Of course," I whisper. A cool breeze hits my face as I step out onto the porch and the door slams shut behind me. I stand there for a moment, wanting to rush back in and save Roger from heart palpitations, but my explanation—sneaking out to avoid him—hardly seems polite.

Apologize later. Tell him you were seeing things. That you need prescription glasses. Or you hadn't slept all night and you'd imagined it. None of the excuses seem valid. I'll come up with something, I promise myself.

I blink at the sun's bright rays as I take the steps toward the sidewalk. A white Mercedes zips by at a speed bound to get anyone a ticket. I catch a flash of blonde hair. Mary Katherine. She turns the corner almost on two wheels. I strain for a glimpse of the passenger, but the top isn't down. I catch only a swatch of dark hair in the seat next to hers. *Shug didn't forget about our meeting, did he?*

It takes me all of five minutes to reach the Hart House. The wooden sign I pass in the front yard is almost too small to hold all of the letters it carries. *Historic Chattahoochee Commission.* I wonder what Chattahoochee stands for and make a mental note to ask Shug. My hand tightens into a fist and I raise it to knock on the door when it opens.

"Oh," I say and jump back, covering my mouth. At least I didn't scream this time.

"Saw you coming up the steps. Just wanted to grab the door," Shug confesses with an adorable smile. "I didn't mean to scare you."

I hold my hand over my heart to slow the beating. "I don't know whether to kill you or thank you, but I guess I'll let you live, since I *really* need this story on the Pilgrimage."

"Why, that's wonderful," Shug answers with a small bow. "And, the first time I've gotten a death threat on the job. From a Yankee, to boot."

"Ha, ha!" I joke as we walk inside.

"Can you give me a minute?" Shug asks. "I have to wrap up a few things before we get started."

"No problem," I hear myself say and try to settle into a wingback chair that's not nearly as comfortable as it looks. The office is plain, with hardwood floors buffed to a shine, one wall of bookshelves, and rows of photos—homes, gardens, and local scenery.

Shug makes a beeline for a small office. "Make yourself at home."

The chair is awful, so I stand up. "So you really live here?" The words spill out before I can catch them and put them back. I need to let him finish his work.

"Um, yes," he calls out, unperturbed. "Let me put it this way, I'm never late for work."

"You haven't found anything else you like?" That seems impossible, given all of the gorgeous homes in Eufaula. But maybe he wants something modern. I wrinkle my nose. That doesn't seem to fit his personality.

It's quiet for a moment or two. Maybe he's going to tell me to mind my own business. It wouldn't be the first time.

"There are a lot of homes I love." His voice sounds matter-of-fact. "I guess the timing hasn't been right or it hasn't been the right place. It's a question of making everything fit."

Reasonable explanation. Sort of like the excuse I've used to break off a relationship. A little part of me in the back of my heart that says 'something's missing'.

The floor creaks under my feet. I glance around at the two clean, empty desks near the windows. Both have the usual on top; a stapler, tape dispenser, and a cup full of pens. Nothing like the haphazard mess in my cubicle at the magazine—my desk is a brewing volcano of letters and to-do memos waiting to erupt.

It seems obvious, but I ask the question anyway. "So, who else works here?"

I hear Shug chuckle. "That would be me, myself, and I." He stops. "I'm sorry, I shouldn't be flip about it. I used to have an assistant, and last year, an intern from Auburn. Funding is tight in the non-profit world."

"Enough for a decent salary and benefits, I hope?" I frown as he sticks his head out of the corner office.

"Nope."

At first, I think I don't hear him right. "Pardon?"

Shug laughs. "No. Because there's no salary."

My mouth widens in horror. I hold back a gasp. "No salary?"

There are faint lines that crinkle around his eyes when he smiles. There's no self-important look, no politician's air. He works here because he wants to. The same shock of hair falls over his forehead as he nods. Already, the motion of him pushing it back is familiar.

"Don't worry, I won't starve. But I do need to scrape up some money for a haircut," he says ruefully.

I squint at him. Compared to my father's usual safari-look, Shug's hair barely grazes his ears, the back just starting to curl up. He's wearing a pressed shirt, orange and blue tie, and khakis that somehow don't wrinkle. Shug looks pretty close to perfect.

"Really, it is shocking," I say dryly.

Shug rolls his eyes at me. "Women."

"So, what are the biggest concerns here?" I ask. "In Eufaula?"

"Convincing everyone that restoration instead of demolition is the way to go. We provide information on grants, loans, and funding for the preservation of historic property." He takes a breath and nods over to a rack of booklets, leaflets, and pamphlets.

"So, you're a right-to-lifer for old buildings?" I quip.

"In a sense," he grins. "I've never thought about it that way." Shug glances down at the tri-fold paper in his hand. "I do spend a lot of my time preparing promotional pieces, going to tourism expos, and recruiting travel writers like you to the area."

He disappears back into the office. David's smug expression flashes before my eyes and I swallow. I wasn't recruited. I'm not the first choice, or the second. I'm the consolation prize.

As I'm having a pity-party for myself, complete with imaginary balloons and streamers, Shug's voice drifts out into the lobby area, over the top of papers rustling. "How's your leg? I think you're the first writer I've known who's been injured in the line of duty."

I chuckle, a deep belly laugh that makes Shug appear back in the doorway. "Line of duty? This isn't exactly Fort Knox." With a sweeping motion, I gesture to the mansions outside the front window.

"Dinner with my family has been compared to surviving a week of boot camp," he retorts, hiding a smile.

I lift an ankle and inspect my war wounds. "I think the fire ant barrage was much worse."

Shug wrinkles his brow. "Have to watch out for them today."

"Well, it's bees, not fire ants, that I really have to worry about, but I carry an EpiPen for that," I tell him and glance down at my leg—still puffy and ugly, but not nearly as angry-red as yesterday. I wonder how long it will take for the bumps to disappear. "I'll certainly think twice before stepping onto the grass."

Just thinking about those tiny ants makes me want to crawl out of my skin. Without much effort, I think about flailing around in the yard of the Jordan mansion, leg swollen as big as a tree trunk, moaning one last sentence. *Tell David he did this to me.*

As I fidget, I notice that Shug is staring at me. I'm saved by the jingle of the phone.

He holds up a finger. "Stay right there." Shug raises a stern eyebrow. "Don't leave. Better yet, take a look at the blueprints next to the back wall." Outside his office, there are large rectangular boards on easels covered with thin sheets of paper.

I force my hands to my sides and stand up. Maybe the blueprints will take my mind off the ant bites. Lifting the parchment paper and flipping it over the top, I scan the lines and lettering. Across the bottom reads *Phase One. Bluff City Inn, Proposed Hotel and Conference Center.* There's a rendering of a new façade, which keeps the same look and feel as the original brick building. The sketch next to it shows the interior design of a spacious guest room with an adjoining sitting area and bathroom.

And what's behind door number two? I lift the sheet from the second easel. *Phase Two, Lakepoint State Park, Proposed Updates.* Before I can glance at any of the architectural details, I hear Shug's voice. He sounds irritated. Very irritated.

The door to the small office closes with a bang.

Very carefully, I slide the parchment paper back in place. I am trying not to listen. Except that Shug is now shouting and I can hear every word.

"No, I don't understand!" His feet pound around his office, making the windows and floorboards shake under my shoes.

As I tiptoe toward the front door, there's another pause. Then Shug explodes, his voice loud and strained. "What do you mean, the Phase Three work?"

I stop walking, transfixed by the conversation. *What is going on?*

The floor groans again. This time, Shug's tone is more subdued. "Yes, fine," he says. "I'll check into it and get back to you, as soon as I can."

I look up, hopeful, as Shug opens the door to his office, walks into the room with the phone in his hand, and presses a button to end the call. Immediately, he dials another number. Evidently, the person doesn't answer, because he stares off into space, his face dark and frowning. He's so lost in thought I'm not sure he remembers I'm here.

"Everything all right?" I ask, trying to stay positive, despite my nerves jumping all over the place. I hate it when anyone's upset, even a stranger. "Minor glitch in the plans?" I nod toward the blueprints in the back of the room.

"You could say that." Shug tilts his head and grimaces. He's not telling the truth. Not the whole truth, anyway.

Shug stares out the window but doesn't offer to explain, and the room fills with an awkward silence. That kind of stillness makes me a little crazy, almost claustrophobic. When you're used to noise, you don't quite know how to act. I search for something else to say, an excuse to go outside and get some air.

Thinking he needs space, I offer it. "If you want, I can go ahead and take a look around the city myself. I'll meet you later."

"No, no. It's fine," Shug says. "I need to get in touch with my father and can't—no surprise. My mother should be at Shorter Mansion this morning—we're headed there anyway."

He doesn't move toward the door, like I expect. He walks over to the architectural boards in the corner, runs a finger along the top of one of them.

I jiggle my leg, anxious to walk off my nervous energy. "Is there something wrong with the project?"

Shug doesn't answer, so I think I've made him angry, too. "Sorry," I explain. "It's just my nature to ask a million questions. I overheard you say something about Phase Three." I stop myself from babbling and watch his broad shoulders tense when I say the last few words.

He pivots on his heel, almost in slow motion. As Shug turns, I watch as his demeanor morphs from soldier-like frustration to that of a person filled with determination and resolve.

"I didn't know there was a Phase Three," I say.

Shug considers this, and answers with three words I don't expect.

"Neither did I."

Chapter Thirteen

SHUG IS OUT THE DOOR before I can ask for details. Based on his demeanor and the fact that he's already made it twenty strides down the sidewalk without bothering to shut or lock the door behind him, the news isn't positive.

I pull on the brass knob, hear the lock click behind me, and hurry after Shug. He's turned on East Barbour Street. I debate kicking off both heels and sprinting after him, but decide that at least a dozen unwritten Southern rules of decorum would frown on that transgression.

He screeches to a stop in front of the mayor's office, taking the steps two at a time. I hang back and catch my breath, clapping a hand to my chest. A hunched man with a stubby cigar in his mouth eyeballs me. He's waiting, too, but not panting like a greyhound that's just finished the race of his short life. I realize that it's Stump from the Citgo.

"Runnin' after Mr. Shug Jordan, eh?" Stump plucks the cigar from between his teeth and rolls it between two fingers. He's leaning on a crude walking stick or cane, hand-carved.

My lips part to offer a smart retort, but I clamp them back together. "No." I shake my head. "No, sir," I add, as it seems the custom for everyone to address everyone else as 'sir' or 'ma'am' even within their own households and families.

He cackles, revealing a sparse set of yellowed teeth. It's obvious he doesn't believe me. "You're not the first," he offers and smiles in a knowing way. "Plenty of 'em chase him. Just none of 'em can catch him."

I cringe, but keep a pleasant smile plastered on my face. There's the rumble of an engine in the distance, and Stump looks away. I take the opportunity to steal a glance up at the dark wooden doorway. Under my breath, I begin praying that Shug will burst out to interrupt the semi-interrogation. In the meantime, I wrack my brain for something intelligent to say to the man who's slightly creepy and seems more than interested in my personal life.

When I turn back to look at Stump, he's gone. The sound of heavy footsteps causes me to whirl around. It's Shug, clearly in no better shape than when he set off on his mission.

"City council, planning commission, special emergency meeting," he mutters as we continue east toward the Chattahoochee River.

"And we're going to the meeting?" I ask, huffing to keep up with Shug. "Is it open to the public?"

"It should be," he answers tersely. "We'll find out soon."

I want to ask how many blocks we're going and why it wouldn't make more sense to drive, but I think better of it. Perhaps his body's forward motion helps him think more clearly.

"The Heritage Association should know about this," he says. "I should've known about this."

"How is the Heritage Association different from the Chattahoochee Commission?" I ask.

Shug gives me a quick synopsis. "Historic Chattahoochee Commission promotes tourism and historic preservation for an eighteen county region in Alabama and Georgia called the Chattahoochee Trace."

I nod.

"The Eufaula Heritage Association has a much more narrow focus," he continues. "It was created in 1965 when the local newspaper announced an auction of the Shorter Mansion and its contents. The mayor at the time, Hamp Graves, appointed an eight-member committee to look into purchasing the Mansion as a city civic center. Pledges from the community poured in and the committee bought the property for thirty-three thousand dollars."

"Thirty-three thousand dollars," I echo with shock.

He nods. "Exactly. The Heritage Association was formed and Eufaula Pilgrimage began that year as a fundraiser for historic preservation. It's been held every year since. The Christmas Tour of Homes was added in 2006."

Shug stops walking, and I pivot to survey the building in front of us. We're standing before the Eufaula municipal courthouse and city police department, a low-lying red-brick building with a green metal roof.

"What's the plan?" I ask, but Shug only sets his jaw and heads for the entrance. After a few twists and turns, he grasps the handles of a meeting room and throws open the double doors. Angry voices rise from inside the room. When I catch up and position myself away from the direct action, I'm able to hear the entire exchange.

"This is a closed meeting," a stern voice announces from inside the room.

"I can see that," Shug replies. "And I'm wondering why the sudden break from tradition? Budget crisis? An emergency? Something the Historic Preservation Board should know about?"

There's an uncomfortable silence.

"You'll be notified when the time comes," another man chimes in. "Now, if you'll kindly leave and close the doors."

"Notified of what?" Shug controls his tone, though there's an undercurrent of irritation. "I look around this room and see City Council Members. I see Planning Board Members. And I know it's not anyone's usual meeting day."

More silence.

"This indicates to me that something important is being considered. Something is being put to a vote. And it's a project y'all don't want me knowing about."

A flurry of accusations and denials are exchanged. I peek

my head around the corner. There's a row of red-faced men all shouting at the same time. Shug's in the middle of the room, standing still, observing the chaos.

Finally, Shug's voice rises above the rest. "Stop! Everyone, stop! What's the meaning of this?" he asks.

"You don't have any right to be here," someone interjects.

"Maybe not, but someone has to speak for the protection of our historic landmarks," Shug lowers his tone. "If that's what this is all about."

I hear the shuffling of papers and whispered conversation.

Shug continues. "If you don't want to tell the Preservation Board members—who have a right to be here—I'll see to it that they're notified, just as soon as I find out *what is going on.*"

One of the men clears his throat and calls for a vote to table the discussion. After the motion carries and a gavel bangs, there's the distinct scrape of chair legs on carpeting. After a group of men filters out of the conference room, I leave my post to find Shug.

When he hears me enter the room, Shug looks up.

"They're going to ruin everything."

Chapter Fourteen

"Can you be more specific?" I ask and sink into a nearby seat.

He blows out a huge breath of air and stares at the stack of white sheets. With his index finger, he thumps the pile of paper.

I cock my head to read it better. *Phase III: Lakeside Condominiums.* Shug pushes the packet closer, then flips to the second page for me to read. *Eagle Investment Properties, LLC, Auburn, Alabama.* I raise an eyebrow. The company name isn't familiar—why would it be?

When I wrinkle my nose, not understanding, Shug grabs the proposal with both hands. He stares at it, not moving.

"So, this is bad," I say, immediately berating myself for stating the obvious. Shug doesn't correct me.

"Remember what we were talking about on the way over here?" he asks me.

I nod, my eyes not leaving his face.

Shug clears his throat. "Back in the 1960s, the town had lost several antebellum homes in the name of *progress.*" He makes quotation marks with his fingers. "There was a movement to modernize Eufaula, construct new homes. But, some community members began to worry about the increasing number of local landmarks that were being destroyed and replaced by new buildings. Other mansions, because of neglect, had been demolished."

"So the Historic Preservation folks—and your organization—fight that, right?"

With a grim smile, Shug confirms this. "We can, if we know about it." His fingers tap the edge of the proposal packet.

I consider the reasons for secrecy. "So, you've been successful so far, but there's someone who'd like to build condos and wants to bypass anyone who might stand in the way."

"Exactly."

"Can they do that?"

Shug narrows his eyes. "It's not supposed to work like that, but I'm sure there are ways around it—a loophole some attorney will find to make it legal." He rubs his chin. "I think they were going for an 'it's easier to ask for forgiveness than permission' kind of deal."

I stand up and walk over to the window. "But now that you know about it…"

"So will the community. They'll be forced to have a public meeting."

"So, how much money are we talking? And who's financing it? And is it just along the lake area?"

This makes Shug chuckle. "You New Yorkers. Don't you ever slow down?"

"Sorry," I apologize and roll my eyes.

"So, the answers are: A lot of money, I'm not sure who's behind it, and the investor isn't talking about lakefront property." Shug wipes his face with one hand. "There's plenty of that to be had. There'd be no need for a special meeting."

It doesn't take me long to realize that whomever is behind all of this is a pro. They've been planning this attack for a while.

Shug leans back. "So far, this is all that I know: An investor who prefers to remain anonymous has made a generous proposal to city council. There are a number of homes—historic homes—close to foreclosure. When all of the other options have been exhausted, banks are forced to repossess the properties when the owners can't pay the bills."

"So, say an investor buys a foreclosed-on property. Then what?"

"Typically, an interested party would renovate the home and flip it, meaning they'd hope to make some money by selling it quick. Right now, the real estate market's so stagnant that no one's buying a shack, let alone ten thousand-square foot mansions."

"So this person—man, woman, whatever—this investor is a Donald Trump sort? A chance taker, a deal maker?"

"This particular investor, from what I can tell from the first few pages of this proposal, plans to develop the land—particularly the parcels nearest to the lake—into a luxury condominium community. There's room for a clubhouse, tennis courts, a pool and spa."

"What?" I cough, aghast at the thought. "What about protection for historic landmarks? What about everything you've worked for?"

"The city leaders might actually entertain the idea because Eufaula—like many other cities in the state—is hurting financially. A big boost to the tax base would be a small miracle. Right now, companies are closing or leaving the area."

"Worst-case scenario?"

"They raze the buildings on the north side of town." Shug levels his gaze. "Six to ten of the homes. Maybe more." He looks out the window and murmurs, "It could happen."

I cross my arms tight across my chest, my emotions locked somewhere between dismay and anger. "So, how did you know? Who called you?"

"A friend," Shug says, looking mysterious. "I'd rather not say. It might get him in trouble, and I don't want to lose my source." He bends his head and begins flipping pages again, scanning each.

The tension in the room is thick.

Wow, and I thought things were crazy at home with journalists and their informants. Who knew about the conspiracy stuff going on in the Deep South?

Suddenly, Shug sits back. He exhales loudly and runs a hand through his hair. "The bastards. I knew it."

I flinch.

"Sorry." Shug stands up and offers an apologetic look. He glances out the window, frowning. "It's worse than I thought." With a quick, sweeping motion, he gathers up all of the pages and tucks them under his arm. "Let's get out of here."

I check my watch as we head back to Shug's office and wonder how in the world I'm going to make my flight. It's almost noon, and so far today I haven't finished a single interview, jotted down any notes of significance, or toured one historic home. My feet are killing me and I'm dying to get out of my suit, which is now binding my waist like a tourniquet. I realize that I haven't eaten, and my stomach—on command—starts growling like a caged lioness.

The sound reaches Shug's ear. "We'll have to take care of that." He doesn't smile or seem to mind the awful noise, just continues his forward motion.

"I have a high metabolism," I squeak in mortification, wishing I'd thought to pack a granola bar, or an apple. Anything. I'd take a spinach sandwich at this point.

We reach the office in record time. Shug throws open the door and storms inside. The message light is blinking on his phone, but he ignores it. He tosses the papers on the nearest desk, grabs a swig of cold coffee from a mug, and squints at a photograph on the wall.

"Julia," he says, swinging his gaze toward me. "I have to apologize. This must be the worst assignment you've ever had." He appears so dejected that I want to hug him and tell him that everything will be all right.

"No," I exclaim. Of course, the moment is ruined when my stomach decides to roar through my skin. "Oh come on,"

I mutter and reach for my bag. I can't—I won't look at Shug. There's at least one Snickers bar or a snack in there somewhere, I just know it.

"Let me get you some lunch," he offers.

"It's okay," I say, thinking I can't field questions from the waitress at the Honeysuckle Diner for a second day in a row—not if I'm famished. I need food—substantial amounts of it—to be prepared. "Really, I'll be fine." I open my bag wider and continue to search like I'm excavating a dig site in the Sahara. *Nothing. Nothing. Nothing.*

"Look," Shug says, clearly distraught at not being able to help. "I'll make you a sandwich. It's the least I can do."

With a sigh of defeat, I raise my chin to look up at him. "Thank you," I say, and then think to explain. "I'm sorry. I get really weird when I don't eat. Light-headed and shaky. It just comes on, all of a sudden. The good thing is…well, the good thing…is that I usually don't pass out. I've only fainted a few times."

His face breaks into a smile. "Come on," he waves me toward the back of the building.

ONE PIMENTO AND CHEESE SANDWICH LATER, I feel like a brand-new person. I won't admit to Shug that the strange concoction was a little scary-looking, with its bright yellow lumps speckled with red pepper pieces, but it was so good I had to refrain from licking my fingertips.

Shug's been reading the proposal, marking pages, and pausing to shake his head or grimace at certain paragraphs. "Better?" he asks when I finish, a tiny grin playing on his face.

"M-hm," I nod, trying not to panic. *Is there something in my teeth?* I run the tip of my tongue along my gumline, wishing I'd stuck an extra toothbrush in my purse.

"Wait," he tells me and reaches for my face. As I shrink back, he takes a gentle finger and brushes the top of my lip.

"Okay, it's gone."

Embarrassed, I cover my face with both hands. "Thank you," I say, my voice muffled through my palms. Can't anything go smoothly? He must think I'm a cavewoman compared to Mary Katherine. So much for the glamorous New York socialite thing.

"You're welcome."

After momentary embarrassment, I decide the best tactic is to pretend it didn't happen. I straighten up, dab a napkin to my mouth for good measure, and take a sip of water. "All right, what's next with Phase III? What are you going to do to fight it?"

"Not on the agenda," Shug shakes his head. "I'm sorry. You're supposed to be at Shorter Mansion in about ten minutes." He stands up. "Besides, this issue doesn't concern the magazine. I had no right to drag you into this."

"Um, I went willingly, remember?" I remind him. "I want to help." An unfamiliar but delicious surge of determination courses through my veins.

"Fine," he agrees with a disarming smile.

My knees buckle the slightest bit. I have to look away for a moment and get my bearings. It's not that Shug's so handsome, with a Southern accent that would melt butter. I'm giddy from the realization that I want to make a difference. Something or someone is trying to ruin this lovely city, and I want to know why and who.

Shug leans on one of the desks, both fists pressed into the wood. "On one condition."

This surprises me. It's not in my repertoire to make deals with anyone on an assignment. As a journalist—it's unethical. And I know for certain David, if he found out, would arrange a public hanging right after I spent a few humiliating weeks in the stocks—my head and arms sticking through openings in wooden barricades.

I decide to hold judgment until he makes his request.

"And that condition is?" I arch an eyebrow.

"Leave Phase III out—" Shug says.

I interrupt. "Look, it's not my responsibility to expose gossip, rumors, or a project that might happen. As far as I'm concerned, all this is right now is a possibility."

"Maybe we should forget the article all together," Shug says. "I'll issue a sincere apology to the magazine for the time you've spent traveling. And replace the broken windshield."

He's not joking. *Forget the article?* "I don't understand."

Shug ambles over to a row of photos on the wall. Each one depicts a city landmarks or homes—likely during recent Pilgrimages. Bright pink azaleas are in full bloom, young girls in frilly hoop skirts adorn the steps of buildings.

"Julia," Shug says, "the Pilgrimage may not *exist* after next year."

Chapter Fifteen

SHUG'S PHONE STARTS RINGING before we can leave. As he answers, a distinct female voice—more than a tad distressed—echoes throughout the confined lobby area. With a hurried gesture, Shug covers the receiver and motions he'll take the call in his office. *My mother*, he mouths before closing the door behind him.

I pace for a few minutes, stop, then repeat, listening to the exchange—until I realize with a start that I am eavesdropping.

To relocate as far away as possible—fifteen feet instead of ten—I park myself at the empty desk in the corner and retrieve a beat-up calendar from my bag. It's clear that going high-tech on my iPhone would really help my organizational ability, but I can't seem to get past needing to scribble and cross out on my little day planner.

Despite my original itinerary, my enthusiasm for making it back to Atlanta tonight is waning. There's too much at stake here and my sorely ignored intuition is buzzing with tantalizing details yet to be uncovered.

On impulse, I grab my phone and hit speed dial. The familiar Delta Airlines jingle reaches my ear, with the recorded message following. I press zero for an operator, doodling on what looks like a scrap piece of paper.

A live person answers after a three-minute wait. "I need to change a flight, please," I tell the person, and recite my departure information from memory. While keys click and clack in the background, I continue to scribble, sketching out what looks like a lopsided version of Shorter Mansion after a nuclear explosion. It's a good thing I write for a living.

The chirpy voice is back. "The ticketing change fee and difference in the two fares comes to…" Her voice trails off and is lost in the noise of the Delta Airlines call center.

Shug opens the door, cheeks flushed, with a worn leather messenger bag slung over one shoulder. "I'm finished," he calls out, but stops as soon as he sees me talking.

I hold up a finger while the operator quotes me an exorbitant price about equal to a month's rent for my New York apartment. There's only one seat left, and it's in first class. For a moment, I don't breathe, letting both sides of my brain duel it out.

How can I justify the cost? I can't expense this, because I'm the one who changed it in the first place. If I don't stay in Eufaula, how can I go back to the office—and David—with no story? If I do, I'm as good as fired. And if I'm going to be fired, I might as well drive my junky Expedition rental into Lake Eufaula.

"I'll take the seat," I tell the Delta representative.

Shug is frowning. He thinks I'm leaving. I try to smile as I confirm the last four digits of my credit card number, praying that I've not gone over my personal spending limit.

It doesn't. I almost whoop with joy. Hey, I'll be broke, but I'll still have a job.

The woman rattles off my confirmation number and I jot it down. "Thank you for flying Delta. Have a wonderful day," she tells me.

I let out a sigh of relief and hit the 'end' button on my cell. "And thank you," I mutter to the air. With flourish, I toss the silver rectangle back into the side pocket of my purse.

"Wait, you're going? Now?" Shug walks toward me, forehead creased. "But I thought—"

"I'm staying," I cut in and jump up, "at least a little longer. Things are just getting interesting, Mr. Jordan." I snap my fingers in his direction. "Ready? We have work to do."

It might be my imagination, but despite all of the uproar about the Phase III project, despite the panicked phone call from his mother, I think Shug is pleased at my announcement. He sweeps an arm past my waist and holds open the door.

"After you, then."

"SO THE WORD'S GOTTEN OUT ABOUT PHASE III?" I shield my eyes from the sunlight as I watch Shug's reaction as we walk—fast.

"My source is spreading the word. There aren't very many secrets in this town," Shug replies. "And my mother isn't taking the news well."

I raise an eyebrow and quicken my pace.

Shug checks his watch. "Lunch isn't until tomorrow morning at 11. There's plenty of time to calm her down."

"Where's your sister? Or your dad?" I ask, thinking that many fathers are useful in an emergency as long as the name isn't David and he isn't editor of *Getaways* magazine.

At the mention of his father, Shug offers a wry look. "Who knows," he says flatly. "He's never around. Especially in a crisis. The more dire the emergency, the longer it takes to find him."

I swallow and don't ask for details as we near Shorter Mansion. The tall windows and center door are draped with fresh pine garland and holly branches. Inside, a towering tree flickers with lights, sparkling ribbon, and glittering ornaments.

"It's lovely," I stop walking, thinking that I need to grab my camera, but that I don't want to spoil the moment. Past the leaded-glass windows, I can see women moving back and forth, preparing for the visitors. "So, your sister and mother are inside?"

"I imagine my sister is busy getting ready for tomorrow.

She's become quite the chef. Every year, since she's been little, PD's helped my mother make a signature treat for the Pilgrimage."

"So she's talented?" I ask. The most I can do on a good day is toast bread.

"Very."

"I hope I can try some of her recipes," I say and remind myself to stop being so judgmental about PD. Shug seems like a great guy. Why wouldn't his sister be just as nice? *I just have to get to know her better.*

"She's a really hard worker. I'm helping her with a grant application—economic development funding—so that she can open her own bakery," Shug explains, his face animated.

"That's really generous of you," I shake my head and smile. "My mother was the same way. She would have done anything for me." The words tumble out of my mouth. I didn't intend to share that, but it's too late.

"Would have?"

"She passed away. Lou Gehrig's," my voice catches and I look away.

Shug reaches over and squeezes my shoulder. "I'm sorry, Julia."

I clear my throat and sniff back tears, attempting to compose myself. "It's okay," I lie and force myself to think of something else. Something or someone awful or mean. David's face appears before my eyes and I mentally whack him down with a branch from the huge Magnolia tree towering above our heads.

I change the subject. "So, tell me more about PD and this bakery."

"There's a great spot that's vacant downtown. Plenty of space and room to grow, plus the rent is pretty reasonable."

"Sounds perfect," I agree.

Shug rubs his chin. "It is. It's PD who's holding back, but with a little help and some more confidence, she'll change her mind. There's nothing I want more than for my sister to succeed."

I want to offer some reassuring phrase, a tidbit of wisdom, but every sentence that forms in my mind seems trite. Probably because I was almost fired two days ago and have no business weighing in on anyone's career. I vow to do better with this assignment. I have to.

We turn up the sidewalk and make our way to the front steps, where both the American and Alabama flags grace the double doorway.

Shug raises his fist to knock. Before his knuckles make contact, I see a figure through the glass. A slender woman opens one of the doors.

"It's your mother, Shug," she cries, the mascara pooling under both eyes. "Aubie's locked herself in the bathroom."

Without a word, I follow Shug and the woman into the airy, open foyer. We step noiselessly onto a patterned red and blue oriental rug. I can't help but admire the ornate staircase that rises and disappears from view.

"What happened?" I hear Shug ask. When I train my attention on his broad shoulders, I see that he's already clasped hands with the distraught matriarch. "Where is she?"

The woman, dressed in canary yellow silk, wrists dripping with diamonds, sniffs and lowers her eyes. "Some awful person started a terrible rumor about a secret government meeting, Shug darling. One of the girls—bless her heart—overheard her daddy, who's kin to one of the city council members. By the time she tried to ask him, he was out the door, and driving off."

My head spins, trying to link the connections, but Shug is following it all—as if she's drawn a huge flow chart on the wall in green crayon.

"Word is…an investor's made a substantial offer on some local property." The woman sniffs. "Probably one of those Yankees."

I swallow hard. Shug blanches, but nods for the woman to continue.

"As you can imagine," the woman waves her hands for emphasis, "everyone's as nervous as a long-tailed cat in a room full of rockers."

The phrase tickles me so much that I have to fake-cough to stifle my giggles.

"Julia, are you okay?" Shug looks ready to whack me between the shoulder blades, so I shake my head vigorously and cover my mouth.

Satisfied I don't need immediate rescuing, he turns back to the canary-lady. "Where is she now? My mother?" Shug looks past her, up to the second floor. I follow his gaze, almost expecting to see a pair of expensive heels and stockinged legs dangling from the chandelier.

The woman puts a hand to her jeweled throat and exchanges a worried glance with an elderly lady in a trim navy suit who's been listening at the edge of the foyer. They both answer in a chorused response. "She's locked herself in."

"In *where*?" Shug's terse question reverberates against the antique glass windows, bouncing off the brocade curtains and carved mahogany sideboards.

The women seem startled. "She's been in the powder room upstairs for the last thirty minutes and won't open the door," the canary-lady answers.

Without pausing for more details, Shug takes the red-carpeted stairs two at a time. I catch a glimpse of the back of his loafer as it turns at the hallway and disappears.

"Shug, honey, we tried our best," the woman in navy calls out after him, then rests a hand on canary-lady's arm. They both turn and look in my direction at the same time. "Hello dear." Again, the two ladies speak in perfect stereo. "You must be Julia."

I blink in surprise, then recover my composure. It's all I can do not to back away slowly. A few of the other women drift closer to observe the exchange.

"We're sisters. I'm Pearl," the lady in navy explains. "And this is Shirl."

Now, the connection explained, I see the resemblance.

"Oh, how nice!" I exclaim. "It's lovely to meet you both. And I'm so pleased to be here." With my biggest, friendliest smile, I thrust out a hand in greeting. When I'm only offered three fingers from the woman in navy, I squeeze the tips gingerly and release. *Gosh, I need a how-to manual for this place. Or private lessons from Miss Manners—the Southern version.*

There's an awkward pause. I find myself darting a furtive look at the staircase. *Where is Shug? Where is Aubie? Is she really locked in? What are they doing and why isn't anyone coming back to save me?*

The twins tilt their heads together and whisper. When they straighten up, Pearl—or Shirl—I can't remember who is who, waves me toward the back of the mansion. "We're forgetting our manners, dear. Come have some tea."

I follow, praying it won't take long for Shug to extricate his mother from her place of hiding.

Chapter Sixteen

"WHAT'S ON THE MENU, LADIES?" I ask, digging into my bag for a notebook and pen as we parade through the corridor.

When we arrive in the kitchen, the sister in navy presents me with an embossed card with swirling gold trim. It reads as follows:

Eufaula Christmas Tour Lunch
Saturday, December 1, 2012
Chicken Salad Croissant, Pimento Cheese Ribbon,
Cream Cheese & Dates on Raisin Bread, and Cheese Straws
Pecan Tassie, Lemon Dainties, Cream Scone, Devonshire
Cream, Homemade Lemon Curd, and Strawberry Preserves

When I finish reading, four eyes are watching me closely. It's the sort of stare that makes a girl feel as if she's about to be blasted with a shrink-ray beam.

"Wow," I exclaim, searching for proper praise. "This looks…wonderful," I say. "And quite delicious." I add for good measure.

My lavish compliments do the trick, as their anxious faces melt with giddy delight. The women cluck and coo around me, each sharing a knowing glance or wink.

Shirl links her arm in mine and pats my hand. "I just knew you'd love everything, New York City girl or not. Just wait until you taste the lemon dainties. And the pecan tassies are so scrumptious, if Paula Deen were here, she'd beg us for the recipe!"

"Hey, y'all," a voice calls from the foyer. "Where is everyone?"

Pearl and Shirl exchange a worried glance, but assume smooth, refined demeanors when PD steps into the kitchen, stacks of trays in her hands.

"Here, sugar, let me help you," Pearl tiptoes over and takes a platter off the stack. "These look marvelous, Patricia Dye. Your mama is going to be thrilled when she sees them."

I lean to catch a glimpse of the coveted contents.

"Cheese straws. A little on the spicy side this year," PD grins at me and sets the rest of the trays on the nearest counter. "Hey Julia."

"Good morning," I answer, then hang back and watch the ladies crowd closer to admire her handiwork. PD is in her element. Surrounded by confections and savory treats, she even looks different. Happier. Content. And she doesn't know a thing about Aubie.

Then, as if she could read my thoughts, she stops fussing over the platters and stands ramrod-straight. "Y'all, where's Mama?"

A hush falls over the room. No one speaks or moves, except me—and that's because a hair is tickling the back of my neck and if I don't scratch the spot I might jump out of my skin. The movement signals PD like a police helicopter searchlight.

"Julia?" she asks with an arched brow.

My neck and cheeks flush hot. I must look guilty.

"Um," I begin, rolling my eyes to the ceiling. "So, your brother found out about a Phase III project. Basically, an investor wants to buy up some historic homes. The houses closest to the water."

"And. Do. What with them?" PD swallows, her eyes darting from Pearl to Shirl, then back to me.

"Condos," I squeak and shrug. There. I've said it. Every-one in the room offers a collective exhale.

PD presses a hand to her brow and winces, like someone's stabbed her in the forehead. "I don't believe it. No, I *do* believe it. There's money involved," she says. "But the idea is about as smart as nailing jelly to a tree," PD shakes her head and starts to pace the floor, continuing the debate with herself. "Of all the low-life, no account—"

I shrink back against the counter to let her pass by me for the second time.

"Wait," she stops. "Do we know this for certain?"

The women around me nod and murmur meek affirmations.

"And so where's Mama?" PD asks. Her hands are locked on her narrow hips and her chin is tilted ever so slightly, making her look like a cat about to pounce on innocent prey.

I wait for someone else to chime in. When I glance around the room, they're all busy checking the time, looking at their manicures, or inspecting a crack on the floor.

Fine. I'll be the bearer of bad news. The messenger who gets killed. With that lovely thought, I remind myself that if I don't finish this story on the Pilgrimage, I'll be dead anyway.

"She's locked herself in the bathroom. I'm sure your brother would have told you, but he's upstairs with her."

I expect her to freak out, but she does the exact opposite.

PD sighs and bites her bottom lip. "Well, in that case, she's in good hands," she says, letting her eyes fall to the floor. "It's his turn anyway," she says under her breath.

With a sudden flash of energy, everyone around me goes back to the preparations. I loosen my grip on my notepad, now damp from my hand clutching the pages, and sidle closer to Shug's sister.

It's terribly sad to think about, but perhaps—in public—PD has conditioned herself to accept Aubie's meltdowns.

I take my cue from her and get back to my own job. I decide that since Shug's busy dealing with his mother, I'll try to get some background from his sister. Chatting about the Christmas Tour might even be a welcome distraction.

"PD, when you have a moment, would you share your thoughts about the Pilgrimage?" I ask, as she arranges the cheese straws in neat rows. "Your brother's filled me in on some of the basics. But, I'd love a woman's perspective."

She pauses, a bit surprised, and looks up at me. "Oh, I'd like that." With deft motion, she adjusts one last piece on the tray and stands back to admire her work.

"Looks wonderful," I say.

"Thank you," she smiles—for real this time. "Let's sit in the parlor for a few minutes. I need to rest for a moment anyway. I've been on my feet for days." She nods at Shirl to take over in the kitchen and strides to the front of the Mansion.

We settle into two dainty chairs and I balance my notebook on one knee. "Could you tell me, specifically, the differences visitors might expect with the spring Pilgrimage versus the December tour?"

PD smoothes her skirt. "The Christmas tour is a much smaller affair and lasts only one day. Guests can enjoy lunch or a formal dinner and visit a small number of select homes. There's also the Mistletoe Market, sponsored by the local businesses downtown. The tour is always held on the first Saturday afternoon in December."

My pen moves across the page at breakneck speed as she talks. "All right."

"The Pilgrimage—always in the spring—features more homes and an entire weekend of activities. We like to have ten or twelve homes open on the tour, several gardens, local churches, Superior Pecans, as well as the Carnegie Library."

I scribble furiously, wishing I'd thought to grab my digital recorder.

"The Pilgrimage always begins with the firing of the cannon," PD smiles at this. "It's loud! There's a ghost walk at night, a fun run Saturday morning, an antique show, book signings, and more southern food than you can imagine." She taps her chin. "Of course, there are the princesses. No queen anymore."

That makes me pause. "Why?" I try to think of a tactful way to ask if she's talking about a beauty pageant.

"Until this year, a queen and two princesses were selected from the Pilgrimage Court to preside over the events. It was suggested that perhaps sixteen young ladies could represent the city of Eufaula—all princesses—making it enjoyable for the girls, instead of a competition."

"Everyone's happier?" I guess.

"And there's a better sense of unity. Plus, everyone looks so lovely in their dresses and can act as ambassadors for each of the homes on the tour, instead of just Shorter Mansion. It's a big honor, something that the little girls in this community dream about becoming when they grow up. A little like a fairy tale."

"Exactly what I was thinking," I nod. Of course, I never was partial to hoop skirts and big bows. I'd rather climb trees and hang upside down, though I won't share that with Shug's sister.

PD stops and laughs a little. "It must sound so trite and silly to someone from up north. In a big city like New York, no one cares about being a princess."

"Oh, I don't know about that." I wrinkle my nose. "There are all sorts of divas in the Big Apple. You'd be surprised," I say. "So, I have to know…did anyone in your family wear the crown? Or tiara? Or whatever you wear when you're selected as royalty here?"

There's a creak behind us in the foyer.

"The answer's yes," a familiar voice says. "Mama and PD both. And it's a tiara."

Chapter Seventeen

"ONLY A MAN FROM THE SOUTH would know a tiara from a tire iron," PD says, and nods approvingly at her brother as she gets up from the chair.

Shug waves at me with a brave smile. He and Aubie are standing in the foyer. Well, I should clarify that Shug is standing. His mother is half-leaning, half-hanging onto her son by one shoulder and what looks like the tail end of his sport coat. There are streaks of black down her cheeks and her hair is smashed on one side, like she's been laying on a bathmat. "Excuse me, Julia, while I take Mama home." PD strides toward her mother, circling an arm around her waist and leading her toward the front door.

"Of course," I say to her back and remained perched on the edge of my seat, ankles crossed. It feels like I'm in day one of finishing school, and I half-expect Martha Stewart to breeze through the door and start overseeing the progress in the Mansion. Well, except that the queen of domesticity spent some time in the slammer, and she's a Yankee. Forget that.

Shug opens one of the doors for his mother and sister, then ambles back over to the parlor, hands buried deep in his pockets. "Surviving?"

"Oh, yes," I say and wave a hand in the air, feigning nonchalance. "I'm learning a lot. So far, we've covered Southern delicacies, the official canon firing, and princess management." I tick off the items on my fingers and grin.

"Nice," he laughs. "Now, how about that tour I've been

promising you? We'll spend more time here tomorrow at the luncheon."

"Great!" I gather my bag and notebook. "I'm ready to hit the town."

"OUR FIRST STOP IS FENDALL HALL," Shug announces as we cruise through town. The top's down, as it's a balmy seventy degrees and sunny.

As we turn onto Eufaula Avenue, I remind myself to be thankful for the break from New York's endless gray clouds and snowstorms. Here, a thousand miles south, the sky is so vivid turquoise blue and pure that it almost hurts my eyes.

"Is it always like this?" I ask, yelling as we pick up speed. My hair blows wildly around my face, catching in my eyelashes.

Shug laughs and gestures above our heads. "You mean the weather?" He shrugs and nods. "Yeah. We're lucky, I guess Summer can get a little brutal when it's ninety-nine degrees in August, but it's hard to beat sunshine in the forecast more than two hundred days a year."

I settle in against the seat and enjoy the warmth on my shoulders and legs. There are amazing houses I can't wait to see inside, towering structures in Greek Revival, Victorian, and Italianate styles of architecture. We come to an intersection and wait to turn right.

Staring down at the road is the towering confederate soldier. The statue must reach thirty or forty feet in the air. He cuts a distinguished figure in Italian marble with his long coat and focused expression, his body 'at rest' with both hands gripping the barrel of his musket.

"The United Daughters of the Confederacy donated the monument in 1904," Shug says, following my gaze. "And there's another interesting fact here," he points to the street signs. "This area is the Seth Lore Historic District. Captain Lore is the man who laid out the city's main streets in 1834. Broad Street, in front of us, runs east-west. The four main north-south routes, including the one we're driving on, were named Livingston, Orange, Randolph, and Eufaula." He pauses and waits for my reaction.

"Ah, L-O-R-E. Got it," I smile over at him. "Smart guy, that Captain Lore."

We ease into the turn once the intersection is clear.

"So, the name Eufaula?" I ask. "Where did that originate?"

Shug shifts his gaze to the road. "The Creek Indians, who lived along the portion of land above the banks of the Chattahoochee River. From what we can gather from historical records, Eufaula means 'high bluff' and Chattahoochee translates to 'river of painted rocks,' though there is still some debate about that between historians.

"I see. And the locals decided to keep the name Eufaula?"

"A group of Georgia men looking for crop land adopted the name for the first settlement in 1823. When William Irwin built a steamboat wharf and post office to support trade—just south of here—for a brief time, the city was called "Irwinton". The mail kept getting sent to Irwinton, Georgia, so the people went back to using Eufaula."

"And the Indians were forced out?" I ask, wrinkling my nose and knowing the answer.

Shug frowns. "To the West. The Creek Trail of Tears." He pulled up along the side of the road and stopped the car. "Not our finest moment in history. But cotton became king and the economy boomed in the 1840s and 50s when all of these magnificent homes were built."

I brush a stray hair off my face and gaze up at a home nestled among towering trees and lush shrubbery. Fendall Hall is three stories tall, with a glass-encased cupola and widow's walk stretching across the massive rooftop.

Shug opens my door. I step out, still drinking in the exquisite architecture and sprawling porch. The home, painted in tan and trimmed in rich brown and white, is immaculate and stately.

"Fendall Hall was built by the Young family in the late 1850s. It stayed in the family until 1973 when the state of Alabama bought it. It's a museum now, operated Monday through Saturday by the Alabama Historical Commission." He nudges my arm. "Wait until you see the Italian marble tile in the entry. And there are some amazing murals—"

"Oh," I wander over to a blooming azalea bush loaded with candy-pink blossoms, stepping closer to inspect the flowers. "I love these."

"They're confused," he grins. "One warm spell and the plants think it's time to bloom."

"I would, too," I say and reach out to touch a few of the shiny dark green leaves.

"Don't," Shug warns with a yank on my arm. "I think—"

Too late, I hear distinct buzzing.

"Ow! Ack! No!" I screech. I'm blinded momentarily, intense pain searing my cheek and eyebrow like a laser beam. I stumble back, hands flailing, grabbing the air and finding nothing. Holding a hand to my eyes, I moan and slump over. Shug's arms are around my waist. He's half-dragging, half-carrying me away from the angry insects.

During the attack, one of my shoes slipped off, and I dropped my purse, but I'm clenching my teeth so hard I can't force my jaw open to say anything.

Shug is breathing hard and trying to pry my palms away from where I'd clamped them onto my skin, as if the pressure might prevent the worst from happening. Underneath, a chemical reaction is taking place. In seconds, I'll swell to the size of a hot-air balloon and lose consciousness.

Shug manages to wrestle me to a seated position on the concrete steps of Fendall Hall. "Talk to me, Julia. Talk to me," he urges. He's gripping my upper arm so tight my veins start to throb.

"Pen-th," I garble. "Pen-th," I repeat, my tongue thick. With effort, I force my eyes open.

A door creaks open behind us and I hear footsteps. "Shug Jordan, whatever are you doing on the front steps?" A female voice asks. "And who's this with you?" she chirps brightly. "Oh, there's your pocketbook. Bless your heart, dear. Let me get that for you."

The sharp click-click of her heels go by, and I catch the scent of sweet, pungent perfume. I want to sneeze, but my sinuses have expanded to the size of breakfast sausages.

Shug doesn't answer. Instead, he tries again to pull my arm away from my head. This time, he's successful.

"You're swelling. Julia, your face is…you don't look so good."

If I had the strength, I'd punch him in the shoulder and say, "No kidding," but under the circumstances, I say what's most important. "Pen-th," I sputter one last time, hoping it translates.

Shug finally gets it. He's not panicked, exactly, but close. "Miss Byrd," he shouts. "Miss Byrd. Please, bring me her purse right away! And call 9-1-1."

Darn it all. Sure, bring more people to the spectacle.

And then, for some reason—the most likely being avoidance of another insect sting—Shug throws me over one muscled shoulder like a sack of grain. No doubt, had I been able to see myself, upside down, derriere in the air, being carried up the steps of this lovely Alabama landmark, I would have wanted someone to shoot me.

Inside, on the floor, I lay sprawled against the cool tile of the foyer. There's an ornate chandelier overhead. The glittering lights swim together like an ocean of sequins and diamonds.

Miss Byrd runs inside and from the sound of it, Shug rips the bag from her hands. He unzips the top and dumps the entire contents on the floor. Lipstick cases go rolling, along with my stash of Advil, and other unmentionable feminine products. Spare change, pens, and keys clink and clatter around us.

After digging through the pile, Shug finds the EpiPen, and without hesitation, plunges it into my arm.

An ambulance siren wails in the distance. A second siren joins in. The cavalry is coming.

As the medication works its magic, returning me to a semi-human state, Shug pulls me closer, resting my head against his chest. I attempt to mumble a thank you, but end up with my swollen lips grazing the inside of his elbow. Which would have been nice, had I been semi-coherent and on our eleventh date.

"Don't try to talk," Shug says.

Tires squeal and the sirens reach a near-deafening scream outside Fendall Hall.

"Oh, thank you Jesus. Here they come," Miss Byrd announces.

I struggle to sit up but get my body about an inch higher before I fall back again. My head feels like someone buried an axe in the back of my skull.

"Just rest." Shug puts a hand on my cheek for emphasis, then tucks a strand of stray hair behind my ear. "They'll be here in a minute."

Miss Byrd coughs. "And Shug, here's Mary Katherine, too. She's coming up the walk right now."

Chapter Eighteen

AFTER THE INJECTION, I'm cold and shaking like one of those machines used to mix paint cans. To my intense embarrassment and dismay, I'm now strapped to a stretcher with an oxygen mask over my face. There are monitors everywhere.

The cart I'm lying on shimmies back and forth as the ambulance screams away from Fendall Hall, bumping over potholes, lights flashing. An EMT, who looks about twelve years old, hangs on to the metal edge of the stretcher frame, monitoring my blood pressure and heart rate.

From the angle of my own body and the strain of the engine, I can tell we're heading uphill at a decent clip. I close my eyes and start to count backwards from one hundred, trying not to worry about the back doors flying open. I resign myself to the fact that—if they do—this emergency worker is coming with me, and we'll both look like Alabama road kill in no time.

The hospital ER is housed in a short, small building. The staff mustn't be very busy today, because it looks like every employee in the entire hospital is here to meet us. My stretcher is yanked from the ambulance, and I'm certain the older of the two EMTs is going to trip before he sets me on the ground.

As I'm being rolled inside, Shug and Mary Katherine race up beside me. They jog alongside the cart as we breeze inside the doors and into the lobby area.

"Julia," Shug waves at my face to get my attention. I blink over at him. "I tried to warn you. I'm so sorry." He looks absolutely distraught, like he's the one who pushed my face into the azalea bushes and summoned the bees to sting.

The truth is, I know better, and should be wearing my medical alert bracelet. The last time I saw it, however, was in my New York apartment by the empty fish bowl. Of course, I didn't think for a moment that insects would be trolling for victims in the dead of winter. And, of course, the dead of winter down south is sixty-five degrees and sunny, so that logic is out the window in a hurry.

"S'okay," I offer what I hope is a reassuring smile. My face usually looks like it's been used as a punching bag, so there's no telling what I'm able to convey. "Happens," I add.

"You poor thing," Mary Katherine chimes in, not breaking a sweat or looking the least bit winded, but doing her best to sound the part of concerned citizen.

"We'll be waiting out here," Shug pokes his thumb in the direction of what I guess is the waiting area. He slows to a walk with Mary Katherine as the EMTs drag me into an exam room and shut the curtains behind us.

A cursory exam by the attending physician indicates that I will, indeed, live to see another day—barring any other unseen mishap. The doctor is pleasant and soft-spoken, with an accent as thick and sweet as crystallized honey.

Though I can't understand a lot of what he's saying, I nod and listen the best I can. "Y'all" and "reckon" seem among his favorite phrases, although "fixin' to" and "bless her heart" are running not far behind with the staff.

The nurses, in scrubs and white tennis shoes, scurry back and forth, chatting between tasks. I catch a few of them watching the activity around my bed and staring at my swollen face, but they're discreet enough to turn away when I notice them looking. By now, if it wasn't a blatant HIPAA violation, there might be a magazine article and photo caption circulating in *US Weekly* tomorrow. I can picture the headline: *NY Travel Writer unveils secret identity as Circus Sideshow Act.*

After another hour of watchful waiting to make sure I don't relapse, the physician signs a few slips of paper inside my medical chart. He confirms a minimum of three times that I have another EpiPen in my luggage, a current prescription for more if needed, and then finally releases me to Shug and Mary Katherine's custody.

Drained of all energy and weak from the medication's after-effects, Shug offers an elbow to hang onto as I hobble back to the Mustang. I decline, a little out of pride, but mostly because of the searing look of displeasure that shoots from Mary Katherine's eyeballs into the back of Shug's head.

He's blithely unaware of her sullen expression, even when he shoos her into the back seat, so that he can keep an eye on me up front.

With a flip of her hair, Mary Katherine steps daintily into the rear and wiggles into the space. She dons a large pair of Jackie-O style sunglasses and reapplies her lipstick, which still looks perfect.

"Julia, I'm going to take you back to Roger's in a few minutes," Shug tells me over the rumble of the engine. "He's making up your bed now and putting on some hot tea. I told him we'd be there shortly." He hands me a slip of paper. "Phone numbers. Mine. PD's. My parents' house. Just in case."

"Thanks," I say. My seatbelt clicks into place as we drive away from the historic district.

Shug takes a right, then another into a church parking lot. He laughs when he sees my confused expression. "No, it's not what you think," he says, jumping out of the vehicle.

He walks around and winks in my direction. I don't move or turn my head to look at Mary Katherine, who probably doesn't need another reason to consider throwing me under the wheels of the Mustang.

"I called ahead for your prescription. Doctor's orders," he jokes.

While I ease out of the car one cautious foot at a time,

Mary Katherine screws up her face. "Shug Jordan, whatever are you talking about?"

"It's the one thing guaranteed to make anyone feel better," Shug says, and then hesitates. "You're not allergic to flour and sugar, are you, Julia?"

I shake my head, trying not to smile. His worried expression is adorable. "Um," I point at my face. "I thought you were making a stop. I'm not sure I want to go anywhere in public after this." I don't have to check a mirror to know my eyes and cheek are still puffy.

"Oh, is that all?" Relief floods his face. He reaches under his seat and hands me a worn blue hat. It's emblazoned with an orange embroidered AU.

I take it and turn it around in my hands, smiling.

"It's my lucky Auburn hat—you know, where I went to college," Shug is beaming. "Come on, be a sport. It'll be fine and will just take a sec. I promise," he pleads.

Mary Katherine coughs. I'm not sure if she's trying to hurry me along, but I slap the ball cap on my head and pull it down as far as I can over my forehead. "All righty then."

"Good. Let's go." He points behind us and up in the air.

It's The Donut King shop I noticed when I drove into Eufaula. The small, simple white sign with bright-red letters hangs outside the building. The structure itself is nondescript and plain, but when I inhale, the scent is a heady mix of sugar, flour, and buttery-goodness. Krispy Kreme, but better. It's impossible to ignore and I find myself drifting across the parking lot toward the incredible smells coming out of the tiniest bakery I've ever seen.

Inside is dark and cramped, with conveyor belts dripping with glaze behind the counter. There are stacks of white boxes on one side and a cooler of milk and juice to our right. An Asian woman is waiting for us behind the counter, her hands folded at her waist.

"Hello Mr. Jordan, good to see you," she says with a slight

accent and nods a greeting in our direction.

When my eyes adjust to the dim light, I notice that the glass case in front of us has several shelves, each full of plastic trays. The trays, though, are all empty—strange for a doughnut shop—but I'm not about to ask what's going on or what we're doing there.

Mary Katherine hugs her elbows and tucks her arms tight into her ribs. She seems miserable and is glancing around like a snake might slither up her leg any moment. In my experience, women like Mary Katherine don't frequent places like this. They don't even pretend to eat high-fat anything, so I'm really not sure what she's doing here, other than tagging along to make sure her boyfriend is behaving. After Shug's seen my face blown up three sizes larger than normal, I don't think I'm much competition.

"I really appreciate you waiting for us," Shug tells the owner of the shop. He looks over at me and winks, "They're usually sold out by now—but I told her we had a special guest from out of town and that she *really* had to sample the best doughnuts the South has to offer. I was planning to bring you here earlier today and surprise you, Julia, but…"

Mary Katherine squeaks like a mouse has nibbled her toe. When we all turn to look at her, she covers up her alarm by snuggling up to Shug. "Silly me. I'm just so excited about tonight. Come on, sweetheart, we've got lots to do this afternoon."

"Well, enjoy." The woman smiles and bends over to pick up a white box large enough to handle a dozen doughnuts, then produces several small bags with the tops folded down.

"Perfect," Shug slides a few bills across the counter and scoops up our stash of sweets. He waves at the owner and opens the door, balancing the box and bags in one hand.

Once we're settled back in the Mustang, Shug makes a big deal of opening the box and shoving it under my nose. The doughnuts smell like heaven.

"You're not going to eat in this car, Shug Jordan," Mary Katherine says under her breath.

He throws her a backward look. "We most certainly are," he retorts to her surprised expression. "This is serious."

To emphasize his point, he turns and offers the doughnuts to Mary Katherine, who turns up her nose and declines. He brings the box back to me.

With my thumb and index finger, I pinch the nearest confection and pull it out of the waxed paper wrapping. The doughnut is perfect, with just the right amount of glaze clinging to every nook and cranny. I take a small nibble and swoon with delight.

Shug finishes his doughnut by the time I've swallowed my first taste. "It's good, right?"

I nod and smile, making sure to keep my lips pressed together because I'm still chewing.

Mary Katherine taps the seat impatiently. "Shug, please. Can we go?" She waves at herself. "This sun. I'm going to burn up if we sit out here much longer."

Shug brushes off his fingertips, cranks the engine, and drives toward the B&B. "You can rest up for a bit. We'll grab some dinner at, say six?"

He parks in front of Roger's a few minutes later.

Mary Katherine follows me out of the Mustang, sliding into the passenger seat. She offers a cool smile and buckles the seatbelt, examining me with the strangest expression.

"Julia, heads up!" Shug calls out, looking mischievous. "Go long." He heaves a small white bag at me. As the sack flies through the air, I manage to snatch the edge one-handed.

"Got it! Thanks." I tuck it under my arm and take the steps one at a time, careful to hold on to the railing. When I step inside the building, smiling to myself, Roger is chatting with someone in the kitchen. I tiptoe to my room, unlock the door, and collapse on the four-poster bed, fully-clothed, and kick my shoes off. They land with a thump-thump on the wood floor. When I grab the pillow and stuff it under my head and neck, I realize now why Mary Katherine was staring at me.

When I raise my eyes, the dark brim of Shug's ball cap stares down at me. I am still wearing his favorite Auburn University baseball hat. I slide his prized possession off my head, rubbing the soft blue cotton between my fingertips. With a sigh, I place it on the mattress with the orange AU logo facing me, and then snap off the bedside light.

As my eyelids grow heavy, and I settle in against the coverlet and firm mattress, I remind myself that I need to set my alarm for five o'clock. That will give me just enough time to shower, dress, apply makeup to my war wounds, and look presentable for dinner.

When my mind drifts further away from consciousness, I wonder why on earth Shug Jordan never asked for his ball cap back.

Chapter Nineteen

I WAKE WITH A START and sit straight up in bed. It's so dark in the bedroom that I can't see my feet or my hands. There's a sliver of light coming from outside, though, and after I launch myself off the mattress and trip over my shoes, I pull back the window's heavy silk curtains.

With the back of my hand, I rub my eyes and look out across the street. The sun is rising in the east, casting a warm, red glow over the homes and buildings I can see in the distance.

Panicking, I leap for my watch, which I'm certain that I left on the bedside table. In my hurry, I bump my hip into the wood and knock the silver band to the floor. Still half-blind and now smarting from the bump, I drop to my hands and knees, pawing around on the floor, reaching my fingers beneath the bed frame.

It can't be morning. What time is it? As that thought exits my brain, I wonder this: *What day is it?*

I snatch my laptop out of its carrying case and open it on the room's tiny wooden desk. The light from the screen pours out and I wince from the brightness. My Mac powers up, chiming to signal the system is loading. With a clumsy finger, I hold my breath and punch the volume button half a dozen times before any other obnoxious noises wake Roger or the B&B's other guests.

The black letters and numbers on my Mac tell me what I've already guessed. It's six-twenty in the morning, it's now

Saturday, December 1st, and I'm about thirteen and a half hours late for dinner with Shug Jordan. I cover my face with my palms and try to inhale. When I've sufficiently replaced the oxygen in my lungs, I swallow hard and click on my email.

Gmail tells me that I have one hundred and thirty-five new messages. The senders include a multitude of spammers, who cloak their sales messages in miracle cures for infertility, impotence, and hair loss. Another two dozen announcements claim they have located a distant, wealthy relative who has left me a million dollars. The final spam-mail is from a minister in Kenya who urgently needs to send me money with absolutely no strings attached.

After I hit delete, I open the important messages, starting with the person least likely to chastise me for something I've done wrong. There are four from Marietta, two from Andrew, my long-suffering boyfriend, and a lone message from David, boss from hell and unfortunately, also my father.

Marietta's emails are brief and snappy, detailing the latest office escapades and late-night hook-ups. She spends an entire page describing Dolores Stanley's makeover and new ward-robe, no doubt spurred by an effort to please the new man at the helm of Getaways magazine. *Actually, Dolores looks pretty good. Someone at Macy's helped her pick out the clothes. Here's hoping someone tossed the tangerine polyester pants and paisley print tops. Off to grab a snack. I'm starving! Love, Marietta.*

At the mention of the word, I remember Shug lobbing the Donut King bag at me before he and Mary Katherine left for home. I sniff the air, trying to locate where I might have dropped the package—please, not the hallway—on the way into the bedroom last night. After tripping over both of my shoes a second time, I give up and flick on the small overhead light.

Phew! The small white bag is sitting just inside the door. I kneel down and cradle the bag in one hand, unrolling the top with the other. Without hesitation, I pop one of the doughnut holes in my mouth and sink back into the chair. My taste buds immediately wake to the golden goodness that dissolves on my tongue. The sweet glaze is just enough balance for the lightly fried flour and yeast confection.

I steel myself with a second and third sample as I open Andrew's emails. His writing is typically sparse and factual, and these messages don't stray much from the established format, mentioning work, the weather, and my return to New York, in that order. He offers condolences for my rushed departure, the change in assignments, then throws me a curveball in the last sentence, which I almost skip because I'm so engrossed in popping doughnut holes into my mouth.

The cursor blinks next to his question. *Where would you like to go for our anniversary?* I'm at a loss. Anniversary. Tuesday. I do a mental calculation and, to my dismay, realize that Andrew's correct. I'll be back in the City in time for whatever he has planned.

In the past, Andrew has tried hard to be very creative. Our adventures have included a trip to New Orleans, which ended up with a pickpocket stealing Andrew's wallet and a homeless person following us back to the hotel. For my birthday, a sunset cruise was a marvelous idea, until a freak storm cropped up and washed the captain overboard. At the time, neither one of us realized he was drunk. Andrew and I did enjoy meeting the coast guard crew when they rescued us from drifting across the Atlantic in a thirty-foot sailboat with a semi-functional engine.

Andrew outdid himself last year by giving me a surprise skydiving trip. Of course, he'd forgotten my fear of heights. Like a good sport, I decided I'd try it—with a borrowed Valium—but the bumpy air and sight of the earth thousands of feet below only served to feed my unrelenting terror. In the end, I tossed my cookies twice into someone's spare backpack and never got out of the airplane.

I'm assuming, this year, Andrew will choose something

standard and safe. I type a vague response about my return, promise to call when my flight lands, then add a few guilt-induced x's and o's for good measure. Andrew, one of the world's nicest guys, deserves better than a lot of 'maybes' and a string of broken romantic dates. So far, we've avoided the big commitment talk, but I feel that it's coming. And to be fair—and honest with myself—I love him, but he's not my soul mate. We need to talk. It'll be first on my list after I finish the article for *Getaways*.

I turn my attention to business. David's message. It's a not-so-subtle reminder about my current assignment. *Deadline: Wednesday, December 5, 2012. Five o'clock.* There's no greeting, small talk, or signature. Duly noted.

With a sigh, I tap 'reply' and pick up a brochure left for me by the Eufaula Chamber of Commerce. I flip through the photos and descriptions, turn down a few page corners, and type up a brief description of the area, being careful to mention Shorter Mansion, the Hart House, and Fendall Hall. I decide to leave out my run-in with the fire ants and yesterday's bee sting incident, choosing instead to share my ambitious plan for touring Eufaula today: the Christmas Tour of Homes, Carnegie Library, Fairview Cemetery, Reeves Peanut Warehouse, and the Confederate Hospital on Riverside Drive.

With flourish, I hit send and close my laptop.

IT'S NOW SIX FORTY-FIVE IN THE MORNING, which I confirm with a cursory glance at the clock in the bathroom. I splash my face with cold water and inspect my cheek and temple. There's not much evidence of the assault on my skin, other than some redness and puffy areas around my eye, which a dab of makeup will fix.

I consider leaving a message for Shug, but decide to wait, do a little exploring on my own, and show up full of apologies on his office doorstep at precisely eight o'clock. After a shower and clean clothes, I run a comb through my still-damp hair, grab my camera bag, and slip out into the hallway. I pass Roger's library on the way out the door and spy a copy of *Back-tracking in Barbour County*. I tuck the book under my arm and adjust the purse on my shoulder as I step onto the street, estimating that it is less than a mile to the old Confederate Hospital.

The morning is pleasant and crisp with a slight breeze. There isn't a cloud in the sky and birds chirp from treetops, hurrying me along. At the corner of Broad and Randolph Streets, I admire cascades of water splashing down from a fountain in the center of the intersection.

After I cross Orange and Livingston, I pause to read the inscription on a tall silver and black monument marker embossed with gold letters. It reads *Central Railroad of Georgia Freight Depot* and bears the date 1865, when the Southwestern Railroad of Georgia became the first rail line to connect with Eufaula and Georgetown, Georgia. The Depot was abandoned in the late 1980s, when the City of Eufaula acquired the structure.

I move to read the opposite side of the marker, and snap a photograph of the long, yellow building with a red metal roof. According to the sign, the refurbished Depot now houses the Chamber of Commerce, Tourism Council, Main Street Eufaula, and other community groups.

As I continue toward the reservoir, which divides Alabama and Georgia, I pass North Forsyth Avenue. I flip open the reference book I've borrowed and search for information on the old Confederate Hospital. I recall from looking through the tourism material that the building, erected in 1836, is considered the first permanent structure in Eufaula. The building also served as a tavern and, for a brief time, an Episcopal Church.

On pages 204 and 205, *Backtracking* recounts the memories of Mrs. Serena Hoole Brown, the granddaughter of Confederate General Hunter. She describes Eufaula on April 29th, 1865—the day General Sherman declared an end to the war between the states.

"...the upper floors of the stores were filled with ill and wounded soldiers...The private homes were like hospitals ... the houses on the hill, on Eufaula and Randolph Streets. The old O'Harro house, a large hotel, was a hospital, and the two-story wooden court house was a separate ward for commissioned officers."

Mrs. Hoole Brown goes on to describe that "...the large wooden two-story house on the bluff, at the foot of Broad Street was the ward for "the blood-poison cases-the gangrenous cases"...Every day had found the women of Eufaula nursing the soldiers, sending their servants on foraging expeditions for eggs and chickens, and seeing to it that the surgeons and physicians were supplied with instruments, chloroform, morphine, quinine and such stores as were necessary. Dr. Hamilton M. Weedon, who was in charge of the hospital on the bluff, depended upon the efforts of the heroic women to supply him with a very excellent healing salve...made of alder pitch and blooms."

I close the book and continue walking. The Old Confederate Hospital—now a private residence—sits nestled among the trees that drip with Spanish moss. It's a lovely building, painted yellow with white trim. Double porches stretch the entire length of the façade.

For a moment, I can almost see the women in hoop skirts and shawls, tending to broken and bloodied confederate soldiers, many just boys. I can imagine the acrid sting of chloroform in the air and the sound of moans and suffering. It is a painful, heartbreaking thought, and I wonder how many families were ripped apart by the battles, how many men— fathers, brothers, and sons—lost their lives in this small part of the state. I shudder and blink against the tears trying to spill over on my lashes.

With a shake of my head, I regain my composure and focus. It's time to hurry back and find Shug. I adjust the strap of my purse and reach for my camera. Though the city is full of historic landmarks, and the residents are used to tourists, I am mindful of not disturbing anyone. While the street is still peaceful and quiet, I snap a photograph.

The familiar purr of a Mustang engine rumbles behind me. "Hey stranger," Shug calls. "I thought I'd lost you for good."

"Hey, I am so sorry—" I begin to explain.

He waves away my explanation. "Ah, I thought you'd need some rest after yesterday. When I came by to check on you last night, Roger said he hadn't heard a sound from your room." He smiles up at me. "We peeked through the keyhole to see if you were still breathing."

"You did not—" I accuse him and wag a finger. "I'll tell your mother on you."

Shug holds up both hands. "Please, anything but that."

"All right, but no spying," I offer a stern look. "It was early when I woke up, so I decided to take the solo tour." I hold up the camera. "I was on my way to see you next. And apologize."

"For standing me up?" He laughs. "Well, had you been able to make our date, I would have taken you to a really upscale place…" Shug lets his voice drift off. When he lets his eyes roll back, I know that he's joking.

"So I blew it?" I play along, ignoring the word 'date.' I put both hands on my hips. "Well, don't leave me guessing. What did I miss?"

"Phil's down-home barbeque." He grins in delight. "Best butts in Alabama."

"I'll bet you they sell a t-shirt with that saying," I tease back.

"Only if you eat enough pork and potato salad. You can get gifts for all of your Yankee friends," he winks. "But, first, you have to try some other Alabama favorites—collard greens, ham hock, and butter beans."

"Now you're scaring me," I cross my arms. "What is ham hock and butter beans?"

"Well, you'll have to find out later," Shug says and pats the seat next to him. "We have to get to Shorter Mansion first. My mom's had her nerve pill—or two—Ella Rae's dressed and ready, and PD's so spun up, she might not sleep for weeks. Wait 'til you taste what she's come up with."

"Something better than Donut King?" I say and arch an eyebrow as I walk around to the other side of the Mustang and ease into the passenger seat.

"Well, I don't know about that," he says, cranking the engine. "But she is my sister. I'd like to stay on speaking terms with my family. I think…I think I'll let you decide."

"And what if I don't like it?" I squint and wrinkle my nose.

Shug turns the wheel and eases to a stop. "We'll have to put you in there." He gestures out my window to a small one-story brick building.

"It says Old City Jail Salon," I read the sign, puzzled. "As in a *hair salon*?"

Shug rubs his hands together. "It is now, but it was the old city jail. Still has the original iron grille, doors, and threshold. They moved it here from behind the courthouse in 1985."

"And?"

"And if you get out of line, we'll just lock you up in there until you behave or I get you a flight home," Shug explains, his face serious. "It's nice and cozy, with only two cells and not much chance of escape. The brick walls are a foot thick, the ceiling has three layers of boards."

"Only two cells?" I blink my eyes.

His voice gets low. "One for men, the other one for women and lunatics."

I frown at Shug. "What lunatics?"

"Don't worry. You're still okay." He's trying not to laugh.

"Me? Worried?" I throw up my hands, let them drop, and settle back against the seat. "Oh, not at all." I giggle. "Just remember, Shug Jordan. If there's no me, there's no article."

"Ah," he slaps his forehead, "I knew there was something I was forgetting."

Chapter Twenty

WE ARE STILL LAUGHING when Shug pulls up and parks in front of Roger's B&B. My host is standing on the bottom porch step, looking dashing in a trim, dark suit and polished shoes.

When I step out of the Mustang, Roger ambles forward, bows, and offers me a hand.

"See you in about an hour?" Shug asks, looking from me to Roger. "Better make it forty-five minutes, just to be sure."

Roger winks at me. "I'll make sure Sleeping Beauty gets to the lunch, is wearing something lovely, and has both of her glass slippers. Go on, Shug. Never you mind. Go see about Aubie and PD. And I'll escort Miss Julia to the soiree."

Shug seems relieved.

"Oh, and by the way, someone *else* is looking for you… rather urgently." Roger knits his eyebrows together and jerks his head in a not-so-subtle way toward Shorter Mansion.

With a jolt, I realize that it's Mary Katherine.

Shug knows it, too. He frowns and waves. We watch him drive off, my arm linked in Roger's, and I try to shake off the feeling that Mary Katherine is just wound a little tight. She's over-protective and perhaps a tad jealous. There's nothing but my assignment between me and Shug Jordan. After I leave, there won't be a reason to come back to Eufaula, and the two of them won't ever have to see me again.

For some reason, the thought isn't reassuring and warm.

"May I?" Roger asks, watching me closely. He sweeps past me to open the door.

"Thank you." I nod, pushing away my worries about Mary Katherine, and follow him inside.

"Now, Miss Julia, you just let me know if you need anything at all." My host taps his fingertips together. "I'll be right here, keeping an eye on the time."

With the picture of a digital timer ticking down in my head, I scurry back to my room and open the armoire doors. When I reach inside to pull out my dress bag, there's nothing inside. I feel all four corners, then the floor, with my hand. Empty.

Oh no. Where is it? I can't have left...

I sit down and think hard about my luggage. After checking it with the ticket agents, I don't recall picking it up at baggage claim. I was in a hurry. I was scattered and worried about getting the rental car. Rental monster truck, I think ruefully.

The digital clock is counting down. I race back out of my room to find Roger. He's on his cell phone, but hangs up the second he sees my face. "Kisses, bye," he whispers and presses end on his iPhone. "Julia, darling. What is it? You look like you've lost your best friend."

"Maybe my best friend's dress?" I squeak. "I can't find my luggage. My garment bag. I think it's still at the Atlanta Airport. No," I add. "I'm sure that it's at the Atlanta Airport. In baggage claim."

Roger nods, never taking his eyes off my face. "All right. So, we'll fix this. We have..." he looks at his wrist. "...not much time." He thinks, types a rapid text message and sends it into cyberspace, then takes my hand. "Come with me. Everything's going to be fine."

WE END UP A FEW DOORS DOWN in a dress shop filled with enough sequins to stock the World Bank top to bottom. When I shoot an anxious 'I'm trying to trust you' look in Roger's direction, he doesn't respond. Instead, he points me to the dressing room, snaps his fingers, and smiles.

Right before I pull the curtains closed, he mouths, "Go on."

I shrug out of my jacket, kick my shoes into the corner, and then shimmy out of my jeans and top. In my bra and panties and a pair of wool socks, I shiver. A male hand tosses a stack of dresses on top of the rod for my inspection.

"Um, I don't know, Roger," I say. "Aren't they awfully bright?" *And short?*

"Miss Julia, do you need something to wear?" he asks in a school principal's tone of authority. "Something dressy and worthy of a New York City journalist?"

I almost salute. Dutifully, I hang up the shimmery cocktail frocks and pull on the first one, zipping it up. It's red and sparkly. I feel like a human fire engine. The second is lemon yellow and not as laser-beam blinding, but it only covers an inch or two past my underwear line. Definitely not.

"I need to see these," Roger prompts and knocks on the wood near my dressing room. "Julia, don't be shy."

"All right," I compromise and wrestle the third dress over my head. It's charcoal gray and long-sleeved with beading at the hem and sleeves. I dive through the curtains and appear to a half-circle of women and Roger. "Oh, hello."

"Hey," they all chorus at the same time.

Roger inspects the lines of the material and nods his approval. He puts his hands on my shoulders and turns me around. "More to try on," he says, giving me a gentle push toward the dressing room. "You need two gowns, not just one. There's dinner tonight, don't forget."

Of course, that detail had completely slipped my mind. "You don't think—"

"No," Roger says, ending the discussion. "You cannot wear the same dress."

I duck back into the changing room and check the price tag dangling under my arm. When I read the numbers, I almost pass out. The tiny little white tag tied with a pink ribbon says four hundred dollars. I check again to make sure. Now, I do feel sick because I've indeed read the amount correctly. Down to the last zero.

I peek out at Roger from between the curtains. "I don't know. There may be a slight issue with my—"

The look on his face makes me falter and stop. I'm about to say 'credit card,' but his expression forbids it. He's all business and obviously has something worked out with the owner and staff. I'm hoping it's a 95 percent discount program for wayward Yankees who lose their luggage in Atlanta.

Roger doesn't look much like a fairy godfather, but I'm starting to believe that he can work a little magic if the situation calls for it.

He takes another few dresses from a girl who's been madly searching through the racks. With his hip stuck out to the right and a stern gaze, Roger holds the hangers in two fingers.

"We're not discussing it," he tells me in a clipped voice. He shoves the new stack in my direction. This group is fluffy and ruffled, not at all my style, but I accept the half-dozen selections without making a peep.

"You need two and it's going to be taken care of. End of discussion." With a flick of his wrist, he whirls his finger in the air for me to continue wrestling on the gowns.

I close the curtains. With a twist worthy of an acrobat, I unzip the dress and let it drop to the floor. I snatch it up in a hurry, hanging it back up as best I can.

Holding up the next pick with both hands, I bite my lip and grimace. It's not my style at all. I hang up the rest and flick through them, pausing long enough to decide that none of them are appropriate for a thirty-two year old woman who's attempting to maintain a shred of dignity.

Until I reach the very last frock Roger's minion has chosen. It's more subtle than the rest, the material in an off-white with gold trim. The design is sleek and formfitting, but enough so that my mother won't turn over in her grave. With the right heels, it might work.

I slide it up my legs and over my hips, letting the silky satin graze my skin. It's cool to the touch and makes me shiver, but the dress fits like a dream. When I turn around to check my figure in the mirror, I am amazed at the transformation.

"Knock, knock," Roger booms from outside the fitting room. "Time's a wastin', sugar. Come on out, Julia."

With another long glance at my backside, I straighten my shoulders and walk out into the center of the room. Roger, with his forehead almost touching one of the store workers, looks up and beams with joy. "That's it. Perfect." He nods, then jumps to attention and claps his hands. "Ladies! Shoes, we need shoes."

Three minutes later, we're loaded down with plastic dress bags and shoe boxes, traipsing back to the B&B. Roger is semi-smug and self-satisfied, though not in an unkind way. I have a feeling that he's missed his secret calling on Project Runway or America's Next Top Model.

When we reach the bedroom, I throw both arms around him and kiss his cheek. "You are amazing," I tell him. "Thank you."

"My pleasure," he says, the color rising in his neck and ears. He shakes his head and releases me, clapping his hands for attention. "Now, Miss Julia, you have five minutes."

IN RECORD TIME, I run a comb through my hair, pin it up, and pull on the new outfit. The shoes pinch a bit in the toes, but I ignore it in my rush. I throw my cell phone and notebook into a small bag Roger thought to add to the ensemble. With a brush, I powder my face, sweep on eye shadow, then apply lipstick, and a light coat of mascara.

Roger's waiting outside the room, checking his watch for the umpteenth time this hour. We race out the door and down the street. My thighs start to burn after a block, and I'm wishing I would have slathered my dry legs with lotion. But I'm keeping up the best I can, and am only slightly winded when we reach Shorter Mansion.

The foyer is full of women, and I can hear the chatter from outside the double doors. Roger doesn't bother to knock, just steps inside, pressing an arm against the door to hold it back so that I can pass through. Once inside, I check the four corners of the room and strain my neck to see over the tops of well-coiffed heads.

Roger waves over a trio of women and exchanges air kisses. He introduces us, and then moves on to the next swarm of ladies in the opposite corner.

I trail behind him, absorbing the ornate décor, admiring the antique furniture, smiling at the unfamiliar faces. The female guests, with subtle glances, take time to appraise my dress and shoes. So far, I seem to pass inspection.

The men, packed in the left side of the house, are busy holding court. Roger leans in. "If I had to guess, the testosterone junkies behind us are busy discussing Auburn football and the number of days until the college season kicks off next August." He rolls his eyes and straightens his suit and yellow tie. Peeking out from his sleeves are intricate gold cufflinks adoring each wrist glint. They wink at me under the light of the chandelier.

We say hello to a couple in the parlor, then move through a whirlwind of introductions in the dining room. The mayor, the city council members, business owners, and the president of the chamber of commerce all thank me for traveling to Eufaula. I make small talk, answer questions about New York, Central Park, and Rockefeller Center, but keep my eyes roving for broad shoulders and a shock of dark hair.

"Oh, don't worry. He's here," Roger says in my ear, taking my elbow with his fingertips and steering me toward the kitchen.

I raise an eyebrow and slide him a perplexed glance. "He who? You mean Shug?" I am rambling, babbling, and I close my mouth before any additional information tumbles out.

Roger squeezes my arm. "It's okay, sugar. You'd make a lovely couple. I can see it now," he murmurs. "The cake, the streamers, the decorations. We can hold the service on the front lawn—or the back—if you prefer a more intimate ceremony." He chuckles, the deep laugh of someone who knows more than they're letting on.

"Oh, now, Roger, I'm surprised at you," I chide and cluck my tongue. "You are absolutely making that up. How did you ever came to that conclusion? As a matter of fact," I whisper, "I have a boyfriend in New York, and it is our anniversary next week. Tuesday." With a rush of exhilaration, I defend Andrew and my honor like a knight protecting his kingdom, forgetting all about my plan to cool things off the moment I step off the plane.

"Poor Andrew. You might be fooling the rest of Eufaula, but there's no mistaking—"

With a sharp intake of breath, I turn on my heel to clear up any misunderstanding about my relationship with Shug Jordan. Before I can utter a word, the sound of a hard snap echoes in the room. I don't move. Roger blinks and looks down at my ankle.

"Sit down," he clenches his teeth into a grin. I oblige in the nearest place I can find, eye level with wrists and ring fingers decorated with thick bangles and jingling jewelry. "It might be *you, too*," he whispers.

I stare at him, trying to figure out what Roger means, but he's already turned to wave at someone else.

"Hey, y'all," a Southern voice carries over my head. "Yoo-hoo." It's Mary Katherine, honing in on our position, making a beeline for my pink tapestry-covered antique settee. She's dragging Shug, who appears to have developed the flu or another illness that causes a person's skin to appear a light shade of green and walk as if fifty-pound weights are attached to his feet.

"Mary Katherine," I greet her, unable to get up, as Roger is holding me down with one hand, attempting—from the look on his face—to send telepathic thoughts to my muddled brain. "Hello. How are you?"

When I turn to greet Shug, she blocks my view. "Well, after I found my sweet boyfriend," she pauses for effect, staring at me with the mirth of a prison guard, "I was able to gather myself together and come down here and help the other ladies with all of the festivities."

While I wonder why Shug was needed for a decidedly female-run event, I nod politely.

Mary Katherine scrunches up her mouth in a pretty pout. "Whatever were y'all doing wandering around by the reservoir? I can't image whatever could be that interesting, especially at that hour of the morning," she feigns a yawn and bats her eyelashes at Shug. Her tone is laced with vinegar and there are sparks of anger beneath her smooth, ladylike demeanor.

I can't help it. I am simmering, two seconds from explosion. *I was the one minding my own business*, I want to bellow. But I don't answer, especially since Roger has gone from patting my arm to pinching it. Hard.

"Ow," I yelp and cover my mouth. When I glare at him, Roger looks bemused. It's his attempt to remind me that there are several hundred witnesses—I mean, guests—standing within earshot, just in case I decide to say or do anything stupid.

Mary Katherine gives me a funny look.

"Oh, it's just my...arthritis kicking up," I lie. "Terrible this time of year. In fact, I think I need my medicine. Roger, can you walk me back? It'll only take a moment."

He nods, "Of course. Just a moment. Stay here, will you, Julia?" Roger traipses over to chat with a tall woman in a huge hat and floor-length mink coat.

With Roger distracted, and Shug still behind her, Mary Katherine looks a shade happier. If she could figure out a way, I have no doubt Shug's girlfriend would lock me out of Shorter Mansion until tomorrow morning or until everyone's gone home. Maybe forever.

She puts a finger to her lips. "That's such a shame about your arthritis. I had no idea. I thought arthritis was for older people." Mary Katherine takes a dramatic breath, then waves her fingertips in the direction of the street. "If y'all don't hurry, you'll both miss the luncheon. And that would be such a shame, considering the magazine article and all…"

This causes Shug to frown and look in my direction.

I swallow and consider if she's just offered a veiled threat. Surely, she's beyond tattling on me about missing five minutes of Eufaula's Christmas Tour lunch. Then again, it's better not to underestimate one really pissed-off Southern belle.

There's a moment of caustic silence.

"Well," I smile brightly, "I'd better get going, then. And hurry back."

On cue, Aubie claps her hands together and calls for everyone's attention. "Lunch is served, everyone. Please join us. You'll find a place card for your name."

After the announcement, there's a rush of bodies toward the rear of the Mansion. The swell of excitement carries almost everyone toward the lush tables filled with food. Mary Katherine locks her arm in Shug's, preparing to steer him away from me and the front door. Desperate for help, I try to signal Roger, who's still talking.

It's the perfect time to escape for a moment, regain my composure, and pretend to take a few pills. *What's taking him so long?*

I cast a glance toward the front door and see PD through the glass. Her arms are loaded down with trays and she's struggling with the latch. Shug's sister teeters and rights herself, still jiggling the door handle.

I'll help!

Without another thought about Roger's strict warning, I spring up, wobble on my right ankle, and promptly collapse on the floor.

Chapter Twenty-One

"IT'S BROKEN," I cry out, holding my ankle. The shoe has snapped in two, leaving a gilt-covered cylinder nearly five inches long in the palm of my hand.

This is what I get for trying to balance in stiletto heels, I tell myself.

Shug rushes over and kneels down; Roger is two steps behind, with his hands fluttering in the air like bird wings. Mary Katherine is glowering red hot between the two men, so angry I think that she might self-combust into flames.

"Julia, are you hurt?" Shug asks, taking my foot in his hands and examining for broken bones. With careful fingers, he slips my toes out of the broken shoe. At his touch, I tremble. His dark eyes find mine and I can't help but feel lightheaded.

"She's fine, sweetheart," Mary Katherine pulls at his coat sleeve. "Now, be a good boy and let PD in the door. I'll look after Julia."

With the mention of his sister, Shug relinquishes his position and gets to his feet, brushing off his pants. "Be right back," he murmurs.

Wide-eyed, Roger shoots a look of pure terror in my direction, then watches as Mary Katherine sidles nearer to inspect the damage.

"Oh, Julia, my goodness, bless your heart," Roger exclaims as he practically pushes her tall figure out of the way to get to me first. He bends down and pulls me closer, tilting his face toward my ear. His voice is hushed but emphatic and clipped. "Didn't you hear me the first time? I said—it might be *your shoe*."

"Oh no, I thought you..." I cover my eyes and shake my head back and forth.

Mary Katherine is closer. Hovering. Circling like a bee to pollen. And ready to sting.

Roger stops talking. Shug's girlfriend is inches from my foot.

"Princess?" Roger shoots a half-annoyed, half-amused look in her direction. "You run along with the other girls and play nice." He shoos her with an adoring look. "Pretty please? Don't miss all of the fun. Besides, Miss Shirl is dying to know where you picked up those stunning earrings."

Mary Katherine brightens, "Oh?" She tosses her long blonde hair over one shoulder to reveal an intricate design of gold and diamonds.

"They are lovely," Roger gushes. I sit still, not breathing, watching in awe as Shug's girlfriend softens before my eyes. "I took a guess. That little antique store in Charleston? Or the one in Savannah?" He taps his upper lip. "But, when she asked me, I told her to go straight to you." Roger takes Mary Katherine's hand in his. "Let's walk, shall we dear? Shug and PD will be along in just a moment."

Open-mouthed, still sitting on the floor, I yank off my other shoe. My toes are red and pinched, but when I stand up, I almost sigh in relief. I hobble to the foyer of the Mansion, feeling much like Cinderella after the ball, and step outside. The naked soles of my feet retract against the cold marble and I practically dance down the steps, my broken heels swinging next to my bare thighs.

"What happened?" PD exclaims from the curb, hoisting another tray from the trunk of her car. "Shug? What's going on?"

"Wardrobe malfunction," I explain.

Her brother, who's pulling another stack of desserts from

the back seat, stands up and sees me. "Julia," he says. "Wait. Why aren't you inside? I thought Mary Katherine and Roger—"

"It's all under control," I nod for emphasis, and step carefully over the cracks in the sidewalk, watching for fire ants. "They're fine. And I'm fine. Really. I just need to run back to the room."

PD is taking this all in. "Shug, be a sweetheart and carry the rest of these in for me? Pearl's in the kitchen—or Mama—and they'll take it from there."

"Are you coming in?" He glances from his sister to me. "Aren't you?"

PD answers for me. "Shug, honey, I think Julia needs a new pair of shoes. She can't go traipsing into the lunch with bare feet—someone would snap a photo and it would end up on the front cover of the *Eufaula Tribune*."

I nibble the edge of my lip and inch closer to PD's car, trying to look helpless so that she'll take pity on me and rescue me from further humiliation.

To my relief, Shug's sister waves me over. "Jump in." I waste no time, dance across the blacktop and slide into the front seat.

PD turns back to her brother. "I'll run her back to the B&B while you smooth things over with Mary Katherine. We'll take a little girl time, freshen up, and take a drive around town," PD suggests. "I can play tour guide for a bit," she offers.

Shug rubs his jaw. He knows she's right, but offers a mournful scowl. "Julia?"

"I'm fine," I confirm this with a shrug and a wide smile— all teeth.

His sister reaches over and pokes his arm. "Hey, we'll be back in a bit. I need a teensy break. I've been in the kitchen since five o'clock this morning; I've memorized that menu in there." She waves at Shorter Mansion. "I've cooked most of it—

including my new masterpiece, yet to be unveiled—which you hold in your hands."

Shug perks up at the thought. "Really?" he asks his sister, putting his nose close to the edge of the tray and peeking under the edge of the coverlet. He pretends to swoon in delight.

I laugh out loud at his reaction and PD giggles. "Go ahead. Be the first. Well, actually, the second, since I let Ella Rae sample one this morning."

"Great!" Shug says and unwraps the edge. He unearths a pastry that is golden brown and flaky. It's in the shape of a triangle, and he takes no time in biting off half. "Mmm," he is chewing and raising his eyes in ecstasy. When he swallows, he asks, "Sis, what is this?" before popping the last of it into his mouth.

"Haven't named it yet," PD muses. She looks up at me. "Want to have one, Julia?"

Shug offers the tray through the open window.

"Absolutely! Yum. Ingredients?" I ask, taking one of the delicacies in my hand and taking a small nibble.

"Puff pastry, marshmallows, Nutella," PD offers a sly look. "Then a sprinkle of powdered sugar."

I finish the treat and lick my fingers unabashedly.

Shug is watching me and I blush in spite myself.

"Totally. Absolutely. Fabulous."

"Are you okay with this?" PD asks as we leave Shorter Mansion in her rearview mirror. "I know you'd like to be in there, but you'll have plenty of time tonight to chat with folks. It'll be the same crowd, maybe a few extras."

"Whew. Good. Actually, Roger introduced me to about a million people before…" I look down at my toes and wiggle them.

PD purses her lips. "Well, I hope you've got something a little safer for tonight." When I don't answer, she slows the car. "Julia?"

"Left my bag in Atlanta. The one with my dresses. And good shoes," I explain. "Roger came to the rescue and took me shopping."

Peals of laughter bubble up and burst from the other side of the car. She is laughing so hard, tears run down her cheeks, creating wet lines through her blush and foundation. When we pull up in front of Roger's, she gasps for air and regains regular breathing. "That explains a lot," she coughs and fans her face.

"Not exactly my style, was it?" I cock my head and grab my purse and shoes off the floor before I push open the car door.

PD puts a hand to her lips. "Bless your heart," she murmurs.

I stop and turn my head. "You know, when I first got here, I thought that particular phrase sounded exceptionally sweet, but I'm beginning to think that you Southerners use it as 'code.'" I shape my fingers into quotation marks and narrow my eyes. "Like, *oh gee, she really messed up—*or—*that dress belongs on a dancing hippo.* Am I that far off the mark?"

After I've slung the question across the seat at PD in true Yankee fashion, I realize that I've probably just overstepped another unwritten boundary of politeness. What's worse, that means I've also insulted Shug's sister, and all others who use the same phrase—three words most likely to be included in a linguist's bible containing two hundred years of honored Deep South colloquialisms. I don't say another word.

Shug's sister blinks at me for a moment, speechless, like I've shouted John Besh's cooking sucks. Or worse, that the Confederate soldiers could have done more to win the so-called "War of Northern Aggression."

Then, PD looks down at her lap, and smiles. "Not at all."

"Sorry," I blurt out. "I just say things. And they don't come out right. It was just an observation and I should have kept it to myself. I get into such trouble sometimes…"

PD reaches a hand across the seat and pats my knee. "You're funny. And not afraid to speak your mind. It's a rare quality."

"Um, thank you," I sputter and wrinkle my forehead. "I think." I twist and put my bare feet on the sidewalk, thinking about what she's saying. PD's not upset at all. In fact, the girl I thought I would really dislike has turned out to be pretty spectacular. I close the door behind me and lean on the frame of the open window.

With a twist of her lips, PD continues. "I'll admit, at first, I was skeptical about a Yankee coming to Eufaula to cover the Pilgrimage. But, you're funny and real. You have an awfully good sense of humor, especially since my daughter smashed your windshield five seconds after you rolled into town."

"It's a rental," I remind her and roll my eyes.

"Thank goodness." PD leans back against the seat and headrest. "Well, I'm glad you came. I like you, Julia. And my brother does, too."

"I'm flattered," I manage to get out. "The feeling's mutual." I rush to clarify. "In a very professional, friendly, business way of liking. Right?"

PD is trying hard not to smirk. "Go get changed. I've got a little tour all planned out. We'll hit Reeves Peanut Company and swing by a creepy cemetery or two." She makes her voice low and mysterious. "Hope you like ghost stories."

WITH PD'S WORDS RATTLING AROUND inside my head, I pull the dress over my head and toss it on the bed, while setting my beaten-up shoes in the corner. With pleasure, I slip on my favorite jeans, simple flats for walking, and a light sweater. I grab a jacket just in case, my camera, and check the mirror on my way out.

After running a brush through my hair, catching it in

a ponytail holder, and swiping on lip gloss, I realize that the face staring back at me in the mirror is flushed and glowing. I ponder this for a moment.

Sure, I've taken dozens of glamorous trips to exotic locations, but it's been a long time since I've been excited and near giddy for a little off-beat adventure. There's a part of me that I didn't realize existed. A part that likes the quiet and easy charm of a small town, the warmth and friendliness of complete strangers, and the elegance of homes that have stood for hundreds of years, surviving war, weather, and the test of time.

My romanticizing ends when I remember Phase III. With a sigh, I throw my purse under one arm like a football, close the door, and remind myself to ask PD about it later. For right now, I'll play tourist, and let her show off the beauty of her hometown.

She's waiting where I left her. As I buckle in, she snaps her fingers.

"I want to show you something else, too," PD says as she cranks the wheel left and eases into the traffic. We travel less than a mile, ending up in front of the brick building on East Broad Street.

It's a sprawling brick structure built in the Renaissance Revival style, with twin gables, arched doorways, and windows. In the center of the façade, there are painted white letters which spell out Reeves Peanut Co. Above that, a rectangular cement insert is etched with the numbers '1903'.

"So, why does it say 'Cotton' at the top?" I ask.

"Back at the turn of the century, cotton was crucial to Eufaula's economy. The Chattahoochee River was used to transport hundreds of bales to far away ports, like New York and Liverpool. The building used to house the Eufaula Grocery Company, and likely carried cotton in addition to other staples people needed. I'll have to ask Shug to make sure."

"And now?"

"It's still a functional warehouse for Reeves. They shell peanuts here, and have since 1932. You can see the ventilators—those metal lattice pieces in the center of each façade."

I get out my notebook and pen to scratch down the dates and details. "I'm going to grab a few photos," I tell PD.

We step onto the blacktop, and I crouch down to get a better angle. "What was the other thing you remembered? Something else that you were going to show me?" I adjust the camera's viewfinder to capture the blue sky and wisps of white clouds behind the red brick.

"Over here," she cups her hand and gestures me closer.

I brush off my pant legs and follow her to the smaller building to the right of Reeves Peanut Company. She's only gone a few steps—when she takes out her keys, fumbles through half a dozen of them, then chooses one to insert into the locked wooden door.

"All right," she warns me. "Come on in. But keep an open mind."

The sweet smell of brown sugar and melted butter tickle my nose and I inhale deeply. There's the scent of cinnamon, with a hint of cloves. On the far counter, fifty-pound bags of baking flour sit like old men on a broken-down sofa.

"This is what Shug was telling me about? Your bakery?" I exclaim, walking around and running my hand on the worn stainless steel appliances. "It's amazing. Wonderful."

PD beams with pride. "I'd been looking at the property for a while now, but I couldn't afford it. My brother signed the lease a few days ago and surprised me. MeeMaw gave him some money. She really wants me to pursue my dream of opening a bakery. We're supposed to bring her over here tomorrow and show her."

"Wow," I say, truly happy for PD.

"Even Mama and Daddy don't know," she adds. "It's kind of a secret right now."

"Of course," I rush to agree. This means, I assume, that

Mary Katherine isn't privy to the project, either. I'm a bit puzzled by this, but considering it's family—not my family—I don't interrupt.

"For the big picture, the long term, I'd like to expand and grow. Maybe hire someone, a few people, actually. I'd really like some of the local restaurants to partner with me—maybe feature some of the pastries on their dessert menu? There's always the coffee shop option, too." She clasps her hands tight to her middle. "I don't know. I have so many plans and ideas that I'm a little overwhelmed."

With a deep breath, I hug my arms to my body and gaze around the room. It's warm and cozy, in serious need of a paint job, but has lots of potential and room to expand. PD's bursting with excitement and I can hardly believe a sibling would be so generous as to take care of all of this for his sister.

Deep down, the nagging problem of Phase III is still poking at me, like an annoying stitch in my ribs on a long run. I tamp down my questions, not wanting to dampen PD's enthusiasm.

"All right," she says suddenly, "onto the next stop."

The small building is locked up and we're back in the car before I can count to ten.

"What's next on the agenda?" I ask, poking an elbow out of the window and enjoying the rays of sunshine as they sparkle through the trees.

"We'll save the library for last," PD decides. "And take a drive by the cemetery. There are several in town," she adds. "Fairview and Shorter are the largest. Shorter is named for Alabama's governor during the civil war—John Gill Shorter. Some of the graves date as far back as the 1840's."

"And that's the same Shorter as the Mansion?"

PD nods. "Very good. Same family," she confirms. "Fairview, though, is the largest cemetery, and the most unusual in the city. You'll notice—when we get there—there's a distinctive fence that sets it apart from the area's other burial places. The iron work around the property was once used at the city's Union Female College." She nods and points over the steering wheel as she parks next to the curb.

Our shoes make a crunching noise as we step over pebbles and make our way inside the entrance, which is lush and covered with foliage. The sloping ground is marked in long, rectangular sections with brick edging. Gravestones, weathered and worn, mark the resting places for a multitude of Eufaula families.

"Here, read this," PD stops at a marker and stands back to let me get closer.

The earliest burials in this cemetery date from Eufaula's pioneer days in the late 1830s and early 1840s. Formerly known as the "Old Cemetery," this public burial ground has been expanded through land purchases and the consolidation of other cemeteries including the Jewish, Presbyterian, Masonic, Odd Fellows, and Negro. At the suggestion of his daughter, Claude Hill, Mayor P. B. McKenzie named the cemetery "Fairview" about 1895.

PD touches my arm, steering me to the other side of the iron sign, which, across the top, reads "Old Negro Cemetery."

I catch my breath as we both read in silence.

Interred on this gently sloping hillside are the remains of many of Eufaula's early black citizens. Their names are known only to God because the wooden grave markers which located the burials have long since vanished. This burying ground was used until about 1870 when black interments were moved to Pine Grove Cemetery.

"It's so sad," I say and look off into the distance. "To not even know where your grandparents are buried. Or their grandparents. I can't imagine." My voice catches and I clutch at my chest, feeling it tighten like a rope's been wrapped around me and pulled tight.

In that instant, I see families, all in mourning, wandering the acres of land, in search of a sign or a clue. My own mother is buried, and it's awful to think of her lying in the cold, dark earth, but I have a place to go. I can visit. And it's more comfort than not to know that her spirit was there, if just for a short time.

"Okay," PD takes a hold of my arm. "Let's take a little break." We walk back to the car at a brisk pace. "For the article, or anyone who asks, there's a Ghost Walk and Tales from the Tomb at the Pilgrimage in the spring. But, we don't have to worry about that now."

She opens my door and helps me inside. PD leans over me and buckles my seatbelt. "Are you okay?" Not waiting another second for my reply, she cranks the engine and drives off, spinning gravel and dust in our wake.

Chapter Twenty-Two

"OKAY, SO NO MORE GRAVEYARDS," PD attempts a smidge of humor as we put the acres of Fairview Cemetery into the rearview mirror.

My breathing eases the further we get from the iron fence surrounding the property.

Shug's sister doesn't ask me anything—I chalk it up to her good Southern breeding—but I can tell by the way she keeps glancing over at me that she knows something is not right.

In that moment, all I want to do is head straight to Rog er's B&B, work on my story, and return to the comfort of my apartment in the City. A place devoid of ghosts, history, and hard questions.

I roll down the window and try to enjoy the breeze in my face as we drive back downtown, but the silence hangs between us. It's oppressive and deafening. The unspoken truth pushes at my conscience. I don't have to share my sorrows, but today, for some reason, they're seeping out of my mind and mouth.

"It's my mother," I blurt, exhaling the words. "She passed away two years ago. I feel cheated. There are so many questions I want to ask her."

PD nods, keeping her eyes on the road. "It sounds like you miss her a bunch. My own mother—well, you've seen her—she's a piece of work. We've never been really close, and I've never understood her. She didn't have a bad life. She had everything growing up right here in Eufaula. Aubie was beautiful, popular, became the Pilgrimage Queen. Then she married TJ and started a family."

We stop at a red light, both counting the beats until the glowing circle turns green.

"From what everyone says, Aubie promptly went off the deep end." PD is tapping on the steering wheel as if her life depended on it.

"Something about marriage—or maybe the men they marry," I muse aloud. "I think my father broke my mother's heart," I say with another sudden confession. "And that's what killed her." I shift in the seat. "Of course, she did have ALS," I include, "but the realization that my father had a secret life the entire time?" My voice reaches a high-pitched octave that might break glass. "I think she stopped fighting."

PD slows down to a crawl, locked on every word. We stop at an intersection and let the cars blow past. I burst into tears. The sobbing, gushing sort of crying that makes your nose run and your eyes rimmed with red. PD hands me a few tissues and I blow hard, the force a person uses when she's held back emotion for years.

"It's family," PD says, her mouth twitching when I catch a breath. "Isn't it our parents' job to mess us up?"

The statement strikes me funny—being that I've spent years trying to avoid David, my own father, and now he is my new boss. I don't share this, but we both laugh until my shoulders hurt from shaking. I'm not sure where we're parked, but I hope that there isn't a tourist group in sight.

When the hilarity subsides, PD looks me square in the face. "I can tell that you're hurting."

"It does hurt," I admit. "I'm sad, and I'm angry that she's gone. And, I really miss her." The statement is so raw and honest I feel like someone's ripped a band-aid off the inner lining my heart.

PD turns her body toward me, puts an elbow up on the seat back, and rests her chin in the palm of her hand. "Don't you think she knows that? And she wants you to be happy?

And wouldn't she tell you to really live—because she can't?"

The idea she presents is so simple, I gasp. The truth is this: I've spent the time since my mother's death running away from life, not toward it.

And it took traveling one thousand miles from home to figure it out.

Yet, coming here, being here, and living in the moment, everything makes sense.

AFTER MAKING SURE THAT I WAS IN POSSESSION of functional, sturdy heels, and a glitch-free outfit, Roger went on ahead—an hour early—to the dinner. I assure him that I have a few calls to make, work-related emails to return, and important notes to type up. While my to-do list was accurate, and I diligently tackled each item in turn, what I really needed was solitude.

When I finally emerge from my room, step onto the sidewalk, and make my way up North Eufaula Street, I am struck by the beauty of the city's historic district.

It's not that I haven't noticed the fresh pine garland and wreaths strung with red velvet ribbon. It's not that I haven't seen the flicker of candles gracing every window. It's not that the city hasn't been dressed and ready in its finest splendor since I arrived a few days ago.

Every home on the street is decorated in similar fashion, and the streetlights provide a soft ambiance as I walk.

Tonight, though, I slow down. Deliberately walking at half my caffeine-charged pace. The sky is a midnight blue pricked with pinpoints of stars. They glitter overhead, scattered like jewels on a sea of fine silk. A few are so bright and close, I feel that I could almost catch them in a butterfly net.

The air has grown chilly. Roger warned me a huge temperature drop was forecasted for tonight, but I don't hurry. I pull my borrowed wrap a little tighter around my shoulders.

Spending time, here in Eufaula, has helped me realize that barreling through life at a breakneck pace—while exciting, sometimes glamorous, and always loads of fun—has been, at best, a distraction. A useful tool in avoiding personal introspection or thoughts of the future.

It's always been the next stop, the next flight, and the next assignment. There hasn't been a day in the past decade that didn't include stress-inducing tasks and multiple deadlines.

All in all, I conclude, my raw wanderlust and suitcase-required career has, in a way, prevented me from really seeing and understanding the magic waiting to be discovered—both in people and places.

That said—inside my brain—I promise myself that I will enjoy tonight and experience it fully, with no thought to my watch or the clock on the wall.

I arrive on the steps of Shorter Mansion. When I push the door open, a rush of warm air swirls around me. Roger immediately spots me and winks across the room. I wave, slip off my wrap, and hand it to the waiting coat-check girl. With careful steps, I meander through the parlor, stopping to chat with the mayor, his wife, and their closest friends.

In the next room, I share a giggle with PD, who's still getting praise for sharing her latest inventive treats. There's talk of holding a contest in the *Eufaula Tribune* to name them, and I second the idea.

"What fun," I say, giving PD's hand a squeeze. "What did your grandmother and the rest of the family think of them?"

"MeeMaw's pretty much in love with them," PD grins and looks down at the floor. "TJ and Shug will eat anything I whip up, so I'm planning to do a second 'sampling' and serve more after dinner with coffee."

Ella Rae chooses that very moment to barrel through the crowd, holding two of the puffed, golden pastries in her right hand. There's a telltale streak of white powdered sugar from her upper lip to her earlobe.

"Well, that answers that question," I whisper as PD excuses herself to apprehend her daughter.

Suddenly, there's a warm hand on my shoulder, and I flinch when several long fingernails dig into my skin. Without having to look, I realize that it's Aubie. The pungent scent of her flowery perfume mixes with the distinct smell of hard liquor.

"S'c-cold outside, sugar," she slurs, attempting to wave outside. "Temp-ture down to the thirties, s-someone said."

"Have to bundle up tonight," someone comments.

I want to take Aubie's hand and drag her to the nearest bedroom, and lock her inside until she sobers up. When I scan the room for TJ, her husband, as usual, is nowhere to be found.

"If it fr-freezes, J-Julia sh-should be right at h-home, then," Aubie leans to her left, her head lolling with her body. She attempts a smile, but the corners of her lips don't move more than a millimeter.

"Sure," I agree, trying to manage a bright smile.

The couple to my left exchanges a pitying look, and the two men front and center cast doubtful glances at Aubie's much-deteriorated condition. She was fine at lunchtime, I seem to recall, but anything could have happened in the hours during my tour of town with PD.

Shug's mother exhales deeply as her arm drops to her side, and a gust of strong whiskey floats past my nostrils. The odor, combined with the heat from the crowd, causes me to sneeze not once, but three times in succession.

This, fortunately, makes everyone around me laugh and takes the focus off Shug's drunken mother. I cover my mouth with one hand and excuse myself, pleading a need for the ladies' room before dinner.

As I make my escape, I catch a glimpse of MeeMaw in the corner with Ella Rae. For once, the child is quiet and sitting still. I wave over at them as I wind my way through small groups of women deep in conversation, knock on the closest powder room, but find it locked. There's another upstairs, I think, so I round the corner and make my way up the red carpeting.

When I reach the top of the steps, I'm standing at the edge of a short hallway. The second floor of Shorter Mansion is just as large as the first, and the upstairs landing opens into at least five different rooms. Under the sound of my own breathing, I hear a man and a woman talking—or arguing—in hushed tones.

My first instinct is to turn and hurry back down the stairs. I press a hand to my abdomen and bite my lip. With a hand against the wall, I ease forward. The full sensation in my gut is making me uncomfortable, and now, a little desperate. I decide that the urgency of finding a ladies' room significantly outweighs the embarrassment of being caught opening random doors.

With a gulp, I try the first door. It's is a simple bedroom with a small bed and dresser. The second, much bigger, contains glass-encased displays of period clothing, long, faded dresses, and children's outfits from the 1800s. With a sigh, I move on to door number three, which ends up being a small, dark closet containing quite a few dingy gray cobwebs and a number of perturbed spiders that scuttle away in the light. I muffle a yelp and close my eyes, easing a few steps away from the opening.

The hallway is silent, though my heart is galloping like a racehorse at the Kentucky Derby. I don't hear the voices anymore, so I chalk it up to my overactive imagination and the glass of wine I polished off downstairs.

With a hesitant hand, I grasp the doorknob on one of the two remaining doors. It's stuck for some reason, but I give it a frustrated yank, and pull it wide open.

This time, there is a scream, but I'm not sure if it's mine, or Mary Katherine's.

Chapter Twenty-Three

"IT'S YOU!" Mary Katherine leaps to her stiletto-clad feet as if she's been stabbed in the derriere with a dinner fork.

"Julia?" A bewildered Shug shifts his gaze from his girlfriend to me.

I begin to stutter. "I-I was only looking for the ladies' room," I explain. "The one downstairs…" But, I realize that no excuse matters when it comes to a jealous girlfriend.

Mary Katherine stalks toward me, pointing a manicured fingertip. "You were following us. You've been lurking over my shoulder since you got here. Why can't you just leave us alone?" She is seething with anger, her voice scaling a few octaves.

I step back from her, trying not to trip over my own wobbling ankles. "Listen. I am simply doing my job. I have to write a story on Eufaula's Pilgrimage. That's it." If I had a white flag, I'd be waving it.

Shug pulls us apart. "Mary Katherine, that's enough. Do you want all of Eufaula to hear you having a hissy fit on the night of the Christmas Tour? Is that how you'd like this evening to be remembered for the next three-hundred and sixty-five days?"

I press my lips together, holding back from launching another verbal attack on Mary Katherine. Shug seems to be holding his own.

His girlfriend juts out her bottom lip and scuffs the floor with the toe of her silver shoe. "No," she mutters like a child who's been caught drawing on the wall of her Sunday school room with bright pink permanent marker.

"I'm surprised," he continues, "at both of you." Shug shoots me a look that borders on disappointment—or contempt—I can't tell because my eyes are filling up with tears faster than I can wipe them away.

There's a knock at the door and the three of us look up to see PD in the hallway with Ella Rae at her side. "We were looking for you," she says, confusion filling her face. "Dinner's going to be served in a few moments and I didn't want y'all to miss it."

No one answers.

"Uh, Mama, Uncle Shug? Why are y'all three in the bathroom together?" Ella Rae twists her face into a sly smirk and eyeballs Mary Katherine. "That's weird."

There's an awkward pause, and Shug walks out of the cramped space to scoop up his niece. He lets out a forced chortle.

"Now, we were just having a little meeting about how many of those treats you've been eating. You know, the ones with the marshmallows inside them?" He is tickling her and she is giggling with laughter. "Are there any left? Any at all? I'm going to be mighty hurt if there's only a crumb."

The steps creak as Shug carries Ella Rae downstairs. PD remains standing in the doorway, looking back and forth from me to her brother's girlfriend. Finally, she manages a bewildered smile. "Well, okay then."

I hang back, clinging to the windowsill while Mary Katherine flounces past. I can hear the thump of the steps as she descends to the foyer with a decidedly un-ladylike stomp-stomp. "Can you give me a moment?" I ask, not able to read her face. "I'll be right down."

PD nods. "Take all the time you need."

Less than ten minutes later, the incident upstairs is forgotten, overshadowed by the sumptuous spread of food. I slip an engraved menu card in my purse for safekeeping, but not before reading over the extensive list of Southern dishes laid out on the table.

Fried Green Tomatoes, Deviled Eggs, Fried Okra
Squash Casserole, Collard Greens, Buttered Yeast Rolls
Fried chicken, Smothered Pork Chops, Chicken Pot Pie
Homemade Banana Pudding & PD's Pillow Pockets

My plate is heaping with samples of everything but dessert. Wine is poured, water glasses filled and refilled. I'm seated—thankfully—next to Roger, who carries the conversation with ease and grace. Not surprisingly, my appetite has waned, and I move the delicious portions of food around on my plate, hoping that it will appear like I've sampled a little of everything and am just watching my figure.

Roger leans toward my ear. "Just try to eat something. A bite or two, or everyone will think you don't like it. And they'll never forgive you." He smiles and laughs at someone across the table, but keeps a strict eye on me. I raise my fork and take a small bite of collard greens, which are bathed in butter and cooked to perfection.

After I set my fork down, my stomach twists in protest, and I dab at my lips with my napkin. In the next room, I can hear Mary Katherine's shrill laugh. Shug's deep voice follows and, for now, it seems that peace has been restored in their little corner of paradise.

Silly me, I chide myself. I am here to do a job. Report on an event and go back home. My place is in the City, I tell myself, and there will be another story and another town to visit next week. I steel myself with thoughts of finishing the article tonight, flying back, and presenting a perfect specimen of my writing—on time—to David's shocked face. Somehow, even that tiny amount of anticipated satisfaction has lost its zing.

Perhaps it's because—somehow in the last few days—I've realized that my life is better spent being happy and moving forward than getting back at people who've hurt me. Perhaps it's because I've figured out that my job—my career—is more than writing about a pretty place, with lovely food and plush hotels. My career is about sharing stories about people, and how those individuals and families, not geography, makes up the lifeblood and future of that city or place. And finally, perhaps it's because I like it here and I'm a little more than sad to leave.

As the conversation swirls around me, and dessert is served, I absorb the remaining moments of the evening. When the chairs are pushed back, and everyone chats over coffee, a shout of excitement comes from the foyer.

There's a rush toward the front of the mansion and a clatter of heels on the wood floor. I can hear Ella Rae calling for her mother. Mary Katherine rushes by the table, dragging Shug by the hand. Even Aubie totters toward the parlor windows, pushing MeeMaw in her wheelchair.

Roger and I are the only two left at the table. He grins in my direction and shakes his head. "It figures," he says.

"What is it?" I ask. "What are they saying?"

"Sugar," Roger laughs and points to the top of the windows. "Can't you see it? It's snowing."

By the time Roger and I reach the front door, the entire dinner party has drifted outside. The night sky is like a snow globe, with swirling white flakes drifting down and melting on everything they touch.

"It's amazing," someone shouts.

"This hasn't happened in forever."

"Someone get a camera."

There are squeals of excitement and more than one person trying to catch the frozen particles in their hands. Aubie is twirling around in circles and I'm not sure why she hasn't fallen, though it's a little magical to watch her so happy.

One by one, the outside lights on other houses flick on and the owners step out on their front porches. There are greetings exchanged, more laughter, and the sound of children squealing in delight. Ella Rae is spinning, curls bouncing, both arms outspread. PD is laughing and clapping her hands. Our eyes meet across the street and we share a smile.

"I think you brought the weather," Roger accuses me.

"You may be right," I tease him back and link my arm through his. "All right, now—do what I do. When you catch a snowflake in your mouth, make a wish."

I tilt my head back and motion for Roger to do the same. It's what my mother and I used to do on the first day of any snowfall. As a child, dressed in a scarf and mittens, holding my mother's hand, I remember wishing for a puppy and a pink bicycle with streamers on the handles. One year, I wished for a trip to Disney World so that I could meet Cinderella in her castle.

Tonight, though, as the cold touches my tongue, cheeks, and eyelashes, I don't wish for a gift or something a person can buy in a store or find in a glossy magazine or catalog.

Tonight, I blink up at the velvet night sky and wish for my heart's desire.

When I lower my chin and glance over at Roger, he is wiping his eyes. He grins and puts a finger to his lips. I smile back at my friend and wonder what he was wishing for. I don't ask, not wanting to break the spell, and look around for the one person who'd truly make my night complete. I'm still clinging to Roger's arm when I see him.

Shug has his arms around Mary Katherine, her long hair like a golden waterfall cascading down her back. As the snowflakes dip and twirl around them, they've pressed their foreheads together and are whispering. I want to look away, but can't bring myself to do it.

It's like a scene out of a fairytale, when the rest of the world melts away with a kiss. And the prince and princess live happily ever after.

That's how the story goes, isn't it?

Chapter Twenty-Four

Despite my exhaustion, I pack my bag. It's close to midnight. My feet are aching and my body is yearning for a nice, hot bath.

Can't rest yet. Too much to do, I tell myself, and force my fingers to dial the phone. By now, I've decided that Delta Airlines could have a dedicated line for Yankees in the Deep South who change their plane reservations at the last minute. I'm daydreaming about this when the operator answers and greets me with a nasal, but cheery tone.

The sound in my ear is familiar and oh-so-New York, but the effect is jarring. In the span of four days, I've become accustomed to the languid drawl of Southerners; the adorable accent and the way everyone says 'y'all.' Even phrases like 'bless your heart' have grown on me.

"Ma'am? Can I help you?" the operator repeats, not quite perturbed yet.

"Yes, yes," I recover, shaking my head to clear it, and inquire about securing an earlier flight.

"No seats open right now." There's a pause, and the clicking of a keyboard in the background. It sounds like a fast-forward version of Morse code. "You can fly standby," she offers. "Just get to Hartsfield as soon as you can."

She rattles off possible flight times, departure gates, and change fees so quickly that my hand cramps as I jot down the details. A reminder that my life—and everyone else's north of the Mason-Dixon line—functions at warp speed 24/7.

I hang up, hold the cell phone to my chest, and watch the snowflakes still drifting toward the ground. It's as if the wintry weather is beckoning me home, no matter that my heart and head are in a bitter struggle to leave or stay.

When I say 'stay,' it would only mean half a day—prolonging the inevitable departure, really. A quick breakfast, a polite chat, and perhaps one last stroll along the magnificent homes that line North Eufaula Street.

The snow would be melted by then, the sidewalks wet and glistening in the morning sun. And there would be Mary Katherine to face, with my luck, simpering and parading Shug around like a trained show dog.

No, it's just not something I'm willing to witness. The tug I feel in my heart is an adolescent crush, I tell myself. And an unrequited one at that. He's polite, a Southern gentleman, anyone could misinterpret the signals.

I allow the curtains to fall closed, as the snow has stopped. I switch off the overhead light, and then turn on the small lamp at the tiny writing desk. Out of habit, and years of hotel room-life, I pull out the middle drawer of the desk. The scent of cedar hits my nose and I breathe it in. Without looking down, I know that there'll be a pen, a small pad of notepaper, and a red Bible.

My hand sweeps the back of the opening, and my fingers find what they are seeking: a small stack of glossy postcards. I pull them out and hold them closer to the light bulb. There's Shorter Mansion with its pillars, Fendall Hall, and the Confederate Monument, followed by Carnegie Library—which I'd still love to see, but is closed on Sundays. Last, there's a postcard declaring Lake Eufaula the "Big Bass Capital of the World." The fine print describes the 640 mile-long shoreline, Lakepoint Resort State Park, and a nearby National Wildlife Refuge.

With the clock moving ever forward toward morning, I pick up the pen and paper and begin to write. First, a note to Roger for his hospitality and another to PD, for listening. When it comes time to write the third, I hover my pen over the page, thinking about Shug. Writer's block isn't something I've experienced, so when my fingers refuse to form letters, I know that I'm in trouble.

After the fourth crumpled note, I straighten my arms, shake out my hands, and focus. Polite. Proper. To the point. When I'm finished, I sign my name, fold the papers, and lick the envelopes. I tiptoe to Roger's oak roll-top desk, where I prop the cards under the lamp. He's sure to see them in the morning. By then, I'll be long gone.

When I stand back from the desk, my gaze falls on a basket. It's out of place for Roger's formal parlor, tied with pink ribbons, and stuffed with tissue paper the color of cotton candy. There's a floral tag attached, and my name is written on it with a delicate script.

I lean closer. The smell of home-baked goods wafts up, sugar, chocolate, and hazelnut. Somehow, PD knew I was leaving. This is my care package for the trip home.

IT'S A MIRACLE, but my missing bag has been located and is waiting for me when I arrive in Atlanta. I check in, head for the gate, and manage to snag the very last seat on the plane.

The flight back to JFK is noisy and bumpy. There's a toddler kicking my chair, his baby brother wailing every time the plane hits turbulence.

Because of storms along the east coast, we're belted in, tethered to our chairs until the jet touches down in New York. I'm a veteran of trans-Atlantic flights, and am comfortable at thirty-five thousand feet, but this may be the longest two hours of my entire life. Even the flight attendants look nervous.

My normal routine is to whip out my iPod, insert earplugs, and zone out for the duration. Sometimes I sleep, other times I pretend to nap. This flight, however, I can't ignore the passenger next to me.

My seatmate, a woman in her mid-forties, is sweating and clutching the armrests for dear life. Her upper lip is beaded with moisture.

She's been talking non-stop since takeoff. I've learned about her job (chef and restaurant owner), her boyfriend (taxidermist), her parents (now deceased), and her recent escapades (being searched) at every airport security checkpoint. After listening for an hour and forty-five minutes, I'm starting to agree that Homeland Security has it out for her.

When she pauses for oxygen and a sip of water, I realize she has the drawl of a person born and raised in the South. And decide to try some intervention.

"Where are you from?" I ask, making direct eye contact. "Is Georgia home?"

The woman nods. "Dahlonega. North of Atlanta." She attempts a small smile, which I consider a major breakthrough, until the body of the plane drops into an air pocket. Everyone around me screeches or yelps. The baby is crying harder now, with loud, wet gulps. My neighbor begins sobbing.

"It's going to be okay," I say, keeping my voice soft and even, then I reach out and pat her hand. To my surprise, she grips it with the strength of a welterweight boxer. "Really. We'll be landing soon."

The aircraft is shaking like the lead car of a wooden rollercoaster. If my seatbelt was any tighter, it would cut off the circulation in my legs like a tourniquet. Any moment, I expect to see the oxygen masks dropping from the plastic ceiling panels.

As we descend through the clouds, slamming and careening like the aircraft is hitting invisible bumper cars, my seatmate starts hyperventilating. The flight attendant call lights go off like little red fireworks around us.

I snatch an airsickness bag from the seat pocket in front of me. "Breathe," I instruct her, snapping open the paper sack and pressing it around her mouth.

With wide eyes and a pink face, she blows into the bag. It expands, then contracts with her inhalation. "Good," I smile encouragement. "Very good," I repeat, noticing that she is still gripped onto my arm like a bird of prey.

I scoot forward as best I can, closer to the aisle, on my seat cushion-floatation device. "All right. So, tell me about Dahlonega. Is it pretty? Lots of trees? Some mountains?"

Nothing moves but her chin, and that is barely perceptible.

"How about lakes?" I attempt to conjure up a picture of North Georgia. Everything in my brain is programmed to Eufaula. It can't be terribly different, I decide. "Did you swim a lot or go fishing, growing up?"

Another slight nod. Now we're getting somewhere.

"I just visited the most wonderful little town," I tell her, pressing a hand to my chest for emphasis. "Have you ever been to Eufaula? For the Pilgrimage?"

The woman's face lights up. Behind the airsickness bag, her cheeks lift, the slightest hint of a smile. Her knuckles aren't white anymore, and I notice that the woman's grip is no longer pinching my hand.

"Oh, it's lovely," she murmurs after the sack drops from her mouth. Her fingertips rub the edges. "It's been years."

I explain that I'm a travel writer for *Getaways* magazine, sent to preview the Pilgrimage. In full detail, down to collapsing in the front yard of Fendall Hall, I recount my bee attack, the subsequent trip to the ER, and my shoe snafu at the Christmas Tour dinner. By the time I finish, my seatmate is laughing, almost unaware of the occasional rough patch of air.

"So, you're heading home?" she asks, settling back against her seat. The peaches and cream color has returned to her face and I'm no longer fearful she'll stop breathing.

I consider the question. The answer, of course, is an obvious one. "Yes, I have a small apartment there, not far from the magazine office." It's my turn to shift in my seat. I glance out the window at the silver-grey of the cloud cover. "The City is my home base, but I live like a nomad. Pets are out of the question, I can't keep a plant alive, and I'm sure my building manager thinks I'm a ghost. He always jumps when he sees me."

This also makes her giggle. Then, her eyes fall on my left hand. "So, what about a fiancé? Or is there a special guy in your life?"

"Also tough to manage," I try to flash a grin. "Andrew—that's my boyfriend—he's pretty neglected. We're supposed to go to dinner tomorrow night. I promised I'd call when we land," I turn my wrist to check the time. We've been descending for ten minutes.

My new friend looks me up and down. "That's not much enthusiasm," she observes with an arched brow.

"He's great," I rush to say, sounding a little bit ridiculous, since I'm about to break off our relationship. Or put it on hold. Indefinitely. I clear my throat. "Um, Andrew's really the best. He's sweet and nice and thoughtful…"

"But, maybe for someone else?" she fills in. She says the words in a gentle way, treading as if my boyfriend—or spies from his family—might be lurking a few rows up.

Tears fill my eyes and they drip down my cheeks before I can wipe them away. My throat closes as I try to swallow, making it impossible to do anything but choke. The woman hands me her airsickness bag.

"Thanks, no." I wave it away, coughing again into the crook of my arm.

"So," my seatmate taps her fingers on the seat rests. "You're coming home, you're not in love with him, and you've been dating Andrew for how many years?"

"Two," I answer as the aircraft breaks through the dark ceiling of cloud cover. A bell dings twice, signaling we've reached ten thousand feet. The flight attendants, somber and exhausted from the bumpy flight, walk through the aisles with open plastic bags, pausing to nudge a seat forward or collect a water cup.

The crackle of the intercom sounds, and the pilot announces we'll be landing at JFK in a few minutes. He thanks us for flying his airline and wishes us a happy holiday season. The intercom scratches again and clicks off.

"Thank you, Jesus," someone squawks in a thick Jersey accent from a few rows back. There are murmurs of agreement, and a single sneeze. "Bless you," the voice speaks again. Then, for a few moments, everything is still except for the sound of the wind rushing against the body of our silver jet.

I keep my eyes trained out the window, checking my seatbelt to make sure it's tight. The pilot lowers the flaps, and the change in airspeed registers in my head and stomach.

New York sprawls before us in thousands of towers and buildings, the blocks divided with intersecting strips of blacktop. Taxicabs and cars, five rows deep, inch along, snaking around corners, splitting off in twos where the roads divide. Everything below, every square mile, is in motion.

As we hover over the runway, my seatmate leans closer. "By the way, I'm Dean Alice Waters," she introduces herself.

"Julia Sullivan," I reply with a smile. "It's been a pleasure talking to you." I glance at her travel bag and try to read the tag. "Are you here on business or pleasure?"

"A little of both, I hope," she presses her fingertips together and shrugs. "I think I mentioned that I'm in the restaurant business. I'm here for a food show. Many of the top chefs will be there—Cat Cora, Bobby Flay, Rachel Ray, Emeril Lagaisse—"

"How fun! Sounds like you'll be eating well."

Dean Alice rolls her eyes. "You have no idea. The food never ends. Last year, I gained five pounds in two days. Don't tell anyone, but I brought my super-secret elastic waist pants just for grazing the dessert tables." She sighs. "I'm addicted to sugar. Carbs, too. Anything with butter, flour, and sugar."

We're jolted in our seats as the wheels touch down on the runway. The sound of air rushing against the wings is almost deafening and I close my eyes. My stomach grumbles at the thought of food and I remember tucking a few of PD's treats into my carry on.

As we taxi to the gate, I unzip my bag and reach inside, and I offer one of the golden marshmallow puffs to Dean Alice. "If you love sweets, you have to try these," I gush. "My friend made them."

Dean Alice takes one of the small pillows of flaky crust, examines it on all sides, sniffs the edge like a wine expert sampling a vintage Cabernet, and takes a dainty bite. I, on the other hand, pop an entire treat into my mouth. As I chew, the marshmallow, Nutella, and sugar dissolve on my tongue like cotton candy. The plane comes to a final stop as I swallow and brush the crumbs from my hands.

"What do you call these?" Dean Alice blinks in amazement, powering on her phone as she's talking. It begins to bleat immediately. "Fifteen text messages," she exclaims, scanning each one. She taps the touch screen and puts the phone to her ear. "And ten voicemails."

The flight attendant in the front of the aircraft announces we're free to go, and everyone jumps to their feet, eager to escape the confines of the jet. The baby behind us begins wailing again. It's mass chaos as passengers flood the aisle, jostling for position, reaching into overhead bins for luggage and laptops.

Somehow, Dean Alice wiggles her frame into the fray and joins the other bodies, pressed together, shuffling along the narrow, carpeted path to the front of the plane. As an afterthought, black cell phone still pressed to her head, she turns and offers a wave.

"Thank you," she mouths and winks, then disappears into the first-class cabin.

With a grin, I wiggle my fingers at her, saying good-bye. I

know she'll be relieved to put both feet on solid ground.

The cabin continues to empty, but I remain standing, resting my elbows on the seat in front of me. My legs seem locked in place. For once, I'm not in a hurry. At all.

Behind me, a few passengers are still wrestling bags from under seats, looking around for keys, and locating ticket stubs. A couple is conversing in Chinese as they brush by me, and the sound of their heated exchange slices through the stale air, thick and guttural.

At last, I am alone. More than two hundred seats—all of them empty—surround me.

"Ma'am?" One of the flight attendants strides back toward my row, hesitates, and touches me on the arm. "Is everything all right? Are you missing your carry-on?" She glances down at my feet. "Or can I help you with gate change information?"

"No," I shake my head.

"Rough flight?" she asks, her expression sympathetic. "Try getting a ginger ale on the way out. It always helps when I'm feeling queasy. There's a shop that sells it on the way to baggage claim."

I want to explain that it's not the turbulence or any amount of rough air. I want to tell her that my anxiety has nothing to do with her, the pilots, the landing, or the weather. I want to reassure her that it's not my stomach that's bothering me.

If I don't get off the jet, I won't have to face Andrew.

If I stay on the plane, in my seat, I won't have to see my father, David.

If I can stop time, I won't have to face my empty apartment and my equally empty life.

No, ginger ale won't help at all. And what's hurting can't be fixed.

It's my heart.

Chapter Twenty-Five

BUOYED BY A SOLID EIGHT HOURS OF SLEEP, my looming deadline, and thoughts of a hot Starbucks latte, I manage to wake up before my alarm, shower, and wrestle myself into warm winter clothes before seven in the morning. As I pull on my favorite pair of brown leather boots, I glance at the meteorologist on my small flat-screen.

The volume's down, but the weatherman isn't smiling when he points to the map of the east coast. From the looks of it, there's a stubborn cold front clinging to New England. When the five-day forecast pops up, I am sure of it. Neither the highs nor the lows stray far from zero. With a shudder, I pull on my wool coat, throw a knit scarf around my neck, and grab for my gloves. They're next to Shug's Auburn hat, which I have to return to him at some point. I run a finger along the brim and smile.

Almost as an afterthought, I snatch up a few postcards from Eufaula and stuff them in my purse. Inspiration for the story, I decide. Then, I grab the bag of treats PD packed for me. Something sweet to offer David—a way to soothe the savage beast, perhaps. I'll warm them up when I get to work.

It's so early that I am the only person in my building riding the elevator. When the double doors heave open on the ground floor, the sound echoes off the floor and pressed tin ceiling tiles. I step outside, and a gust of cold air stings my face, stealing my breath. The sky is mottled with gray cloud cover—not a pinprick of blue anywhere. After I pull the scarf over my mouth and hunch my shoulders against the wind, I prod myself forward.

A deceptively clear coat of ice covers the sidewalk, the tricky sort that causes tourists and elderly women to wipe out. I shuffle, one foot, then the next. It's not attractive, but at least I won't need a hip replacement.

The corner Starbucks is jammed, every table full of hands, coffee cups, and laptops. At the counter, there's a line nine-people long, and I take my place as number ten. As I bask in the warmth of the building, I feel a stab of pain. It's an elbow, jabbed by mistake—I think—into the tender part of my ribcage. When I turn to look, expecting an apology, the owner of the offending arm has moved on without a backward glance.

It's all right, I remind myself, just as someone's heel comes down hard and crushes my toes. "Ouch!" I muffle a shriek, as an Amazon-like woman in a powder blue ski jacket wobbles in front of me, her other massive snow boot threatening to land on my uninjured foot.

I jump back, out of the way, jostling into the people behind me. With a murmured '*I'm sorry*' for invading everyone's personal space, I turn back toward the counter. The line has moved about three inches.

My stomach grumbles as I glance around the room. Every ear is pressed to a cell phone—there are dozens of conversations going on in here—just not with each other. Another gurgle surges in my midsection. I press a hand to my abdomen, trying to distract my body from outright rebellion. Thankfully, ahead of me, the blender starts to whir, steam hisses, and coffee grounds begin to percolate.

This is my routine. Whether in Rome, Paris, or New York, I wake up, wait in long lines, and pay exorbitant amounts of money for a paper cup, a lid, and hot liquid.

I wrinkle my nose. Wait—I love the hustle and bustle of a city, exploring new places, and people watching. But now—

something's changed—I'm smitten with small-town life. Not just any small-town life. The wide streets, the sprawling yards, and huge oak trees of Eufaula, Alabama. I even miss the sound of crickets chirping as the city's blue sky fades into twilight.

"Miss," a sharp, nasal voice yanks me back to the present. "Can I help you?" A pair of coal-black eyes peer at me below a choppy head of red hair. The hair belongs to the girl behind the register. She is snapping her gum and raises a pierced eyebrow in my direction. "Anytime."

There's a hurried exhale on my left, and the sound of coughing to my right. *Hurry up*, the cough says. *Hurry up*.

"Um, I—" The black sign looms down at me. Coffee choices, chai tea, and an entire shelf full of calorie-laden breakfast sweets. There are several brews, a dozen flavored syrups, three cup sizes, and the choice between a cold or hot beverage. It's all too much. I begin backing up.

"Never mind," I say. "Thank you."

The redhead behind the counter rolls her eyes, exasperated. She leans over and looks past me. "What can I get started for you?" she says to the next customer.

Before my hands hit the glass and metal door, she is ringing up an order. And another. And another.

And I am running full-tilt from the Starbucks store, kicking up slush in my wake.

AT SEVEN THIRTY-FIVE, after a quick cab ride, I arrive at the bottom of my office building. As I pass the glass-framed structure, I catch a glimpse of myself. I screech to a stop, and almost lose my balance. *What?*

My hair is disheveled, my makeup streaked, cheeks flushed berry-pink. My jacket is on crooked and the bottom of my scarf is dirty and wet. I must have dragged it on the sidewalk all the way from Starbucks. If someone hands me a quarter, I'll know for sure I've joined the ranks of the thought-to-be homeless and crazy.

It's still ice-cold outside, but I take off my hat and smooth my hair. I lick my lips, straighten my scarf, and wipe the black from under my eyes. This isn't any time to lose it. I have a job to do, a story to write. A boss who is expecting me to fail. And I have to prove him wrong.

I stop by the restroom, unbutton my coat, and splash cold water on my face. With a tissue, I dab at my makeup and blow my nose. I reapply lip gloss, check my purse for powder, and discover that my phone screen reads five missed calls and three voicemails. Of course, I neglected to charge my cell, so the battery is blinking red.

"Cripe," I mutter and begin tapping the screen. Please don't let it be David. Please don't let it be David.

The first name that pops up is Marietta's. Phew. Then Andrew, twice. I note from the time and date stamp both calls were from last night. I close my eyes tight. Darn. In my rush, I didn't check in. Not even a text message. I promised I would and I didn't. With trepidation, I scroll through the other numbers. There's another I don't recognize. That's four. I inhale and read the name from the last caller.

Shug Jordan.

I blink at the screen and erase his name. The empty black background stares back at me. With a shake of my head, I type a quick message to Andrew. "Dinner tonight? Seven-thirty at O'Reilly's?" It's a loud Irish pub near the office, not the least bit romantic, but safe for a face-to-face 'talk.'

I hit send and power down the phone, not waiting for a reply. No distractions, I tell myself. Not today.

Ten seconds later, at seven forty-nine, I'm sitting in my cubicle, notes stacked neatly beside my laptop, postcards pinned where I can see them on my bulletin board. And I start to type.

I'm so engrossed in my story that I don't hear Marietta sneak up behind me. She taps my shoulder. My chest seizes and I jump out of my chair.

"Sorry," she laughs. "It was so quiet over here I wasn't sure you were back." Marietta wags a finger at me. "I tried to reach you last night."

"I know, I'm sorry," I apologize and hold up my cell phone. "*This* was about to die, so I had to shut it off."

My friend smothers a laugh and hugs me anyway. "Ah, Jules," she murmurs into my hair. "Some things never change."

I stiffen at the comment, even though she's right. Another classic Julia Sullivan snafu. This time, instead of sulking into my empty coffee mug, I draw back, untangle myself, and wink at Marietta. "Well," I reply with a sly grin, "I don't know about that."

"Really?" my friend eyes me with both hands on her hips. "And just what did they do to you down there?"

"They didn't *do* anything," I protest, pushing at the air with both hands. "Oh," I say, and spin in my chair to find PD's treats. "If you're hungry later, pop these in the microwave. Delish!"

Marietta grins and takes the paper sack. "Hmm. Thanks. David's at a meeting 'til lunchtime, by the way..." Her voice trails off. No boss. Until noon.

She's waiting for me to change my mind. Usually, I'll chit-chat for a good hour, spilling the details of my latest trip before getting to work on a story. Not today.

"I'll give you all of the details later. I promise," I cross my heart, running an imaginary 'x' across my ribbed red sweater. When my friend raises an eyebrow, I tuck my legs, swivel back to my laptop, and resume work on my keyboard. With a flick of my wrist, I shoo her away. "Love ya, but a girl's gotta make a living," I tell her over my shoulder. "Work to do. A deadline to meet."

She grins, raises the bag in the air as a mock salute, and heads for the employee break room.

No distractions.

A quick time-check tells me I have only a few hours before David strolls back in the building. With a glance at my Shorter Mansion postcard, I settle in, focus, and try my best to block out the rest of the office.

By eleven-fifty, my fingers are stiff. I've edited my piece, reread, and edited it again. I fact-check, making sure dates are correct, the history is accurate, and my quotes are attributed to the right people. And as promised, I don't mention Phase III.

I linger over the last lines, a quote from Shug. It's the perfect ending to my story. "Past and present meet seamlessly in the heart of Eufaula, Alabama, home to breathtaking natural beauty and magnificent architecture. A living tribute to our nation's proud history, Eufaula is a treasure to experience with the senses; one that must be preserved for generations to come."

My hands hover above the keyboard. What will happen to Eufaula? To the Pilgrimage? I can picture PD and Ella Rae, Aubie, and TJ around the dinner table. Roger at his B&B. And MeeMaw. I can only imagine how she must be taking the news about this developer. Then, Mary Katherine flashes before my eyes. Her laugh, her laissez faire attitude and complete brush-off of Shug's concerns about preserving the city's history. Why didn't I think about this before? Other than the city council, she seems like the *only* person in Eufaula unaffected by the plans to build vacation condos.

The realization hits me like a brain freeze—one of those sudden awful stabbing headaches from too much ice cream, too fast. I press my fingers to both sides of my temples and rub in gentle circles. I close my eyes. I'm caffeine-lacking and a little fatigued. My eyes are crossing from staring at the computer screen. I need a break.

With a pang of worry in my chest, I check my email again. PD promised to update me on any big news, including city council and dreaded developer announcements. There are about a zillion new messages, but none from Eufaula.

I close out of the screen, spell-check my story a final time, attach it to an email, and hit send.

Chapter Twenty-Six

I SLIP OUT AT LUNCHTIME with Marietta at my heels. We steal across the street to a loud Jewish deli, where orders are yelled across a glassed-in display case. After a five-minute wait, we get lucky.

We pounce the moment two well-dressed men vacate their barstools. Marietta and I scoot up to a long slab of wood that serves as a counter, balancing sandwiches, drinks, and napkins. We're sitting so close that our knees bump together— an odd sensation if the body parts belonged to anyone other than my best friend.

Marietta is concentrating on her Reuben—a thick mess of meat, Swiss cheese, Thousand Island dressing, and sauerkraut on Rye. After she pauses to take a breath and wipe her lips with a folded napkin, she launches into a rapid-fire set of questions.

Why haven't I called? When did I get back? What about Andrew? Have I talked to him? Did I finish the article?

"Whoa!" I lean back and raise both hands in the air, fingers spread. "I've been crazy-busy. Got in last night. I'll see Andrew later. And yes, the story's waiting in David's inbox."

Marietta takes another nibble on her Reuben. "Mhm," she says, thinking and chewing. When she swallows, my friend wrinkles her forehead. "Really?"

"Which part?" I ask, taking a long drink of ice water.

"All of it," Marietta adjusts her glasses to peer at me, as if she's trying to make sure I'm not joking. "You stayed longer than you needed to…in *Alabama*." Her voice takes on an in-credulous tone. "And, you didn't call."

"It's complicated," I shrug and raise my eyebrows. "I'm the first one to admit I was wrong—totally wrong—about Eu-faula. It's wonderful. The architecture is amazing, really lovely. And the people there are sweet, funny, and interesting. And they are so proud of the history there," I catch my breath and smile.

Marietta is sitting up straight. There's a strange look on her face. Disbelief? Wonder? Amazement?

She reaches out and pinches my forearm, twisting the flesh.

"Ow!" I yell and swat her hand.

There's a brief lull in the conversation around us. A few heads turn in our direction, curious, then look away when there's no drama to witness.

"What was that for?"

"I'm checking to see if it's really you," Marietta pushes her plate away and puts both elbows on the table. She inter-laces her fingers below her chin, her eyes never leaving my face. "That you are the real Julia Sullivan, and not some robot replacement. Please tell me the magazine hasn't brainwashed you into a Stepford wife-travel writer."

I pretend to freeze, then make jerky movements like bolts have been screwed into my joints and my flesh has turned to metal. "Does not compute," I say. "Reprogram my hard drive."

Marietta smirks. "I see. Very nice. The old avoidance technique." She brushes her hands together with a brisk mo-tion. "Fine. You don't have to admit that there's anything's go-ing on."

"There isn't anything going on," I repeat in a normal voice, rolling my eyes toward the ceiling. It's not a lie. As far as my personal life is concerned, the statement's true. Shug's with Mary Katherine. I'm back in the City. I'll talk to Andrew tonight.

Of course, my best friend is not buying it. "Liar. Liar. Pants on fire," Marietta accuses me, flipping a stray curl out of her eyelashes. She's hurt. A smidge.

Ugh. I'm going to give in. "You have to promise not to laugh. Or make fun of me," I tell her with a stern gaze.

With a triumphant grin, Marietta holds up three fingers pressed together. "Girl Scouts' honor. Now out with it, missy."

"All right, here's what happened," I say, and lean in to whisper, just as my cell starts buzzing. The vibration—complete with flashing light—sends the phone and its bright purple case inching toward the edge of the counter. I snatch it up and set it in my lap. But the buzzing doesn't stop and I wonder if it's an emergency.

"Just a sec," I tell Marietta. When I glance at the screen, I start coughing. There are three messages from David. Each one says 'urgent.'

AFTER TROMPING THROUGH two blocks of slush, Marietta and I arrive back at the magazine in record time, sprinting through the double doors, flashing past a few coworkers. We screech to a stop in front of the guard to flash my badge. He's tall, with a chiseled jaw and close-cropped dark hair. I make a point to read his nametag.

"Hey Frank," I say, breathless. "How are you?"

The tall security man in blue blinks at my badge, then back up at me. "Hi Marietta," he says to my best friend. He turns to survey me. "And, Julia Sullivan. I didn't think you knew my name."

Although I can't see her, I know that Marietta is grinning at his assessment. I blush red and get hot under my scarf and wool coat. "I'm sorry," I apologize. "I'm always in such a hurry. Usually running late."

"Today being no exception?" he asks, revealing two rows of almost-perfect white teeth.

"My boss," I groan a little and glance the clock above his head. My feet are itching to race toward the elevators. "My article. He probably hates it."

"Nah," he shrugs. "You'll be okay. Get going," Frank waves me through. "Have a good day, ladies."

I scamper toward the bank of silver doors and punch the up button. There's a chime, signaling that the elevator to our right is about to open. After waiting for a dozen people to filter out, Marietta races in behind me.

With a sigh of relief, I shrug off my coat. "Did you know that guy's name?" I ask her when my breathing returns to semi-normal.

"Frank? The guard?" Marietta pulls off her scarf and shakes out her curls. "Sure. He's been here for years."

I purse my lips. *Years.* And I've never said hello. The pit in my stomach gets a little deeper.

"Hey, so now, you know."

The elevator dings, signaling our floor. We step out and Marietta grabs my arm, pulling me toward the wall.

"Um, I've been meaning to ask you. Are you okay? Because there've been a couple of strange calls," Marietta whispers. "The person was quite persistent, and I think the front desk got tired of talking to her, so she got routed to my desk."

I'm baffled. "Who was it?"

Marietta frowns. "You met recently? I think her name is Buffy or Muffy, something like that. Anyway, you and her friend shared a taxi?"

"Oh, them!" I laugh. *Chanel Lipstick and Cashmere Wrap. Has to be. What in the world?*

"They wanted to send an arrangement, to cheer you up," Marietta purses her lips. "But you were out of town. So, then, she asked for your home address. They wanted to mail a card. I didn't give it to her. She wasn't very happy. Something about Athazagoritis?"

I cover my mouth with both hands and shake my head.

Marietta squints at me. "What's going on, Julia? No B.S. Are you really sick and not telling me?"

"I'm fine." I widen my eyes and stare at her, not blinking. "*Really*."

My best friend squares her shoulders. "You'd better not be trying to save my feelings or something dumb like that…"

"They think I'm at death's door," I exhale. "And it's my fault."

"What? Why?" Marietta tries not to smile.

"Right before I left for Alabama, there was this snow-storm. It was awful. I was freezing. There were no taxis. No one would stop. So, after twenty minutes, a cab finally pulls up and these ladies tried to steal it from me."

"So you made up a story—"

"Yes. I don't even want to talk about it," I shoot Marietta a threatening look.

"What?" She makes a face, choking back a laugh. "That's not even—"

"I know. Don't even say it," I sigh. "I feel bad enough as it is."

"So, what if she calls back?"

"Um," I wince and drum my fingers on the side of my leg. "Oh, I don't know. First of all, give her my address so that she'll leave you alone. And…how about tell her that…I'm cured?"

Marietta frowns at me.

"I promise I won't ever do it again." With my index finger, I cross my heart with a huge 'x' and make cow eyes. "Please, I know better now. It sounds crazy, but in the past week, I've really grown up. Tons. Forgive me?"

Marietta considers this. She pecks my cheek, still cautious, as if I might decide to nip her on the heels like a wild dog. "Don't do it again," she lectures.

We part ways at the hallway. I head for David's office, steeling myself for the lecture he'd likely prepared. Lucky girl that she is, Marietta escapes, turning left, toward the cubicles.

When I round the corner, Dolores is sitting at her desk, shoulders hunched, fingers flying over the keyboard. There's the unmistakable scent of Chanel No. 5 floating through the stale office air. That's when I decide to look up.

Her hair is different, I notice, and then remember Marietta's email about the makeover.

Instead of rapping my knuckles on the filing cabinet to let her know I'm waiting, I walk around the desk. "Hi there. David wanted to see me?" I say.

With a quick yank of her hand, Dolores pulls off her earbuds. Marietta was right, she does look good. Her hair is colored a dark brown and is styled in a cute pageboy. She's dressed in a black pantsuit with a tasteful white blouse underneath. Her makeup is light and plays up her eyes, which are hazel-green.

"Look at you!" I exclaim, reaching my arms out for emphasis. "You look amazing, Dolores. Your hair. The clothes."

She flutters her eyelashes in shock, and jumps a little, startled at the compliments. But instead of snapping back, ignoring me all together, or frowning in typical grumpy-Dolores fashion, she looks quite pleased. "Um, thank you," she squeaks out, her voice barely above a whisper.

We stand beaming at each other when David opens the door to his office.

"Julia," he beckons me with a straight face. "I thought I heard your voice."

My legs quiver and a tickle of worry creeps up my spine. I paste on a brave smile and give a thumbs-up to Dolores.

Of course, as I cross the threshold into David's office, I realize that maybe I shouldn't be acting so jovial and chit-chatting about trivial matters like outfits and hairstyles. He's probably going to send me home, so I'd be safer walking the plank off Captain Hook's ship, straight into the mouth of that hungry crocodile, ticking clock and all.

He settles into his leather chair, looking every bit the

corporate magnate. I take a seat and grip my hands in my lap, preparing for the worst.

"So, I received your story," David says, his eyes piercing into mine. His mouth barely moves, but his body language is saying 'less than thrilled.'

I press my lips together and nod.

"Interesting angle you took on this assignment. It's a big step away from the usual style of the magazine." David is still not smiling. He's staring at me. Not blinking. He's waiting for a response.

If it were possible by some miracle of quantum physics or magic, I'd make myself vanish. Poof! Gone! Or shrink myself to microscopic proportions. Of course, I'd run the risk of getting stepped on, but I'll take my chances.

"So, why the change?" he prompts, swiveling in his chair to get a better angle on his laptop. He flicks his gaze toward the screen and scrolls through what I'm guessing is my Eufaula article.

"Um," I hedge for more time, jiggling my leg up and down. "I guess because it was a different kind of story." My voice cracks on the last two words. I'm not the best at defending my work. Actually, I can't remember a time that I've had to. The routine has been the same since I started at the magazine: Write the article, submit, make recommended edits. Clearly, David wants more. He blows out a breath and leans back in his chair, thinking.

I shift an inch in my seat. There's an itch on my left knee, like something's crawled up my leg. My neck is starting to cramp. I start praying for an interruption. Dolores, Marietta, the fire department. Anyone with a crisis.

David drums his fingers on his massive desk. "Maybe I'm not being clear, Julia. I'll refresh your memory. The question was why?"

My vocal cords tighten. My throat thickens. I reach for the armrest and grip the fabric. *Why is he torturing me? Can't he just say what he means?* I am suddenly incensed.

"Wait, just a minute," I bark out like a Chihuahua. "I am proud of that article. I did a lot of research. I toured homes, learned the history of the city, and talked to tons of people, one of them named 'Stump'—did you know that there's an entire family named after Auburn University football coaches?"

David is trying to get a word in, but I wave a hand in the air and continue my tirade. "I drank iced tea with about a hundred packs of sugar, had to wear a ball gown because I lost my luggage, and very politely endured countless 'Yankee' comments, thank you very much." I suck in a breath. "Not to mention that my windshield was smashed, my heel broke off at a party, and got a ride in an ambulance after being attacked by killer bees."

My boss raises an eyebrow.

"Okay, so there weren't any 'actual' killer bees," I say. "I'm allergic."

David nods. "I remember."

You should, I want to say, but bite the inside of my cheek instead and think of my mom, which makes me want to cry. My father was at work when Mom figured it out. I was in the backyard by her hydrangeas, got stung, and blew up like a balloon. She rushed me to the hospital, sat with me in the emergency room, and held my swollen hand.

When she was still alive, she always reminded me to pack my EpiPen.

Stupid tears. I brush at the moisture on my cheeks and stand up. I'm not going to let David torture me any longer. I'll pack up my cubicle, go back to my apartment, and send out resumes. No, better yet, I'll have a glass of wine, sleep, and then look for a job tomorrow. I won't be so upset then.

"Julia. What's wrong? Where are you going?" he asks, pushing his chair back.

"I'm leaving," I reply, bending down to grab my bag. "I'm fired, right? Isn't that what you told me would happen? So, now you can have your fun."

David stares at me like I've grown a second head. "Fun? Is that what you think?" He chuckles. "You were always sensitive."

Jerk. I turn and walk away, reaching for the door handle, when I hear his voice.

"Stop," he says. "Please."

I bite my lip and concentrate on the swirls of woodgrain. I stare longer, but don't see the office anymore. Instead, I see Shug and PD. Aubie, MeeMaw, Ella Rae. They all trusted me and I let them down. How am I going to break the news that the story's been scrapped?

I pivot on my heel, raise my chin, and force myself to look at David.

My father's face relaxes. He takes a seat on the edge of his desk. "You didn't let me finish," he explains. "I was trying to get you to explain what caused you to write that way—from the heart. The article is very good. The best you've written in a long time. I think you did a marvelous job."

Chapter Twenty-Seven

"YOU HAVE TO UNDERSTAND MY SITUATION," David says, motioning me to have a seat again. He unbuttons his jacket and smoothes his tie. "Having a daughter working for me in the business looks a lot like nepotism."

I perch back on the chair, relieved about postponing a frantic job search.

"Even," he underscores with a direct look, "a daughter who hasn't spoken to me in several years. It's all about avoiding the appearance of impropriety."

Image is huge at any magazine, but I admit that I hadn't given our family connection that much thought. I was too busy focused on me, my job, and soothing what was left of my bruised ego after David informed me that my job might be on the chopping block.

"So, you were just threatening me for no reason?" I ask, a bit incredulous.

David rubs his chin. "That was the tricky part. Your work had slipped. There were a few complaints, mostly deadline-related, but the overall consensus was that your writing had lost its pizzazz."

I feel my face grow hot.

"I was faced with a very odd predicament, so I made a deal. One last assignment, a tricky one, and one last chance to succeed."

"Or fail," I add.

"No one had an office pool going, but you needed to

know I meant business." David runs a finger along the edge of the desk. "If anything, I had to be tougher on you. Set the standard higher."

"So, I was being taught a lesson," I say. My skin prickles with embarrassment. I didn't realize the position David was in. I almost blew a wonderful career. And I was oblivious to it all.

David shrugs. "Did it feel like punishment?"

"Maybe at first," I say, hesitating at coming out with the God's honest truth. David crinkles his forehead. "Well, yes, it did feel like punishment," I admit. "I was a little angry. A little resentful."

He nods.

"But, as it ended up, despite all of the craziness, once I settled in, it was really wonderful." I allow myself to gush a little bit. "The homes, the people. Everything was great, the weather especially. But—" I stop myself.

David tilts his head expectantly. "But what?"

I want to rewind the last word, pop it back in my mouth, and swallow it like a piece of candy. It's too late. I've already said too much. As I watch the expression on his face, I suspect that David knows more than he's saying.

There's a knock on the door, and the handle turns.

Dolores sticks her head inside the office. "Sorry to inter-rupt, Mr. Sullivan. There's a visitor. He says it's urgent."

David is nonplussed. "I don't remember anything on my calendar. Who is it? What do they need?"

With a slight cough, Dolores pauses and looks at me. "Actually sir, there's a man here to see Julia."

My father nods at me. "Go ahead and see what it's about. We can talk about the rest of this later. I have your next assign-ment for you, by the way. And a photo you might find interest-ing." He hands over an envelope.

"Oh?" I arch an eyebrow, immediately intrigued.

David smiles, "I think you'll like New Orleans this time

of year. Festive, lovely decor, parties in the Garden District. I've got you staying at the Roosevelt. You leave Wednesday."

"What happened to Route 66?"

He checks his watch. "You're still on that beat. Dana? Dena? The new hire? She has the flu, so you're covering her assignment. We'll talk more about it tomorrow. Let's meet at ten-thirty sharp." He looks at Dolores. "Can you get me Steve Jabowski at Hearst on the phone?"

"Yes sir."

I follow Dolores out, still clutching the envelope. In a fog, I walk to the front lobby where I assume the surprise visitor is waiting for me. On the curved receptionist's desk, there's a huge bouquet of flowers, dripping with lilies and roses. It's so enormous that I have to squat down a few inches to see the girl who answers the phone.

"Hello?"

"Julia," she smiles.

"Nice flowers," I comment. "Special occasion?"

She tilts her head to the side with a coy look. "I wish. They're for you."

I whirl around to see who delivered them, but the reception area is empty. "But it's not my birthday, or anything…"

The receptionist giggles behind the arrangement.

I bend down. "Do you know who brought them? Is there a card?"

She points to the left side of the vase. "I think there's a message."

"Oh, I see it," I say, stretching to reach the tiny white card. I pluck it from between the blossoms and tear it open. There are three words printed in block letters.

Meet me downstairs.

A sudden thought crosses my mind. It's Shug. He broke up with Mary Katherine, flew up to New York, and tracked me here. I float toward the elevators, not able feel my own feet, and press the down button. The light passes from number to number, getting closer.

On impulse, I dial his phone. *I'll beat him at his game.*

The instant the elevator dings, I hear a deep, masculine voice answer. "Hello?"

The massive silver doors slide open and I step inside. "Guess who this is?" I giggle into the phone. As the doors close and the car descends, there's only the low hum and soft whir of the elevator mechanism.

My stomach drops. "Hello?" I say again, perplexed at the silence.

The connection begins to fuzz out as we drop deeper inside the building. Fifth floor, fourth floor.

Between crackles, I can hear him say something. "Em?" I make out. His voice is gruff and I can tell he's older. His tone is familiar, but I can't quite place it.

"No, it's not Em," I reply, making my voice cool. "Who is this?" I start to ask, but before I can get the words out, he's gone. On my screen, the number flashes, signaling I've lost the call. Instead of five bars, my cell has none. Lips pursed, I exhale, blowing all of the air out of my lungs. *What in the world is going on?*

The doors open at the second floor, and a man in a dark suit steps inside. He offers a curt hello, but I'm too upset to do anything but nod and grimace.

I called the right number, but it was definitely not Shug who answered. And who is this mysterious "Em"?

With a jolt, the elevator stops at the first floor. After another ding, the double-doors heave open. I blink and step into the bright lobby, the heels of my boots click on the marble tile. I stop and stand still, craning my neck like a goose, searching for a glimpse of Shug's dark hair and broad shoulders.

Oh, I am going to give him a piece of my mind…

Someone taps my shoulder. I whirl around, holding out an accusing finger, ready to launch into a mini-tirade about the phone call and "Em."

But it's Andrew.

"Looking for someone?" He smiles and takes my limp hand. He's holding yet another bunch of flowers, perky white daisies and bright pink tulips, this time.

"Andrew!" I widen my eyes and try to form something else to say. My brain is stuck in reverse. I want to go back upstairs, back to my office, back to David's office, even.

He laughs, showing off his perfect teeth and boyish dimples. I can feel a few jealous looks as we stand in the middle of the lobby. Andrew always attracts admiring glances with his sea green eyes and blonde hair.

"I know we're supposed to meet a little later," he grins and rubs his gloved hands together, "but I called your office and arranged for you to have the afternoon off."

I bite the inside of my cheek and I try not to look furious.

Andrew takes me by the elbow, turns me around to face him, then leans in and nuzzles my forehead. I used to love that, I think to myself. I used to love everything about him. I swallow the gigantic bubble in my throat.

"Who? How—?" I sputter out and shake my head. We begin to walk toward the street and I'm glad I don't have to look Andrew straight in the face.

He chortles. "Oh, I have my ways."

I nudge his ribs with my elbow, encouraging him to tell the rest of the story. I need to know who I am going to have to kill when I come to work in the morning.

"Marietta?" I ask.

"Nope," he raises his chin in satisfaction. "I talked to the top man. Your new boss. He was in a great mood, said you just finished a fantastic assignment."

I slow my pace. "You. Talked. To. David."

"He was great. Seems like he really likes you," Andrew winks down at me like we've just shared a juicy secret.

It's my turn to laugh. Of course, it comes out sounding

more like a sharp, halting bark. Like a dog that's had his paw run over with a child's bicycle wheel.

Andrew holds the door open for me and gives me a curious look. "What's the matter?" he asks and frowns.

The December wind whips my cheeks and, for once, I'm glad, because it helps me calm down. I take a deep breath and review the facts: Andrew doesn't know David. They never met. By the time we started dating, my father had already left.

But David could have warned me. Given me a sign. A clue.

Andrew whistles and waves down a yellow taxi. As the cab pulls up, wheels gripping the packed snow, I step back from the curb and wait. Always the gentleman, Andrew opens the door and beckons me inside.

"So, did David, my lovely new boss, happen to mention his last name?" I ask as I slide inside the back seat.

Andrew pauses for a moment, then shuts my door. He leans forward to the cab driver's open window, murmurs an address, and walks around to the other side of the taxi. After he's settled in next to me, he thinks for a moment. He's usually good with names. He remembers everyone. He drums his fingers on the seat beside him. "Sanders, Sherwood, Silver?"

"Try Sullivan," I say.

"Sullivan, that's it," Andrew snaps his fingers in delight.

I don't respond. I watch him. And wait for it all to click. Not thirty seconds later, Andrew gets it. The name. My name. The whole story. His eyes meet mine. "As in?"

With a small nod, I acknowledge he's correct. "Yes. David's my father."

Chapter Twenty-Eight

IN MY POCKET, MY CELL BUZZES. Andrew hears it, I can tell, but he doesn't ask who's calling me. I pull out my phone, and my fingers fumble to shut it off.

Without looking at the screen, I power it down. "Not important," I say. And right now, no matter who it is, I owe Andrew my full attention. And an explanation.

"Where are we going?" I ask.

Andrew gives me what passes for a broad, but uneasy smile. "Don't you want to tell me more about the big reunion? With David?"

He doesn't really expect me to talk. Andrew is well aware that my father isn't quite stellar in the categories of parent and husband. David is an expert at leaving, my own wanderlust proof of his lineage. *At least I have someone to blame it on.*

Andrew reaches across the seat to squeeze my hand. I don't pull away, though I'd like to sprint back up 5th Avenue, head back to West 57th and Central Park. My comfort zone is calling.

I chew my bottom lip and shake my head. "Not much to say. It was a bit of a surprise." I actually smile, remembering my reaction—a cross between sick and shell-shocked. "I'm over it now. He's there. He's staying. He's really smart and will do a great job."

"What about you?" Andrew gazes at me.

I shrug. "I'm gone so much. On the day I found out he'd been hired, he sent me off on assignment. I'm leaving Wednesday for New Orleans."

"Happy holidays from the Big Easy, eh?" Andrew murmurs. He's not thrilled.

"Something like that," I say. "I don't have all of the details yet."

The cab driver eases to the side of the street and parks. We've arrived in the Flatiron District, East 20th Street, to be exact. Andrew glances at the fare, peels off a few bills from his wallet, and gets out of the taxi.

He walks around the cab to my side, opens the door, and offers me a hand. Safe on the sidewalk, we watch the cabbie drive away. "Thanks. So, where to?" I ask, raising my eyebrows at the buildings surrounding us.

I'd suggested O'Reilly's for the casual atmosphere and proximity to work. I'm actually longing for the simple menu at McGee's on West 55th Street or The Gin Mill on Amsterdam.

The sumptuous Gramercy Tavern looms ahead. Any other evening, I'd be thrilled to be dining on Shrimp or Sea Bass. I adore the restaurant's Bok Choy and have been known to polish off an entire course of Snapper with a side of Radish, Turnip, Bacon, and Beet Broth.

Despite my voracious appetite, and the huge bill when we leave, Andrew takes me here once a year. It's our special place, as those things for couples go, and my heart sinks a little lower in my chest with every step we get closer to the entrance.

I've already meandered though our relationship with no intention of long-term anything. In my defense, I've been honest. I'm a commitment-phobe. Certifiable. More broken relationships than anyone I know. And Andrew entered into this knowing it.

But our unheard of stretch of romantic bliss has survived because we're long-distance without being long-distance. I have an apartment in the City and a job that takes me around the world. The separation doesn't make my heart grow fonder, it helps me endure. I know that I'm leaving, and therefore, can commit to another day, another week, another month.

But it's not fair to Andrew, who, on more than one occasion, has stated his desire for domestic bliss, a house in the suburbs, and two point two children. True, I've overhead him saying it to friends or colleagues. He hasn't addressed it directly with me. Not yet.

I think he still believes he can change my mind about marriage and forever after.

Tonight, I have to let him go.

We're seated at the bar while we wait for our table. The table, covered with a lovely, crisp cloth, fresh flowers, and shiny silverware. The table that I have no intention of going anywhere near. The bartender takes our order—Andrew's scotch on the rocks, my glass of Pinot Noir. As we wait, I run my hand along the smooth mahogany wood and try to settle my nerves. With a sly glance, I eye the slight bulge in his jacket pocket. A small gift? Some jewelry? My chest tightens. An engagement ring?

Our drinks arrive, and while Andrew takes a conservative sip and chats up the overweight man beside him, I down the entire pour in one gulp. The bartender eyes me and I nod vigorously, conveying my urgent need for a refill.

After the second glass in five minutes, I'm loosening a bit. My shoulders relax and I'm able to stop clutching my purse. As it turns out, Andrew's new friend is quite funny, and we spend the next twenty minutes laughing at his off-color jokes. At one point, I have to dab at my eyes with a cocktail napkin. I can't even remember the punch line.

I'm on my third glass—or perhaps my fourth—when the hostess sidles up to inform Andrew our table is ready.

"No, thank you," I grip the stem of my wine glass and flash a look of pure terror at the restaurant worker. My stool seems to shift to the right and I try to sit up very straight. I put a hand on the bar and steady myself. The hostess takes a step back, frowns, and decides to ignore me. She's drilling her eyes on Andrew, who's making short work of vacating his seat.

"Julia?" Andrew touches my arm. His hand burns on my bare skin. I contain a yelp and pull away, sloshing my wine and nudging the innocent bystander to my right.

Andrew's brow furrows. He sweeps a hand through his blonde hair, confused. "Julia," he repeats. "Ready?"

"I'm not," my voice strains above the crowd. I grip both sides of my chair for emphasis and lock my feet on the legs of the stool.

Andrew pivots at my acrid tone. For a moment, he looks stunned. Or perplexed. The wine's altered my judgment, so I'm not able to read his expression with any clarity. I decide on basic unhappiness.

"Can we go?" I plead and pull on the sleeve of his navy sport coat.

He brushes off my hand. "Julia," he hisses. "I don't understand." His jaw is set, eyes hurt.

"Not here," I say and sweep a hand to indicate we're in a crowd. Of course, my judgment of spatial relations is impaired, and I manage to knock off a row of six martinis the bartender's just poured and garnished.

The crash and shatter of glass momentarily stuns the entire room full of people. The counter becomes a lake of gin and vermouth. A toothpick full of olives rolls by as the martini river continues to run toward unsuspecting elbows. The bartender chases the liquid with a dishrag, shooing patron's elbows and hands along the way. I shrink down in my seat and raise my eyes to meet Andrew's, expecting disappointment or disapproval. He's not one for scenes, and this is a doozey.

Andrew's face has lost all color. He's as white as the cocktail napkin under the fluorescent lights. "Julia," he says, voice tight and intense.

"I'm sorry," I wince and close my eyes. "Andrew, I've

wanted to tell you for a long time." There's no response. My eyelids flutter open. He's not looking at me. He's looking at my knees, or my lap. "Andrew," I clear my throat, trying not to get irritated that he's not paying attention. "I really care about you, but—"

"Julia," Andrew grabs my hand tight and drops to one knee.

"What are you doing?" I pipe up. "Do not propose, Andrew. I can't accept."

Instead of whipping out a small jewelry box with a bow, Andrew shoves me off of my barstool, wraps my hand in a white towel he must have grabbed from one of the wait staff, and points me toward the front door. "You're bleeding," he yells in my ear. "I think you need stitches."

I drop my eyes to my hand. Bright red liquid is soaking through the wrapped fabric. Blood, my brain tells me. Not wanting to accept it, I decide to ask anyway, hoping that someone spilled a bucket of cherry Kool-Aid. "Is that...?" My voice trails off and I gasp.

"Yes," Andrew says, whisking me out of Gramercy Tavern.

Beneath the bandage, my palm begins to throb.

A DOZEN STITCHES AND A CUP OF COFFEE LATER, I am very sober and completely mortified. We're standing on the concrete steps of my apartment. Thanks to a Novocaine block, I can't feel anything below my wrist, and for that I am grateful. For the fiftieth time this evening, I wish there was something similar for my brain.

"So," I finally say, "you were never going to propose."

"No," Andrew shakes his head. He reaches into his jacket pocket and pulls out a letter. "I've been offered a job in London. Great opportunity, and I've decided to take it. I wanted to tell you myself. Face to face."

"Thank you," I whisper.

"You are a wonderful girl, Julia," he continues. "But, I don't see a future for us. Maybe you can come visit. Or someday we could try—"

I stand on my tiptoes and put a finger to his lips. "Shh. It's okay. You don't have to say anything. Go to London, meet someone wonderful, get married. You deserve it. You deserve to be happy."

Andrew pauses, reading my face. His eyes redden. With an awkward grin, he takes me in his arms, hugs me tight, and kisses the top of my head. "Be good."

"You too," I murmur as he releases me. "Thank you for taking care of me."

Andrew runs a finger along my cheek, his face full of emotion, and turns to leave. "Anytime." His voice breaks a little.

I wave, tears coursing down my cheeks. Then, I clutch my bandaged hand, smile, and watch him until he disappears into the ink-black night.

"Good-bye," I say to the night air. He didn't say the words, but it is obvious. He's moving on. He's leaving. And I didn't try to stop him.

For Andrew and me, our "anytime" ends tonight.

Chapter Twenty-Nine

THE SOUND OF HONKING TAXICABS and a rumbling trash truck jerk me out of a deep sleep. My head throbs. I press two fingers to my temple and open my eyes a millimeter against the bright light. The clock on my bedside table reads nine-thirty-two.

Nine-thirty-two in the morning? No. No. No. My brain rewinds. I'm scheduled for a meeting with David in one hour. *One hour.* I scramble to kick off the covers, bump my bandaged hand, and fight the nausea welling up in my throat. *The new Julia doesn't sleep in on workdays. The new Julia shows up on time. The new Julia is responsible.*

After wrestling off the cap, I swallow three Advil, throw a plastic bag over my wounded appendage and jump through the shower. One-handed, I run a comb through my wet hair, scrub my teeth, and pull on my favorite dark-rinse jeans and a black turtleneck. After I locate my scarf, gloves, and coat, I dial Dolores, tucking my cell under my chin while I wiggle my feet into my leather boots.

"David Sullivan's office," Dolores answers in her usual clipped manner.

"Good morning Dolores," I say, breathless, "This is Julia. I have a ten-thirty with David. Please tell him I *will* be there. I was...delayed this morning."

There's a disapproving silence and the sound of rustling paper.

I squeeze the phone tighter to my shoulder and squint

at my reflection in the mirror. "Dolores?" I say, "Thank you. I appreciate you taking the message. I know you're really busy."

After a beat, Dolores answers, her voice almost civil. "You're welcome, Julia."

Whew.

With a glance around the apartment for any last, needed items, my eyes fall on the envelope David handed me yesterday. I snatch it up, stuff it into my briefcase, and lock the door behind me.

When I reach the elevator, there's a huge construction sign and yellow tape. I grit my teeth and take the stairs two at a time, the motion jiggling my aching brain and stitched-up hand. The ground floor has never been such a welcome sight. I burst onto the sidewalk and look for the yellow flash of a cab.

After being ignored by five drivers and being splashed by the sixth, one takes pity on me and pulls over to the curb. The hems of my pant legs are soaked, and I'm shaking when I slide inside the taxi. I smile at the man behind the wheel, rattle off the address of *Getaways*, and say a proper thank you. He nods in the rearview mirror and we take off, launching into traffic like a NASCAR pace vehicle.

As we weave in and out of lanes, I settle back against the seat and focus my thoughts. Andrew, my long-time boyfriend, is moving to London. The idea still shocks me, and I cringe when I remember our conversation. What I wouldn't give for a mind-eraser device or a machine to zap a few hours from existence.

Andrew wasn't proposing engagement. He was quitting the relationship, escaping, moving on. I blink back tears and gaze out at the hundreds of people moving down the New York sidewalks—all going somewhere, all meeting someone.

It had been over with Andrew for quite some time. He was the only one brave enough to say it. I'm not certain he would have stayed, even if I'd begged him last night. He'd had enough.

I owed him the truth. He deserved that—and more. But all I did was run away. My father did it to my mother. I'd done it to my father, my college boyfriends, and now Andrew.

It was time to grow up. It was time to stop. Even if it meant hurting someone's feelings—or my own.

The driver pulls up to the tall silver building and I hand over the fare and a generous tip. I ease out of the cab with one hand, step onto the sidewalk, and check my watch. Thirteen minutes and counting until my meeting with David. It's a miracle.

In the elevator, I squeeze into the corner behind two men and a group of six women, take out the manila envelope, flip it over, and lift the metal tabs. When I peek inside, my breath stops like someone's clamped a vice on my windpipe.

It's the same photograph Aubie Jordan gushed over at the dinner table.

The elevator stops and dings. The massive doors slide open and shut. We begin to move again, but I don't look away from the young girl in the picture.

Snippets of that evening's conversation come back to me in a rush. I can almost hear Aubie's voice. "There was this reporter...I was just seventeen, and it was the first Pilgrimage, 1965...he took that photograph...that reporter. I can't remember..." In my mind, I can see Aubie rubbing her forehead. *Was she trying to remember his name? The newspaper? Something about the day?*

TJ was quite annoyed, I recall that. PD appeared nervous, and Shug dashed to the rescue when his mother fell apart. *What was the last thing she said?* I strain my memory.

And then, like a long-lost letter, it comes back to me. Aubie had drifted into a dream-like state, her tone soft and hopeful, with the flush of young love. "He was so handsome... A real gentleman. And I wore that dress. I still have it, you know, in the closet ..."

The man next to me clears his throat, an obvious prompt

aimed at me. I glance up at him, then over at the elevator doors, yawning open. It's my floor. He's holding the 'open' button and seems annoyed. I swallow. *How long have we been standing here?* I murmur an apology, hunch my shoulders, and rush into the office lobby.

While I'm attempting to sneak past the front desk, someone spots me.

"Julia," a voice calls out.

I stop, square my body toward the desk, and sneak a look at my watch. *Darn it.* With a quick adjustment of the briefcase strap cutting into my collarbone, I raise an eyebrow at the receptionist and lower my voice. "Um, I'm in a hurry. I have a meeting with *David*," I emphasize this by widening my eyes. "Who is it?"

Before she can answer, the office phone rings, and I hear the click of high heels and an unmistakable Southern drawl. "Julia, darlin'!"

I whirl around and come face to face with Dean Alice Waters, my seatmate from the Atlanta flight. She squeals and throws her arms around me, hugging me to her chest like she'd just won the lottery.

When I can breathe again, I manage a smile. "It's great to see you, Dean Alice. I'm so surprised. How did you find me?" I blurt out in a not-so-discreet way.

With a peal of laughter, she touches my arm. "Sugar, you told me that you worked here." She winks at me with long mascaraed lashes. "Even for a little old Southern belle like me, raised in tiny Dahlonega, Georgia, you aren't that hard to find."

I blink at her. For being so traumatized by airport security checks and two hours of severe turbulence at thirty-five thousand feet, Dean Alice is quite astute and has an incredible memory for details.

"Oh, Lord have mercy. Sakes alive! Whatever happened to your hand, darlin'?" She examines the bandages.

"Long story, but I'm fine," I confess, then feel a stab of panic when my eyes fall on the clock above the reception desk. It's ten-thirty. On the dot. And David said ten-thirty sharp. He's likely to blow a gasket. "Look, Dean Alice, I hate to say this, but I actually have to run. I have a meeting—"

The receptionist behind us calls out. "That was David. He's running late."

"Thanks," I reply, desperate to race back to my office, study the photo again, and figure out what the heck is going on with my father, Aubie Jordan, and Eufaula, Alabama. "Could you let Dolores know that I'm here, please? And ask her to buzz me when he gets in?"

After an affirmative nod from the receptionist, Dean Alice throws an arm around me and squeezes again. "Perfect! Then we can chat for a few moments."

Her perfume wafts over me. I am light-headed enough as it is. I need food and strong coffee. Two or three cups of coffee, lots of cream, and a big pile of sugar. Instead of trying to delay the inevitable and ask Dean Alice to come back—or make an appointment like everyone else—I paste on my most polite and welcoming smile and wave for her to follow me.

Marietta watches as I lead Dean Alice back to the maze of office space. She notes the wrapping on my wrist and palm, pursing her lips with a concerned look in my direction, but says nothing in front of my guest. I make the introductions, the two women shake hands, and I collapse against the chair in my cozy cubicle. It's still a mess, with piles of papers everywhere, but my visitor doesn't seem to notice.

I jerk a desperate look at my best friend. "Food?" I mouth at her, grimacing.

"Have a seat," I gesture to the only other seat in the cubicle. It's a beaten-up chair that looks like rummage-sale material, but it's the best I can do. As I'm the one usually off on assignment, it's not often I entertain visitors.

Marietta hands me a pack of cheese crackers, an orange,

and a bottle of cranberry juice. "I love you," I say, then turn to Dean Alice, "Would you like some?" When she declines, I rip into the package with abandon and pop a cracker in my mouth. I chase it with a swallow of juice, and then get to work on peeling the orange with one hand.

"Bless your heart," she clucks her tongue, watching me. "I had no idea you hadn't eaten." Dean Alice cocks her head to one side. "Since I just about dropped in on you out of the blue, and you have a meeting, I'll make this quick, sugar."

I nod, still chewing. I've given up on the orange but pop another cracker into my mouth.

Dean Alice clutches a hand to her heart. "I must have the recipe for those delicious little treats you gave me on the airplane. I've spent the past few days with some of the finest chefs in the world and tasted some scrumptious desserts, but I can't stop thinking about those little marshmallow puffs." She straightens in her chair. "Whatever the asking price for the recipe, I'm willing to pay it," she adds.

Marietta, who's half-listening to the exchange, now eyeballs me over the cubicle divider. I ignore the face she's making and turn back to Dean Alice.

"That's really kind of you," I say. "But it's not my recipe. A friend made them. They were a gift."

Dean Alice presses her lips together and thinks for a moment. She clasps her hands together and rests them on her crossed knees. "Well, now, that's all right. Would you mind terribly giving her a call? Tell her that I would *love* to speak with her about this *creation*."

I slide a glance at Marietta, who wrinkles her nose. It's obvious she thinks the entire situation is a teensy bit bizarre. I don't make friends on airplanes. I don't share food with strangers. And I don't have people show up at my office unannounced. We exchange another glance, then Marietta looks down and starts typing on her keyboard.

As I turn the idea over in my mind, I begin to consider

the positives for PD and Eufaula. If Dean Alice is a chef and restaurant owner, and if she has all of the amazing the connections she says that she does, there's no limit to the potential exposure, recognition, and profits.

A ping on my laptop startles me. A new message.

I shimmy my body in front of the screen and hold up my index finger in front of Dean Alice. "Could you give me just a sec? Excuse me."

The message is from Marietta, who's just wrapped up a little research on the visitor and her background. It's short and sweet. "She's legit. The real deal."

When I swivel my chair back to Dean Alice, she's waiting patiently.

"Let me call her first," I say. "She's very talented and is just starting her own business. I'm not sure what she'll say about all of this, but I guess that's for you both to discuss."

Dean Alice beams at me. "Wonderful."

I flash a look in the direction of David's office. Still no boss. No Dolores. No call. So, I pull out my cell phone and scroll to PD's number. My finger hovers above the call button.

"My friend lives in Eufaula, Alabama. Her name is Patricia Jordan," I say. "Well, it's really Patricia Dye Jordan," I correct myself. "But she goes by PD."

My visitor brightens. "As in Coach Pat Dye? As in Auburn University?"

"From what I'm told, yes. Everyone in the family is named after a coach, or player, or mascot." I start to tick off names, "There's Aubie—that's her mother. TJ, or Toomer—is her father. And Shug is PD's brother."

Dean Alice claps her hands in delight. "How adorable. I absolutely cannot wait to meet them."

"All righty," I breathe out and hit 'call.' After three long rings, PD answers.

"Hello?"

"PD," I say, making my tone brisk and business-like. "Hi!

It's Julia Sullivan here. I have a favor to ask. Do you have a few minutes? Is this a bad time?"

"Julia!" she exclaims. "Oh, of course. Anything. We've all been wondering how the story's going. Did your boss love it?"

"I-I think so," I say.

A dark shadow crosses my desk. Dolores is hovering over Dean Alice's shoulder. Her face is grim and set. She's back to unhappy. She raises a painted on eyebrow and jerks her head toward David's office.

I stand up, almost knocking my phone to the floor. "I met someone," I begin. "On the flight back to New York. She's a chef and owns a restaurant. She wanted to talk to you about your Pillow Puffs."

"Really?" PD says, her voice measured and slow.

I can't tell if she's excited or upset. I keep talking anyway. "Her name's Dean Alice and I'm going to hand the phone over to her right now. She stopped by the office. And I have to rush off to a meeting. Thank you so much. Take care of yourself."

PD says something else—I think about Phase III—but I can't wait any longer. I jam the phone into Dean Alice's waiting hand, grab my bag and the envelope with Aubie's photograph.

The day is proving to be full of surprises, and it's not even half-done. I stride to David's office, trying not to break into a run. Whatever happens inside those closed doors, one thing's for certain. I'm going to get some answers.

Chapter Thirty

DAVID CLOSES THE DOOR BEHIND ME. "Bar fight?" he asks, noticing my wounded hand.

"Something like that," I grimace and try to tuck my arm out of sight.

"I hope it won't affect your trip to New Orleans?" It's not a question. He expects me to go, no matter what.

I shake my head. "Not at all."

"Good," he says. "I have you on a tight schedule, leaving early tomorrow morning. You get back Sunday evening." David leans back and surveys a pile of papers. "Here's your contact information and hotel reservation." He hands the stack across the desk.

"David," I interrupt. "Why did you send me to Eufaula? I understand that you needed to make a point, scare me into doing better work, but it wasn't *all* about that, was it?"

My father looks thoughtful. He props his elbows up on the arms of his office chair and presses his fingers together. "Perceptive."

"So," I say again, irritation creeping into my voice, "why send me there?"

David half-smiles. "It was a favor, of sorts."

I let this sink in. "A favor for whom?"

"A friend—no, an acquaintance—someone I haven't seen or spoken to in a long, long time. She wrote me and asked for help."

I keep my face calm. My father is being cryptic on purpose. "So, what sort of help? Coverage for the Pilgrimage help? Anyone could do that. Why me?" I'm shooting questions at my father as fast as they pop into my head. He's watching me, amused, and it makes me angrier. I fire off another question for good measure. "What do you owe this *friend*?" I emphasize the last word, making quotation marks with my fingers.

Though I don't want to hear it, I know it involves a female. *Did he hurt someone? Get someone pregnant? Make promises he couldn't keep? And what does Aubie have to do with it?*

"It's actually the other way around," David says.

My forehead creases as I ponder his reply. This person owes my father? Unusual. David's repertoire doesn't usually include spontaneous gestures of kindness.

David, of course, is reading my mind. "Not making sense?"

For once, I don't answer him right away. I pick up the envelope, reach inside, and draw out the photograph. I hold it up, the image facing my father.

"So, who is she?" David asks, his tone casual. He takes the picture, holds the corner between his thumb and forefinger, studying the image like it's the Mona Lisa. "Is that what you'd like to know?"

"I've met her," I say, trying to keep a defensive tone from creeping into my reply. "I've met her family. I've had dinner at her house."

David's body stiffens and I see the cords in his neck tighten. "Ah, my dear, you've been sucked in already. That Southern hospitality will get you every time."

"Maybe so," I reply, plucking the photograph from his grasp and tucking it back inside the envelope. "But I like them. They're nice people."

My father regards me. "Really? A few days and you're an expert?"

"There's a lot more to it, David," I say, folding my arms across my chest. "If you actually cared about your friend, you'd know that this travel article—even a full-page spread in the New York Times—isn't going to make a bit of difference." I narrow my eyes. "Wait a minute. You know."

"I know what?" he asks, appearing innocent. "Something that's not in the article? Did you leave something out?"

Now, I'm in a pickle. I've said just enough to get myself in trouble. In trouble with Shug, I remind myself. Shug, who isn't here. Shug who's with Mary Katherine.

I try bargaining. "If I tell you, can you promise not to put it in the story?"

David snorts.

"That's a no," I cross my arms and frown, trying to out-think my father, who's been in the business four times as long as I have.

"I don't want to hurt anyone," I explain. "The article is about the Pilgrimage, and I could write all day about Eufaula's amazing architecture. The gothic columns, the antique furniture, the mansions, but it's the people who bring it all to life. How can I include...that the city is considering a huge building project?"

The smile dissolves from my father's face. "You didn't mention this before."

"My assignment was to preview the Pilgrimage," I retort. "With you threatening to fire me, I wasn't about to deliver an expose on how progress and construction are sucking the life out of small-town America."

David sets his jaw. He has no idea a contractor wants to bulldoze half of Eufaula's historic district.

"So your friend didn't mention anything about Phase III?" I ask, choosing to plop down into a hard-backed chair across from my father. My feet are killing me.

David shrugs. "No. I assumed—like everyone else who gets in touch with me—that she wanted a promotion for her pet project. I didn't think it was a distress signal." My father digs into his desk drawer. He produces the card embossed with an illustration of Shorter Mansion.

"I'm not a mind reader," he snaps. "The note didn't say anything about construction or a crisis." With a flick of his wrist, David tosses the note into the trash.

I stand up. "Well, then, I guess you won't care if a builder razes part of the historic district and puts up high-end condominiums."

My father lifts his chin so quickly I hear his neck snap. "Condominiums?" he repeats, and I watch as a vein on his forehead starts throbbing just under his hairline.

"The city council is considering the option," I report, keeping my voice brisk and light. "There are several houses in disrepair, a few more for sale. The purchase would ensure a steady income for the city, a great tax base for Eufaula," I explain and start to walk toward the door. "So, it's a good thing, right?" I pause and place my fingers on the door handle. "Anyway, what do you care? You're done with the Jordans once and for all."

Color flushes my father's face. He's caught and he knows it. "Spill it," he tells me.

For the next hour, I explain what I'd discovered. I detail the city council meetings, the proposal, and reaction from the community.

"Eagle Investment Properties?" my father asks, pulling his laptop closer.

I nod. "In Auburn, Alabama."

David's fingers fly over the keyboard, hunting and pecking the letters in a haphazard fashion. He hits return, waits for the page to load, then angles the screen so that both of us can view it. "Anyone look familiar?" he asks.

"Nope."

He clicks through a few more pages. *Company profile and mission statement. Board members. CEO and CFO bios. Current projects.* He squints at the last page, scrolling down through dozens of photos—documenting celebratory groundbreakings, ribbon-cuttings, and grand openings.

Each one is a carbon copy of the last. Same people, same suits. These men are even standing in the same spots, picture after picture. Only the location changes. After the first fifteen or so, my eyes begin to cross. I wipe my forehead with the back of my hand.

"Who or what are we looking for, exactly?" I ask, rubbing my eyelids with my thumb and forefinger.

"Not sure. Anyone who looks familiar," he says, clicking on the next photo, and the next. "Maybe a location that might offer a clue?"

I glance at the screen and grit my teeth in frustration. *Same people. Same suits.*

My father leans back to look at me. "This company stands to make a lot of money from this project. Eufaula's a substantial distance away from Auburn. Someone's kept an eye on the situation. Someone's been clued in about the city's current financial situation, and they've been told it's ripe for the picking. Believe me, the person behind this isn't going to let a little thing like historical landmarks or the Eufaula Pilgrimage get in the way of profits."

When the last photograph pops up, I almost choke. Same smiling faces, with one addition. They're all standing in front of a brand new red-brick building. A building I've seen before. In Eufaula? No. On the drive from Atlanta? Maybe. I pinch the bridge of my nose, blink a few times, and shake my head. I'm light-headed and dizzy. I grip the nearest chair with my good hand, bracing myself so that I don't faint. Knocking myself out cold on the edge of the desk wouldn't be pretty.

"What is it? Who is it?" Frowning, my father scans the screen.

When I turn back to David's laptop, I take another long, slow look at the row of people holding the huge white corporate banner. The name of the bank and *Eagle Investments LLC* are printed in royal blue. The sign is trimmed in orange.

I'm not imagining this.

I recognize the last person on the left.

Mary Katherine is in the photo. *What the…*

"Uh, um, sorry," I say, "I need to make some phone calls. Right now." I sprint out of David's office, past Dolores and a group of employees who probably think I've just been fired. When I round the corner, craning my neck to spot Marietta over the mass of cubicles, I slam into the mail cart and its driver.

A shriek and a crash later, I'm surrounded by flying envelopes and swirling memos. When the tornado subsides, our newest intern glowers at me.

"Oh, no," I murmur and sink to one hand and my knees, scooping up paper and packages, tucking them under my bandaged arm. "I apologize. I'm in a bit of a hurry."

"No kidding," the skinny kid with the black spiky hair mutters, then freezes. He covers his mouth, realizing the insult.

I stop gathering the mess. I stand up, still clutching the mail, and very slowly, set the bundle down on the cart. I feel a thousand eyes on both of us. The hallway goes tomb-quiet.

The intern regards me, mouth open, face red, expecting a full-on verbal attack.

"I apologized. It was an accident," I tell him in a soft voice. "Now, I'm sorry I can't help you clean this up, but I have an emergency to handle."

In three strides, I'm at my desk, searching for my cell phone.

Marietta peers over the divider. "Need some help?"

I pause, noticing a bright pink and green business card lying next to my laptop. When I read the name in script, I slap the front of my head. "Sheesh, I totally forgot. What happened with Dean Alice?"

My best friend grins and winks. "Well, I wasn't trying to listen, but I did overhear part of the conversation."

Thank you Jesus.

"She talked with PD for the longest time. First, she tried to hire her. When that didn't work, she was going to draw up a contract for exclusive rights to some cookie? Or dessert? She wants to take it national and distribute it in little Cinnabon-like shops."

"Really?" I am bursting out of my skin with happiness for PD.

Marietta sticks a pencil behind her ear and swivels in her chair. "But, then something happened. With somebody in her family…"

My heart clenches. "You're talking about Dean Alice?" I bite my bottom lip.

"Nope, PD," Marietta says, making a clucking noise with her tongue. "She had to hang up all of a sudden." My friend points over the cubicle. "So, Dean left her card. Said to tell you thank you and that she'd be in touch. She had to catch a flight back to Georgia."

"Thanks, Mar," I squat down and move some files under my desk, then finally catch a glimpse of my cell phone case. It must have fallen out of my purse. I run a finger down the screen and find Shug's number. After I press the call key, I drop into my chair and wait.

After three rings, I get his voicemail. I don't leave a message.

I try Shug's office. No answer. *Strange.*

Despite what Marietta said, I try PD. Voicemail again. I press end.

Staring at the screen, I debate my next call. Who would know what's going on?

I try the Jordan house. This time, the phone buzzes about a hundred times. I hang on, praying someone will hear it. Because my ear's going numb, I get ready to hang up. One finger hovering over the button, I hear a woman's voice. Mary Katherine's voice.

"Jordan residence," she chirps.

"Mary Katherine, it's Julia Sullivan. From New York," I say, flustered. Of course she knows I'm from New York, I remind myself. *Get it together, Julia.* "I'm trying to reach PD," I say. "And I've tried Shug's number, too."

There's a long, awkward pause. Mary Katherine's not going to budge. She's probably duct-taped her own lips shut.

I clear my throat. In that instant, I decide that I'm not going to tell her about Dean Alice and the bakery conversation. That PD hung up in a hurry and I'm concerned. I don't have to explain all of that.

"Neither one is answering," I continue. "This might sound silly, but I'm a little worried. Is anything wrong? Did something happen?"

Mary Katherine bursts into an attempt at fake giggles. She doesn't do a good job. "Bless your heart. You are so sweet to worry about *my* Shug. And PD, too."

I count backwards from ten. "So everything's good?"

"As far as I know," Mary Katherine twitters.

In my mind, I can picture her standing in Aubie's kitchen, fingers crossed behind her back, the entire Jordan family bound and gagged in a closet. I squeeze my eyes shut and take a breath. *Calm. Be calm.*

"Tell them I called, please?"

"Of course," Mary Katherine simpers. "Tootles, now."

Then, dial tone.

I check the screen—it's black—and feel the bottom drop out of my stomach. *She hung up on me. What the heck is going on? Where's Shug? What's happened with PD? Who else would know?*

When I look up, the postcard of Shorter Mansion catches my eye. As I gaze at the building and its long white columns, I can practically feel the soft grass beneath my feet, the sun warming my skin, and hear the birds chirping. As I channel energy from the picture, I think about the people who live and work in Eufaula, the men and women who grew up there, and the many generations of families before them. Only to have it all destroyed for a row of garish tourist condominiums?

If there's a way to reach Shug, I have to convince him that it's even more important to stop Phase III from going forward now. I have to tell him who I think is behind the plans. And why.

Even if it hurts him. Even if he ends up hating me.

Chapter Thirty-One

AFTER SPLASHING COLD WATER ON MY FACE, downing a hot cup of coffee, and re-focusing the gray matter in my head, I figure out the perfect person to call. After ducking down to make sure I'm alone in the ladies' room, I lock myself in the last stall.

Like he's been expecting the phone to ring, Roger answers before I can take another breath.

"Julia, darling," he drawls, "I was wondering how long it would take you to pick up the phone."

"How are you?" I ask, trying not to panic, ask a hundred questions, and offend him. My leg is jiggling. My foot is bouncing off the tile floor. I'm a wreck.

"Now, dear, we both know that this isn't a social call," he tells me.

"Where's Shug? Where's PD?" I ask with relief. "I called both of them, they're not picking up. I called Aubie and TJ's house, but Mary Katherine answered." I stop myself from accusing her of lying.

"Ah, yes. Protecting her territory like I'd expect her to," Roger says. "She told you everything's fine?"

"M-hm," I manage to answer, chewing on my thumbnail.

"MeeMaw's had another stroke, darling, but there's not much that can be done now," Roger allows this to sink in.

I gasp. That's why PD got off the phone with Dean Alice. "How? When?"

"Just this afternoon. She had a spell. Aubie called 9-1-1. The paramedics rushed her to the hospital. Word is, she doesn't have much time left. MeeMaw insisted on being taken home. The family arranged to have Hospice come in and help. That way, she can be comfortable. In her own bed, surrounded by family. It's what she wants."

My eyes sting with tears. *Another stroke. Hospice.*

Roger continues. "It's tonight's Phase III vote that upset MeeMaw so much. There's a group rallying to vote in favor of the project, trying to make it look like the logical choice for tourism, the future, and the city's economic growth," he pauses. "Just today, TJ started speaking out *in favor* of the project. He's making the rounds, politicking, chatting up the major players."

"So, Shug's father is in on this?" I exclaim.

Roger snorts. "Bought in, locked in, and sold out, far as I can tell. TJ's suddenly *crazy* for Phase III. The man's always been about the almighty dollar—don't get me wrong—but in the past, he's had restraint. He's been logical and respectful of the city's landmarks. This is different. It's like he's been brainwashed."

I press a hand to my forehead, remembering TJ and Shug arguing fiercely about Eufaula's historic preservation versus the area's future progress. At the time, it was a heated discussion. I saw it as a difference of opinion. Two grown men, agreeing to disagree.

This changes everything.

TJ is willing to harm his own son's career, wipe out the city's historic buildings, and ruin his wife's beloved Pilgrimage.

In my mind, I see a mushroom cloud of destruction. Scenes from Hiroshima and Nagasaki. Okay, I'm getting a little carried away. I shake my head and think.

This all comes down to money. Greed. Positive cash flow for Jordan Construction.

Roger's not saying as much, but it's obvious. It's the only way this makes sense.

"What are you going to do?" he asks.

It takes me half a minute to decide.

I stride out of the ladies' room with renewed purpose. I am a woman on a mission.

"Wait just a minute. You're leaving?" Marietta looks alarmed. "I thought you weren't rushing off until tomorrow. You know, New Orleans? Your job? The Roosevelt Hotel?" She's worried. And suspicious. For good reason.

"I have to talk to Shug," I say, slinging my bag over one shoulder.

"The guy from Eufaula?" Marietta asks. "What kind of name is that anyway?"

"Um, long story. It's a family tradition. Auburn University football. War Eagle, and all of that." I circle around the desk and give Marietta a peck on the cheek.

"You can't just call him on the phone?"

"Not exactly."

"Oh, don't tell me," my friend sighs. "You don't have time to explain it all now."

I clench my teeth into a guilty smile. "You guessed it."

"And when David asks why you've disappeared?" Marietta puts her hands on her hips.

"Don't tell him a thing. Or Dolores," I insist. "Say that I've been working on my new assignment. Doing research. Then, you went to grab a cup of coffee." With a slight tilt of my head toward the break room, I nudge Marietta to get going.

She doesn't move.

"When you came back, I was gone." I shrug and try to look bewildered. "You don't know where I went. And, that part is true, because I'm not going to tell you."

"Julia—" she warns me, not the least bit amused. She hisses at me, her voice straining. "Whatever you're up to…this is not a good idea."

"I'm going to make it to New Orleans. I promise," I say. "Just a day late. Plenty of time to get the story done."

"It's not a good idea. What if something happens? You run late? Or you get lost? Or you miss your deadline?" She rolls her eyes. "You know what David threatened last time."

I level my gaze at my best friend. She's right. "And I love you for reminding me. I *know* what I'm doing. Trust me."

We're both silent for a moment.

"It's him, isn't it?" Marietta lifts her chin, brightening at the thought. "That's why you're running back there so soon."

My first instinct is denial. Absolute, flat-out denial. It's preposterous. It's insane. And my pride tries to take over.

"That's not the only reason," I pipe up in defense of the city. "I care about Eufaula and the Pilgrimage. I care about my story. And I care about the people who live there. All of them." I suck in a breath and can't meet my friend's eyes. But, way deep down, I have to admit that she's right. I can't stop thinking about him.

I throw out one last defense. "Besides, Shug's practically engaged."

"Practically doesn't mean a thing," Marietta argues back.

"She's gorgeous."

"Doesn't matter."

I hug my jacket tight to my body and lock eyes with Marietta. "It's not just him."

She waves me away, fingers fluttering. "Go on, now. Make your escape before I grab a rope, tie you to your chair, and talk some sense into you."

I take a step, wave good-bye, and pivot on my heel. And I keep walking.

My heart is heavy. My body is throbbing with anxiety.

The elevator dings.

Do I really know what I'm doing?

The doors open. I step inside.

Am I risking my career? Can I save part of history?

I press the button. And wait as the floors flash by. Three-two-one.

Eufaula. The Pilgrimage. Shug.

The elevator stops.

Am I too late?

Chapter Thirty-Two

BY SOME MIRACLE, I make it to JFK in record time. Our arrival is like Moses parting the Red Sea. When the taxi drops me off at the departing flight area, I jump out, pay my fare, and head for the terminal. There's no luggage to worry about, so, I breeze up to the ticket counter and explain my situation to the pleasant-looking agent who greets me.

"Tickets and identification, please?" she asks, leaning to one side and frowning when she finds no suitcase sitting by my leg. "No bags to check?"

"Not today, traveling light," I smile and hand over my e-ticket information and New York driver's license. Of course, as I say the words, I realize that this might be code for Richard Reid shoe-bomber-speak. No bags equal big trouble. I lean on the counter and lower my voice. "You don't have to worry. I'm the last person who'd want to bl—"

The airline agent stares at me as if I've sprouted antennae from my tousled hair.

I fake a huge coughing fit. In my rush to explain, I've almost gotten myself a VIP trip to the closest NYPD station.

"Never mind," I say and regain my composure. "Thank you."

The woman slides my license across the counter, flipping it up like she's playing the poker game of a lifetime. With her thumb, she raises the corner of my license, then shifts her gaze from me to my photo, which, I'll admit, looks nothing like me. My hair's darker (missed my salon appointment for highlights), I don't have on makeup (overslept), and I'm not smiling (I stubbed my toe on the way into the DMV).

When I ask to change the destination from New Orleans, Louisiana to Atlanta, Georgia's Hartsfield Airport, she doesn't smile. I realize that the agent is staring at the line of people who've appeared behind me, each one toting rolling luggage and small children. One of the girls, otherwise adorable in pink boots and a matching, faux-fur trimmed coat, begins sneezing every few seconds. *A-choo! A-choo!*

"Bless you," I murmur with an apologetic smile at her parent, then turn my shoulder away from the spray of bacteria.

A-choo!

"Return flight?" The agent sighs, returning her glance to me. She peers through her glasses, purses her lips, and poises her fingers to type.

I hadn't considered this. Though a one-way ticket makes more sense, I decide not to give airport security and TSA another reason to flag my itinerary, so I choose a random date. When I buy the ticket to New Orleans tomorrow, I'll cancel the flight back to Atlanta.

The agent slides my license back across the counter, prints out my boarding pass, and sends me on my way.

A-choo! The girl in pink sneezes. Her mother shakes out a Kleenex and holds it to the child's nose. Obliging, the girl blows into the tissue, then jerks away at the last minute, spewing micro-pellets of sickness on everyone in a twenty-yard radius.

Holding my breath, I sprint away, putting as much distance as possible between the little girl and my deteriorating immune system.

As I clomp along, one phrase echoes in my head. *Please don't be on my flight. Please don't be on my flight.*

It's warm in the terminal, but I loop my scarf tighter around my neck, chin, and mouth anyway, hoping the fibers will somehow offer an added measure of germ protection.

For good measure, I stop by the first kiosk I find and grab cold medication and a bottled water. The sales clerk hands over the pill bottle and my drink, slapping my change down on the counter. Without bothering to read the exact dosage information, I pop a few of the tablets and wash it down with a long drink of liquid. *This is serious business. I don't have time to get sick.*

I head for my gate, joining about a zillion other people heading off to attend business meetings, visit loved ones, or enjoy a much-needed vacation.

Somehow, on the escalator, the moving parts catch the edge of my sweater. I feel myself being pulled back, caught off balance. With a sharp jerk, I rip the offending piece of thread away. As a result, almost half of my favorite cashmere cardigan unravels. I watch as the silken skein floats away, carried by gravity. It now belongs to a four-year-old who's decided that the pretty piece of blue string is the perfect play-toy.

Keeping my dignity, I do my best to ignore the whispers of fellow passengers in the security line, waiting, moving the designated inch, adjusting my jacket, sliding another centimeter. After what seems a million years, I'm summoned through the metal detector. I kick off my boots and drop them, my keys, and any stray belongings into the nearest plastic bin.

The TSA agent waves me through, unsmiling. I tiptoe across in my bare feet, not breathing. The machine lights up, bleating like a branded calf. I'm sent back to empty pockets, shed jewelry, undo belt buckles. I pat myself down, removing my watch and a few bobby-pins. The agent, now licking her lips in anticipation, beckons me like a lamb to the slaughter.

I pass under the metal framework. As my body is scanned by unseen magnetic forces, the alarm sounds a second time, winning me a round in the pat-down Olympics.

I'm led to an area a few steps away from the line of passengers being funneled through security. While I watch, the contents of my purse are pawed through. The findings include a pair of tweezers (tossed), a bottle of hairspray (more than 3 ounces), and a metal nail file (also confiscated as a possible weapon). I refrain from any small talk, and allow the TSA agent to run hands down both legs, under my arms, and pat down my midsection where no one—even Andrew—has been allowed for the last six months.

After it's been established that I am not a threat to national security, I am released to get on my flight. The corridor to my gate is yawning and long—thank goodness, there's a people mover waiting for me—because I am suddenly very sleepy. I clutch at the rubber handle and lean against the side, watching for gate signs. When the wide black strip under my feet comes to an end, I step over the silver threshold, onto the tile floor, wobbling to one side from the sudden lack of motion.

It's another fifteen steps to my gate, and I shuffle forward with determination. I fan my face with my good hand, wondering why the building manager keeps the temperature at a sub-tropical ninety degrees. Before I can sit down, my boarding zone is called.

I'm first in line.

With a contented sigh, I find my seat, flop down, and buckle in. I press my head against the clear plastic window, hugging my purse close, and let my eyes slam shut.

I'M JERKED AWAKE BY A GIANT BUMP, and the sensation of an object being pressed down on my bare forearm.

"Ack!" I shout, brushing at my limbs like tarantulas are crawling over my skin. My sudden screech and jerky movements startle everyone around me, including the small passenger beside me who starts bawling. There's a whoosh of wind against jet wings and the sound of wheels rolling down a strip of cement runway.

I rub my eyes and realize my seatmate is the same child

from the ticket line. She's still sick, because in the next moment, an *A-choo!* sounds in my ear and I feel the faint, familiar spray of sickness covering my unprotected cheek. The girl's mother glares at me, then hugs her daughter and coos into her hair. All I can catch is a few words of the conversation between high-pitched sobs.

"Don't pay any attention" and "She's a bad, mean lady."

I am a nice person. I'm about to jump out of my seat—over the sick little girl—to inform the woman of that fact, when the crackle of the intercom interrupts. With a jerk and the squeak of brakes, the jet parks at the gate.

The flight attendant's voice fills the cabin. "Welcome to Atlanta. We hope you've enjoyed the flight. When your plans next call for travel, we hope you think of our airline first. Have a wonderful day."

There's the usual rush of bodies, jockeying for aisle position, and shoving of luggage when the bell signals we're free to go. I remain seated, seatbelt on, head turned. It's the best attempt I can make to avoid the super-paranoid mommy who's decided I'm the devil incarnate. As the passengers continue pushing toward the jet way, I allow my gaze to fall on my arm.

I shrink back in horror and stifle another outburst. My pale skin has been decorated with marker. Pink, red, purple, in swirls, dots, and lines. There's some black thrown in for contrast, giving my appendage a Halloween-like appearance. Down each finger, dotting my thumb, there's more color. Dazed at the sight, I lift my wrist to my nose and sniff. It's a distinct, acidic scent.

Sharpie marker! What sort of psycho-mom hands over permanent marker to her four year-old and allows them to draw on a complete stranger's skin? A stranger—who, by the way, I feel like yelling—was passed out. I struggle to unbuckle my belt, still groggy from the medication I popped in my mouth at the airport. With fumbling fingers, I pull apart the buckle, reach for my purse, stand up, and promptly crack my head on the plastic ceiling.

"Ouch," I hear from beside me. It's one of the flight attendants. She's staring at me, the expression on her face between confused and concerned.

I expect she's clearing out any stragglers, so they can turn the jet around and head back to JFK. My poking along at a sloth's pace is most assuredly messing with their timetable.

With caution, I duck my chin and ease out of the row. Once safe in the center aisle, I straighten and feel my spine snap back in place.

"Y-you might want to visit the restroom," she blinks up at me with a strange expression I can't read. "Before you deplane," the woman points in the direction of the galley.

I realize that she must be talking about my arm, which is a lost cause. Even nail polish remover and a good scrub with a wire brush won't do much good. It's Sharpie Marker.

"Was I surprised to wake up and see this," I try to appear jovial, as if this random body-art by kids happens to me all of the time. "I'll never take *that* much cold medicine again."

I stop my babbling and attempt to move past her when I notice something. The flight attendant isn't looking at my hand or wrist. She's focused on my face.

"Oh, no," I say, realizing what must have happened. "Excuse me," I yell and push her out of the way, almost jumping over five rows of seats to get to the restroom door. In my hurry, I almost yank the panel off its hinges.

Once I'm inside the tight space, the fluorescent lights flicker on. The glow adds a green cast to almost everyone's appearance, so it's been my practice—on every flight—to avoid my reflection entirely.

This is different. This is desperation. This is… I force my eyes up. I look.

And scream bloody murder.

Chapter Thirty-Three

I'M IN THE BUSIEST AIRPORT IN THE ENTIRE WORLD. And I look like a freak. Worse than a freak. A freak who's OD'd on cold medicine.

In an attempt to disguise myself, I wrap the scarf around my head and face like a hijab. I wish like crazy I'd thought to pack a hat, a proper scarf, or extra clothes. And extra strength makeup remover.

With one last look in the restroom mirror, I bend my head and slip into the empty aisle. I whisper a thank you to the flight attendant and rush into the hollow-sounding jet way, my purse slapping against my side with every step. Airport sounds—clatter, traffic, people—fill my head as I get closer to the terminal. My plan is to plunge into the fray, find the nearest car rental counter, then the closest Walgreens.

"Julia?" I hear a voice over the din.

Of course, I know that whoever it is can't be looking for me, so I keep my head down and hurry off in the direction of baggage claim and car rentals.

"Julia!" It's the same voice again. Deep, male, commanding. This time, the word has a familiar ring. In fact, the tone and quality are the same my father used to use. Especially when I was in trouble.

My body tingles as I inch toward the side of the building, away from the person calling my name. Surely, this man will find who he's looking for. Not me. I don't know a single person in Atlanta, Georgia, let alone Hartsfield International Airport,

Concourse A.

I'm about to break into a run, when a hand grabs my shoulder and spins me around.

"Julia, didn't you hear me?"

It's my father. David Sullivan, in the flesh.

I'm flabbergasted. And begin to cry in the middle of the airport terminal.

My father is holding me, first at arm's length, then tight against his chest. I inhale his warmth, the woodsy smell of his cologne, the smooth brush of his navy Brooks Brothers sport coat. All at once, I'm transported back to my childhood—and the last time I can remember that we ever embraced.

It was junior prom, way before my mom was diagnosed with Lou Gehrig's Disease. My father hadn't seen the dress I was wearing, a Scarlett O'Hara number with a flouncy, billowing skirt and a dark green ruffle that framed my bare shoulders and unadorned neck. My mother and I had shopped for weeks, searching everywhere for a dress no one else would be wearing. When I caught a glimpse of the silken sheen in the window of an exclusive dress shop in Westchester, I knew we'd found it.

My mother had twisted my auburn hair into a chignon and tugged a few tendrils loose to frame my face. She'd applied a light touch of lipstick, a brush of mascara, and blush to make my cheeks rosy. When she finished, and we looked in the mirror together, she was sniffing and brushing back tears.

"You look lovely, Julia. The prettiest I've ever seen," she told me, squeezing my hand. "I hope you have a wonderful time."

To her credit, she didn't give me a last minute lecture about boys and sex, she didn't warn me about creeping in past my curfew, and she didn't lecture about alcohol.

We'd had the talks, beginning when I turned thirteen. I'd asked questions. I'd read books she'd check out of the library on all of the squeamish topics my mother was uncomfortable discussing. I was ready—as ready as I could be. Or so I thought.

I was attending prom with a senior, the guy I'd been secretly in love with since the fifth grade—the same guy who'd had his heart broken exactly one week ago. To everyone's surprise, the girl he dated for the last three years quit high school and ran off with the police chief's son. There were wild rumors—pregnancy, drugs, even that they'd won the lottery and had bought a small island in the Caribbean. I didn't care. She was gone.

So, when this same neighbor showed up on my front doorstep and asked if I'd like to be his date for the prom, I was out of my mind with glee. After floating on a cloud for a few days, my mother—ever so gently—yanked me back to earth and reality.

"Dillon's hurt," my mother said, draping one hand over the steering wheel at a red light. She looked at me long and hard, her big hazel eyes wide open. We were driving home from the dress shop, my gown in the backseat, wrapped in a white plastic bag, my matching shoes in a pretty pink box on the floor.

"I know," I frowned over at her, annoyed that she'd bring it up.

The light turned green and my mother pressed the accelerator. I reached over and snapped on the radio, ready to change the subject and keep the mood light, but my mother took the first opportunity—the next traffic light—to press a finger and turn the music off again.

"Julia," my mother continued. "I am not one to lecture and am only going to tell you this once," she drew in a breath. "But being second choice has its challenges."

Deep down, I knew she was right. I didn't want to hear it. I wanted to revel in the thought that—I Julia Sullivan—was going to prom with the most handsome senior at my high school. I wanted to bask in the warmth of it. I wanted, desperately, to enjoy it.

Second choice. But my mother had said the words, making them real. Making them stick. And, after all, that was her purpose. *Second choice.*

At the time, I wanted to spring out of the car, I wanted to yell at my mother, and tell her she was wrong. I wanted her to drop me off on the corner and never come back. At the time, I thought she was the meanest woman in the world. How could she say those things? How could she be so hurtful? Didn't she love me?

Second choice.

I sniffed and lifted my nose, trying my best to appear unaffected at her words. Even though I wasn't looking in her direction, I knew she was watching me. Caring about me. Loving me, even though I was rejecting her.

"What are you talking about?"

"Dillon's still in love with that girl," she said, turning the wheel toward home. "I need you to understand that, Julia." She allowed that to sink in.

Try as I might to shake off the message, it seeped in, little by little. I could ignore it, but the words were true. Dillon didn't suddenly come to his senses. He didn't wake up and realize that I was his first and only love. He didn't worship me. Not even close.

"How do you know?" I tried asking, certain that she wasn't an expert on love and relationships. Sure, she'd married my father in a white dress with a small ceremony. I'd seen the photographs, a few. Pictures of her looking up at him. He was twenty-two, she was twenty-one. I'd come along a year later. As far as I knew, it was fate and magic and all of that.

Not that it seemed that way now. I was sixteen and naive. Selfish, concerned with my own life and future. I didn't pay much attention to my parents' marriage and certainly didn't keep track of kisses and romantic moments.

My mother parked the car. We were blocks away from

the house.

"What's going on?" I asked, confused.

With both hands clasped above the steering wheel, my mother closed her eyes. "I'm telling you this—something important—because I don't want you to make the same mistake I made."

I shifted uncomfortably. Was I adopted? Were my parents not really married? Was there some problem with our family?

"You see," she said with a gentle whisper, "I was the second choice." She swallowed. "I met your father and he was so handsome, and smart. But he was in love with someone else. Someone he could never have." My mother blinked back tears. "At the time, I was okay with that. I would make him love me. We'd be happy. And a baby would help us become a family."

A truck roared by, its engine drowning out everything but the grinding of machinery.

"And we were happy, we are happy," my mother corrected herself, trying to reassure me. "And your father loves you the best he can. But, for me, there's always been this distance, this part of him that I can't reach. I can never get him to open up and let me in."

At the time, I sat stone still, wishing that I could melt away, become invisible, or disappear. I didn't want to hear it. I didn't want to know that my father didn't—or couldn't—love my mother enough. And I didn't want to think the same thing about Dillon.

So I blocked it out. I blocked everything.

Including my father's reaction that evening. The look on his face when I walked down the stairs, when I reached the landing, and twirled around on the wood floor. I remembered the click and flash of cameras, the admiration for my dress, the admiring glances thrown at my handsome date. Dillon was nervous, I remembered that, carrying the wrist corsage across the driveway, ringing the doorbell, stepping inside like he'd never been in our foyer, when actually he'd run in—in a ripped shirt and gym shorts—smelling of fresh-cut grass and dirt more times that I could count.

My father stood to the side. Thinking back now, he was paralyzed. His eyes didn't leave me. In fact, it made me so uncomfortable that I ignored him until it was time to leave.

We stood in the doorway, enjoying the cool night air, and he didn't speak for a long time. "Daddy?" I asked. "Are you okay?"

"You remind me of someone," he confessed, his voice rough and gravelly, but his eyes soft and dreamy. "From the past. A long time ago."

He hugged me then, tight, for a long time.

Then, Dillon walked over and my father snapped himself back to reality. He pulled away, offered some gruff advice about having me home at a proper hour, and that Dillon needed to behave like a perfect gentleman.

There was the mention of a shotgun, I vaguely remember, and a joke about a shovel and one hundred acres where no one would ever find a person. I think my mother finally rescued us, pushing my father away, waving good-bye, and giving me a kiss.

"Have a good time," everyone chorused. There was another flurry of photo taking and flashes blinking, cameras snapping until we slid into his borrowed BMW.

Dillon and I went to the prom. We danced, we laughed, and we even kissed goodnight. My date was sweet, but distant, and I felt the longing, an undeniable urge to tell him that I could be his one and only, solve all of his problems. I would make him love me. But, in the end, I didn't say any of it. In the end, I knew that my mother was right.

In the end, I thanked him for a wonderful evening. And I told him good-bye.

I'D REPRESSED ALL OF THE MEMORIES and ignored any hidden meanings. In the Hartsfield Airport, all of it came rushing back. My mother's words, the gentle warning, the message she was trying so hard to tell her young, teenage daughter who didn't know a thing about life or love.

"Why are you here?" I demand.

"I could ask you the same question," he says, "unless you have a connecting flight to New Orleans."

When I don't answer, my father trains his eyes on mine, and I can't hear anything but the sound of my own breathing. The moment envelopes us like a titanium shield, cutting out the squawk of overhead announcements, the bleep of vehicles transporting passengers, the dull noise of everything moving at once.

I break the silence. "Marietta told, didn't she?"

My father shakes his head. "No, she wouldn't tell me," he chuckles, "even when I threatened to fire her."

My lips twitch, but I don't smirk. It's refreshing to know that someone will stand up to my father. While David wouldn't hesitate to hand me a pink slip, there's no way reliable Marietta would get cut loose over another one of my screw ups—the key word being 'my.' If anything, her loyalty probably won her another notch in my father's employee of the month tally—if such a thing exists.

"So, you're here to stop me, talk some sense into me?" I ask and settle my shoulders against the airport wall. "Tell me what a gigantic mistake I'm making?" A minuscule piece of dust or dirt tickles my nose. *"A-choo!"*

I sneeze again, and David steps out of the line of fire, and takes a spot next to me. "Bless you." He gazes out into the crowd. "You going to tell me what happened to your face? And why you're wearing a scarf wrapped around your head?"

A harried mother rushes by. She's pushing a stroller and I catch a flash of golden curls, but the child tucked beneath the blanket is decked out in lime green and purple. I grimace. It's not my marker-wielding attacker. Lucky for her, and me, too.

"Long story," I mutter, pulling the frayed edges of my

sleeve to cover my marked-up skin. The fringe catches on my watch and I notice the time. "I have to go anyway. I need to get cleaned up and make a quick stop—before I catch a flight to the Big Easy."

With a furtive glance, I dart my eyes to the right. My father's smiling at the comment. He's pleased with my determination. But, without even asking him, I can also guess that he's completely convinced I won't be able to pull it off.

I can't let him have the satisfaction. With a sniff that I hope comes off like total disdain, I start walking. I don't say good-bye. I step up my pace, feeling triumphant, edging around slower travelers, dodging suitcases. I begin to run, knowing that in another five seconds, I'll be around the corner, down the escalator, and I can get lost in the chaos of baggage claim.

Except that I hear David's Italian-made leather shoes slapping against the tile floor behind me. Up ahead, I see a slack-faced security guard. He's almost asleep, from the look of his drooping eyelids, but I start waving anyway, wind-milling my bandaged arm.

"Help, officer!" I yell, hoping my outburst will force my father to give up the chase.

Just as the security guard springs to life, a hand catches my sleeve.

"Julia, quit it," my father, red-faced, is clutching his chest. "Let me drive. We're going to the same place."

Chapter Thirty-Four

TOO LATE. After the Hartsfield Airport security guard assumes my cries are related to a terrorist plot or kidnapping attempt, three uniformed men with guns tackle my father and throw him to the floor.

"Stop," I call out, waving my arms for someone to listen. "I didn't mean it."

No one hears me. As if a 7.5-magnitude earthquake just rocked the terminal, people run, scream, or duck to the floor for safety, covering their heads. Children cry, service dogs bark, and more alarms sound.

I watched in horror as my father is shackled, yanked to his feet, and dragged into a lock-down room, where I know he'll be interrogated like a criminal.

"Please wait," I say, racing after the swarm of security personnel, trying to stifle a sneeze. *A-choo!* "This is all a big mistake. He hasn't done anything wrong. That's my father."

After repeating my plea to everyone who will listen, one of the female guards takes pity on me. She does a double take when she sees my pink and blue marked-up face full-on, but gives me the benefit of the doubt. "You're his daughter?" She raises both eyebrows, her dark eyes suspicious.

I nod.

"All right, sister," she says, taking my arm. "Let's hear what you've got to say."

Amid a few more sneezing fits, I manage to tell my story. Halfway through, I pull out my driver's license, the last name of which matches my father's, recite his birthday, and spout off the phone number of our workplace and one Dolores Stanley, executive assistant.

After that information is checked and verified, I produce my boarding pass and ticket information. I find the of bottle cold medicine in the bottom of my bag—as well as the receipt for the pills—which includes a helpful time and date stamp. The security guard then confirms that exactly four tablets are missing, and admits that the medicine may explain my vegetative state during the flight to Atlanta.

When I describe the little girl, the Sharpie markers, and her mother, the agent coughs and covers her mouth. *She doesn't believe me.* Now, even more self-conscious, I run a hand over my scarf, pulling the edges together under my chin.

"I needed to disguise my appearance," I gesture at my face and roll my eyes toward the ceiling, "until I could figure out how to get this stuff off," I explain.

There's a knock on the door, and another uniformed officer hands the woman across from me a handful of white squares.

"Give these a try," she tells me and slides the pile across the table.

Alcohol preps. Individual wipes. *Smart.*

With a bit of a struggle, I rip one of the packets open, releasing the scent of antiseptic. My eyes begin to tear, but I hold the square against my chin and begin to scrub. The white cloth turns an awful shade of purple-brown when I lift it from my skin, but I'm thrilled. It's working.

While I reach for another alcohol prep, and repeat, my captor presses her knuckles against her bottom lip. "So, back to the disguise. That's when your father saw you?" I can't tell if she thinks I'm crazy, or if she believes me.

"Yes," I answer. "We haven't had the best relationship

since I lost my mom." Her face flashes in front of me, and I have to stop talking and inhale to regain my composure. "Now, we have to work together. He's my boss." My nose tickles, but I manage not to sneeze.

The woman nods with a flicker of empathy, but she doesn't interrupt.

"He followed me here. I think it's some bizarre attempt to help me. Or maybe, to make himself feel better. I don't know."

"So you didn't really need help?" she asks.

"No." *A-choo!*

"Bless you. And your father isn't a terrorist or kidnapper?"

"No." *A-choo! A-choo!*

"Bless you again," the lady says with a heave of frustration. "You do realize that—in the event there was a *real* safety threat at the same time you pulled this little stunt—you could have jeopardized the lives of hundreds of innocent people?"

"Yes ma'am," I say, my voice barely audible. I lower my chin.

"And, are you aware that we could hold you on criminal charges?"

The room spins. A bitter taste surges in my mouth. I'm terrified and can't look up. I focus on a speck of dirt in the center of the table.

From the corner of my eye, I see the woman stand up.

"Perhaps next time, no cold medicine?" she asks.

That's not at all what I thought she was going to say. I glance up, hopeful, anxious. Directly in my field of vision, she clasps her hands together, fingers interlaced. She's not reaching for handcuffs, I notice. She's relaxed.

"And can you promise no more false alarms? No more scenes in the airport terminal?"

"Yes, ma'am," I say.

"Ah, then we agree." Her cell phone buzzes. She checks it and smiles down at me. "You can go."

"Thank you," I gush, so relieved that I almost fall out of my chair getting to my feet.

"Your father's waiting. Right outside baggage claim. He says look for the red car."

After a quick stop in the ladies' room and another five wipes, I find my father waiting for me, leaning against a fire-engine red corvette, top down, chatting up one of the security guards.

David slaps the man on the shoulder. They shake hands and he stands up to greet me, noting my scrubbed-clean face. Only a few traces of Sharpie marker remain.

"Now then, you look *a lot* like my daughter," he says, his eyes dancing as he opens the door for me.

"Alcohol preps," I say, sliding into the seat with a wry look as he walks around to the driver's side. "I've got another half dozen wipes, so be prepared for the smell."

"After what you already put me through today, I think I can handle it." With that, my father presses down on the accelerator and we roar away, leaving Hartsfield International Airport in the rearview mirror.

THREE HOURS LATER, the entire vehicle smells like rubbing alcohol, but my face is clean and I've stopped sneezing. My father theorizes that the chemicals may have killed whatever bacteria was lurking in my system since the flight.

I'm hoarse from talking. My father hasn't complained once. I've shared my theories and suspicions about TJ and Jordan Construction. I've worried out loud about MeeMaw, her stroke, and Hospice. I've described her grandson Shug and his mother Aubie, explained about PD's bakery business and mentioned her daughter, wild-child daredevil-in-training Ella Rae.

"Sounds like you," my father confirms.

Near the end of our journey, I tell him about Mary Katherine. I'm careful to say that she is Shug's girlfriend, she's very beautiful, and she works at a local bank. I don't say that she tends to be very jealous, she doesn't like me, or she's not to be trusted.

I do mention the Eagle Investment website. And wonder out loud why she was in one of the photographs.

To this, David raises an eyebrow.

We rumble into Eufaula. It's dark, except for the flicker of streetlights, and the residential streets are empty. My iPhone tells me that the public hearing was scheduled for eight o'clock. According to the corvette's clock, and thanks to the time zone change from Eastern to Central, we're already a half-hour late.

My father turns toward the city council building, easing the corvette around one corner and the next before I can offer directions. There are lights blazing from the courthouse, and the double doors are propped wide open. A few people mill around on the steps, but I can't make out their faces. As I peer into the night, David slows and maneuvers down the next block.

Cars and trucks are parked three-deep in every available space. There are vehicles on the sidewalk, on the grass, and for as far as my eyes can see.

Without warning, my father jerks the car into reverse and backs into a sliver of space next to a humongous black pick-up. He reaches into his sport coat pocket and whips out a small, laminated sign. It reads "Press" in black capital letters. He slides it onto the dashboard where it's plainly visible, then hands me a laminated pass bearing the *Getaways* magazine logo, loops a matching one around his own neck, and shuts off the car engine.

"I hope we're not too late," I whisper, more for my own benefit than David's.

He hears me, though, and gives me a grin. "Didn't I ever teach you that it's not over 'til it's over?"

Side by side, we hurry up the steps and enter the building. The room is packed, people sitting shoulder to shoulder, others in the aisle and standing against the side and back walls. The air is warm, almost stifling, the fans swirling overhead doing little to ease the heat.

The mayor and his council members sit at the front of the room on risers. There's a podium in the center, a few feet away from the city leadership. At the moment, there's a woman speaking. She's an ancestor of one of the families who settled Eufaula, and she's sobbing so hard that it's difficult to hear what she's saying. My heart aches for her, and I am desperate to find out if Shug has had his turn at the microphone. His calming presence, his rational demeanor, and reasonable arguments are what the city council and mayor need to hear.

When my eyes adjust to the bright lights, I search the rows. Since I'm shorter than most of the men standing in the back of the room, I do my best to wiggle into a space where I can stand on my tiptoes and peer between shoulders.

There's a row of businessmen in the front on the left—I assume they represent Eagle Investments. I don't linger on the backs of their heads, I want to find the people I know and care about.

It doesn't take me long to find Pearl and Shirl in matching hats near the front. Stump is sitting on the far right, spit cup in his hand. He sees me and nods. I grit my teeth into a weak smile and continue searching for familiar faces. I find Elma from the Citgo seated next to a man in denim overalls. Further toward the back, Roger is seated, back stiff, dressed all in black as if he's attending a funeral.

My father nudges me and nods back toward the line of gray suits on the left. I shake my head and shrug. *I've already seen them.* Then, just as I'm about to look away, David tugs my arm and urges me to take a step in front of him.

I see then what—or who—he is trying to point out.

With an unobstructed view, I find the Jordans. Some of them, anyway.

In the middle of the room, I see PD with an arm around Ella Rae. Further down the row, my eyes land on TJ. But instead of Aubie's generous curves, I see Mary Katherine's slim frame. Her hair's done up in an elegant twist and she's wearing a black suit with a white ruffled collar. Like she's already part of the family.

The sight causes my stomach to drop. I don't mean to, but I squeak in dismay. The shrill noise makes Mary Katherine look. We lock eyes.

I can tell she's shocked, but then, Mary Katherine looks right past me, shields her eyes, and turns back to the front of the room.

I glance at my father, trying to ignore Mary Katherine's obvious brush-off. There are much more important issues to worry about, I remind myself. First and foremost—there's no sign of Aubie or Shug, which can mean only one thing.

MeeMaw is dying.

THE MAYOR BANGS HIS GAVEL FOR ATTENTION. When the room is quiet again, he asks for any final statements from the public. There's some activity from the center of the room, and I watch as TJ rises from his seat.

With everyone's full attention, he makes his way up to the front podium, nodding this way and that at select people in the audience. I frown, watching him. This is a side of Shug's father I haven't seen. He's preening, reveling in the spotlight, almost as if he's a political candidate running for office. I half-expect he'll stop and kiss a baby, if he can find one. Then, TJ settles behind the wooden stand, adjusts the microphone, and begins speaking. I can only guess that this is a strategic move, waiting until the end, and giving everyone else an opportunity to speak. Everyone's tired. The people won't want to keep arguing. And the council is ready to vote.

"Mr. Mayor, city council members, ladies and gentlemen of our fine city," he clears his throat. "I come forward tonight after much deliberation. My heart is heavy with worry about the future of Eufaula."

There are murmurs of agreement.

"As y'all know, Jordan Construction has been part of the backbone of our community for decades. We provide jobs, stability, and health insurance for the people who live here. I believe that our company makes Eufaula a better place to live. We've been preserving and restoring the city's historic landmarks for decades."

A spatter of clapping breaks out on one side of the room. TJ waves his acknowledgement and grins his appreciation.

"Thank you. We're so blessed at Jordan Construction. Truly fortunate."

Shug's father sounds more and more like a voodoo doctor promising to heal the sick and raise the dead. My chest tightens and I brace myself to hear the rest.

My father eases closer to my shoulder. I shift my gaze to his face. His mouth barely moves. "Look up Jordan Construction's financials." He glances back at Shug's father, frowning. "Hurry," he whispers.

I pull out my iPhone and begin searching for clues while TJ continues his speech. After scrolling through three different sites, I hit pay dirt. With a nudge to my father's elbow, I ease the screen into his line of vision. He nods, checking the numbers.

With a sudden burst of curiosity, I go back to the Eagle Investments website. When I found the photograph of Mary Katherine, I was so flustered that I didn't notice the name of the project or the type of property that had been built.

As I search, TJ, thank goodness, is still droning on. His voice fills my ears. "I want you all to know that I'm committed to the future of Eufaula," Shug's father says. "The city, the people, the growth. I've studied the Phase III plans," TJ pauses. "And I've given each detail careful consideration."

My finger hovers over a page with the title "Recent Projects." I tap it, and it begins to load. When the page comes up, I scroll down to find the one with Mary Katherine. I squint at the photograph and enlarge it, trying to see the huge white banner hanging on the building.

In all capital letters, the sign reads "Tiger Paw Landing." There's a familiar blue and orange logo with an intertwined A and U.

I adjust the page again, examining the angles and details of the property.

There's no doubt about it.

Behind Mary Katherine's smiling face, there's a set of brand-new, luxury condominiums.

Chapter Thirty-Five

I SHOVE THE IPHONE AT MY FATHER, point at Mary Katherine's image, and gesture to where TJ was sitting. "Read the banner," I mouth at him. David studies the screen, and then manipulates the photograph. His eyes widen.

Coincidence? Or not.

I'm about to stalk up to the front and announce my entire, outlandish, awful, but probably-true conspiracy theory when my father sticks out an arm to hold me back.

TJ is wrapping up.

"In closing," he says, "I ask that everyone support Phase III. Mr. Mayor, members of the city council, we need your votes in favor of this project. Thank you."

There's a beat of silence, then a clap. Another follows, and a portion of the room picks up the momentum. Mostly businessmen are nodding and clapping. Of course, the representatives from Eagle Investments are smiling. When I search for Mary Katherine, she's gone.

Traitor.

There's more gavel banging. "Attention!" The Mayor calls. "If there is no one else who wishes to speak, we'll consider the matter closed and the city council will now vote."

"Wait just a minute," my father calls out, waving his arms.

The mayor peers into the crowd, trying to establish who's talking.

David squeezes through the crowd and takes his place

behind the podium. "Good evening. It's so nice to see every-one," he begins. "It's been a long time."

I blink and frown, wondering what on earth my father is talking about. *A long time since when?*

"I'm David Sullivan. I run a travel magazine in New York City. And I have some concerns about Phase III."

There's a burst of chatter and my father waits a moment for it to die down.

TJ stands up, red-faced. "Now, hold on, sir. Who do you think you are barging in here like this?"

David turns around, smiles, and nods at Shug's father. "I suspect you don't remember me. We met back in 1965, Mr. Jordan," he says, allowing the date to sink in.

My knees buckle. *What?* The announcement causes TJ to lower himself into his seat.

"We can get to all of that later," my father says, turning back to the row of city council members and the mayor. "But right now, I want to share some details you all might not be aware of. It won't take long, so don't worry." He taps a finger on the podium. "First, Jordan Construction is almost bankrupt."

There's a collective gasp and looks of horror exchanged throughout the audience.

"Second, if and when Phase III goes forward, Eagle Investments will accept bids from many construction com-panies. Strangely enough, the bank that will likely be chosen to finance Phase III has—shall we say—a special interest in Jordan Construction."

The mayor is pulling at the collar of his shirt. One of the city council members has turned white. Another keeps clench-ing and unclenching his fists.

"Of course, you'll want to do your own research on this, but it stands to reason that Phase III will save Jordan Con-struction." My father holds up both hands. "Actually, that's not true. The condominium project will actually net Jordan Construction several million dollars."

My father's last comment triggers total bedlam. There are angry shouts and accusations flying. The city council is exchanging harsh words with the mayor. People begin to stream out the doors of the building. I stand on my tiptoes, searching for my father in the chaos. Between two burly shoulders, I catch a glimpse of his face. He's smiling.

Without warning, an explosion rocks the building.

With a sonic boom echoing in my ears, I'm thrown to the floor and the entire building shakes under my hands and knees. A huge boot nearly crushes my fingers. I scramble back to my feet, calling my father's name. Women are screaming, children wailing, and all at once, there's a mad scramble for the doors.

Fire sirens wail in the distance. A hand grips my upper arm, guiding me out the back of the room. It's my father.

After fighting our way out the back exit, we burst outside, both gulping at the cool night air. All around us, there are people running, car engines being started, and the sound of crying.

"Wh-what happened?" I'm shaken, and my legs don't want to work.

"We're going to find out," my father says. "Come on."

He drags me to the car. With the click of a button, he opens the door, shoves me inside, and drags the seatbelt over my lap. My door slams shut. A moment later, he's behind the wheel, turning the key, and throwing the car into drive.

"Where are we going?" I wipe at my eyes, blinking at all of the headlights.

"Historic district," David says, setting his jaw. "I think someone decided that Phase III was going forward, vote or no vote."

My father presses the accelerator and I'm thrown back against the seat. Gripping the door handle, I hang on for dear life. As David proceeds to drive with expert precision, weaving in and out of traffic, I brace myself for a crash and shut my eyes.

"Don't worry," I hear my father say. "I'm a careful driver."

"For who? NASCAR?" I open my eyes, leaning away as we almost miss the bumper of a silver Ford Focus.

My father chuckles. "I've never known you to be frightened of anything."

"Well, let's just say that I'd like to stay alive a little longer," I force out with a gasp.

David cranks the wheel, making a hard right. I'm pressed against the door as we careen around the corner. I notice that this street is almost empty.

I look behind us. "Everyone's leaving. They're all getting out of the city."

My father nods, his eyes following the trail of taillights.

"What if someone had tried to bomb the building where the meeting was being held?" I shudder. "We all would have died."

"Think about it," my father glances at me, then pins his eyes back onto the road. "If you wanted Phase III to go forward, and you were desperate, what would you do?"

As we near the historic district, something flickers in my memory. I almost jolt out of my seat. *Mary Katherine.* The story about leaving the gas stove on. Telling me she could have blown up the whole house. *Whoosh!* I can hear her say the word.

"Oh my God. Mary Katherine. She's going to try to get rid of all of those empty homes. The ones they wanted to tear down for Phase III."

My father hits the gas. "Almost there."

My mind spins. "She was at the meeting. Mary Katherine saw me and left. We have to warn Shug," I say. "He's with MeeMaw at Aubie's house."

David screeches the corvette to a stop in front of a barricade and flashers on North Eufaula Avenue. Three police cars are parked there, doors open, and at least four men are patrolling the area.

One of the uniformed officers walks up the corvette, face grim. "You'll have to turn around, sir. It's not safe."

"Could you tell us what happened? Please?" I ask, leaning my head so that I can see the man's face. "Is everyone okay?"

The officer shakes his head. "Sorry, I'm not at liberty to say. The scene is under investigation, ma'am. We're evacuating everyone in the neighborhood."

My throat constricts. "Has everyone gotten out? Is everyone else safe?"

The policeman regards me with serious eyes. "We're doing the best we can to make sure of that. We're going door to door, asking everyone to leave the area."

"The explosion," David cuts in. "Was it one of the empty homes?" he asks, hands gripping the wheel.

Something changes in the policeman's eyes. He flinches. "Again, sir, I can't share that information."

His walkie-talkie crackles to life and a voice calls for back up.

My skin tingles. I hold my breath.

The operator lists the address, then repeats it.

It is one of the empty houses slated for tear-down during Phase III.

The officer switches off his walkie-talkie with a firm click. "I'm going to have to ask you to leave. Sir, it's not safe for either of you to stay here."

I half-expect my father to pull out the press card again, but he doesn't argue. I don't say a word. My father eases the corvette back, does a quick u-turn, and creeps away from the barricade. Ten yards up the street, he puts the car in park, but keeps the engine running.

He shifts in his seat to face me, brow arched in concern.

"You were right," I breathe. "That address. It's one of the abandoned houses near Aubie and TJ's. I have to get to Shug and MeeMaw."

My father grips my arm. "It's too dangerous. You heard the police. They've gone door to door. They've told everyone to evacuate."

"But what if they can't hear them? Or they can't leave? What if all of them are passed out? From the fumes?" I'm getting hysterical just thinking about it. I'll start hyperventilating if I don't calm down. I force myself to inhale. *In, out, slow. In, out, slow.*

"Let's try and call him," my father suggests.

I pull out my cell, scroll through the numbers, and hit dial when I reach Shug's number. "It's ringing," I tell David and press the phone to my ear. But there's no answer. After six or seven rings, Shug's voicemail clicks on. I shake my head and hang up.

David turns his head, frustrated. We both watch the policemen. We're stuck. At a dead end. Backed into a corner. At least it seems that way.

But I'm not giving up. I won't. I can't.

With a burst of inspiration—or maybe, insanity—and before my father can catch me, I unbuckle my seatbelt. In one smooth, swift motion, I open the car door, jump out, and start sprinting toward Aubie and TJ's house.

By the time one of the officers notices me, I'm already way past him.

There are frustrated shouts, the sound of feet pounding the pavement. My father is calling my name, pleading with me to stop.

Arms pumping, legs burning, I shut everything else out. I run as fast as I can. Past all of the homes I've grown to love, past all of the towering columns, and blooming azaleas. As my eyes adjust to the dim light, I make out the shape of Shug's car in the driveway.

I push myself harder, forcing my burning lungs to draw in more oxygen. My thighs are screaming, my feet are killing me. I'm almost there.

Twenty yards, then fifteen yards.

With a flash, there's another explosion. I'm thrown into the air, sailing, drifting before I hit the sidewalk.

My cheek and hands scrape the cement. I taste blood, warm and salty. The ground rocks with aftershocks. And everything goes black.

Chapter Thirty-Six

EVERYTHING ACHES, my ribs, my legs, even my toes. Breathing is hard work. My mouth is talcum-powder dry. I'm so thirsty.

As I force my eyelids open a millimeter, I wonder if I've woken up in Northern Siberia. It's freezing cold. And everything is white. Is the mattress packed with ice? It's possible that I've been cryogenically-preserved, except that I'm in a bed, not a transparent, upright tube like you see at the movies.

And it's laser-bright in this room. Sunshine streams in through the double-window pane. It's morning.

Oh. No. It's morning!

Alarms ring in my head, sounding danger. I'm going to be fired. That's it. My career is over.

My shoulders twitch, trying to lift my body up. My abdomen contracts, then turns to mush. Every limb is shaking, down to my fingers and toes. With monumental effort, I inch my head to the right.

There's movement. The swish of someone walking. Then a man's hand on my bare arm. It's so warm against my chilled skin that I almost dissolve into the sheets.

"Julia," a man says. "Can you hear me?"

My pupils don't want to focus, but I train them toward the voice. Like gazing through binoculars and making tiny micro-adjustments to the lens, my father's face comes into focus.

"Daddy," I murmur, blinking away the cloudiness.

He strokes my hair. "Don't try and talk. You're pretty banged up from last night, but the doctors say you'll be fine with some rest."

There's an IV pole nearby, medication dripping from a clear plastic bag into tubing that ends with a strip of thick tape on the back of my hand. My other arm's been cleaned up and re-bandaged; any exposed skin shows off bruises and abrasions.

It's likely I could pass for a female boxer who lost her last fight. And I don't need a mirror to confirm it. No question, I'm battered, inside and out.

"Do you remember what happened?" my father asks.

I press my eyes shut, trying to dredge up a memory—a clue—anything that brings it all back. So far, my mind isn't functioning. There's a big, gaping black hole of nothing, like someone sucked out my brain cells with a vacuum cleaner.

An ear-ringing crash sounds in the hallway, and a humongous clatter follows. It's as if an entire drawer of silverware has been upturned on a metal tray, then shaken back and forth for good measure.

And it all comes back to me in a rush.

The meeting. The explosion. Everyone panicking and screaming. Racing off in David's rented corvette. The police barricade. Shug's car in the driveway of his parents' home. I'm running as fast as I can. The officers are chasing me. My father is calling my name. I'm almost there. Just a few more steps.

Then, I remember the second blast.

With a small cry of anguish, tears course down my face. I try to wrench my head away and bury it in the down pillow. *They're gone. They're all dead. And whatever messed-up plan TJ and Mary Katherine came up with…they got away with it.*

In the next moment, there's another blow. I'm supposed to be in New Orleans. Covering for someone else. Another writer. I have reservations at the Roosevelt. I can hear Marietta's voice. *It's lovely this time of year…*

"Where's my boarding pass? My ticket? Did I forget a piece of luggage?" I spasm at the thought, arms flailing for my suitcase. *I should be in the terminal. Did I miss my flight? I'll be fired for sure this time.*

But there's no overhead speakers. No elbow-to-elbow crush of travelers. No carry-on to keep track of. No plane to catch.

"Julia, everything is fine. It's going to be okay," my father says.

"No, it's not," I say, my chest heaving between sobs. "It's all ruined."

My father places both hands on my shoulders. "Look at me." He drills his dark eyes into mine. "Would I lie to you?"

"Yes," I murmur, attempting to wipe at the wet streaks on my cheeks.

This gets a chuckle, which makes me furious.

"How dare you joke around at a time like this?" I demand, trying to sit up in the hospital bed. I can't, so I flop back down, eyes filling again with tears. My father is a heartless bastard. How can he laugh when people I care about are dead?

"So, nothing I say is going to convince you?" David asks, folding his arms across his chest. "Right?"

Obviously. I close my eyes tight and shake my head. I can't bear to look at him. I want him to leave.

"Then, I'll find someone who can," he whispers.

Don't bother, I want to yell after him, but my throat is raw and my tongue feels like sandpaper. Arguing is pointless. It won't do any good. And I'll just get more upset.

There has to be a call button. On the bed, next to the bed. I run my fingers along the rail. If I can press the call button, I can get a nurse in here. The nurse can tell my father he's not welcome. Better yet, that he can't come back. Ever.

The door hinges creak. The hallway light shines into my room. First, only a sliver, then wider. And I hear footsteps. A man's, but it's not my father. The person stops.

I'm not going to open my eyes. I'll pretend I'm asleep. I lay still, motionless against the white cotton sheets and pillow. Until my nose starts tickling. It's awful. I can't stand it.

Three agonizing seconds later, I explode. *A-choo!*

"So you are awake." The voice is low, musical, and familiar. The sweet Southern accent makes me snap to my senses. It can't be. Am I dreaming? Hallucinating? What kind of drugs have they given me?

Through the fringe of my lashes, I peer out, barely breathing.

But it's real. He's real.

And now, his lips are touching mine.

Shug Jordan is kissing me.

And it's the most delicious feeling in the whole world.

"All right, lovebirds," my father calls out.

I come up for air, a little dizzy and bewildered, swiveling my head from Shug to David.

"How? What?"

The two men burst into laughter.

"It was all a set-up," my father says.

"And most of it went as planned," Shug adds.

"Just a minute," I say. "This was a set-up? Me in the hospital? You planned this?"

"No, not this part," David tells me, back peddling. "But when you were finishing up with security at the Hartsfield Airport, I called Aubie, who put me in touch with Shug."

My mouth opens. "But how—"

"Long story," my father says. "I'll explain that part in a minute."

Shug interrupts. "I was suspicious from the start about who was behind Phase III. And I was beginning to realize that Mary Katherine wasn't really interested in me, she was after the family money—"

"Except there wasn't any," my father cuts in with a knowing smile. "Jordan Construction was almost bankrupt."

"My girlfriend, unbeknownst to me, discovered this little problem. And she made a deal with my father. Her bank did business—almost exclusively—with Eagle Investments. She knew the CEO, the VPs, all of the key people," Shug adds. "Mary Katherine understood their financial information inside and out, what they looked for in a construction company, how they made decisions on who would do the work on a project. She was in a position—not to make the final decision—but to heavily influence which company would be awarded the winning bid."

"She was in that photo," I murmur, remembering.

"She was in more than that," my father adds, rolling his eyes.

I swallow, not certain that I want to know what he means. I don't ask. Not now, anyway.

Shug rubs his chin. "So as the vote got closer and closer, Mary Katherine grew more and more worried that the city council wasn't going to vote in favor of Phase III. You remember that when the news first came out, there was a lot of opposition."

"What changed?"

"My father," Shug admits. "I didn't want to believe it. My father, the man who took so much pride in this community and its history. The man who has run a family business here for decades—a company his own father started from nothing." His voice chokes.

I can't speak. My father looks pale.

Shug clears his throat. "My own father wasn't upset about Phase III. He wasn't trash-talking Eagle Investments. Everyone else was freaking out and I was trying to play tour guide."

"Great timing," my father winks at me, teasing.

I shoot him a mocking look.

"Julia," Shug turns to me. "That night you left. When it was snowing? You just disappeared and didn't say a word."

"Roger and I—we saw you outside—you and Mary Katherine. We thought everything was great. I thought maybe you had proposed. You looked so…happy," I admit. "So I left."

"There was no proposal," Shug explains. "She was jealous of you, Julia. She was trying her best to distract me because she guessed that I had feelings for you—" he breaks off.

My face grows hot. I can't help but smile.

"It was all an act," he continues. "When she found out you were gone, Mary Katherine started scheming again."

I think back to the white Mercedes convertible I saw zipping around Eufaula one early morning. There was a man in the other seat. Someone I'd assumed was from the bank, or a brother, or friend.

"Were they?" I pause and try not to choke on my own words. "Together?"

Shug nods. "For some time. Mary Katherine was careful, but my father began acting like a teenager. He really fell for her, hard."

Oh my God.

"There was a text message. I'm sure my father was supposed to delete it. The day after you left, Julia, I found it." He draws in a deep breath. "At first, I wasn't sure what it meant. But then, when I thought about it, I realized. She was going to make sure Phase III went forward—vote or no vote."

My eyes widen and my stomach clenches tight. I'd suspected, but hearing it out loud makes it real.

"I'll give her this—Mary Katherine thought it all out," my father says. "She planned everything. If the city council voted in favor of the project, everything was golden. Jordan Construction would get the contract, and with TJ wrapped around her finger, that money would eventually come to her."

"So, what happened?" I ask.

"I decided to test my theory. I needed to make sure I wasn't overreacting or jumping the gun. I went to MeeMaw and my mother and confessed everything I suspected."

"Really?" I'm horrified and fascinated.

"My mother came up with the idea to avoid the public meeting all together. We decided that if MeeMaw got 'sick,' we'd have a perfect excuse to stay home. Everyone would know why, and everyone would know where we were."

"So," I say slowly, "MeeMaw didn't have a stroke? And she's not dying? And so the Hospice workers and everything Roger told me…"

"Gossip," Shug nods, his mouth curving into a smile. "Very reliable way of getting the word out. It worked pretty well, I'd say. All I had to do was get in touch with Stump."

"Stump is your 'source?'" I wrinkle my forehead.

Shug nods.

"So, when I called you and PD no one answered. That was on purpose?"

"Yes," Shug looks sheepish. "I would have told you. After the vote. When it was safe."

"But I talked to Mary Katherine," I tell him, biting my bottom lip. "She said everything was fine. She didn't say anything about a stroke or the hospital. Why wouldn't she say anything? That's just awful. Even if it wasn't true in the first place."

My father interrupts my mini-tirade. "Isn't it obvious? She didn't want you here." He laughs. "You're a journalist. An investigator. What if you came down and messed up all of her plans? She wasn't about to tell you anything."

"So she lied," I say, "but then I talked to Roger."

"And then I talked to Shug and told him we were coming," my father adds. "We swapped information. I told him we were going to the meeting. He made me promise not to say anything until after. So I didn't."

I look from Shug to my father. "So, we arrive, Mary Katherine gets frightened that we're going to speak out against the project—or that we might know something—so she leaves to launch her contingency plan?"

"Right. If the council voted *against* the project, it was all over. No Phase III, no condos, no money for Mary Katherine.

Unless...she somehow got rid of the houses."

My father nods. "And that's where the text message came in handy."

"What did it say?" I ask, barely able to contain my curiosity.

Shug hesitates, and then looks into my eyes.

"P3 back-up. Boom."

Chapter Thirty-Seven

"THERE'S ONE THING I DON'T UNDERSTAND," I say, still reeling from Shug's story. "But it has to do with my father." I shift my gaze toward David.

He cocks his head, a smile playing on his lips. "Yes?"

"It's about Aubie. Why do you have that photo?"

My father is grinning now, and so is Shug. Like they've shared a big secret. And I'm not in on it.

"Come on. No more secrets. Why are you here?" I ask David. "Why come with me all the way here? Why do you care so much?"

My father walks to the hospital window and looks out. "Do you remember me telling you that I started out my career as a newspaper reporter? I was just a kid. Barely twenty years old."

"Okay," I wrinkle my nose. What did that have to do with anything?

"So, I covered stories all over the Southeast," he glances at me.

I swallow. "Like, in Alabama?"

David crinkles his eyes, remembering. "Like in Eufaula, Alabama."

For a moment, I can't speak. My brain is racing with numbers, adding, subtracting. My parents were fifteen years apart when they got married, but how old is my father now? I concentrate on the math. He was born in 1945. When he turned twenty, it would have been 1965—the same year as the first Pilgrimage.

"No way," I blurt out. My jaw goes slack. "You were here? You covered the first Pilgrimage?"

"I did." My father exchanges a glance with Shug. "My first job was working for a small newspaper out of Georgia. I covered everything from obituaries and weddings to breaking news and barbeques."

I nod, familiar with that part of the story.

"In '65, the mayor of Eufaula announced the Pilgrimage, and yours truly was sent to cover it." My father stops and smoothes the lapel of his sport coat. "Back in the days when I didn't have to wear a suit and tie." He smiles at the memory.

"So, you met the Jordans," I say in a soft voice.

David glances back at me, his ears and cheeks tinged red. "I met Aubie first, at Shorter Mansion. She wasn't a Jordan then." He shakes his head. "Pretty as a spring day, sweet personality, and full of life."

I blink, not able to believe the words. *Aubie? My father is talking about the same Aubie I know?*

"We spent every moment we could together. She took me around, showed me all of the homes, the railroad station, the jail, just like an official tour guide," David laughs to himself. "By Saturday evening, her family was ready to rally a search party."

"She was what?" I do a quick calculation. "Seventeen years old?

"Just a baby," my father confirms.

"And you were twenty?"

"Twenty and old enough to know better, according to her fiancé's mother." David rolls his eyes and grimaces out at the traffic moving below. "I was taking advantage of a young girl, I was a terrible influence, causing her to misbehave."

"Wait a minute. You're talking about MeeMaw? TJ's mother?" I wrinkle my nose as a mental picture of Shug's grandmother forms in my mind. Her wizened body, the white hair, the ropy veins in her white hands. She hardly seemed like an authority figure, much less a person who went around threatening young reporters.

David frowns. "One and the same."

"Let me get this straight. You were in love with Aubie?" My mouth fills with a bitter taste, like I've brushed my teeth with vinegar. "And she was engaged to someone else?"

My father nods. "I was smitten—a goner—like Cupid had swooped down and shot a dozen arrows into my heart. We were going to run away together."

I choke back a burst of hysterical giggles. Shug's mother and my father? Together? It's so far fetched and ridiculous that I don't know whether to laugh or cry. I'm exhausted and not thinking straight.

A week ago, I ended my own relationship with the man I'd been with for years. Today, I discover that my father has been in love with someone else—maybe for my parents' entire marriage.

"I realize that it all sounds insane," David says. "But I really cared about her. I thought that she was the one." With the confession, his shoulders sag.

"What happened?" I ask in a quiet voice, watching his face for clues.

"TJ's mother found us and sent Aubie home. We had a little chat." My father rubs his mouth with his hand. "She told me it was time to leave. That I shouldn't come back to Eufaula if I knew what was good for me. She had her son's life all mapped out and she wasn't about to let some Yankee ruin it."

"MeeMaw threatened you?" I realize my mouth is hanging open and close it, pressing my lips together.

"When I refused to go, she offered to pay me. A year's salary, which was big money at the time—"

"Please tell me you didn't," I interrupt with a high-pitched squeak.

David offers me a withering look. "I may have been an

absentee father and a bad husband, but I'd never take a bribe. Not from her, not from anyone."

I'm relieved, but a dozen other questions volley back and forth in my brain. *Why did she care? Weren't there other girls? Why was it so important to get David Sullivan, newspaper reporter, out of the way?*

My father draws in a breath. "When she figured out that paying me off wasn't going to work, she threatened to ruin my career. This included calling my boss, the owner of the newspaper, anyone who would listen. She was hell-bent on making my life miserable and I believed she'd do it. The last thing she told me was that I'd never amount to anything." A bitter laugh rises in his throat.

"How did you say good-bye? What did you tell her?" I ask, suddenly desperate to find out how the romance ended.

"Nothing." The word is flat and final. His face reveals no emotion, but his eyes are distant and stormy.

"Nothing?" The answer shocks me. My heart races. I am so upset, imagining Aubie's tears and broken heart, that slapping my father across the face—actually, for a moment— seems like a logical idea.

David, sensing my angst, sinks down in his chair, leaning back against the dark leather. Putting more space between us is wise, I decide, like an invisible buffer. I'm able to breathe and regain my composure. Instead of wild accusations, I ask one simple question.

"Why nothing? I don't understand."

"She had a shotgun," David pauses, then raises an eyebrow. "And it was loaded."

I press a palm to my forehead. The story sounds like an old B-movie, with a crooked sheriff, damsels in distress, and a posse of deputies running the good guy out of town. If MeeMaw was the sheriff, what was she trying to protect from an outsider? I think about the Jordan's sprawling mansion, the antiques, and fine furnishings.

"So, MeeMaw obviously had some money to throw around," I say out loud, though I'm really talking to myself. Then, it hits me. I stop walking and stand still on the thick carpet. "But, if Aubie's family was the real deal—old Eufaula money—with a family tree tracing back to the 1800's..." I frown.

David doesn't speak. He doesn't move. Which probably means I'm right.

I put the rest of it together, rehashing the details, tapping my fingers against my elbow. "So, Aubie's family had the real money, gobs of it, and she stood to get a substantial inheritance. You show up in town, sweep Aubie off her feet, the two of you fall in love, and it messes up MeeMaw's plans for her darling son."

I close my eyes, trying to imagine my handsome, dashing father meeting an adorable, naive seventeen-year old Aubie back in 1965 Eufaula. When I picture the two of them, I see the antebellum homes, the blooming azaleas, the blue sky. Add in the festivities of the first-ever Pilgrimage, the excitement, the parties—what a perfect place and time to fall in love.

My father leaving without a word would have devastated any young girl with hopes and dreams of true love. Hurt like that can damage a person, cut them to the bone, leaving a raw, empty soul that might never be filled. A broken heart like that can make a person seek out ways to stop the pain—wine, hard liquor, sleeping pills. Did Aubie drown her sorrows because my father left? Or was it marrying TJ? Or did she find out about MeeMaw, the money, the threats, the shotgun? Or all of it?

I realize that my father is watching me. And grinning. "You know, as far as careers go, you should really think about becoming an investigative reporter. Or a detective."

"I'll take that into consideration," I reply with a grin, and then realize my father hasn't answered my original question. "So, back to the beginning. Who was the friend who sent you the note? And what did he or she want?"

"Believe it or not, it was from MeeMaw," my father says. "After all these years. After the threats and the shotgun. And though I don't think I'll ever get an 'actual' apology, as strange as it sounds, I believe it was her attempt to make a peace offering."

I shake my head in disbelief.

David smiles, "And even after all of this time, I couldn't say no."

Chapter Thirty-Eight

IT'S A GLORIOUS APRIL IN NEW YORK. Not too cool, not too rainy. I'm walking to the office, swinging my red umbrella, and there's a bounce in my step. I've been globe-trotting again—Nicaragua, then Japan, and back to Montreal, Quebec—but as of this evening, I'm on vacation. Seven entire days of absolutely nothing.

A real vacation. An honest-to-goodness break. Not the working, interviewing, racing-around madness to which I've become accustomed. There has to be rest, sleeping in late, and a bit of indulgence—whether it's the bliss of absolute quiet or the freedom of going barefoot for the entire week.

I'm counting the minutes until five o'clock.

My office building looms in the distance. Imposing, massive, glass-encased. Awards hang on the walls. A few new ones are mine. An impressive number are from last year, when the industry decided to smile on the *Route 66: Back Roads to Big Dreams* column that my boss created.

I kept my job. And I've been promoted.

And I *did* make it to New Orleans—several months later. In March, I enjoyed the Tennessee Williams Writers Festival, the *Stella!* Shouting Contest, and dining at John Besh's *August* restaurant.

Through the lobby, up the elevator. Fourth stop.

I step out and smile, shaking my head as I pass the gleaming, silver frames. It still amazes me how one article about a small Alabama city captured the minds and hearts of America.

But it happened.

After a near-fatal bee sting, a near-death experience, and the deliberate destruction of two Eufaula, Alabama landmarks, my *Getaways* column generated national media frenzy.

I pause and chat with the receptionist, wave hello to the new intern, and pick up my mail. After I drop off my latest article with Dolores, I stop at my cubicle and hug my best friend.

Marietta squeezes me to her, clinging like Velcro. Tighter. Tighter.

"Okay, I can't breathe," I gasp, wriggling out of her grasp.

She smiles and ducks her head. "Sorry. I'm just going to miss you."

"Mar, I'll be back in a week," I insist, frowning at her to emphasize that my little trip to Alabama is no big deal.

"Uh-huh. We'll see," Marietta nods, making no attempt to hide that she doesn't believe me.

"It's the Pilgrimage," I insist. "I have to be there."

"Right. I know," she says breezily. "You can't miss it. Everyone's expecting you. That's what you keep saying." Marietta eyes me up and down knowingly. "But, girl, it's as plain as day. You are in L-O-V-E."

I won't admit she's right, but an hour later, I'm still grinning.

Even after an hour of stop and go traffic, one detour, and a thirty-minute wait at airport security, I can't help but smile. I say hello to strangers. There's a bounce in my step. I give the Starbucks barista an extra big tip.

When the gate attendant announces it's time to board the flight, I can't help myself. I jump to my feet, ready to be first in line.

The jet banks right, hovering at ten-thousand feet.

I adjust my seatbelt, tightening the strap, checking the buckle. According to the cute flight attendant, we'll be landing in a few minutes.

Out the window, I can see green peanut fields, lush blooms, and wide-open spaces. In the distance, there's the dark swath of runway. The jet lowers down, banks, and turns toward the blacktop.

We're minutes from touchdown.

I'm overjoyed and anxious. I'm frightened and thrilled. Will it feel the same? Will I fit in? Will I want to stay?

The explosion changed everything—but I remind myself that it's over.

For good. For always. Forever.

That's what Shug tells me.

And how can I help but believe him?

He risked so much to protect everything and everyone he loves. Shug spilled his concerns about Phase III to MeeMaw, Aubie, and PD. He explained what he knew about Eagle Investments. Then, bracing himself for denial, backlash, or incredulity, he shared his suspicions about TJ and Mary Katherine.

The trio of women believed him. After my father's testimony at the public meeting—so did everyone else in Eufaula.

Aubie, sadly, had long suspected TJ's infidelity. PD confessed that she'd never really liked Mary Katherine, that it felt strange for her brother's girlfriend to spend so much time with their father. MeeMaw, knowing her own son better than anyone, concurred on both.

So, Shug invented MeeMaw's stroke, setting his plan in motion. He told everyone—including Roger and Mary Katherine—there was no hope of recovery. He called in Hospice to ease her final hours of life. Of course, Shug lamented in public that the timing was terrible, he wanted to speak out against Phase III, but that being by MeeMaw's side was more important—vote or no vote.

After the explosions, it took all of twenty-four hours for Aubie to file for divorce.

She produced a valid, notarized copy of their ante-nuptial agreement cutting him out of any share of her family money, then opted for a two-month long stay in a very private, very expensive alcohol rehabilitation facility in Miami.

All reports from Shug indicate that she's recovered quite nicely, trimmed down fifteen pounds, and has taken up speed-walking. Best of all—Aubie will be back home this week—just in time to resume her duties for the upcoming Pilgrimage.

There won't be any divorce drama with TJ, thanks to an Alabama Bureau of Investigation probe into Phase III and Eagle Investments. Despite maintaining his innocence for months, the state's fact-finding mission resulted in a very public arrest for conspiracy and related white-collar crimes. If convicted, he'll spend ten or fifteen years behind bars.

On the flip side, Mary Katherine came clean. Her high-priced Hollywood attorney advised her to cut a deal. In exchange for sworn testimony against TJ, Shug's former girlfriend is on house arrest for a year, ala Martha Stewart. Wearing her ankle bracelet for all the world to see, Mary Katherine admitted her role in the Phase III project during a satellite interview with Nancy Grace. After a tearful apology, sobbing through a promise to continue extensive therapy and rehabilitation, she blamed her actions on Shug's father.

I've only seen the show once—Marietta recorded it and swore she'd fast-forward through all but the best parts. We split a carafe of wine and dined on a bag of Chili Cheese Fritos. We'd finished both by the time we reached the grand finale. It was a good thing, because I might have choked to death on a chip during her final confession. As it was, I could barely watch as her face filled the TV screen.

"I was in love with TJ," Mary Katherine paused and sighed, smoothing back her blonde hair. "He was this hand-some, powerful businessman. I adored him, respected him.

And he took advantage of my youth and innocence. I believed all of his lies. He promised me he was leaving his wife, he told me that Phase III would make us rich, and that Jordan Construction winning the contract would mean I'd never have to work another day in my life."

Gripping the sofa, I was transfixed. Marietta rolled her eyes and let the DVR play.

"I was under his spell, it was like he'd brainwashed me," Mary Katherine lets a tear trickle down her cheek. "He knew I'd do anything for him. Anything for his company." She sobs here, then catches her breath, bosom heaving. "So when he asked me to turn on the gas stoves in two houses the night of the public hearing, I didn't think twice. I did what he told me to do. I did it *for love…*"

At the word 'love,' Marietta clicked off the remote. The television goes dark.

I clapped both hands over my face. "And they bought this story?"

"The right people did," Marietta said dryly.

"So, they believed this ludicrous fabrication of facts—that TJ convinced or manipulated Mary Katherine to blow up not just one historic home, but his own house, too—with his mother, wife, and son inside?" I laugh.

"She's sticking to it, telling everyone who will listen, and TJ's not saying a word," Marietta confirmed. "I think Aubie's divorce lawyer worked out some kind of gag order."

After *Nancy Grace*, Mary Katherine started her own blog, posting original articles on relationships, love, and dating. Marietta tells me that her Facebook Fan page boasts five thousand 'likes.' Apparently, Mary Katherine also landed a literary agent. She's begun writing her memoirs and is in the process of negotiating a lucrative book deal.

The wheels of the jet touch down and jerk back.

I grip the armrests and hold on. There's a rush of power, and air pushing against the body of the airplane. We roll for what seems a million miles, sucking in the landscape, the lights and the air around us. Finally, the pilots ease the jet to a stop. *Welcome to Atlanta. It's now safe to move about the cabin*, the flight attendant tells everyone.

Next to me, my father stirs. He's dozed most of the trip, giving me plenty of time to think. When he brought up the idea of both of us going to the Pilgrimage, I admit I wasn't at all convinced it was a good idea.

But, we're in this together, he told me. And despite any arguing to the contrary, I've decided that he's right.

We both have our reasons for coming back.

My father's reason is simple. Mine is a bit more complicated.

As all of the passengers shuffle together in the aisle, I reach for my red suitcase, grasp the handle, and carry it until we reach the terminal. Holding on tight helps stop my hand from shaking. After a forever-long hallway and a trip down the escalator, we reach baggage claim. The swirling, circling silver tracks mimic my insides. I'm a nervous mess on so many levels.

My father wants to talk to Aubie. He wants to apologize for leaving—and explain why he disappeared out of her life so many years ago. Even if she doesn't forgive him, he'll know he tried. Which is better than doing nothing at all.

I'm fine with it. Really. His attempt to make things right.

In the past few months, I've come to understand my father a little bit more. He's a tough boss, sparing with praise. He wants the best out of his employees. He demands it.

At the same time, on the weekends, I glimpse a different side of David. He's funny and smart. He has actual feelings. He's not a jerk one hundred percent of the time.

I believe that he cared deeply about my mother. They had moments they were happy. They had me. They'd made a commitment—which they kept until my mother got ill.

This subject, we've never talked about.

David left one month after her diagnosis. I was angry. Furious. I wanted to hate him. When my mother passed away, I told myself that my father was dead to me, too. We didn't speak after that.

But then, fate, dumb luck, coincidence—and yes, maybe our careers—brought us back together.

Before I go one step further, I decide that I need to know the truth. *Right now.*

My father grabs his bags off the conveyor belt and waves to catch my attention. He stacks the pieces, rolls them toward me, and stops.

"Julia, what is it?"

"Why did you leave? Why did you leave Mom? Right when she—" My voice breaks and I start to cry in the middle of baggage claim. Big, dripping tears, pent up from years of wondering and guessing. My shoulders shake with sobs and I swallow, trying to stop. I wipe my face with my sleeve.

Passengers who notice pause and detour around us. A few glare at my father. One kind stranger hands me a tissue.

With one hand, my father takes my elbow and leads me to a small bench. We sit down, knees touching. I'm still sniffling.

"Your mother didn't ever ask me for anything. She never made any demands. She was the kindest, most gentle person I've ever met," my father begins. "And when she found out she was sick, she didn't admit it, but she was devastated. So was I. We were shocked. She was dying and didn't have much time left."

I press my knuckles against my lips and listen, watching every movement in my father's face. His eyes are red-rimmed, his jaw is tight. He's uncomfortable. But he keeps talking.

"So, not long after we found out, your mother did a lot of research on ALS. She knew Lou Gehrig's disease was awful. She would be debilitated, helpless. And according to the specialists, it would happen soon. So, she made one request."

I wrinkle my forehead. "What? What was it?"

My father swallows. "That I leave. That I say good-bye. And remember her as she was. Vibrant, healthy, active. Beautiful. And a woman who loved you and me."

Everything stops.

The noise quiets. People freeze. I can't breathe.

"But—" I blink, trying to digest what he's saying. It doesn't make sense. She wanted him to go. She knew she wouldn't see him again.

"I told her no. I fought it. Told her she was being ridiculous. She made me promise not to tell you, until...after. Your mother was stubborn. She kept insisting it was the right thing—for me to go. Then, a few weeks later, she started having trouble swallowing."

I nod, ever so slowly. In my mind, I can visualize her struggling.

"Your mother asked me one last time. Told me that if I ever loved her, if I respected her at all, that I would say good-bye."

My eyes fill with tears again.

"So, I hired the best nurses, made sure your mother had around the clock care. You were there day and night." He sighs. "I did what she asked, Julia, because it was her dying wish. It wasn't my choice."

Using the back of my hand, I dry my cheeks. I'm shocked. And bewildered. *My mother told him good-bye. Asked him to leave. She made him promise not to tell...until after.*

I think back.

At the funeral, I didn't speak to my father. After my mother's burial, I disappeared from the cemetery. At home, I wouldn't return his phone calls. At work, I refused to see him. There were letters, but I sent them back. I blocked his telephone number, his email.

I never let him explain. And finally, my father gave up.

After all of this time, I finally understand.

Epilogue

IT'S ONLY BEEN THREE MONTHS, but driving into the city's historic district, I can feel that Eufaula has survived and flourished. It's the first day of the forty-eighth Pilgrimage and the candlelight tours are about to begin.

The azaleas are in full bloom, the deep green foliage bursting with every shade of pink and purple. The Dogwood trees are flourishing, each decorated with a trimming of white, lacy flowers. Curtains of Spanish moss drip from tree branches making a soft canopy overhead.

In front of Shorter Mansion, young girls in hoop skirts wave with gloved hands to passersby. The sidewalks are full of tourists of all ages—there must be a thousand people here. Everywhere I turn, visitors are taking photographs, scanning tour guide pamphlets, and enjoying the balmy evening.

We cruise through the historic district, and I feel a thrill of excitement as we pass several new construction sites. They're not condominiums—the Phase III project was rejected after the explosions. After the public outcry, it's likely that any similar projects won't be attempted or approved.

There's a new coat of trim and fresh paint on at least three of the mansions. Down the street, two historic homes are being rebuilt from the ground up. One plot of land belongs to Aubie Jordan. The other property was purchased by an investor—and Shug promised to tell me all about the new owner tonight.

My curiosity satisfied, David turns the car around and we travel back up North Eufaula Street. We turn, pass Roger's

B&B—we'll be staying there tonight—and look for the gourmet restaurant and boutique where we're meeting all of our friends. I spot a jaunty painted sign up ahead, set high above a parking lot full of cars. There are swirls and dots of blue and yellow, with the outline of a cupcake under the fancy lettering. My friend, PD Jordan, is now the proud owner of Alabama's newest and finest gourmet bakery, *Ella Rae's Sweets*.

Tonight is the grand opening, and PD's throwing a party to celebrate. Everyone who's anyone in Eufaula will be there: MeeMaw, the Jordan matriarch who gave her granddaughter the seed money to get the business started, Ella Rae, PD's seven-year old daughter and tasting supervisor, as well as celebrity restaurateur Dean Alice Waters, famous for her signature desserts.

As we pull up and park, I see Roger waiting by the door. My favorite innkeeper, shopping savior, and occasional knight in shining armor finally made it to New York for a whirlwind weekend in February. I swear that Roger didn't sleep one wink the entire seventy-two hours. We saw four Broadway shows, dined at the Four Seasons with my father, and took in the skyline from the top of the Empire State Building. He's already making plans for another visit.

My father cuts the engine, and I bound out of the car. Letting out a small squeal of delight, I walk into Roger's waiting arms.

"Darling." He hugs me, then kisses both of my cheeks and holds me out in front of him. "It's been too long. Forever."

"It's been—what? Six weeks?" I shoot him a coy look. "Did you miss me?"

Roger winks like he's got a big secret. "Not as much as *someone* else did…"

"I can only guess who you two are talking about." My father's voice calls out behind me. David walks up, thrusts out an arm and grips Roger's hand. "Good to see you again."

"Ready?" Roger tilts his head toward the bakery entrance.

I peer over his shoulder to look inside the open window. Music, soft jazz, floats outside, along with the scent of fresh-baked cupcakes and cookies. The room is thick with people, groups of three and four gathered around tall, skinny tables. Everyone's carrying small plates of frosted delicacies or sipping glasses of champagne.

In one corner, a camera flash goes off, followed by peals of laughter. On the opposite wall, I spot PD and Dean Alice surrounded by a crowd of admirers. They're wearing matching ruffled aprons with blue and yellow trim to match the bakery décor.

"Shall we?" Roger nudges me.

My father, taking the hint, opens the door for me. His eyes roam the room, no doubt looking for Aubie.

Pearl and Shirl grab me as soon as I take a step over the threshold. "Welcome back," they greet me in unison. I wave hello to Elma and blink to make sure I'm seeing the same Stump I met back in November. After a much-needed haircut and shave, I have to admit he's a changed man in his dapper seersucker suit.

Roger follows close behind me and snatches a pair of delicate champagne flutes off the nearest tray. "Let's go visit with the ladies of the hour," he says, linking his arm with mine and steering me toward Dean Alice and PD.

With a small twist of anxiety, I can't help but wonder what's happened to Shug. *He said he'd be here. Did he change his mind? Did something happen?*

There's a change in music, a few familiar notes play, then a huge spotlight clicks on the exact spot where I'm standing. I throw up a hand to shield my face, then grope with the other for Roger. I need to steady myself, but he's gone, too. I squeeze my eyes shut against the glare, wait for someone to turn it off, and try to balance.

A booming male voice croons out the first line of the song: *Start spreading the news...I'm leavin' today...*

My brain flickers with recognition. *Frank Sinatra. New York, New York.*

I swear that I can hear my father singing along. Roger's voice chimes in. *These vagabond shoes...are longing to stray...*

Then, the strangest thing happens. The entire roomful of people joins in. *Darn this spotlight anyway.* I force my eyes open, squinting to see. PD's grinning at me. So is Dean Alice. How does anyone here know this song?

To find I'm king of the hill...top of the heap...

Aubie eases out of a shadow singing her lungs out, holding hands with Ella Rae and MeeMaw. Shug's right, Aubie looks great. Ten years younger.

Somehow, Roger now has half the room formed into a Radio City Rockette kick line to wrap up the song. He's conducting the dancers, urging their legs higher. If this keeps up much longer, someone is going to get hurt.

Come on. Come through, New York, New York ...

Everyone whoops with laugher and offers a round of rousing applause. Roger takes a bow. More clapping. The man's obviously missed his theatre calling.

When the noise dies down to a reasonable level, someone whistles for quiet. PD holds out both arms, waving for attention.

"Thank y'all so much for coming out tonight. What a great party!" She pauses to catch her breath. "I'll bet a few of you—especially those of you from out of town—are wondering about the choice of music." PD winks at me. "And that particular selection was chosen for tonight's guest of honor!"

There's a drum roll from somewhere, and I'm dragged, pushed, turned around, and stuck in between PD and Dean Alice. Everyone here is staring at us. The three of us. And I'm smack-dab in the middle.

I catch Roger's eye and make a frantic 'help' face. He

shrugs and covers a smile, then leans over to say something to my father. They both chuckle.

PD claps her hands a few times for attention.

"Most of y'all have met Julia Sullivan—or at least remember seeing her around town back during the Christmas Tour. Julia's a talented writer and a fine person. I'm proud to call her my friend. You might not know this, but she nearly died when someone decided to blow up two of Eufaula's historic homes."

There's a hush in the room.

I glance over at PD. Her eyes are shining with tears.

"Julia wrote an amazing article about Eufaula, which drew national exposure for this year's Pilgrimage." She throws an arm around my shoulders, squeezing tight. "As a gesture of our sincere appreciation, we'd like to present Julia with a small gift—a key to the city!"

The crowd parts. Through the opening, I glimpse the person I've been longing to see. Shug walks toward me, holding an ornate iron key cupped in the palm of his hand.

He steps toward me, smiling, and wraps me in his arms. "Hi stranger," he whispers.

And then, he kisses me.

The next ten minutes are a delirious blur of clapping and yelling and congratulations.

And without interruption, the party resumes in full swing with Lynyrd Skynyrd's "Sweet Home Alabama."

"You knew and didn't tell me?" I try to yell at Shug over the din.

He puts a hand on the small of my back and guides me out the back door.

In the moonlight, we press our hands together. We are alone. Outside. Under a canopy of glittering stars.

"I missed you," Shug says, his lips finding mine again. His arms circle my waist and draw me close. When he lets go, I'm trembling. My heart thumps, sounding out the pulse of my breath.

"I missed you, too," I whisper as he presses his forehead against mine.

Inside Ella Rae's, the music grows louder. A champagne cork pops, there's a whoop of excitement, and glasses clinking.

"I have another surprise for you," Shug tells me, sounding mysterious. He puts a finger to his lips. "Wait right here. I'd like to take the credit for this one, but I can't."

As I sway to the music, Shug returns with my father in tow.

"I'll let your dad explain."

My father holds out an album. For a second, I don't understand. He opens the first page. It's full of postcards. Eufaula, the Pilgrimage, and places in Alabama I haven't visited yet.

"Turn the page," my father urges.

When I lift the corner and let go, I can't speak. Somehow, my father kept all of the postcards my mother and I collected. The cards I threw at him that day in his office. All of the memories I was sure he'd just thrown away.

My father holds up both wrists and twists his hands in the air. "You can have the cufflinks, too."

I'm laughing and crying, shaking my head, hugging the album to my chest. It's the best gift anyone could have given me.

"Oh," I clasp a hand over my heart. "Thank you."

"So have you changed your mind?" My father eyes me, winks, and then looks over at Shug.

I raise an eyebrow.

"About Alabama," he prompts. "Your assignment here, remember?" He wiggles his eyebrows.

Oh, no. He wouldn't.

But when I see the grin on my father's face, it's clear he's never going to let me forget what I said. Very slowly, I set the album down on the closest bench, flushing red from my toes to my head. "Don't you dare—"

But my father keeps talking, "So, after I tell my daughter she's not going to Bali and inform her that she's traveling to Eufaula, she looks me straight in the eye, puts her hands on her hips, and has a good, old-fashioned hissy fit. You won't believe what came out of her mouth next—"

"No!" I shriek and hold up both hands, signaling him to stop.

My father, playfully batting me away, keeps talking. "She says—"

"No!" I am jumping up, trying to clamp a hand over his face. I'm making a total fool out of myself, but it doesn't matter.

Shug looks positively bewildered. And I'm doing my best to keep it that way.

My father takes a step back, satisfied he's made his point. He puts a hand to his ear and leans to one side, listening for an apology.

"You're right. You were right about everything," I say, breathing hard. It took almost getting fired to find myself. It took coming to Eufaula, Alabama to find love. It took everything in between to trust my father again.

"Julia?" Shug takes my hands in his and squeezes. "Would you mind explaining?"

"Well, *Dad*, where should I start?" I say, taking David by surprise. A look of amazement spills over his face. He's glowing. It's the first time I've called him 'Dad' since my mother passed away, but it feels right. We're family again. And this time, I'm not letting go.

"Aw, shucks," my father reddens and grins sheepishly. "I'll let you explain. I have my own amends to make. And I'm long overdue."

He means Aubie, but neither Shug nor I say a word. We watch him turn, smooth the sleeve of his sport coat, and head back toward the party. As he rounds the corner, my father begins to whistle.

I was wrong.

So wrong.

About my career. My father. My life.

I summon all of my energy and look into Shug's eyes. "Ever since my mother died, work has been total chaos. I was always late, I missed deadlines. My career was on a crash course."

Shug is staring intently at me, his brow creased with concern.

"In November, just back from Rome, David—my dad— became my boss and he handed me an ultimatum. Pull myself together or find a new job." I close my eyes for a moment, praying Shug won't hate me.

"What happened?"

"I behaved like a child. When I was told I was going to Eufaula, Alabama to preview the Pilgrimage, I said something awful." I wrinkle my brow, trying to crumple up the memory. "And if I don't tell you, my father will."

"And then?" Shug argues.

I drop my arms to my sides. "It'll come out. In public, at a party, in the least appropriate moment of my entire existence."

Shug steers me down the sidewalk, away from the party. "It can't be that bad."

"I said…" *Get it over with, Julia.*

Shug waits.

"I said that…I'd rather…*dance naked* for my next assignment than go to Alabama."

I'm not breathing. I'm afraid to look at Shug. When I finally pry open one eye and peer at him through my lashes, his face cracks into a huge smile. He wraps his arms around me and pulls me close. His heartbeat is strong and steady, comforting.

It feels like home.

Shug reaches to caress my cheek. His eyes are twinkling.

"You're not angry?" I choke out. "About what I said?"

He laughs, his entire face lighting up. "Are you serious? I want a full description. Will there be music? What kind of dancing? And let's talk more about the nak—"

I kiss him before he can say another word.

"I forgot to tell you, there's one more surprise." Shug looks mysterious.

"Um…uh." My insides flare with panic.

"Don't worry. It's a good surprise," he says with a slow wink. "Do you happen to have your new key?"

That's all? Relieved, I pull the heavy iron key from my pocket, and dangle it between us. "Of course," I flash a smile. "Do you have plans for this already?"

"Actually…" Shug leans in and whispers an address.

It takes only a beat and I make the connection.

"Really?" I squeal and pull back from his embrace, bouncing on the sidewalk with excitement. It's a property in the historic district. The site of the first explosion, where construction crews are rebuilding. Shug Jordan is the investor. It's going to be his new house. And he wants to share it with me.

I'm the luckiest girl in the world.

I'm in the very place where my father found love forty-eight years earlier.

Eufaula, Alabama.

Exactly where I was supposed to be all along.

Readers Guide

Readers Guide

1. At the outset, Julia is harried and unorganized. How much do you think her mother's death and her father's subsequent absence affect her ability to focus on her job?

2. Is travel a way for Julia to escape her past and avoid dealing with the pain?

3. Julia is, at first, upset about her assignment in Alabama. Did it surprise you that a person so well-travelled might be unhappy about being sent to a small town in the Deep South?

4. Southerners, by nature, are open, friendly and gregarious. Contrast that with the people Julia encounters in New York City.

5. Shug Jordan's relationship with his father is tense and strained. Should TJ have pushed Shug to follow in his footsteps or embrace the fact that his son wants to forge his own career path?

6. What was your initial view on Aubie? How did other women in the community and her own family handle her alcoholism?

7. Mary Katherine appears to be a superficial Southern Belle with aspirations to marry Shug and secure her portion of the Jordan family fortune, but it's later revealed that she has a tough, scheming side. Why didn't Shug see this?

8. When she first meets Julia, PD isn't as warm and welcoming as the rest of Eufaula's residents. Why do you think this is?

9. Julia is accident-prone and often lands in embarrassing or awkward situations. How do the people of Eufaula take care of her? How does that kindness change the way she sees her career and the focus of her article for *Getaways* magazine?

10. Does David Sullivan, Julia's father, redeem himself with his daughter? How did you feel about David at the end?

11. Discuss a time when people were at odds with a new building project in your own community. What happened? At what point does "progress" interfere with an area's history?

12. Spoiler Alert! In the last chapter, Shug tells Julia he's bought property in the historic district and is building a home. What do you think will happen with their relationship? What else is next for Julia and her career?

PD's Pillow Pockets

- 2 packages Puff Pastry (frozen, let thaw slightly)
- 1 jar of Nutella Chocolate Hazelnut Spread
- 1 bag of Mini Marshmallows
- 1 Egg White plus 1 tbsp Water (whisk together in a small bowl)
- Powdered Sugar (sift)

Cut each pastry sheet into four equal pieces. Spread a tablespoon of Nutella in the center of each piece, leaving an inch border. Add 6-8 mini-marshmallows to each piece and fold over to form a triangle. Press edges with fork to seal. Brush with egg wash and sprinkle with powdered sugar. Place on a parchment paper lined cookie sheet to prevent sticking. Bake at 350 for 22 minutes or until just golden. Remove and let cool, sprinkle with powdered sugar. Makes 16 Pillow Pockets. *Enjoy!*

Acknowledgements

To my husband, Mark, my biggest supporter and partner in everything. Love you, honey! Patrick and John David—you are my world—forever and always. Loads of appreciation to my entire family, especially my Mom and Dad. We can't wait to see you at the Lake this summer!

I am indebted to my wonderful early readers: Ashleigh O'Dowd, Kimberly Kinrade, Tara Turner, Laura Pepper Wu, and my mother, Maxine Kidder.

Further thanks go to Melissa Ringsted of *There For You* blog, and Kitty Bullard of *Great Minds Think Aloud,* for proof-reading *Dixie.* Kitty, you were divine to work with, as always. Big Hugs! And Melissa—if you can dream it—someone can make a movie about it! Let's find out if Reese is available...

To Laura Pepper Wu, my adorable and sweet publicist—I will try to quit emailing you fifty times a day. Thank you for your advice, guidance, and friendship! To Laura's husband, Brandon Wu, technical expert extraordinaire, I can't thank you enough for helping with my website.

Much praise goes to the very talented Damonza, who created the fabulous cover for *Dixie* in the midst of moving his family to a new home! You are amazing.

Kudos to my fantastic formatting team at DuoLit who managed the task while welcoming a brand new "Indie Ninja" baby into the world! Congratulations!

A late-night text message to Jen Neese…you always make me laugh! A bottle of wine and any missing Lego bricks go to Yvonne Edeker—the best neighbor in the entire world! Lisa Daughtry—thank you for listening—even at midnight.

A big *Hey, y'all!* to Lizz Gentry Wodrich, Lynnette Spratley, Doug McCourt, and Ron Wright for all of your support these past months! You have been unbelievable!! I am so blessed.

A plate of mystery rolls to Jane McEnerney, who shared delectable recipe ideas for PD. Hugs to Stacey Howell, who introduced us and welcomed me into her lovely home for book club.

I'm so fortunate to know Mary Epps Ellingwood, Rebecca Castillo, Jen Gallaspy, Jana Simpson, Karen Alford, Ashleigh O'Dowd, and Julie Flotte—who's up for another Pensacola trip?

I raise a delicious latte to celebrate my favorite bloggers, among them Liz & Lisa at *Chick Lit is Not Dead*, Samantha Robey at *ChickLitPlus*, Marianne at *Goddess Fish*, Amanda La-Conte, Roxanne Rhoads, Majanka Verstraete, *Novel Girl* Rebecca Berto, Julie at *AToMR*, Melissa Amster, Jessica Sinn, Ashley Wiederhold, Shah Wharton, Mandy Reupsch, Marie Borthwick, Lucy D'Andrea, Lindsay at *Turning the Pages*, BK Walker, Jencey Gortney, Lucy D'Andrea, Laura Chapman, Kathleen Higgins-Anderson, Kaley Stewart, and Jen McGee.

A wave of my magic wand and three wishes to each of my fellow authors Dina Silver, Tracie Banister, Jen Tucker, Cindy Roesel, Kate Rockland, Kevin Carey-Infante, Melissa Garrett, Kimberly Kinrade, Kira McFadden, Samantha March, and Emlyn Chand.

It's been such fun getting to know the gang at Page & Palette Bookstore in Fairhope, Alabama. A special thank you to Doug for believing in *Stay Tuned* and *Dancing Naked in Dixie*.

And finally, a perfect summer sky full of incredible fireworks for all of my readers. I adore getting your emails and I am humbled by your many lovely comments on Amazon, BN.com, and GoodReads. A heartfelt review is the highest compliment an author could ask for! Thank you so very much.

About the Author

Lauren Clark writes contemporary novels set in the Deep South; stories sprinkled with sunshine, suspense, and secrets

A former TV news anchor, Lauren adores flavored coffee, local book stores, and anywhere she can stick her toes in the sand. Her big loves are her family, paying it forward, and true-blue friends. Check out her website at www.laurenclarkbooks.com.

More from Lauren Clark

The Pie Lab

Coming February 2013

Visit www.laurenclarkbooks.com

Read on for an excerpt from

Stay Tuned
by Lauren Clark

Available from Monterey Press

Stay Tuned

Chapter 1

ALYSSA ANDREWS WAS MISSING.

Gone, vanished, MIA with just minutes to airtime.

"Melissa, where is she?" Our news director, Joe, shot a harried look in my direction. After dealing with a broken studio camera, spotty satellite reception, and last-minute script changes, his nerves were fried to a crisp.

"She'll be here," I promised, knowing my confidence was a front. Alyssa, one of WSGA-TV's main news anchors, was a constant source of angst in my already-stressful job.

She was young, talented, gorgeous…and chronically late.

This lack of punctuality was a problem, especially when WSGA ran a show at exactly six and ten o'clock every night. Not a moment later.

WSGA was Macon, Georgia's number one news station and had been for two years running. If we wanted to keep it that way, timing was everything. Every second mattered.

I produced both evening shows, which meant—among a dozen other tasks—organizing the day's stories, writing copy, and checking video. Each segment had to run seamlessly between three-minute commercial breaks.

Deep breath, Melissa. Send up a little prayer. She'll show up.

The red numbers on the clock continued to march forward.

Another deep breath. Everything's in place. Alyssa just needs to walk in and get on set...

"Tighten up on camera one." Joe peppered the room with demands. "Mic check, now, not yesterday."

Tim Donaldson, Alyssa's co-anchor, obliged, counting backwards from the number five.

Joe's thick fingers punched buttons on the massive keyboard in front of him. "Bring up the live shot."

Still, no Alyssa.

Joe raked a huge hand through his long gray hair. "Five minutes!" he growled, with a glare into his empty coffee cup.

At this point, it was Joe's show to run. He was in charge. I shuffled my scripts. "How about I call her?"

"She's an adult," he grumbled. "You shouldn't have to."

Joe expected nothing less than perfection. He was experienced, hard working, and a stickler for detail. Alyssa's nonchalance made him crazy.

Which, at 9:55:36 on a Friday night, gave him the patience of a gnat. On crack.

This was particularly dangerous for an unsuspecting new employee, all of twenty years old and pimple-faced, who crept up behind us.

Joe ignored him at first, barking an order to me instead. "Fine, fine. Melissa, tell Princess A. she's needed in the studio."

On autopilot, I punched her extension, eyes focused on the row of monitors above my head in case she decided to appear.

While the phone rang, the new kid rocked on his heels nervously. I flashed a smile and shook my head gently in his direction, hoping he'd get the hint.

Not now.

Nope. The kid stood there, coughed lightly, and waited for one of us to turn around.

"*What?*" Joe finally snapped.

The force of the word made the kid's body jerk back. Jaw open, unable to speak, his face turned crimson.

Joe waited about a second for the kid to talk, and then leaned back over the control panel. He pressed at switches, clearly annoyed. The kid looked sick. Joe rolled his eyes. My anxiety level cranked up ten notches.

9:58:09. Less than two minutes.

Wait…a flash of an ivory suit and blond hair.

"There she is," I interrupted the tension with a cool nod toward the monitors.

Front and center, Alyssa sauntered into the studio, lips puckered, blowing her shell-pink nail polish dry. She slid into her seat next to Tim, and gave him a playful pat on the shoulder.

Joe muttered something I couldn't repeat.

I stifled a loud sigh of relief and glanced around the room. The new guy was the only one in the building unimpressed with Alyssa's arrival. With a shaking hand, he reached out and tapped Joe's burly shoulder.

"Mr. Joe, there's a problem with one of the machines—"

Joe's back stiffened. He turned a millimeter in the kid's direction and exploded. "Get your butt back there. Get one of the engineers. Fix it. Call someone."

I caught the now-completely mortified kid's eye, and motioned for him to come toward me. Grabbing the nearest piece of paper, I jotted down the engineer's extension and held it at arm's length with a kind smile. Poor guy. Lots to learn.

With a grateful look, the new kid plucked the scrap from my fingers and darted away.

Time to get started.

I settled in, gripped my pen hard, and looked up.

Okay. Alyssa's collar was turned under. Minor detail, but sure to garner at least five viewer complaints. You wouldn't believe what people called in about.

I leaned toward the microphone to let Alyssa know.

"Dare you not to tell her," Joe muttered. It wasn't a secret that the guys would willingly let Alyssa go on air with underwear on her head. She hadn't made friends. Or tried to.

Tim, her co-anchor and current boyfriend, didn't count.

"Just part of those darn producer duties, Joe. You know that." I flashed him a smile and pressed the button to talk. "Alyssa, fix your collar."

Her mouth parted into an O. Alyssa frowned, glanced down, and straightened the pale edge. Just in time.

Like a well-directed movie, the WSGA-TV opening video flashed across monitor one. Macon, Georgia's skyline filled the screen.

My body tingled with a familiar rush of excitement. It happened every time we went on air. The cameras and lights, the beat of the music, the thrill of live television.

Here we go.

Seconds later, Alyssa and Tim appeared under the lights, their bright anchor smiles pasted on.

"Good evening, I'm Alyssa Andrews.

"And I'm Tim Donaldson."

And on it went, without a blip, for the first ten minutes. I started breathing again after the third break.

Stanley and Sunshine, the weather cat, were ready for the five-day forecast, check.

Commercial break, check.

Sports, check. I didn't worry about that three-minute slot. Plenty to talk about, visual stories; the anchors could get away with jokes and ad-libbing. Viewers loved it.

We rounded out the show with an inspirational kicker about a local scholarship winner, a kid first in his family to go to college. He'd won forty thousand dollars and was going to Georgia Tech to study astrophysics.

The show wrapped with a standard goodnight, credits, and a wide shot of the WSGA set.

The second the master control operator switched to

break, Alyssa flounced off the set in silicone fashion. She barked into her jewel-encrusted cell phone about her min-pin puppy's cancelled spa appointment and stomped out of the studio, teetering precariously in four-inch heels.

Yikes!

I climbed the flight of stairs back to the newsroom, relieved the night was almost over.

The phones started to ring five seconds later.

Made in the USA
Lexington, KY
06 April 2013